THE
SALT
ORACLE

Also by Lorraine Wilson

This Is Our Undoing
The Way the Light Bends
Mother Sea
The Last to Drown
We Are All Ghosts in the Forest

THE SALT ORACLE

LORRAINE WILSON

First published 2025 by Solaris
an imprint of Rebellion Publishing Ltd,
Riverside House, Osney Mead,
Oxford, OX2 0ES, UK

www.solarisbooks.com

ISBN: 978-1-83786-574-1

Copyright © 2025 Lorraine Wilson

The right of the author to be identified as the author of this work has been asserted in accordance with the Copyright, Designs and Patents Act 1988.

All rights reserved. No part of this publication may be reproduced, stored in a retrieval system, or transmitted, in any form or by any means, electronic, mechanical, photocopying, recording or otherwise, without the prior permission of the copyright owners.

This book is a work of fiction. Names, characters, places and incidents are products of the author's imagination or are used fictitiously.

10 9 8 7 6 5 4 3 2 1

A CIP catalogue record for this book is available from the British Library.

Designed & typeset by Rebellion Publishing

Printed in the UK

To Mr Short,

My secondary school science teacher who told me, repeatedly, that girls weren't cut out for science. My PhD and I beg to differ.

The Bellwether

DRAFT DOCUMENT SENT *by Professor Vienna Simon to Professor Valdemar Olander, University of Helsinki, six years after the Crash. Three weeks after the 'Helsinki Incident'.*

The recent tragedy has demonstrated that the child must be moved – to protect her from certain factions as much as the public from her. We therefore propose relocating the child to a purpose-built facility as a matter of urgency [*I'm thinking repurposing a rig, or those floating turbine bases?*]. This facility should be located offshore to minimise risk to infrastructure and the public but must also be easily navigable within our new limitations. See attached map for two viable suggestions.

Such a facility [*think up a catchy name, would you? You know I'm awful at those*] will need to be defensible, as both positive and negative attention is likely to increase with time. We anticipate a significant proportion of the budget would need to be allocated to an autonomous security team.

Likewise, the facility will host a permanent research staff specialising in the extraction and reconstruction of data channelled by the child. We attach preliminary figures, obtained prior to the recent incident, demonstrating our ability to combine these digital 'ghost' fragments – particularly climate models, oceanic sensor databases, maps and navigational records – into viable reconstructions. Such data resources have obvious humanitarian and financial interest, given the joint impacts on fishing and shipping across the region, of climate unpredictability and the loss of navigation tools. [*Do we need to summarise all the reasons why the seas are fucked? Or do the number of wrecks visible from shore suffice??*] The ability to source external contracts will be vital to maintaining such a facility, but this child holds a vastly untapped potential to improve maritime movement, and we anticipate no particular difficulty securing funds.

Research success will depend on optimising both the visible ghosts attracted to the child, and the ghosts she channels 'remotely'. [*Are we using 'channels'? Might get confusing re: mapping!*] Thus ghost-avoidant tricks, e.g. the use of valerian root, will be tightly controlled, and the building itself designed to be both permeable to ghosts and resistant to the fires they cause. Safety on board the facility will remain a priority, but the overwhelming value of the research will require significant relaxation of university standards.

[*Check the enclosed numbers make sense? Val, I know you have your doubts about safety, but Dr Karttunen believes the child is stabilising, and there are bound to be researchers willing to commit to such a venture. I can think of several, if they're still alive, and can make the journey. It's worth it, isn't it? If we don't try this, someone else will.*]

Chapter One
Auli

WHILE THE ORACLE hummed broken arpeggios, swaying with the movement of the Bellwether, Auli stood at the railing, watching the ghost of a tern dive into a ghost of the sea. The real sea soughed and scintillated twenty metres beneath the tower walkway, and the breeze was summer-warm as the video fragment drifted west, its long dead bird hunting endlessly. Auli stopped sketching it when the humming behind her cut off.

Turning to face the girl, she checked the datacloud ghost flickering above the tower – already recorded and far enough away to near-ignore. The Oracle swayed, the carer perched on her stool, knitting.

'The Ship of Fools,' the Oracle whispered and Auli raised her eyebrows wordlessly, writing it down beneath the tern sketch. 'Stultifera Navis, a common allegory...' The Oracle faltered, canted her head, tangled strands of wheat-pale hair rising around her thin face with the static of her own legion hauntings.

Voices rose inside as a seminar ended. But here at the top of the Oracle Tower, only Auli noticed. The Oracle wove her fingers through the air, while her carer, Ursula Poronen, had her gaze firmly on her sienna-red wool; firmly disinterested in lipreading anything the Oracle might say, which was likely why she'd lived longer than all the previous carers. Before recruiting her, they had theorised her inability to hear the Oracle would protect her. So far, they'd been proven correct. Her needles clicked steadily, and the air smelled of the wind-bent pines on the islets, of the hot metal, hot wood walls of the Bellwether. All the Oracle had done since Auli came on shift was sing the ghost of some poor musician's rehearsal recording and recite a menu for a lost ship's restaurant. An easy duty; not enough to distract Auli from the meeting later. From all the questions she needed to ask Boudain, and how to do so without revealing her hurt.

'The whole of humanity drifting,' the Oracle murmured. Auli wrote it down.

The datacloud ghost slipped closer to the Oracle, crackling static. Ursula paused knitting long enough to touch the glass vial hanging at her throat, and a raven flew an expectant arc past them. Auli pulled two bread crusts from her pocket to lay out on the railing beside an old metal button. The raven croaked, banked, and the Oracle drifted further around the tower, so Auli followed, close enough to hear her cantations over the breeze, but no closer.

Then the Oracle stiffened, lifted one hand out to the empty sea as if to halt a stranger, and whispered in English, 'Ye and each of you are adjudged and sentenced.' She spun to stare unseeing at Auli, who blinked, dropped her gaze to her clipboard, and wrote.

'Ye and each of you are adjudged and sentenced,' the Oracle repeated. 'And there within the flood marks to be hanged by the neck until you are dead, dead, dead.'

She fell silent. Auli read the words she had written.

It would be from a story, of course. Bea might know it.

The Oracle took a step closer, and whispered, 'There within the flood marks to be hanged.'

Auli jerked backward, nearly losing her clipboard over the railing to the four-storey drop to the sea as Ursula looked up curiously, briefly. Auli touched the vial at her own throat. The whole of the Bellwether shifted as the tide turned, the giant floats tugging against their anchors.

'Race cancellation,' the Oracle said in French, staring down past a map fragment ghost to the tide eddying between the Bellwether's giant floats. 'The incoming storm means we are taking the decision to cancel today's races. Keep your eyes on tomorrow's forecast, but it's not looking hopeful.'

Auli wrote it down, but it was useless without a date and a location. If one of the Principal Investigators were here, they could ask the Oracle, nudge her rudderless mind to trawl for useful details. But Auli, fortunately, wasn't allowed to speak to her.

THE DAILY BOAT from Mariehamm came and went a little later, taking with it whatever forecast the Weather team had extracted from their incomplete models and the day's cantations. Tomorrow the research boat should be returning, if the inshore forecast flags stirring atop West Tower stayed blue – meaning no storms predicted, no fog or freak events, at least as far as they knew. It wasn't much to stake a life and a livelihood on for the local fishermen, but it was all they had and reconciled them at least a little to the presence of the Oracle in their waters. It wasn't much to aid the returning research boat either, which was why Auli was refusing to think about it.

The departing forecast boat however, meant that Auli's listening shift was up. And on cue, three quick knocks sounded in the stairwell below, then rapid footsteps, and Bea Roselwicz bounced through the tower doorway, saying, 'Anything good?' as they checked for ghosts, touched the stump of their severed wrist to the vial at their neck, and extended a hand to Auli.

Auli passed the clipboard over, eyeing the book stuffed into the Oceans assistant's pocket. 'Do you recognise the story fragment? And if a PI catches you with that book out of bounds, I'm not covering for you this time.'

Bea grinned at her. 'Yes, you will, because you're too nice. But they're checking stores in the underdeck.'

Rather them than her, Auli thought. The lowest deck, right on the Bellwether's floats, was fortified and windowless, and earned its name because despite the heat from the kitchen and batteries, it remained a shadowy, briny place where the water knocked constantly against the floor like a hundred drowned sailors trying to get in. That sound in the dark had joined Auli's endless nightmares and she avoided the place as much as she could.

'Wow, cheerful,' Bea added, reading Auli's notes.

Auli opened her mouth to ask if they knew the quote, but an invisible woman shouted, the Oracle began to murmur, and Bea gave Auli a last smile through their windblown curls before turning away to start transcribing. Auli nodded farewell to Ursula then slipped past them all, down the steep stairs into the Oracle Room and out onto the third deck, the research deck. Nothing now between her and the meeting she'd been steeling herself for all day.

She skirted the edge of the wide space in between offices and corner towers, that was filled with desks and patched drawers for filing, and the shabby sofas gathered in the 'Centre' beneath the library dome. There were a handful of researchers at their desks, nowhere near as many as the Bellwether had been built to hold and yet still enough that Auli kept her face averted as she knocked on Boudain's door.

'Come,' he said. And then, 'Ah, Auli dear, good.'

* * *

SHE SAT IN his untidy office as gulls too changeable to be ghostly called beyond the open outer door, chasing the fading afternoon. It was usually a comfort to be in here at the tail end of a day, talking research with her mentor. But Auli's hands were restless in her lap and Boudain's eyes were too perceptive.

'I know what you want to ask,' Boudain said fondly.

Auli flushed. 'You do?'

'Why didn't I tell you I recruited an assistant?'

'Until the boat arrived yesterday evening with him on board,' Auli agreed. She couldn't quite meet his eye. He was her Principal Investigator, he didn't really owe her explanations, but she couldn't imagine Gabrielle or Uoti recruiting new researchers without consulting their seniors. And the QD team had only been the two of them for two years... she wasn't sure she wanted that to change.

Boudain was doodling idle shapes on a piece of paper, forgetting yet again about scarcity. 'There was no guarantee he'd make it, so I didn't want you to worry.'

Auli stilled, tomorrow's returning boat back in her mind like a thorn.

On the research deck, Bea's partner, Pertti, laughed vastly, and Auli winced even though Alexis, the cook's adoptive child, would not be up here to be startled. He rarely strayed far from the garden barges or the underdeck kitchen for fear of the boatmen's guns, and he slept curled against the heat of the kitchen stoves like a puppy. Auli, seeking insomniac coffee, had stumbled upon him almost a year after her arrival, and thought him dead. Then, when they had both recovered from the shock, she had fled to the upper library and wept for her brother for the very first time.

Boudain raised a grey eyebrow at Auli now, appearing to read her mind. 'Wouldn't hurt you to have a little companionship, dear. I don't like seeing you lonely.'

As if loneliness mattered. As if an assistant equated to family.

'I'm not lonely,' she lied. 'I have you and my work. And you didn't recruit him just—'

'I didn't,' he said gently. 'But I do want you to be happy, as well as content.'

She smiled at him, affection catching her up like a bird. Perhaps he really had meant the secrecy as a kindness, she could hardly begrudge him that. 'And now I have Leigh,' she added. 'So, who's funding him anyway?'

'Ah, Leigh, good timing. Come in,' Boudain said, switching to English as a figure materialised in the doorway. 'Settling in well? Good, good. Now, come, let's chat.'

Auli forced herself not to react. But she'd asked to meet Boudain alone, and he'd invited Leigh Alvarez anyway?

The sting faded as Boudain talked. Softened by the warm familiarity of the room's almost-organised disorder, Boudain being affably professorial with a student new to the work. It was as if the last sixteen years had not happened and they were back in Helsinki, and later she would walk the busy streets, checking her phone, hopping buses with her head ducked into her scarf, planning the dinner she would cook for Mama Sara and wondering how late Mama Márjá would come home.

'And now onto your own research focus. You read my summary?'

His tone made Auli focus abruptly.

'I'm very excited about it, sir. Experimental studies will be a new thing, right?'

'Experimental?' Auli said.

Boudain shot her a guilty glance. 'Ah, yes. Something I cooked up last minute for young Leigh here. A new investor approached me recently because, well, with these new redeployed buoys and our better grasp of the Oracle's fugue state, we are at a watershed moment for the Bellwether. All that's needed is—'

'Wait,' Auli said, sitting forward. 'Wait, what—'

Boudain lifted a hand. 'Let me explain. Your work identifies the ghost *types* most cantated by the Oracle, and potential, ah, causative events in her childhood. Well, with the data she picks up from the new buoys, Leigh can pinpoint the precise ghost *transmission frequencies* she's most attuned to. Combined with biochemical datasets, we can predict how we might reproduce specific Oracular states. We'll start with mechanical reproduction. An Carline will be able to—'

'Reproduce Oracular states,' Auli repeated, aware of Leigh watching her, of how her ignorance must look. She didn't recognise the light in Boudain's eyes.

The wind curling in through the door seemed colder now than a minute ago, the researchers' voices further away. The Oracle was cantating somewhere outside, and when Auli sat back she could see the carer out on the walkway, knitting.

'Boudain,' Auli said quietly, 'why would we want to reproduce Oracular states, when she's in one permanently? And *what* biochem data? We don't collect any.'

Leigh frowned, then turned back to Boudain.

'Niki has records,' Boudain said vaguely of the Bellwether doctor. 'We'll need a month or two to run prelim analyses from the buoy data, then we can combine the biochemical variables. Leigh, you'll join Célestine's stats tutorials. You'll pick up what you need in no time.'

Leigh glanced sidelong at Auli again. 'I don't know much about biochemistry.'

As if any of them were meant to know about that. As if she hadn't proposed several research projects to Boudain a month ago and none of them sounded remotely like this. Auli inhaled carefully.

'Boudain, what's the planned output for this?'

Boudain smiled. It might have looked mild to others.

'The contractors are a shipping consortium. They want direct access to Oracle output, their own onboard forecasting and navigation source. The satellites are gone, the ghosts make even *compasses* unreliable, and everyone wants our data yesterday—'

Not theirs, particularly, Auli thought. The data from the Oceans team, and the Weather team, yes. Qualitative Data was no one's priority.

'—we rely on one single erratic source for all the lost maps and forecasts. But there's an obvious solution.' He spread his hands. 'They are offering considerable funds for us to develop oracular powers, Auli. Not unregulated Oracles like this one, but trained Oracles, able to control their cantations, who can be hired out to ships and harbours all around the Baltic.'

Somewhere a door slammed and the Oracle shouted then cut off.

No, Auli thought. People died, she thought. *Boudain* nearly died.

'Who would conceivably volunteer for that? It's impossible,' she said and abruptly was nineteen again, panicking about her dissertation in Boudain's office. He had handed her a coffee and said calmly, *Nothing is impossible. We only need the right tools, and the right motivations. Or the wrong ones.* And she'd laughed, unwinding for the first time in days.

'There will always be someone willing to risk it for a price.' Boudain shrugged. 'My only concern is it might be easier with younger subjects. She was six when she was picked up.'

The walkway outside creaked, almost hiding Auli's gasp. Everyone had *died* last time. 'The Oracle is unreplicable,' she said desperately. 'If she weren't, there'd be more like her occurring naturally. She's unique, that's why' – Auli made a tight gesture at the Bellwether and everything in it – 'she's so protected.'

Boudain blinked, the faded blue of his eyes intent and unperturbed. But it was Leigh who spoke first.

'Has... has it been tried before?'

He hadn't heard? Though they'd tried to hush it up, rumours had persisted of those disastrous early trials to replicate the Oracle. Enough to have stopped anyone trying to create their own private navigational sacrificial dolls, which considering the voraciousness of the shipping barons and the pirates, spoke volumes.

So someone somewhere had not bothered to tell Leigh.

'Yes,' she began. 'It fail—'

'We lacked the data then, and were aiming for full replication, not partial.'

'People died,' she said flatly.

Leigh drew in a sharp breath.

'Which is why we stopped. But we have considerably more data now, so the situations are incomparable,' Boudain said, his voice holding an edge that would normally silence her. But this was different.

'I don't want—'

'I'm not asking.'

Auli flinched. Leigh coughed awkwardly and Auli wished for the thousandth time she was better at confrontation. She ought to at least be capable of confrontation with *Boudain*.

Boudain's expression softened. 'I'm not asking you to alter your research, Auli. I admit there is a high chance of failure, but not' – raising a hand even though she had not moved – '*not* a risk to anyone here. We will test it on electrical devices first, hence bringing An Carline in. Then animals – corvids, I thought – and only then step up to humans.'

No one spoke. The Oracle's voice drifted in through the door.

Boudain switched to Russian. 'We could change the world, dear.' Leigh clearly didn't understand. Boudain leaned forward, his pale hands heavy with arthritis and his gaze on Auli keen. 'You and I and this boy here. Imagine if instead of trailing after a facsimile of a girl, hoping for breadcrumbs, this College instead trained specialists with the ability to tap into the world's ghosts, or the captain's restored buoys. Walking satellites! Sentient, controlled and expert Oracles!'

'Building something better,' Auli said softly. Boudain's entire demeanour eased. 'Gabrielle will oppose it,' she added quickly.

Boudain laughed. 'Once we've got trial data, I'll get the funding locked in. Gabrielle believes in the infallibility of our political neutrality, but you cannot hold something powerful and call yourself neutral, it is oxymoronic. We hold power, so it is power that keeps us safe, your captain understands that. And what greater power than to be the only place in the world training Oracles and sending them out to serve across Europe? Christ, across the world, why not? Someone has to rediscover America someday!'

'Does Gabrielle even know, or Uoti?'

'Do they ask my permission for the contracts they take on?' Boudain said, not smiling now. 'Gabrielle, much as she wants to be, is not in sole charge here.'

'It's too risky,' Auli insisted.

'So is everything that is worth doing.' He switched back to English. 'This one fallible, frail, unpredictable Oracle saves lives. Think how many more could be saved if we succeed. How many more lost if we refuse to try.'

It was a cruel argument, knowing her as he did, and crueller, too, in English. Auli stared at her clenched fists, fighting the hurt.

'It sounds exciting,' Leigh said into the silence.

Boudain leaned back and nodded. 'It is the only way we will survive long-term. The Oracle will not last forever.'

Live forever, Auli thought.

He was right, though. It was an inescapably ephemeral existence, an institute centred around one young woman already broken beyond repair. And yet this place, for all its ghosts and boatmen and isolation, was Auli's haven still. She suspected no one who had lived through the Crash was entirely whole. She suspected everyone in the Bellwether was here because the Oracle and her gathered ghosts were far, far better than whatever ghosts they had left behind. The thought of losing this place made it hard to breathe.

He was right, too, that the mission mattered most. The potential to save lives at sea, surely she more than anyone knew that was worth a little risk. Auli touched her hand to her own throat to check she was not drowning. She trusted Boudain implicitly. And yet...

'Then sign me up,' Leigh said. 'Though I'm no expert on, well, anything useful, I guess.' He laughed, and Boudain laughed, too, because who was? The researchers came here because they were mathematicians or because once long ago, they had been the scientists creating the data they now desperately sought to claw back from the void. No one came here fully prepared, but everyone came knowing it might kill them. Auli was foolish to think this was any different.

The girl

She is a storm cloud chasing a lifeboat home, silver-purple light and the boat's orange hull glimmering along her arms like an excised sun. She leans into the waves, the wind counting down her bones... and she is a quiet man's voice in the empty air; she is audio balance and listener log, all enfolding in the gravity of that excised sun. She is a dying star made into pixels, made into indices of infrared, made into words.

The sea whispers, she falls from sun into waves and is the flicker, shimmer-twist of a shoal of fish, frozen into stasis for eternity. The fish turn their flat eyes as if she is the predator, as if she is the prey.

Ye and each of you are adjudged and sentenced, the fish become words falling from her mouth all silver and blood. *And there within the flood marks to be hanged by the neck until you are dead, dead, dead.*

Please, she thinks, in the moment between the shoal of words dissolving and the wind catching her up. Please.

But she doesn't know what she is yearning for, only that she is a deepwater current now, pressure values in a long series like a song sung into the darkness.

Chapter Two

Auli

BOUDAIN SENT THEM away after that. 'Show him the library, would you?' he'd said. 'He'll need it.'

Auli walked to her desk too tangled up in her own thoughts to realise she'd left Leigh behind and then could not help but smile as he hurried after her.

'Still feeling sick?' she asked.

He shook his head, but his arms were slightly spread and his gaze a touch too fixed. 'No, that tea really helped. Thanks.'

'You get used to the motion,' she said. He grimaced comically. 'Honestly, you do. You only notice it when the tide changes, or there's bad weather.'

'It was worse last night.'

She wondered whether he really meant the motion of the boats. He was right: the two dorm barges everyone other than the PIs and the captain slept on lay across the prevailing swell, so they did rock. A hungry motion exacerbating Auli's endless dreams of drowning. But she suspected he meant instead the strange, lonely exposure of the Bellwether, impossible to ignore at night in your restless cabin with the waves and the constant come and go of the ghosts, the twice nightly calling of the guard as a reminder you were adrift on an unforgiving sea at the very centre of a gathering of ghosts that terrified any half-sane person away.

After some early deaths, the cabin portholes had been enlarged to allow escape if a ghost cornered you in your room. You learned to sleep lightly.

'You get used to that, too,' she said simply. 'Now, someone will be with you for your first listening duty, but gardening duty is just getting on with whatever jobs are listed on the board. Ready to meet the forbidden books?'

Leigh smiled with surprising sweetness. 'Not forbidden anymore back home, though you wouldn't know it by the way people act,' he said, trailing her across to the library ladder. Auli scaled it quickly, moving aside on the steel walkway so he could follow.

He waved a cheery hello first to the second Oceans assistant at his desk. 'That's Tobias,' Auli said. 'He was the newest until you arrived. Came in the spring to replace—' She cut off and turned to the shelves lining the round tower. Every few paces, long windows rose the full two storeys to the dome, and at the base of each window, was a metal barrel filled with kindling. But both floors were mostly taken up with shelves, and shelves, and shelves. 'On this floor all the books have their ghosts, so they might be a little restless but they're safe.'

Leigh eyed the bookshelves. 'They're safer possessed?'

'Yes. The ghost has found its data match, it's stable. The ones up there' – she pointed to the upper library floor – 'are not possessed. So only the three Principal Investigators and Senior Researchers are allowed up there. We keep an eye on them and relocate them if they are found by their ghosts.'

She expected him to ask about the infection rate. He hadn't done so yet but surely, he'd want to know. She had asked. Quietly, in Boudain's office the day after she arrived. *How many of us die?* she had said almost apologetically. He'd shaken his head and said, *Enough, but it's better now than the early days when we let everyone talk to her.* Better, but still an immovable truth to their shifting home: there were more ghosts because of the Oracle, so more people died. Whether you were put off by that depended very much on two things – where you would be if you weren't here, and whether you thought the Bellwether's mission was worth it. Everyone here balanced those scales differently and Auli had no idea how Leigh was doing so. She waited for him to ask; he didn't.

'No one told you about the first trials?' she said.

He was looking at the shelves rather than her. 'PI Caron said it's not the same now? We can do it better?'

I doubt it, she wanted to say. But instead only moved ahead of him, explained that books stayed within the research deck, always within three metres of a fire barrel or a window. The library shelves were labelled with strips of paper written over and rubbed out until the paper was too thin for anything else. Most people didn't relish coming up here, which was why it was Auli's favourite place on the Bellwether. That and the feel of a book in her hands, the sheer beautiful ambition of entrusting written words to the world, the prickle of static against her palm as a reminder that knowledge was fragile and easily lost.

She didn't say any of that.

'There's all sorts,' Leigh said, trailing along the walkway, staring up at the labels. He was in his early twenties; a child when the Crash happened. The children of those first post-Crash years were a species apart, Auli thought – perhaps that was why he seemed undaunted by the thought of... God, of replicating the Oracle.

She had been the age he was now, a student in Helsinki worrying about what she would do once her PhD was complete. Whether she could leave her mothers behind like her brother had done or was as bound to them once she graduated as she had always been.

But then it hadn't mattered at all. And two years later, her mothers had gone north, with a hug and a command to send any news of her brother. And nearly four more years had passed, grim, lonely and unrelenting, surviving on invisibility and the university's crumbling bones before a letter had arrived from the mysterious New Baltic College of Oceanographic Research, and her old supervisor, Boudain.

'We've got some fiction, if you're interested,' she said, pushing the memories away. 'All loosely maritime, of course. Helps us identify the book and film ghosts attracted to the Bellwether.'

'The Bellwether?' Leigh said, pulling a book out very gingerly. It was a French guide to smallholding, understandably rather worn, and as soon as Leigh opened the cover, the pages riffled and flipped to a section on vine fruits. Leigh yelped, nearly dropping the book before mastering himself.

'They remember the last page read,' she explained. 'Some boatmen are determined to grow grapes for wine.' Then, answering the other question, 'The Bellwether, because that's what we are doing. Trying to lead people across the waters safely.'

She'd read his psychological assessment last night. *Sociable, optimistic, ambitious*, his interviewer concluded; *good problem solving, adaptable under pressure*. Nothing, she realised, about physiology or psychology training, and she couldn't remember which languages he spoke either. All the researchers were polyglots of necessity, defaulting among the researchers to English, the boatmen, Finnish.

'So is it?' he said. The book turned a few more pages, this time he didn't react at all. 'Leading people across the waters safely?'

Below them, one of the boatmen stood in the now emptied

Centre, calling an idle insult in Finnish. The bearded Finn Joar, Célestine's current fling, emerged quickly from the Oracle Tower and laughed loudly, shaking his head.

'Yes,' Auli said. 'There's only so much we can direct the Oracle, of course, but we're rebuilding datasets steadily, reconstructing climate models, fish stock models, navigation maps. The restored buoy network means we are re-starting short-term forecasts.'

The boatmen moved away; Miika Puhakainen, the tall sniper missing three fingers, glanced up at her and nodded carefully.

It was strange, how the boatmen treated her with the same wariness the researchers felt around them. As if Raphaël had left some mark on her his boatmen could still see.

'Come on,' Auli said. 'It's nearly dinnertime.'

Leigh set the book back and looked up at the rows of unhaunted books visible through the bars of the upper walkway, then turned to Auli with that boyish smile again.

'You said we all do listening duty but can't speak to the Oracle. How do we direct her, umm, oracling then?'

'Cantations,' Auli corrected. 'The PIs do that twice a day – it's called "Seeding". They will say lat and longitudes or buoy ID numbers, or dates; anything that might trigger the Oracle to connect to the ghost containing the data we're after.' She shrugged. 'It's erratic, and understanding what works best is another of our research areas. But they generally get much more targeted data than listening does.'

Leigh nodded thoughtfully. 'Why just the PIs? Is it…'

'Dangerous?' she supplied. A shout came from West Tower, echoed from East. The guard change. 'Yes. They limit it to three samples, but still, Boudain' – she hated even thinking it – 'is the only original PI but we're also the newest department. Oceans and Weather have both lost several PIs. Seeding has about three times the infection risk of Listening.'

Auli studied her knuckles on the ladder, then looked up at her new responsibility. 'Don't talk to the Oracle,' she said.

He nodded without speaking, serious, but not nearly unnerved enough. He reminded her of her brother, she realised with a bolt of pain.

'On that note,' she said gently, 'you'll need to sign the form giving your choice.'

'Oh, the thing about if I get ghost infected?' Auli nodded, while Leigh smiled a little uneasily. 'I guess I choose the morphine, if it's free. Like, no one wants to go through that, do they?'

No, Auli thought. And yet still they were all here.

LATER, LEAVING LEIGH making friends with startling ease, Auli returned to her desk and tried to focus on her draft paper on why the Oracle existed. Why a girl from inland Russia cantated maritime ghosts and somehow did not die of it. Four years after arriving here, Auli wasn't sure an answer existed. There were patterns in the data suggesting certain... resonances. But the initial cause? She may have been born around the time of the Crash — did that matter? She had been orphaned and saved from drowning — did *that*?

None of it was enough, despite Boudain's confidence, to risk people's lives on. Auli sighed.

'Still working, Fraser?'

Auli dredged up a smile before turning around. Amidst the constant murmurings of the sea and people chattering beneath the library dome, she'd not heard Célestine approach.

'Just catching up,' she said. The Frenchwoman tilted her head to study Auli's papers uninvited and Auli glanced beyond her, expecting her Weather colleagues, but Célestine was alone, and had unfortunately put the brake on her chair.

It was surprisingly stable on the constantly shifting floor, and Raphäel's work, of course, which didn't help Auli's mood.

'How is your new assistant?' Célestine ran one brown hand along the arch of her wheel. 'What is he working on? Boudain isn't planning any more experiments, I hope.'

'What?' Auli said, startled heat rising in her face. 'Why would you think that?'

But she didn't, she was only saying it to rattle Auli, tapping her nails against her wheel in satisfaction.

Auli forced a smile, wishing for the courage to hold the other woman's gaze and tell her to fuck off. She hadn't been here when Boudain had tried to create more Oracles, so she hadn't been here when all of those test subjects had died. But Célestine had. She and Raphaël had arrived from France within three years of the Oracle being found, not quite two years after the incident in Helsinki that led to the Bellwether being built. Raphaël in a moment of sleepy confidence had once told Auli she still resented being manoeuvred out of the PI post by Gabrielle when the Bellwether's founder had died.

This was one of the reasons Auli did not like talking to Célestine – it made her think about Raphaël. It made her remember Célestine leaning in to murmur beneath the hubbub of the Hall two years ago, *Your face hides nothing, but he has no interest in love, only in distraction. Ask him when he is back and he will tell you this. It is better to know, no? Have a care for your heart, Auli Fraser.*

She'd been right, of course. For all her sharp edges, Célestine wasn't prone to lying, and Auli would have made a less easy target if she hadn't been so assiduously lying to herself.

'Has the forecast gone?' she said now.

'Yes. Did you hear the news from Helsinki?' Célestine didn't wait for an answer, because Auli rarely read the weeks-old newspapers the forecast boat sometimes delivered. 'Those Survivors have stopped picketing the university.'

Auli raised her eyebrows sceptically. Célestine laughed. 'I know. Only until another one of us dies, no? Then they'll start again. But it is good to know someone cares, even if only lunatics who want the Oracle hung.'

Auli wasn't sure she wanted that kind of pity. 'So,' she said, eyeing the emptying deck, 'are you waiting for your boatman?'

In the oblique light, Célestine's eyes were fleetingly almost sad. But it didn't last. 'Trying to get rid of me? Anyone would think I intimidated you, Fraser. Can you imagine?' She threw her arms wide to signify the wheelchair, as if the gesture did not emphasise her strong arms, her beauty, the bold angle of her jaw.

Yes, Auli thought, I can well imagine, actually. But she only gave a tight smile and watched a video ghost drift up between desks towards the books above.

When the pause began to stretch, she said, 'The flag is still blue, that's good.' For the boat returning tomorrow, she did not say; if they returned, if they were okay. They'd been gone two months and Auli had almost succeeded, most days, in not thinking about all the ways a ship could come to harm out there beyond their walls.

Célestine unlocked her brakes in a quick, sharp gesture. 'Yes. It is. Don't work too hard.'

Auli ignored the mockery, watching her wheel to the winch that would lower her to the second deck, knowing full well what had driven her away. The unspoken reminder of Raphaël's return. The fact that this morning the Oracle had cantated data from one of their restored weather buoys, of a freak rainbomb two weeks ago, near the Latvian coast exactly where Raphaël and his team had intended to be. Auli may not like her, and God knew the feeling was mutual, but they both feared for him when he was away. It was an odd kind of hostile complicity.

IT HAD BEEN Raphaël who'd brought Auli here the very first time. In the smaller boat that was right now tied up to the dock below. The *Meri Noita*. The *Sea Witch*. And the name ought not have added to her nerves that day, but honestly, how could it fail to do so? Sailing over feckless water where oceanic ghosts drifted almost invisible in the refracted icy light, trusting to the navigational skills of men who looked better equipped for taking lives than saving them. Auli clung to the seat the dark-eyed captain had told her not to move from, and flinched each time the patched sails snapped in the bitter wind. The ghosts they passed taunted them with glimpses of the lost – radar, bathymetry maps, a black and white image of wrecked submarines, a video of a fisherman's nets. Occasionally, when there were no ghosts close enough to interfere, that captain checked his compass, but mostly he navigated by the island shorelines they tacked between. Even then on that first day his unwavering calm had been a comfort against the fear of the hungry water beneath her, the heartache, the dread of the girl she was sailing towards.

When it finally came into view, the Bellwether, her mysterious new home, was cloaked in pale afternoon light that failed to soften the looming walls and corner towers, but that reflected off the glass dome high in its centre as if the whole stark edifice was cradling a fire gently.

You get used to it, the captain had said, almost kindly but still startling her.

Which bit? she'd wanted to ask. The guard towers and the guns, or the gathering of ghosts visible even from here? The isolation? The... *What's she like?* she'd asked, over the wind and the chink-chink of the rigging.

He shrugged, watching a ghost, his crew, the shore. *Strange. As dangerous as they say, but less frightening.*

Up on the walkway circling the largest tower, a slim figure of a girl was standing alone amidst the ghosts. Fear tangled around Auli's throat. She had written to tell her mothers about the job, assuring them the danger was likely overrated, and she was excited to work with Boudain again. She had not said *I am skipping meals because the university cannot pay me*, she had not said *I do not know why I am alive; I need to do something to make myself worthwhile.*

Boudain says you are saving lives, she'd said when the captain added nothing more.

He glanced at her, held her gaze until her heart skittered. *That's the idea,* he'd answered. *I'm Raphaël, by the way.* Then he called something else, the sail sang, the boat canted onto its other side and Auli ducked her head to stop herself screaming her brother's name.

The girl

THEY COME AGAIN as the night sky is remembering itself. She is a close-cropped moonrise, greyscale pixels, layers of contrast and sharpening. She drifts between code and impact craters, echoing.

Latitude fifty-nine minutes, fifty seconds. Longitude twenty-three minutes, zero seconds. Date, twenty-six, seven, sixteen pc...

...come on Oracle.

She is the sea of dreams; she is a focal point.

Here is a hook.

Latitude fifty-nine minutes, fifty seconds. Longitude twenty-three minutes, zero seconds. Date, twenty-six, seven, sixteen pc. Twenty-hundred hours. Come on, girl.

She is snared. All torn tissue and rain, pain red as an error message scrolling through her flesh. The numbers come and her mouth fills with them, inverse drowning. The ocean within her is undying and full of hurt.

Fifty-nine minutes, fifty seconds. Twenty-three minutes, zero seconds. Twenty-six, seven, sixteen. Two thousand. Twenty-nine, seven, eight point five, eight hundred and thirty-four, seventy-six percent. Fifty-nine minutes, fifty seconds. Twenty-three minutes, zero seconds. Twenty-six, seven, sixteen. Two thousand and one. Twenty-nine, seven, eight point five, eight hundred and thirty-three, seventy-six percent.

The numbers stop and there is a cloud sailing through her. *A rabbit!* someone calls, laughing. *No, a dragon!*

That's it? Well, give it to her then. You've already added it? Good.

Heat, familiarity. The cloud flickers and the child's laughter crackles like fire. The hook is gone and everything flickers but does not fade.

Night falls.

And is full of stars. Each one singing a single note rippling outward, every vast fire a dropped pebble in a black well. The sky sings and her skin hurts with resonance and she... she is lying in her bed, the windows curving around her like a hand halfway to a fist. She remembers falling through the sea, fish galaxies, she remembers lightning in all of her bones...

The room. The room is round and familiar and warm. She knows this place, she moves her arms and the blankets hush against her, one voice hangs in the shadows talking softly, another unspools numbers into her mind, and another tugs at the blood in her veins all deep currents and undertow.

Hello, it says. *There you are.*

Hello, she thinks, here I am.

She does not move, because if she does the numbers or the green strobe of a radar will take the place of that thought, and she will be lost.

Hello, she thinks wonderingly, here I am.

The deep dark tugs at her veins. It has teeth clear as glass and sharp as broken bones, it has waited a long, long time. She thinks perhaps so has she.

Chapter Three

Auli

AULI SLEPT FITFULLY that night, dreaming yet again of a small boat and climbing flames, of leaping into dark water and drowning, and drowning. Gasping awake to the sound of a boat's engine. Or the ghost of one.

It took her a long time to fall back to sleep and she woke again with the early summer dawn, ash on her tongue and the otter family running along the ledge below her window all claws and chatter.

From the prow of the barge, she paused to stare northward. Tendrils of mist hung over the surface of the sea, but the islands were clear sage-green and granite beneath a tannin stain of fire on the burned blue horizon. She thought of her mothers, far north in the melting sphagnum forests of Lapp. They'd last written six months ago, because paper was scarce. They'd said she mustn't lose her place here. That had been Mama Márjá's voice, Mama Sara worried instead about the ghosts, when the pain gave her space to.

The barge rocked as Dunya the cook crossed from the crew barge to theirs, then onto the slim gantry to the looming bulk of the college. Auli shook herself and followed, cutting around to the two garden barges on the south side. There were white-caps out where the deep channels lay, and she tried not to think of the returning boat. Tried not to fear. Bent fixedly to the underplanted vegetables on the first garden barge, to begin weeding.

When the man first shouted, Auli assumed it was a ghost and ignored it. But then a door slammed shut and she straightened, her shadow tangled in the peas. Someone came fast along the third deck walkway, and Auli's gut twisted. Infection, she thought.

'Hej!' It was the boatman, Miika. When he saw Auli he stilled. 'Oh good, you're a medic, right? It's PI Caron. Come.'

No. Auli rose slowly. *Not Boudain, no.* 'Boudain's infected?'

The boatman spun on his heel on the walkway above, headed towards a door. 'The Oracle Room,' he called back. A raven croaked from the library dome; out over the water its mate answered.

Auli ran through the Bellwether and met Miika at the Oracle Room door. He moved as if to stop her, and she remembered an evening years ago when he had been two aquavits past drunk and had told her woozily, *You remind me of my little sister. She was not meant for all this either.*

The past tense, far more than the near-insult, had hit her like a blow and the way he looked at her now hit her the exact same way. She moved past him into the room.

Two steps inside, she stopped, bewildered.

Boudain lay on the floor against the northern curve of the wall, legs crooked and his head tipped up to the sky, his mouth open. He had wet himself before he died.

AULI HAD ALWAYS thought the Oracle's eyes were unseeing, blinded by their own lightning, but she realised now how wrong she was.

'Fraser... you're a medic?'

Auli jerked. She hadn't even noticed Gabrielle but now threw herself across the room to kneel by Boudain's body. Because that was what it was. The man she had followed here to the middle of the Baltic Sea was gone. She set his cold hand back on his chest, then simply stared at him until Gabrielle spoke again.

'Well?'

Auli still didn't look away from Boudain's face. 'He's dead,' she said, as if they hadn't known.

'How? Clearly not ghosts.'

Auli shook her head wordlessly. How was she supposed to know that? She, along with a few others, had been trained by Niki enough to deal with most things when they were away on expeditions. But they hadn't trained her for this. She tried to close Boudain's eyes, but they wouldn't obey and horror shuddered through her.

She checked for burns, pushed up his sleeves but found nothing other than the Bellwether tattoo of a lighthouse on his forearm. Behind her, Miika had vanished but Hellä Novikova, Raphaël's second, stood against the closed door, her pale eyes wide, Gabrielle was in the middle of the room with her arms crossed, and Uoti was just that moment coming down the stairs from the Oracle's bedroom above. The acting head of security, and the PIs of Weather and Oceans. They all watched Auli.

'When was he found?' Auli said faintly.

'Suvi found him when she came on first listening shift,' Uoti said.

Gabrielle shifted her weight. 'Heart attack,' she said. 'Surely. We'll announce in the Hall, move his body...' She hesitated, her stern, dark face made sterner by the tight scrape of greying hair away from her temples. They weren't used to having entire bodies to deal with – even the ones who chose the morphine were usually too slow or too hopeful to die whole.

'The underdeck storeroom furthest from the kitchen,' Hellä Novikova supplied. 'It's the coolest place.'

Gabrielle nodded without turning. 'The funeral will be this evening.'

'We don't know how he died,' Uoti said, and Auli sagged with relief that he'd said what she wanted to. 'We need to know before we bury him.'

Gabrielle fixed him with a flat stare. 'It's midsummer. We can't delay burial.'

'He was healthy,' Auli whispered. 'He didn't have heart trouble.'

'Confided everything in you, did he?'

Like his research plans? Auli looked away, tried to treat her mentor's body the way Niki would, but still tentatively, as if he would wake.

'The Oracle is sleeping,' Uoti said.

Auli paid no attention. There was no blood that she could see, no signs of… what, Auli? she thought to herself. What is it you are looking for? Put it into words.

'Good. Once we've Boudain moved, we can get the listeners back on task. Hellä? Use Célestine's winch.'

The door opened and closed.

…signs of a struggle, Auli thought. There were no signs of a struggle.

She checked his fingernails for blood. The tie that he alone insisted on still wearing had loosened, his throat vulnerable and bluish, the vial of valerian hanging sideways. A song ghost drifted through the window, a man and a guitar singing in an English from a continent no one had heard from in sixteen years.

'What are you doing?'

She turned his head very gently, fighting against revulsion, horror, pity, panic. No bruising.

'Fraser?'

She didn't even know why she was looking, because who would want to kill Boudain Caron, the least important of the Bellwether's ruling triad?

We could change the world, dear, he whispered.

'He was healthy,' she repeated. And then, a little desperately, 'Niki is due back today.'

'There's no guarantee they'll arrive.'

Heat climbed Auli's throat as she rose and looked to Uoti rather than Gabrielle. 'But they might. I just... I'd feel better if an actual doctor examined him. Isn't it standard?'

Gabrielle recrossed her arms tightly.

'It's true, Gab. Rule out disease.'

'Or ghosts,' Auli added, although she didn't know why and regretted it immediately.

Gabrielle looked from Auli to Uoti. 'It's none of them. Look at him, do you see *any* signs of disease? And the fact we have a body at all rules out ghosts. Which one would hope you knew, Fraser. He's an old man in a world that's lost half its medical capabilities.' She turned to Uoti, the conversation abruptly binary. 'Let him rest.'

Auli looked from one to the other. How must it feel, she wondered, to be the person in the room everyone obeyed?

The thought might have been enticing, if you were not Auli.

'If Niki's back today, they can examine Boudain's body. Either way we proceed with the burial tonight,' Uoti equivocated. 'We follow infection protocol, Gab.'

Gabrielle shuddered very slightly. 'I've no objection to Niki examining him, did I say that? But' – she turned and Auli forced herself not to quail – 'you understand, Auli, we are a small community dependent on rationality. I appreciate wanting to do right by Boudain, but rein in any flights of fancy.'

'Yes,' Auli said. Her throat was full of dust and spiders. 'I just want Niki to look at him. I am' – she gestured at herself despairingly – 'unqualified for this.'

Uoti rested a hand on her shoulder. 'You have done just fine. We'll take care of him, you know we will.'

The inner door opened and two boatmen entered, tall and blond and bulky in Auli's peripheral vision, but she was trapped by the sorrow in Uoti's eyes and the knowledge that she was in shock still. That she had all of her sorrow to come.

'Right, I'll make an announcement in the Hall at breakfast.'

Uoti nodded at Gabrielle and dropped his hand. 'Fraser, will you cover the listener duties until Suvi returns? It won't be onerous.'

The boatmen crouched beside Boudain, a hammock stretched between them, and they handled his body as if that were all it was. Auli couldn't watch.

URSULA PORONEN LIFTED her head from her knitting when Auli reached the top of the Oracle Tower. Too sparsely furnished to feel quite comfortable, this room was just two beds fitted awkwardly into the curved walls, a table, a long cupboard, the necessary luxury of a tiny bathroom, and the door out to the walkway. No electrics up here, for the fire risk. Instead, old brass oil-lamps sat oddly elegant in this slipshod exposed space that was the metaphorical lightroom in the tattoo on Auli's arm. The carer was sitting on her bed, and the Oracle curled childlike on the other, so Auli perched on the desk, between a jumble of shells, a mug crusted with hot chocolate, fish bones, twists of metal and gleaming sea glass. Odd, for the Oracle to sleep this time of day, but Auli was grateful for it.

'You okay?' she said in Finnish. Ursula watched her mouth, then released one knitting needle to point at the stairs.

'They're taking him down to the cold store,' Auli said. Something twisted sharply beneath her ribs. 'They think it was a heart attack.'

Ursula did not move, her eyes on a spot over Auli's shoulder. 'You agree?' she said eventually.

Auli had never said much beyond hello and goodbye to the carer, the rule not to speak to the Oracle seeming somehow to leach into the carer, too. But she found herself wanting to talk now. To talk and talk so she did not have to think.

'I don't know. I can recognise a heart attack happening, not the... aftermath. There were no burns. Did you hear—' She cut off, annoyed at the mistake. Ursula picked up her needle again, seemed to notice the way it shook and lay the whole lot down in her lap.

'The light was on,' she said.

Auli frowned. 'Late?'

A nod, her fingers flexing in the wool. The Oracle stirred, murmured, a tattered photo ghost circling above her. The crew were only permitted the small vials of valerian around their necks, none for scattering. They needed the ghosts drawn to the Oracle, not deterred, and the tonic they all took twice weekly was supposed to be protection enough. But sometimes Auli found herself wishing for the tangible, gritty comfort of the herb within her palms.

'I wonder why. Did he do the late seeding session?'

Ursula glanced at the girl, the slantwise light in her eyes as she nodded.

Auli had not spoken to him after their meeting. She'd left without even returning his smile, and God, but she wished...

Ursula stiffened. Auli realised she had gasped.

No, she thought. There were no wounds, no blood beneath his nails. And besides, only she and Leigh knew he'd planned to resurrect a disastrous experiment; Auli was being absurd, and Gabrielle was surely right. She relaxed her balled hands. Her unease, her fears were only because she needed Niki's authority, and because it was easier to focus on the *how*, than face the *now what*.

Auli stood, making shells clatter to the floor. The Oracle cried out in her sleep. Another ghost echoed her beyond the window, a child crying for its mother, but Auli paid it no attention, already at the stairwell.

The room below was empty now. Some HTML code was spooling slowly where Boudain had been, black and green and static. There were voices on the research deck, people coming up to start work because the Bellwether didn't stop for death. Which meant soon Suvi would return to listening duty, and Auli didn't have long.

Like the room upstairs, this one, too, was kept sparse for avoiding ghosts. Only an old, heavyweight wooden desk tucked beneath the stairs, a worn red rug, and a scattering of chairs. Auli went to the desk, sifted through a clipboard with some corner fragments of torn-off paper, part of a physics textbook, some pens and at the very back, almost invisible in the shadow of the stairs, Boudain's favourite mug. She stared down into the chocolate-scented dregs for a moment before setting it aside.

Two drawers were missing, but in the top one was the skull of a bird, a pencil worn down to a stub, a brass compass whose needle spun lazily, confused by the ghosts or the Oracle or both. A glass bottle with a faded label and black rubber dropper only a little decayed.

Auli held that to the light and then set it beside the mug. None of it was what she was looking for, which was a relief. The notes for his godawful project must be in his room, and she supposed she would have to find them before anyone else did. That was all she could think to do right now. Find the notes so no one could gossip about him – so no one could think less of him.

She turned towards the door, and then, beneath all the varied voices of the Bellwether – another sound. One she'd been listening for since that first moment of seeing Boudain's body in a line of vanishing sunlight.

Chapter Four

Raphaël

RAPHAËL GIROUX – CAPTAIN, Bellwether head of security, unusually irritable – watched the Bellwether rise into view around Grisselkobb headland and called the order for the turn into the bay. The wind was against them but the tide with, so he wasn't wasting precious battery. Besides, it brought him distraction, the work of sailing.

From the cargo he was bringing within the Bellwether's walls. From the echo of Mariehamm's harbourmaster that morning as they loaded the last supplies. He'd been passing on news of ships sunk by unforecast storms, unmapped rocks, mines, wrecks, or simply losing their way on a lying compass out of sight of land. Everyone had relearned the old knowledge fast, but the pole star didn't much help with ghosts, pirates or forgotten munitions. She'd told him about the still-absent cod, the local mood, the rumours.

'Be wary,' she'd said, squinting into the sunrise. 'Fools stirring tempers on the mainland and this weather's got to break soon. A bad combination, hey?'

Very. 'The forecast team are getting another boost.' He'd nodded at the *Meren Rouva*. 'And we can handle a little trouble.'

She'd sucked on her teeth. 'You can, but the islands can't. And if trouble comes looking for you, we're right in its path.'

There had been little Raphaël could say to that. It was true, and he wouldn't make promises he couldn't deliver. 'Be wary,' he'd echoed. 'And wiser than the fools.'

She'd laughed, gone to slap his shoulder then remembered where he was bound, and instead thrown a pointed handful of valerian at a ghost and walked back down the jetty.

THE *MEREN ROUVA* tacked gracefully, close enough now to see the boatman on duty in West Tower, the faint movement of ghosts around the Oracle Tower.

Eight years ago, he and Célestine had stood in Helsinki harbour, eyeing the burned ruins of the harbourfront, and then the cherubic face of the woman who'd met them.

You are a welcome sight, she'd said. *Your letter only got here four days ago so you're lucky we got in. Célestine...* She'd studied Célestine's chair, then both their blistered hands and torn clothes. *We need you and your data brain badly, I'm not going to lie. And as for you, Giroux.* Her perusal of Raphaël left him feeling like a schoolboy. *Not military, but you look capable.*

I am, he said. *If I'm given the autonomy and manpower. What happened to my predecessor – politics or ghosts?*

Vienna Simon laughed. *Oh, it's always the ghosts, on the Bellwether. The politics is just, ah, healthy competition between research departments. And now we've got Célestine, Weather will progress faster than Ocean can dream of.*

Célestine was not listening. She gestured with her chin at the damage to the harbour. *How soon will this happen to us, if we join you?*

As if, Raphaël thought, they would turn away after coming so far, through so much. He'd take ghosts and the need for mercilessness over all the graves they'd left behind.

The Bellwether's founder didn't lie. *It's better than it was, and you've seen what we're working on. Well? Coming?*

Célestine looked up at Raphaël and raised one eyebrow. *Death or glory?* she said. He laughed. And they'd sailed this final leg to the Bellwether, too relieved to have arrived for trepidation.

Two years ago, he'd done the same journey, fiercely anticipating seeing Auli again after a long month away. Then that night she'd asked him a very simple question, and because he was an idiot, he had answered out of instinct carved by loss, and lost her.

Today he was simply bad-tempered and bone tired. Worrying about a solid dozen things beyond his control and only half-pleased to be returning to the place he called home.

'I've not missed the ghost soup,' An said at his side.

Raphaël grinned at the engineer. 'But you have missed the people.'

She snorted. 'Less than the ghosts. At least the ghosts have an excuse for being irritating. How soon do you want those explosives ready for your new toys?'

'Soon,' Raphaël said. He leaned sideways to eye the sky, which was why he didn't see the ghost until Sandesh shouted.

''Ware ghost! Dead ahead!' he yelled from the foredeck, then another voice yelped, and Raphaël saw only a haze of static against the clear air, a dark shape over the prow, before he swung the wheel sharply and the sails lost their wind with a lurch that rattled all the way through the deck.

'Fuck me,' An swore, knocked to one knee on the veering deck. Raphaël shouted instructions and the crew leapt for sheets, ducking beneath the wildly swinging boom, as the hull shuddered again. The ghost hissed and Raphaël very nearly lost his grip on the wheel as the wind caught at the sails again and static swept over the bow along with... 'Fuck me,' An repeated. 'Are those *tentacles?*'

They were, and Raphaël was swearing too, but they were through it now, slower than they ought to be as if it were clinging to the hull. The moment he was sure it wasn't a fire risk, he shouted, 'Reef sails.' And started the engine.

Everyone else watched the ghost slip into their wake as Raphaël concentrated on putting solid distance between them, and it was An, of course, who said what they were all thinking.

'Well, that was bigger and uglier than any ghost has a right to be.' And then, with a laugh, 'You nearly had me in the drink, throwing her about like that. You bastard.'

Raphaël didn't reply. Because it hadn't been his evasive steering that had made the boat shudder like it had hit a rock. It had been the ghost, and that was impossible.

Auli

THE BOAT WAS coming in on its engines, the solar panels across its prow reflecting the light darkly as a gull and a ghost both drifted in its wake. Something shadowy and shifting, perhaps underwater footage, perhaps a movie. Normally Auli made sure not to watch them return, but this time her mind was on Niki, so she didn't care if she was seen and misunderstood.

The door behind her opened, and Auli turned quickly, feeling the fizz of static as her hand passed through a ghost she had not even seen.

'Full fathom five,' it whispered in English as she pulled her hand back sharply, reflexively touching the vial of valerian at her throat.

'Uh, hi, I'm back on duty, is she upstairs?'

It was Suvi, Célestine's assistant. A human calculator, like the women who carried men to the moon, her clever mind half the power behind Célestine's work rebuilding forecasting models that made the local fishermen and the trade ships a fraction more forewarned of some of the dangers on the water. It didn't sound like much, but aside from Uoti's harbour approach bathymetry maps, these piecemeal forecasts were the College's biggest contracts. If you were venturing out without maps or even reliable compasses onto an irrevocably warmed and uncertain sea, you'd pay steeply for fragments too.

The boat swung out of view towards the dock.

'Yes,' Auli said, collecting the mug from the desk, then after a small hesitation, the bottle as well. 'She's sleeping.'

'No wonder.' Suvi moved towards the stairs, then hesitated uncomfortably. 'Are you okay? You knew each other before, and he'd survived longer than anyone.'

'I'm fine,' she lied. 'Thank you.'

'And he wasn't *that* old really.'

'He wasn't old at all,' Auli muttered. 'He was barely into his sixties.'

But Suvi was twenty-two, and the world had changed, and Auli felt briefly ancient in the face of the girl's polite disbelief. She opened her mouth to say something else but then remembered Gabrielle's words and said instead, 'I'd better go. Sorry.'

Suvi nodded, tapped her knuckles three times on the wall, checked her own vial, then climbed up into the room above. No one knew when the tapping had begun, but somehow everyone did it. As she skirted the research deck's Centre, Auli was more fiercely aware of the people there than ever because they were aware of her, too, today. And the whispers weren't about Boudain's death.

She dumped the mug and bottle in her desk, then wove through the Bellwether to the steps leading down to the floating dock. There was no access into the Bellwether on the first level, only blank metal walls and this single steep route up to the second level walkway. Because the Bellwether was not just a college, it was also a fortress, and it did not let you forget it.

Auli paused at the top of the steps, watching the boatmen tying up the big sailing boat. Two men and the terrifying engineer, An Carline, were unloading crates, swaying with the movement of the dock. Raphaël was bent over the engine compartment, probably laying boobytraps and he had his back to her but straightened and turned, looking directly up at her with the sun in his eyes. She ignored both him and the heat in her cheeks, which was frankly pathetic after all this time, and ran down the steps.

'Niki,' she called to the other figure on deck. Raphaël frowned, glanced at the doctor, then at her and took a step closer.

Niki abandoned fighting with a bag strap to push their hair off their glasses. 'Auli, what's—'

'What's wrong?'

An passed Auli, sparing her one curious glance, as the Bellwether door above opened with a creak and everyone other than Raphaël straightened marginally.

'I need you,' Auli said. 'Niki, Boudain's…' Her throat ached abruptly, grief hovering around her like a settling cloak. 'He died last night. Not ghosts. We need an autopsy.' She reached out as if they might refuse, but after a flash of shock, they were already climbing down to the dock, and it would be okay now. Niki would find out what had happened, and she could lay Boudain to rest without this terrible doubt that she was doing her mentor wrong by her own incompetence.

Gabrielle spoke from the walkway as Auli turned. 'Fraser. Very prompt of you. Captain, welcome back. Doctor, sorry to rush you. I hope this is just a formality.'

Auli didn't meet Gabrielle's gaze or look at Raphaël as she led Niki back up the stairs, and down to the underdeck. Joar

Gunnarson was leaning against the storeroom door, turning a knife between his hands in the gloom.

'Ah, Doc, you're here,' he said in Finnish, moving aside. The sea knocked against the floor, slow and erratic, the tide turbines thrummed, and Auli shuddered. Joar grinned at her. 'Scared of ghosts?' He laughed as she ducked her head and followed Niki into the storeroom.

The boatmen had laid a sheet over some crates to make a rudimentary table and Boudain was a pale, shrouded shape in the cluttered room that smelled of vegetable oil, wet iron and flour. And on top of those, of death and ammonia.

How ungentle it was, Auli thought. How disrespectful and sordid, and she wanted to stop Niki from reaching for the sheet but only said cautiously, 'Gabrielle assumes it was a heart attack, but he was fine last night. And I don't know…'

Niki had folded the sheet back and was peering at Boudain's staring eyes, lifting the lids, pulling his lips back from his teeth, lifting his hands and studying the fingers.

'When was he found? Where?'

Auli told them.

They began to undo his shirt and Auli looked away, then shook herself hard. She needed to be useful. 'What are you looking for?' she said.

'Post-mortem stages to estimate time of death. But if there are no injuries, there's a good chance I know what killed him, directly or indirectly.'

'You do?' Auli stepped forward involuntarily. Niki looked up and met her gaze gravely. They'd been here almost as long as Auli, and of everyone on the Bellwether, it was probably the two of them who had liked Boudain the most.

'He had cancer,' Niki said bluntly. 'Of the bowel. I diagnosed it a few months ago.'

Auli stared at them. 'He never told me.'

'He didn't want anyone to know. I was trying to obtain

chemotherapy drugs on this trip. They're nigh on impossible to find but there's a chance…' They looked down at Boudain's pale chest. 'Well, it doesn't matter now.'

Auli didn't understand. 'What do you mean, directly or indirectly?'

Niki gave her a vanishingly quick smile. 'Well caught,' they said, and nudged their glasses up their nose. 'I'll check, but I don't expect the cancer was extensive enough to cause a crisis event. I suspect he instead decided to avoid a drawn out and painful end.' Niki shrugged heavily, their eyes kind.

Auli gaped. 'No. No, Niki. Why in the Oracle Room, not in his bed? Why not leave a note? Why, when he had just…' Shaking her head more firmly with every question. 'He was excited about a new research project last night. It's not possible. He wouldn't do *that* hours after persuading me to agree to a new project.'

'What project?' Niki said.

But the words dried up and she only shook her head again.

Niki waited another moment. 'Perhaps he knew you'd carry it on. Perhaps that was him handing over.'

Handing over?

Auli grasped the edge of a crate for support. The sea knocked mockingly beneath her feet, and she felt briefly like one of the fish shoaling down there, blind-eyed and in the dark.

Niki huffed softly. 'Congratulations on your promotion, Auli. You're one of the holy trinity now.'

'No,' Auli whispered. She'd been trying so hard not to face this.

Niki didn't answer, only bent their head again and returned to removing Boudain's clothes. 'Can you help?' they said after a moment.

No, Auli thought. No, she couldn't help with what Niki was about to do to the body of the man who had given her a home, and she couldn't step into that same man's shoes. She definitely couldn't take over the research project he had been so excited about.

Niki raised their voice and switched to Finnish, 'Joar? You there?'

The boatman leaned in, looked questioningly at Niki, ignoring Auli entirely. God, she thought, *her*, a PI? She almost laughed.

'A tarp please. Two buckets of water, my black case from the boat, and two more lamps.'

'Fresh?'

'Salt's fine.'

Joar vanished.

'Auli?' Niki said.

Auli pried her fingers off the crate edge. And followed Niki's instructions with her mind suspended between the strange, sordid horror of what her hands were doing, and the terrible prospect of what was awaiting her on the decks above.

An hour later they were finished, and Auli's head ached, nausea coiling in her stomach from the smell, the shifting floor, the knocking of the waves underfoot.

Niki was stitching a neat line back up Boudain's torso, their fingers bloody.

'It's so undignified. He'd hate it,' she said.

Niki glanced up through their fringe. 'He was pragmatic. If it answered questions, he'd think it worth a little indignity.'

Auli held her bloody hands out like deep sea creatures. 'And has it? Answered questions?'

Niki tied off, cut the thread and set the needle aside, straightening with a sigh. 'Some, yes. I'd say he died before midnight. There was some fluid on his lungs, but the cancer wasn't what killed him.'

'A brush with a ghost? A shock strong enough to kill him?'

'No burns.'

Of course not. She was an idiot.

'So...'

Niki reached for the bowl of water, then wiped the last of the blood from the suture line with a cloth. 'So I can test the blood and stomach contents, but he took something, Auli.'

Auli poured out the last of the clean water for her own hands, studying the spiralling blood in the bowl, nausea like a weight. 'He killed himself.'

'I'm sorry. I know he meant a lot to you.'

Mentor, almost-friend, saviour, perhaps father figure although she'd never had one so how would she recognise it? 'How did he get hold of it?' she said. When Niki didn't reply, she looked up from her hands. They were drying Boudain down slowly, a frown visible behind their glasses.

'That's a very good question. If anyone has been helping themselves to my stores, then I need better locks.'

'I have the key,' Auli said. 'So do the other medics. That's three.'

Niki shook their head. 'Only to the standard stuff. Don't worry, I'll figure it out. You want to go get a set of clothes for burial? Give him back some of that dignity.'

It was a little frivolous – good quality clothes were hard to find, and opportunities to trade for them even rarer. But he was a PI, that counted for something. He was *Boudain*, which to her counted for far more. Auli dried her hands and escaped the salt-blood-tainted room.

BOUDAIN'S BEDROOM, ON the second deck along from the main hall, was messier than she'd expected of him, but still they none of them owned much. It took only a few minutes to find clean clothes, worn but not shabby, for him to be buried in. She chose a tie the colour of forests, remembered tying her brother's, him pretending to choke, Mama Sara laughing softly.

'Thanks,' Niki said when she returned. And then, 'Go. It must be lunchtime. Tell the PIs I'll report as soon as I'm done here.'

'Don't you need help with—'

'I'm nearly done.'

Auli was moving towards the door before they'd even finished speaking. The Bellwether creaked and swayed, somewhere a ghost emitted an incoherent wall of sound then fell silent.

Chapter Five

Raphaël

RAPHAËL LEANED BACK in his chair, laying silent odds as it creaked on it giving way. After showering for the first time in days, then getting Hellä's report of her command in his absence, he'd come down to the boatmen's barge rooftop. Even in the depths of winter, someone would find something combustible and they'd huddle around the fire here, gossiping like old women about the researchers, the news, each other, the past.

But there was no fire today, nor yet alcohol and there were some subjects they'd not broach in his presence, one of which Boudain's death edged a little close to. Raphaël held himself relaxed, ostensibly studying the distant thumbprint of wildfire smoke on the northern sky, and listened.

'Sweet way to go, though.'

'True enough.'

'I sure wouldn't complain. Quietly, among friends, buried with respect.'

General sounds of agreement. Raphaël had never been a soldier so there were a number of things he only understood slantwise. This wasn't one of them.

'You think they'll let her replace—' The speaker cut off with a grunt of pain.

Raphaël concentrated on guessing which bit of the mainland was burning. He remembered when the wildfires started in France before the Crash. How alien a creature it was; how familiar now. *The world will heal after we are gone,* his mother had said, *and she will not mourn us near so much as she mourns the cricket or the sparrow.*

We cut too deep, he wanted to tell her now. *She's taking her time healing. And I still mourn you.*

'Might scrap his unit altogether. Everyone knows it doesn't bring in the contracts.'

'And Gabrielle's been wanting control forever. This is her chance.'

Someone hissed between their teeth.

'Will you let her, Captain?'

He sighed. 'Thankfully so long as no one's trying to kill or steal the Oracle, I can stay well clear of academic squabbling.' Scattered laughter as he levered to standing. 'Frans, go shower, you're scaring the ghosts. Miika, relieve Joar in twenty, will you? We're fitting the mounts in the towers tomorrow, while Sandesh and An build the explosive heads.'

'Boomtime,' Hellä said delightedly.

'Maybe we'll see the ghost that tried to fry you all on the way in,' Miika said. 'I want to try sticking a harpoon in *that*. Bet I get a clean shot quicker than any of you idiots.'

He would, Raphaël thought, treat the harpoons as just a more dramatic form of snipering. Anything to be better than Joar at hitting small things from very far away, with, as he regularly pointed out, half as many fingers.

The bickering began but Raphaël was already on the walkway to the Bellwether, the sway of it unfamiliar after a month away. He hadn't been especially fond of the dead PI, who'd been far too aware of his own intellect, but he hadn't *disliked* him, and the repercussions of his death were uncomfortable. Auli would do a better job of PI than Boudain, in Raphaël's opinion. But then what?

The research deck was no quieter than normal, Célestine busy at a blackboard and Auli at her own desk, talking to Bea and a young, unfamiliar man. Raphaël looked away and crossed through the middle of the deck towards Uoti's office, nodding to a few folk but not slowing.

'Raphaël,' Uoti greeted him. 'Good to see you. How was the trip?'

'Fine. Here's the updated list of restored and deployed buoys.' Raphaël set a sheet of paper down between them. 'I've messages from contractors and the university – I assume Auli's taking the promotion?'

'Oh.' Uoti looked briefly startled. 'I haven't checked. She's been helping Niki with the autopsy, but I suppose we ought... I'll get Gabrielle.' He pushed to his feet, rubbing a hand over a still-stubbled chin. Niki's herbal substitutes must be working – the pure hormones had long vanished, not enough of anyone's priority and one of the new world's smaller cruelties, Raphaël thought.

He shifted his weight as the Bellwether tugged on the changing tide.

Uoti paused, curious. 'There's bad news?'

Raphaël shook his head. 'I got hold of the salvage we required for the higher power arms.'

'That's good news then. What are they?'

Raphaël crossed to the windows. The walkway was empty and so was the sea – no ghosts, no Oracle and no eavesdroppers, just a loose flock of gulls high overhead, drifting east.

Half-turning, he put his back to the side wall; the walkway and the whole of the office in his field of view. 'Explosive harpoons. The big industrial whaler ones. Sandesh and An will double check the grenade heads and we'll start training with unarmed ones tomorrow.'

'I hear a *but*?'

'But these explosives are old. There's no guarantees.'

Uoti's eyebrows raised. 'How risky is it?'

Raphaël shrugged. 'We won't know until they go bang when we don't want them to, or don't when we do.'

Uoti rubbed that palm over his chin again. 'The danger to the Bellwether…'

'Once made, they'll be stored in the guard towers.' He didn't add what that meant for the unlucky bastards on duty. 'The added safety, though, will be considerable.'

'Worth the risk?'

'Half the Baltic think the Oracle, and by association you lot, are too dangerous to live. The other half are increasingly wondering whether they'd get results faster if they had the Oracle.' He had wanted military grenade launchers, but instead got these things with their ugly history, and the sheer subjectiveness of his distaste was comical. 'Tensions on the mainland are rising, too, and the pirates getting bolder. We were attacked three times—'

Uoti hissed. A ghost did the same, a haze of degraded code. 'You're alright, though?'

'Pfft. They were ill-equipped and desperate. The fishing has been almost non-existent.'

Uoti grimaced, fishing data was his department. Raphaël watched a lobster boat beyond the bay, then returned his focus to Uoti.

'You'll support it with the others?'

The other man pushed off the desk and joined him at the window, hands behind his back, fingers flexing unconsciously. Raphaël waited. The ghost crackled sharply then emitted one low moaning sound of distorted audio data.

'You don't need permission.' Uoti said without turning.

Which was true. The Bellwether rocked, Raphaël shifted again; he'd grown too used to a boat. 'But you'll be fielding questions from researchers. Gabrielle is about to become very unimpressed with me, and Auli doesn't know it was planned and won't like it.'

'Gabrielle was in a foul mood even before your news.' Uoti huffed a laugh. 'Poor Boudain.'

Raphaël didn't answer. He thought of the words of his boatmen, of all the ways a person could die.

'We need defence against vessels. However good your boatmen, they're still just people with rifles and the high ground.'

Which was not an inconsiderable advantage, but still.

Uoti turned around, almost smiling. 'Fine then. I take it this is all so I'll explain it to Auli?'

Raphaël was rather pleased with himself for not wincing. 'Track down Gabrielle. I'll get Auli.'

Uoti eyed him and Raphaël wondered what he was thinking, but in the end he only nodded. 'Gab and I should speak to Auli first, although it's only a formality. Can you send her down and give us twenty minutes?'

RAPHAËL LET HIMSELF back into the main room and started towards Célestine – he'd only managed one insufficient hug earlier – but then the library came into view, revealing Auli on the upper walkway amongst the unhaunted books. He pivoted and scaled the ladders to her quickly.

'Auli,' he said. The sky hung blue and tarnished through the dome above them, the sun high, and he caught himself unconsciously checking the time on his watch, the angle of the sun, reaching into his pocket for the compass that only worked fifty percent of the time. Two months of navigating an unnavigable sea.

'Are you allowed up here?'

Raphaël shrugged. 'Security,' he said. 'I'm not sure anywhere is off-limits to me.' Apart from the obvious.

Auli flushed slightly. She had a book open across her forearms. There was a datacloud ghost floating just behind her and he shoved his hands into his pockets.

'PI meeting downstairs. But first I need to ask a favour,' he said, a little abruptly. 'As the new PI.'

Her eyes widened, and the freckles on her cheekbones stood out like a scatter of ink. 'What, now?' she blurted, and then looked up at the sky, breathed in and out slowly, and looked back at him. 'Okay. Can we talk up here? I'd rather not use his office, it feels… transgressive.'

Raphaël moved two step stools to the furthest point from the datacloud ghost, and sat watching her approach, the sun on her hair catching blue highlights in the black.

Auli

'So what is it?' Auli asked slowly, laying the book on the bars by her feet, notebook and pencil on her knee. Aside from making skirts hazardous, the open metalwork of the walkways meant you could see anyone below. It was an oddly intimate public space up here beneath the dome, with the sea's motion both stronger and quieter than anywhere else.

Raphaël watched her unsmiling. 'Actually, it can wait. I'm sorry about Caron, I know what he meant to you.'

Perhaps he did, but she couldn't talk about Boudain now. 'How did the trip go?' she tried instead. 'Were the buoys deployed last time still working?'

Raphaël grimaced. 'We relocated fourteen of them; nine were fried.'

'Oh.' That was bad news. They'd only been out a year.

'An got eight cleansed, one needed bringing in.' He paused. 'They attract ghosts, the wardings don't last.'

'Yes.' He knew she knew this. She wanted to bristle but resisted. 'The new ones?'

'Half deployed running south to Hiiumaa, the rest east of Gotland. Twenty-three total. Uoti's got the coordinates for seeding.'

'That's good.' She looked at her blank notepad, then back up. 'Is everyone alright?'

Raphaël glanced down through the walkway. 'Everyone is alive. A few minor injuries from a pirate scuffle. Oh, we found two PAM buoys and a satellite tag in a market in Tallinn. Big one, probably from a seal.'

Auli's eyes widened, Raphaël almost smiled.

'Dunya's annoyed about the lack of sugar, but...' He flipped his hands in a *what can you do?* gesture.

'What was the favour?' she said.

He leaned forward, elbows on knees. 'I was going to ask Boudain to look into it, but it's likely nothing. I don't...'

Auli wondered whether it was worry for her, or doubts about her abilities making him hesitate.

'Alors. There was a ghost just beyond Flatskär. It was unusual.'

'Unusual,' she repeated.

He shook his head. 'Bigger, and it came out of nowhere so we ran right through it—'

'Anyone infected?' she interrupted.

'No. A few shocks, but there was...' He trailed off.

'What?'

Raphaël blew out a breath. 'I don't know, Auli. As we went through it, the boat *jolted*. Like we'd hit something.'

Auli stared at him, whispering, 'It frightened you,' before she could stop herself.

He scowled at her, predictably, and straightened. 'Ghosts don't have mass. I don't like an enemy I can't understand.'

She opened her mouth to explain it hadn't been mockery but horror. His unflappability, his sheer competence, was the lynchpin of the Bellwether's safety. She didn't want to even contemplate something that frightened *Raphaël*. But instead, she said, 'So we'll figure it out. What was it of?'

A rock pipit landed on the glass above them with a faint skitter of claws.

'A kraken, would you believe?'

Auli tapped her pencil on her notepad. 'A movie. The jolt was probably the engine shorting. What were the coordinates? Was there any dialogue?' She glanced up and faltered. He was annoyed – it was in the line of his jaw, the way his eyes had shifted from forest brown to something more impenetrable.

'We were under sail, so it wasn't the engine.'

She ducked her head, hair falling over one shoulder. 'Right… So, was it drifting towards the Oracle?'

Raphaël cracked two knuckles, which Auli had always hated, and took her notepad, writing down coordinates in his quick, slanted scrawl. 'It's probably nothing, and you have other things to worry about now.'

Boudain, Auli thought, and his new project and an assistant she didn't know what to do with. 'I'll look into it,' she said, and stood up. 'I should…' Go to the PI meeting. God. It was hot under the dome and she wanted to be outside suddenly, breathing salt air and the mineral tang of the sunbaked islands.

Raphaël was watching her too carefully.

'You alright?' he asked.

'Yes.' She could not bear his pity, not now. 'We'll need the boat this evening.'

He nodded. 'Auli, I'm—'

She cut him off. 'Poor Joar has been standing watch in the underdeck for hours now, you might want to—'

Raphaël raised his eyebrows, that deadly kindness erased. 'You're PI, Auli, not my boss. Or Joar's mother.'

For a long moment Auli couldn't speak, then she simply turned away, sliding down the ladder to the lower deck without looking back.

BEFORE GOING TO the PI's lounge, not that she was delaying at all, Auli took Boudain's mug to Niki. Their room was right beside Raphaël's office on the north-east side, central, where the Bellwether's movement was smallest. No one wanted a wave or a changing tide to interfere with surgery, and they had planned for permanence, building this place. Auli wondered whether believing in it was enough to make it true.

'I found this, too.' She held out the bottle and Niki glanced up from their workbench, took it from her quickly and threw it into a tray of items awaiting sterilisation.

'Just an old bottle,' they said, already looking back at a rack of test-tubes. 'I'll test the coffee if I can't get a clear answer from the blood.'

'It was hot chocolate.' As if that mattered. Boudain had a sweet tooth, and sometimes the carer made him a mug of the rare treat alongside the Oracle's. *There's got to be some perks to being the old man of the Bellwether,* he'd said to Auli once, grinning like a child.

Niki nodded. It was a dismissal and Auli stood for a moment, oddly bereft.

'Can you...' She hesitated, but it was them who'd first pointed out her new position. 'Will you report to me first, with whatever you find?'

She half-expected them to refuse. But they only unscrewed the lid of a bottle, and said, 'It won't be for hours.'

So she left them and forced herself down to the second deck, the room directly below the Oracle Room where Boudain had died. Gabrielle and Uoti were already there, talking about the funeral. Auli sat in a leather chair that was worn to a soft grey nap over the arms, and curled her fingers in her lap.

'Yes, I'll do the sending off,' she agreed, when Uoti asked. 'Shall I write to his ex-wife, or his son? They should know.'

Gabrielle snorted quietly. 'She made her opinion of him clear long ago. It's been, what, twelve years? He's dead to them already.'

Auli stiffened, as did Uoti, and Gabrielle noticed, ran a hand over the tight curls escaping her bun, and added, 'Write to them then, just don't expect a response. And if they've left Lahti there's not much we can do.'

Auli wanted to say she knew full well how hard it was to trace someone now, how easy for someone found to become lost, for someone lost to become dead. She nodded, forcing her hands to relax. 'Okay. The letter can go on the next boat.' She prepared to rise, hoping to delay the other conversation until after the funeral.

Uoti gave her no choice.

'You're happy to be PI? We will formalise things through the university if so.'

Gabrielle scrutinised Auli like a specimen. 'It's a lot of responsibility.'

It was understandable they would doubt her, she doubted herself. But still it stung. Boudain had been the one to tell her she was capable of leading teams, strong enough to stand up to Gabrielle, brave enough to live here. But Boudain had lied to her about his research and then killed himself. So now she had no one.

'What would happen if I didn't take it?'

Gabrielle looked, if possible, more disapproving. Uoti only shook his head slightly. 'We would open the position up to the other Seniors. There are a couple who may be willing to change to… a different research arc for the position.'

A less important research arc, he meant. Célestine would, and would be a better leader, Auli thought sourly, but knew nothing, and cared less, about qualitative research.

Gabrielle recrossed her legs and glanced at the corner of the room where a ghost was turning a slow spiral. A shaky video from a racing yacht. 'There is the option to restructure,' she said. 'Aggregating research areas would strengthen our balance sheets.'

Uoti failed to look surprised.

'Get rid of Qualitative Data?' Auli said bluntly, then wished she hadn't.

'Gabrielle, we can talk about this another time,' Uoti interjected.

Gabrielle's foot was ticking gently. The Oracle appeared beyond the windows, her lightning eyes unfocused; two ghosts trailed her, then Leigh and Tobias with clipboards and a few seconds later, Ursula Poronen, her sewing dangling from one hand. Some crew paid her to repair their clothes or sew entirely new ones. Auli had made do with her own questionable skills so far and it showed.

Once they had gone, Gabrielle reached for a coffee that must surely have grown cold, and studied Auli over its rim.

'We need to demonstrate the College's efficacy at delivering on its mission. Can QD really do that?'

Auli imagined Boudain cocking his eyebrow with mild curiosity and saying *You think reducing our research remit, our vision and potential, would help us?*

She rose abruptly and very much did not mention the new funding he'd just secured. To Uoti rather than Gabrielle, she said, 'I'll take the job, and go write that letter.'

'No rush,' he said. 'We missed the seeding session this morning so there wasn't enough data for a daily forecast. The flag's up; the boat won't come in till tomorrow.'

'Oh, of course.'

Gabrielle's mouth tightened but was it any wonder Auli had forgotten when it was only one more thing on the list of things coming undone today?

'And the captain should... Ah, good timing.'

Auli hadn't heard the door opening, but there was Raphaël, crossing quickly to lean against the window as he always did.

'So, what news?' Gabrielle said in a very different voice.

Raphaël scanned the three of them. 'Uoti has the new buoy specs, supplies trading was mostly successful. Stockholm asked Uoti to present the fisheries research report in person. The Gdansk shipping contract liaison is new and clueless – the old one's dead. There's been a flurry of wrecks through the great belt in Denmark so they're threatening to pull funding if you don't deliver bathymetry and sea mine maps stat. I suggest we deploy the next lot of buoys there – the current patterns sound like they've broken down. There's increasing piracy coming into Riga. They're requesting better current maps. The university are prepping a contract. And we're starting work mounting harpoon cannons on all three guard towers as of tomorrow. We'll be—'

'Harpoon cannons?' Auli interrupted.

Uoti leaned sideways in his chair confidentially. 'Filling in some gaps in our security. I'll update you later.'

Auli opened her mouth, shut it again. Nodded.

'We'll be testing the weapons over the next few days, dummy rounds then live ones.' Raphaël straightened away from the window. 'Anything I need to know about, aside from the obvious?'

Gabrielle smoothed her trousers over her thighs. 'Our explanation for the delay on the Denmark map is that the Oracle doesn't care about research priorities, Captain. It's in progress. And given the new contract, any luck recruiting an Oceans analyst? We're at capacity.'

Raphaël shrugged, uninterested. 'Write to the university or turn down the contract.'

Gabrielle bristled, Uoti moved a hand easily. 'I'll come up with something. And yes, I'll explore subsurface data collection for Denmark, that'll assuage them for a while.'

Raphaël glanced at Auli fleetingly, already moving for the door. 'Boat leaves straight after dinner.'

Gabrielle began arguing quietly with Uoti about priorities and time allocations, and neither of them appeared to notice when Auli also left. She pulled the door gently to, and leaned against the wall, a crackling ghost her only company in the shadowy corridor. She could have stayed, it was her room now, too, as was the bedroom just around the corner with its own private bathroom and great wide windows. She shuddered.

'She's not got the backbone for it,' Gabrielle said, clearly through the not-quite-shut door. 'And the unit is redundant. It makes sense, Uoti.'

Auli stiffened.

'She might surprise us,' Uoti said. 'And people like the QD work, it feels... hopeful to them.'

'It's a waste of time.'

'Says you.'

'Yes,' Gabrielle snapped. Auli pressed herself against the wall. 'Says me. How many boats have they saved from storms? How many navigation guides have they produced, or fish populations remapped?'

'Not sure that last carries much water this year, Gab.' Uoti sounded amused.

'Which is hardly a laughing matter, and might be an argument for assessing *your* team's efficacy.'

This time Uoti did laugh. 'Gab, I know you worry. But look at it this way – now you've got two PIs who aren't remotely hungry for power. Relax. Enjoy it.'

Gabrielle made a short, indignant noise, and Uoti carried on more gently, 'We don't know what will save us in the future, or even if this will all end tomorrow. I say we cast our net wide and pray, not because Auli, or even Boudain, are irreplaceable, but because one day their wide net might be the very thing that keeps us alive.'

Auli retreated out of eavesdropping range.

The girl

THE QUIET PERSON presses something into her hands and lifts them. She is surf breaking along a beach, blue and gold and fine white lace infolding. She drinks and beneath the waves her body is bracing for... she doesn't know. Another wave runs toward the shore and dies.
There, back to normal now.
She is music under an open sky then two voices talking, her bones are wavelengths and attenuation, her veins interference patterns in the busy air. She is trapped, a fly in a spiderweb, two boys in a deep tunnel, dark water. She is falling and falling and...
...the quiet person is holding a mug in one hand. Blood tides and numbers draw tight around her.
You're okay. I'm sorry. Go to sleep.
She does not remember sleeping, only different ways of drowning and being unmade. Perhaps sleep is like being unmade, only without the pain. Her limbs shift, the world is blue-black waves and black-blue sky, and the water rises.
She does not sleep. She drowns.

The Salt Oracle

* * *

YOU'RE BACK? *I'VE been waiting.*

She breathes saltwater, remembers this voice all teeth and darkness.

Me too, she thinks. The sea swirls around her, more familiar than her own skin and for a moment it feels like someone else's skin. Like arms, like lips pressed against her hair but that moment slips between her tentacle fingers, she is kelp fronds floating.

Can we, at last?

She does not understand. The ocean is full of currents and upwellings, and she is only one small flotsam thing, lost.

Can we, child? Can we be free?

Free? Would that be like dreaming undrowned?

Oh, yes, she thinks. *Please.*

The tides in her blood surge, teeth flash in the dark smiling bone-white and oceanic.

Chapter Six

Auli

THERE WASN'T MUCH left of the day now. Auli ought to eat but instead sat at her desk in the abandoned research deck and stared blankly at a half-written research paper. She ought to check in on Leigh's first listening shift, or search their ghost logs for Raphaël's kraken, or finish this paper. But she did none of them, aware of all the ghosts and the hollow spaces around her, and how she'd never really thought Boudain would die. Which was foolish, given everything, but still.

'Here,' someone said, and Auli jerked upright. Leigh set a cup of coffee down in front of her. 'I didn't know how you take it.'

'You're finished? What's your time?' Auli asked, checking her own watch as well. They never stayed accurate here, so time was generally just averaging and guesswork. An kept a wind-up clock running in Raphaël's office, but Auli would much rather correct her watch against other people's.

It was, best guess, nearly time. Auli drank her coffee too fast, her stomach a tangled mess of sorrow, stage fright and the unwavering fear of boats that was honestly ridiculous given her choice of home. She stood. Leigh watched her uncertainly.

'You're doing the... the funeral?' he said.

Auli nodded, straightening her shoulders. 'You can watch from the walkway. I'll see you after,' she said, and turned for the stairs.

A funeral on his second day here might be a record. The last was a boatman ghost infected seven months ago. There'd been, because he had refused the morphine, very little to bury once the ghost had eroded his flesh into binary code and static, but they had wrapped what was left, and the small tawdry things that made him *him* – a ring, a photograph, a pair of boots, a knife – all into a strip of coarse wool and done with it what they would do with Boudain now.

At the top of the dock steps, Auli paused to quell that tangled dread once more. It was evening but the summer sun still lay several degrees above the translucent horizon. The ghost of a small fishing boat drifted cross-channel and up onto the shore of Lindö, bucking on a forgotten swell through the wind-bent trees.

Doors were opening along the walkways as everyone began to gather, so Auli descended to the dock and climbed onto the *Meri Noita* where Raphaël and three boatmen were strapping Boudain's wrapped body to the deck. The weight of everyone's attention felt untenable as she sat on the bench seat, but this was the PI's job, so now it was hers. Raphaël started up the engine, she fought down the urge to leap for the dock, the boat juddered and they moved off, curling around the Bellwether's southern corner towards the deepwater channel west of the islets.

'OH GOD,' AULI whispered. One of the boatmen, Hellä Novikova, looked over with a pale raised brow.

Auli gripped the bench, fixing her gaze on the Bellwether's retreating metal flank. 'It's the first time I've been off in six months,' she said too fast. 'I went foraging on Lindö.'

'I'm not sure that counts,' Hellä said, her gaze shifting from Auli to the skerry of Flatskär, a few redshanks foraging along the shore.

The boat tilted, Auli bit back a gasp, and hoped Raphaël could not see her.

'When were you last off?' she asked, so desperate for distraction she'd even try conversation. Hellä had kept her distance long before Auli was with Raphaël, but Auli had decided it was less personal than that Hellä simply saw the researchers as peripheral to her job at best, a liability at worst.

Hellä scratched her thumbnail over her jaw. 'Five months, two weeks and three days. I'm off next week. Can't wait.'

'Do you have family?' Auli risked a glance up the boat, but no one could hear over the slap of waves and the engine.

'Too far away to count. I'm getting roaringly drunk in Mariehamm, finding someone to shag and blowing my savings on befouling my eternal soul.'

Auli startled herself by laughing. Then the water shifted from inky turquoise to inky grey and she stiffened, bracing for a calamity that had already found her.

'Do you believe in souls?' she asked quietly.

She thought Hellä would ignore her but after a long, slightly derisive examination, she jerked her chin at the shape lying on the deck. 'Best not to. Otherwise your PI will be mighty uncomfortable down there with the bodies of the people he killed, don't you think?'

Auli hadn't thought of that. She steadied her hands between her knees and wanted to defend Boudain, not because she thought Hellä was wrong but because he wasn't able to defend himself. But then the engine cut back and the boat slowed, apace with the oncoming swell, right over the deep channel where they lay the Bellwether's dead. It was a glacial scar, Bea had once told her, the claw-marks of some vast ice sheet bleeding deepwater in its wake.

Auli shivered, then couldn't seem to stop as she forced herself to move to Boudain's wrapped form.

Raphaël caught her eye, but was thankfully too busy coordinating lifting the board holding Boudain to comment. So Auli simply clung onto the gunwale to stop herself drowning before they were ready for her.

In the distance, everyone was crowded on the walkways, ready to speak the words with her despite being too far away to hear. But as she pulled a small packet from her pocket, opened it with quavering hands, it was Boudain's voice in her head, teaching her the words for her first funeral, six weeks after she arrived. The smell of lavender and valerian whipped around them as she scattered the herbs over the wool, and her voice felt unbearably frail in the wide, wild world.

'May the salt in the sea guard you, may the flowers of the land soothe you, may nothing disturb your rest, and no one forget you. May the darkness shield you and our memories ease you.' Her voice cracked, but held. 'May you be forever more peaceful, Boudain Caron, than the world above.'

She stared at the empty herb packet for a long moment, then Raphaël held out a length of chain and she shuddered against the chill in the sunset wind. But wrapping the chain around his feet felt like cruelty, like a worshipper laying alms that were also a noose, and her hands shook, the chain's ends refusing to latch together, the world all fractals and the hungry sea from her worst dreams, his voice again in her mind from even further ago, and never even spoken aloud.

Auli, I hope this letter finds you, and finds you well. I have a job offer for you now I am settled here. It is paid and permanent, which I imagine you are in need of. You have heard of the College, of course, and likely, too, the rumours that the Salt Oracle is dangerous, or the research miraculous or hopeless, or both. Do not be misled by the incident in Helsinki harbour, though. I believe you have the character for this job, and its peculiarities. I need your help, Auli, and I imagine you need mine. Come – we can build something hopeful here.

'Auli,' someone said. Auli tugged on the chain again, but her hand slipped and someone else's hand settled over hers, stilling her. Raphaël. 'Auli. I have it.'

She nodded, which sent the tears spilling over her cheeks, and she stumbled back a pace, caught and steadied by a firm hand before she could fall. Was it better to burn or drown? She wished she knew.

I believe you have the character for this, he had written. *I need your help, Auli.*

And she didn't know what she would do without him to believe in her, or need her. Who was she, if not Boudain Caron's mentee? And why, *why* had he chosen not to wait for Niki's return?

'Alright?' Hellä said quietly. Auli straightened and Hellä released her arm.

'Sorry,' Auli said, scrubbing at her face with one hand and staring fixedly at the wooden board that the boatmen now began to tilt. There was a moment of stillness, the sun spilled itself into the horizon and then in a quick slip and splash, a flicker of herbs on the wind, Boudain's body slid into the water, and sank.

THE WATER BORE no mark of his passing.

Which seemed wrong somehow. Fresh-turned earth or restless ashes would have marked this tiny moment here, but the sea did not care. Auli rubbed her face again, the boat's engine picked up and she threw out a hand for the gunwale once more, too lost for panic.

Raphaël was watching her across the empty stern, leaning back on the gunwale with the wind blowing his hair into his eyes.

'Ça va?' he said. Which meant none of the boatmen on board spoke French.

She pulled her familiar hurt around her like a cloak. 'Joo,' she said; Finnish, which they all spoke. 'Do we have enough battery?' Because the sun was orange and half-eclipsed by the sea, like a cat's heavy-lidded eye, and the solar panels on the cabin roof would be useless.

Raphaël stuck with French, Auli's head beginning to ache. 'Niki told me about the cancer, and the tests they're running. You don't believe it though.'

Christ, Auli thought. In Finnish, she said, 'It doesn't matter what I believe. Niki's tests will tell us what happened.'

The sun bled a wavering line across the sea towards them, and the boat's wake shone indigo and crimson. Three small birds crossed the bloody light, their dark wings high, feet dancing over the waves. They vanished, then reappeared again, and Raphaël said quietly, 'Pétrel tempête,' then in English, 'Mother Carey's chickens, the Brits call them. God knows why.'

'They're late,' Hellä said in Finnish, walking down the deck towards them, the sun in her eyes.

Raphaël's face tightened and he glanced back at the sun-stained sea. 'Of course. I'd forgotten.'

Auli looked from him to Hellä, who explained, 'Omens of death. Bad timing, heh?'

Auli flinched and turned back to the water, but the ghosts had gone.

Raphaël

FIFTY METRES OUT, the West Tower flashed a quick series of light signals across the water.

Raphaël hissed. Alan Woods scanned the sea. ''Ware ghosts.

Not here though, so... infection? Damn, well, we were about due. Seven months since Andrej bought it.'

Raphaël made a sharp gesture and Hellä opened the *Meri Noita*'s throttle as he scrutinised the Bellwether. The Oracle was on her tower walkway, two figures with her – carer and listener. Gabrielle's silhouette in the Oracle Room below. Everyone else already back inside, vigil done. No fire in the library windows, no running figures. The boat canted into the turn and Raphaël swayed with it, filled with a familiar sick frustration. His entire purpose here was the provision of safety and yet he remained powerless against this. And every time it happened, it might be to one of the two people who were the only reason he was here at all.

He left Hellä to secure the boat, told Auli to stay with her, and met Joar on the second deck walkway with Alan and Miika in his wake.

'What's happened?' Still no sign of the infected. They were usually screaming by now.

'I didn't see, boss. They sent me to—'

'Where?'

'Oracle Room.'

Raphaël nodded and moved past him.

Noting the complete lack of tension on the research deck, he sent Miika and Joar away and reached the Oracle Room with just Alan. He was young, but sharp as a pin and his deceptively gentle voice made the researchers less skittish than the two looming Finns. Gabrielle was in the room, with Niki and the new guy who'd been talking to Auli earlier. A ghost just beyond the window, none within.

They all looked up at him, Niki rose.

'Leigh?'

Auli slipped past him to drop down before the stranger, and Raphaël looked at Niki rather than let himself react.

'Leigh, what happened?'

'Doc?' Raphaël said.

Gabrielle brushed her hands down her hips. 'A brush with a ghost but no harm done. He's possibly not fully protected given he's only had one dose of tonic. Doctor? Might we consider a higher dose at induction?'

Niki looked from the kid to Gabrielle. 'When it's not contra-indicated, maybe. We've not had such an early incident before so this may be coincidence.' They paused. 'I'll consider it. Now, if I may...'

Raphaël moved out of their way, spoke quietly to Alan, then when they had both left, he walked to the window, leaning against the north wall and studying the room. Auli was still kneeling, looking up at the kid as he talked, and something about it made him unreasonably cross. She was a PI now, for heaven's sake. She should not be kneeling at anyone's feet, but the sheer absurdity of his indignation brought him up short.

'You okay, kid?' he said, sticking to English for lack of knowing the alternatives.

The kid looked up from Auli, wide-eyed in a way that made Raphaël instantly suspicious. No one was that innocent now, especially not someone recruited to the College, and who'd managed the journey across the water.

'I'm fine,' he said. English then. 'It was just a shock, you know? I'm sorry, you're Captain Giroux, aren't you? I've heard about you.'

Auli twisted around, not quite looking at him. 'Sorry, Leigh. Yes, this is the captain. Captain, my new analyst, Leigh Alvarez.'

'Yours?' Raphaël said, then wanted to kick himself.

Auli said flatly, 'Yes. He's an archivist. Some Portuguese and some Arabic.'

Raphaël switched to Arabic. 'So, you are here for the books? From the Bodleian? I heard it is working hard to reestablish itself, after the fires.'

Leigh smiled boyishly. 'I do not know about the Bodleian, Oxford is unwelcoming to outsiders.' His Arabic was more formal than Raphaël's Darija, and careful, as if he were picking out words rather than thinking in them. But the same was true of Raphaël's.

'I'm fine though, Auli, honestly,' Leigh said, switching back to English and holding out his arms. 'See?'

He was like a puppy, Raphaël thought.

'Good,' Gabrielle said. 'Get yourself another dose but your attitude is appreciated.' She straightened her clothes and moved towards the door. 'Auli, a word. If you're free.'

Auli rose in a quick, smooth movement and Raphaël wished he could apologise for questioning her use for an assistant. For a lot of other things too, but that would suffice.

'Leigh, go get coffee and pulla,' she said gently, then followed Gabrielle without looking back.

Raphaël cast another quick glance over the room, a spilled mug, the electrical burns on the boy's forearms, the evening shadows pooling beneath the stairs.

'Where's the Oracle?' he said.

'Upstairs, Captain,' Leigh said. 'PI Davidson got another assistant to take over.' He switched back to Arabic. 'Where is your Arabic from, your dialect is—'

'PI Fraser gave you an instruction, I believe,' Raphaël interrupted, in English. 'Keep those burns clean. We can't waste antibiotics on carelessness.'

'Yes, Captain,' Leigh said, almost convincingly meek and Raphaël snorted, amused suddenly.

Then the door opened. Célestine grinned up at Raphaël and gestured to the kid. 'Come on,' she said. 'I hear you had an exciting listening shift. Have you met Alexis? He doesn't like new people but makes exquisite cream pastries so he's a good friend in times like this.'

She spun her chair around and the boy obeyed her. Raphaël

watched the door swing shut behind them, frowning at nothing in particular. Then he shook himself and headed for his nominal office.

HELLÄ WAS ALREADY there, sprawled in one of the chairs but straightening with a snap as soon as he appeared. When no one came in with him, she relaxed again, and so did he. He'd told her to ease up on the formality, but she said it served a purpose and she had a point, much as it rankled.

'She escaped,' she said before he could speak. The walkway beyond the windows was clear, while on the research deck, a handful of analysts were gathering in the Centre beneath the library with coffees and cakes, the smell of both making Raphaël sharply aware of his own tiredness. This morning he'd been in Mariehamm, loading supplies onto the boat.

He raised his eyebrows. 'She's twenty centimetres shorter than you and about thirty kilos lighter—'

'Ha! It's all muscle.'

'Exactly.'

'I'm not about to body tackle the new PI, not when there was no screaming.'

Raphaël waited.

'Sorry, boss.'

He let it go. 'It's fine. It was her I gave the order to after all, not you.'

'And she's not yours to command,' Hellä said, then flushed an alarming shade of red, and hurried on, 'Alan said you wanted me?'

He scrubbed at his face. 'I want a guard on the Oracle during the day.'

Hellä lifted her head, surprised. 'Sure thing. But that'll stretch us. Can I ask why?'

'I don't know. One of the juniors got' – Raphaël made claw

shapes with his fingers, then studied them curiously – 'burned on listening duty. And Boudain died after speaking with her. It might be nothing.'

The tall Finn nodded, scanning the room idly for ghosts. 'Within twenty-four hours? It might be something.'

The Oracle was uncharted waters; in fact, in a world of uncharted waters she was another whole level of unknown. Despite Auli's research, they still didn't know why she connected to maritime ghosts the way she did, nor whether she would one day simply stop. Or more likely, die. The College was built to guard her from people who sought to destroy or control her, and Raphaël's job description didn't include protecting the crew from the ghosts – why include a doomed clause? – but that didn't mean he shouldn't try.

It was the old trade-off he'd been balancing since he and Célestine first arrived. This place offered purpose beyond simply surviving, so he worked to make it safe enough to tolerate. Célestine got to build her forecasts that saved the lives of fishermen, Raphaël got to keep her safe while she did so. It was enough, and aside from her friendship, he'd sworn off any entanglements that made the inevitable deaths harder to endure. Auli had been... something that it didn't do to dwell on.

'You think she killed him somehow?'

Hellä's voice pulled Raphaël back with a jolt.

The Oracle kill Boudain Caron? Could she have? It was possible but didn't seem very likely. He thought again of the long, thin burns on Leigh's arms that actually hadn't looked much like electrical burns at all, and a new possibility slithered into his mind, making him wish he'd questioned Leigh more closely.

'Boss?'

'No,' he said. 'I think Boudain wasn't well.'

Hellä's mouth opened. But all she said was, 'Huh.' So Raphaël carried on.

'We can pull the East Tower guard to put on the Oracle for now.'

Hellä nodded and pushed to her feet. 'Anything else?'

The sky beyond the window was as dark as it got this time of year, which meant it must be gone ten and he'd been up for twenty hours with only one meal that he could remember and not nearly enough coffee.

'No,' he said. 'We'll tell them about the harpoons tomorrow, explain the risk.'

'Heh. They're used to deadly things here, boss. Won't notice one more.'

Chapter Seven

Auli

'WHAT DID YOU want to speak to me about?' Auli asked. They were in Gabrielle's office, and Gabrielle was pouring tea from a flask with her back to Auli. It was deliberate, of course. The ribbon of falling tea was as peaty and dark as a bog pool in summer, and Auli absorbed the blow of homesickness. For Lapp and its infinite sky, for the smell of pines and pine smoke, snow; her family.

Gabrielle righted the flask, put the lid back on and set it down.

Auli's fingers were a little unsteady from the delayed horror of another ghost infection and relief at the near miss. She pressed her palms against one another and watched a ghost bat against the window like a moth.

Gabrielle added sugar to her mug. Perhaps it wasn't an insult, Auli thought, perhaps it was a test.

'Thank you for looking after Leigh,' she said. 'I'll speak to Niki before clearing him for listening duty again.' Her voice rose on the last word, and she wanted to kick herself. Boudain had believed in her; she needed to do better.

Setting the spoon aside finally, Gabrielle turned and leaned against her desk, crossing her feet neatly at the ankles. Neither of them had sat down.

'Actually, it was Niki I wanted to talk to you about.'

'Niki?'

'They said you requested blood tests to find out what Boudain took.'

Strange, Auli thought. Niki had wanted to know because no one was supposed to have access to those drugs. So why lay it at her door? She lifted one shoulder stiffly; tried not to sound as weary as the long, terrible day had left her. 'I did. I assumed it was protocol.'

Gabrielle looked at the mug in her hands and sighed, the line of her shoulders dropping briefly. She looked tired, Auli thought, and wanted to sympathise but if she was tired of combative conversations, she could always choose not to start them at ten o'clock at night.

'Had they finished, when they spoke to you?'

'Look, Auli.' Gabrielle set her mug down with a thump. 'Sit down. There's something you need to know since you are PI.'

Auli didn't want to sit. She wanted to fidget, open all the windows and let the night air fill the room with brine. But she obeyed and waited.

Gabrielle watched her intently. 'Niki found a sedative in Boudain's blood. It was a very high dose, so we know he died by his own hand.'

'Oh,' Auli said, quietly, like he might hear. 'Where did he get it?'

'That's the issue. I wasn't planning to…' Gabrielle picked her mug up, set it down again. 'Well, you may as well know. It will answer your questions, and I know you and Boudain were close so—

'The sedative is for the Oracle. Boudain must have helped himself to the stores or switched out the Oracle's evening dose. It doesn't matter. The point is' – Gabrielle turned her palms up – 'it was the Oracle's medicine. That's where he got it.'

Auli felt herself nodding jerkily, unable to tie up all the threads in Gabrielle's words. She unclasped her hands and spread them on her knees. 'You sedate the Oracle? To help her sleep?'

Gabrielle picked up her tea again, moved to sit in her chair and studied Auli through the steam like she had earlier. Hiding her own face, Auli realised.

'Partly. The founding PIs realised everything worked better if a degree of sedation was maintained through the day, too.' Auli stiffened, and perhaps Gabrielle saw it. 'This was all decided after the Helsinki incident and I am not opening up a discussion. I am simply giving you the answers to Boudain's death, so we can move on.'

'Move on?' Auli repeated. 'The Oracle… that child is drugged? All the time? How?'

'We put it in her hot chocolate.'

Oh, Auli thought. Of course. She had always thought the twice daily drink was a small kindness for a miracle child. What a fool she was. 'Boudain knew about this? Who else – the PIs and Niki, and Raphaël? Does Raphaël know?' Not that it mattered. But it absolutely did.

'I imagine he must, but his only concern is security, and neither the university nor our contractors care how we manage the Oracle so long as she's producing the goods.'

It didn't matter, Auli repeated angrily. What mattered was the fact itself, not who knew it.

'This is exactly why I doubt your ability to be PI,' Gabrielle said, just as Auli opened her mouth to speak. 'The College is not for the fainthearted, Auli. Our mission is to make the Baltic Sea safe again, to reduce shipwrecks and provide predictable livelihoods for fishing communities. Decisions must be made that protect the Oracle, whilst allowing her to fulfil her purpose. You can either accept that, or you can step aside and let more committed researchers take your place.'

Auli felt sick. She pressed her hands against her stomach and thought of the lightning flicker of the Oracle's unfocused gaze, her fragile wrists, and knew that Gabrielle was right. She was not cut out for this. No one knew better than her how deadly the seas were now, but wasn't this exactly why she'd come here – to be part of something that saved lives?

God, Boudain had known about the Oracle.

'Why kill himself *now*?' she said without meaning to. 'He only had to wait a few more hours to know whether Niki had found cancer medicines.' Gabrielle studied her perplexedly. 'It's so *illogical*, and Boudain wasn't illogical. He was careful and planned everything—'

Something I cooked up last minute.

He'd said that about his research project. So how well had she really known him?

We have a better idea of the Oracle's fugue state, he'd said. *We have considerably more data now.* And she hadn't understood at the time, but he'd been talking about the sedatives.

Auli's throat ached as if she might cry, grieving him again like she had on the boat in the sunset. Only it wasn't sorrow tightening her chest now, it was horror.

When Gabrielle spoke, it was the kindest Auli had ever heard her. 'He was only human, Auli. He must have feared the prospect of chemotherapy and surgery, here with only Niki.' She shrugged, a small, tight movement. 'Perhaps he couldn't face even having the choice. Sometimes it's easier to have all your choices taken away, even if what you are left with is terrible.'

The Bellwether shifted idly, Célestine's pulley rattled, and if it had been anyone other than Gabrielle here, Auli would have reached out. Instead, she sat unmoving, horror and bewilderment within her like a whirlpool.

It was Gabrielle who broke the silence, laying a hand on a pile of paper and clearing her throat. 'Well then. Are you satisfied?'

No, Auli thought viciously. But she stood and turned to go, then hesitated. 'I want to see the medication records.' Gabrielle leaned back heavily and Auli hurried on. 'It's for some research Boudain planned. Does Niki have them?'

She waited, her shoulder blades like wire.

'They do, yes.' A pause. 'What research?'

Auli stiffened at that, just a little.

I believe you have the character for this, he had written long ago.

She smiled very slightly at Gabrielle. 'I'll let you know once I've decided whether to carry it on.' And without giving herself a chance to waver, she slipped out into the empty research deck.

WITH NO ONE there to watch her, Auli crossed straight through the Centre, past the sofas and an abandoned chess board, and climbed up into the library. To the upper floor with the night salt-stained through the glass dome and the books below murmuring faintly. You couldn't hear it during the day, that constant susurration of the ghosts in their paper flesh, and even at night you might mistake it for an echo of the sea. But this was Auli's favourite place on the whole Bellwether, and this sleepless dark her favourite time.

She moved the fire barrel out of the north-facing window and curled in the nook between bookcases, leaning against the cool glass, and closing her eyes. The day had left her like a window-struck bird. Boudain's death, the lingering feel of his organs cool and wet beneath her fingers, the way the sea had swallowed and forgotten him in one breath, Leigh, and Raphaël's kraken and the way everyone on the Bellwether was watching her, awaiting failure.

She breathed deeply through the tug and sway of the Bellwether, until the nausea clawing at her throat eased.

If she was going to do this – be Principal Investigator for Qualitative Research at The New Baltic College for Oceanographic Research – then she needed to grow a spine.

Her brother had told her so, more than once although never unkindly.

You're too keen to please everyone. You let them push you around. Learn to say no.

In her head she'd thought, *At least I don't leave others to shoulder my responsibilities*, but all she'd said was, *That's easy for you to say, you got Mama Márjá's confidence, I got Mama Sara's gentleness. It's just who we are.*

He'd laughed briefly. *Look, I won't come back to Finland for a year, maybe more. Come visit me. The mamas can cope for a while, it'll do Mama Márjá good to see how much you do. You'll like Portugal. And we can sail to Morocco, look for whales. You've always wanted to see whales.*

Which had been true, and she wasn't sure whether the ghost whales she saw once, breaching in the western sky, counted. But he'd been on his boat when the Crash happened, and three weeks after everything broke it was spotted drifting and aflame, the people on the shore unable to tell which screams were humans dying, and which were ghosts being born.

It took two years for the news to reach her, and she would never know for sure if he had died.

Their mothers had gone north four months before. They'd been hanging on in Helsinki, despite first the riots, then the martial law, the disease, hunger; and all the time, the ghost deaths and the ghost-spawned fires. But those fires and perhaps the fear, too, were a torture to Mama Sara's body, so eventually Mama Márjá had taken her hand and said gently, *Let's go north, love. Home. Auli can send news, and I miss the snow.* Then she had looked at Auli, and barely, just barely flinched, but it was enough. Auli and her brother had always looked alike. *You'll go to the docks every week and ask? You could follow us if the university closes, but Sara can't wait any longer.*

She might want to stay, Mama Sara had said with blood in the corner of her smile. Auli had felt like she was falling. *You might find your wings without me tying you down.*

No, Auli had said. *You never tied me down.* Which had been, if not a lie, then a complex kind of truth because she *had* minded, sometimes, but still the day her mothers left her for the long dangerous boat trip north, she had never felt so abandoned, nor so lost.

Until now.

She opened her eyes and wished a few more lights were out in the research deck so she might see the stars. The north star that would guide her to her parents, if she ever chose to go.

That was a lie, too, of course. She did not feel as lost now as she had then, because even without Boudain, she still had the Bellwether. She had her research papers, the rustle of the books, the knowledge that Raphaël was around somewhere shoring up the walls however much she tried not to think of him. The tiny warm thrill of *belonging* to this strange place the way she'd never once belonged anywhere before. She touched the Bellwether tattoo on her inner arm and couldn't bear to lose this. She definitely didn't want it taken away by Gabrielle.

So maybe it was time to grow a spine. Or some wings. Or both.

A ghost sank down through the dome, sparking in the photovoltaic glass then circling the hollow space. It was a transcript – translucent white screen and audio data all fragmented hissing French. Auli tried not to listen but couldn't help herself.

Alaa will either be free in the next days or he will die in prison during #COP27 as the world watches. Crackle. In the next few days, will die. Crackle. The world watches.

The ghost spun twice around the library as if searching all the unhaunted books for a home, then sank further into the half-lit shadows below. And Auli realised she was crying once again. Not for Boudain or even for herself but for a man from long ago. And perhaps for the Bellwether, surrounded by the sea, with death too commonplace to speak of. This thing of hope she'd learned held a flaw in its heart.

The girl

SHE IS ON the deck of a sailing ship, huge and canted, sail-torn, storm-tossed. All about her men run barefoot, climb the rigging with rain in their unblinking eyes and every one pale and wailing. Begging for rest. Begging for release as the ship gleams darkly in the darkness like it was painted in blood and soot.

And he who sees the Flying Dutchman is accursed, and any ship venturing close to that terrible vessel shall assuredly founder or meet ill chance of every kind.

She turns, and only turning realises she can, that her body is her own all skin and sinew. Forgetting the voice, she holds her hands up to the sky; the rain and the sea fall over her, tasting of winter and hexadecimal places, but her fingers are solid and real.

'Oh,' she says. The word is vast as a planet, because it is hers and hers alone. 'Oh.'

Hmm, the voice says.

The ship is gone, the storm gone, they stand on the sea together although she does not think to look for her companion. She is too used to bodiless voices. The sea now is a green-blue silk skin so nearly motionless she thinks it a photograph until it ripples beneath her feet. Plants curlicue beneath the surface, and the air is heavy with stories, empty of clouds.

The dungeon of lost souls, the horse latitudes...

She sees them, the horses all their scattered bones, their panic and their drowning, the cry of gulls. The water is a great unwavering moon.

The sargasso sea, the doldrums. So many stories, so many captains' logs.

The voice is smiling, she thinks. If it is the kind of voice capable of such a thing. Do sharks smile, she wonders, when they are readying their teeth?

Are these good stories? Would you like to tell them?

No one has ever asked her that before. She doesn't know. She burrows her toes, her own flesh toes into the silky water and remembers another voice asking, *Can you stop it? Can you stop them coming? Lyubimy, you have to try to stop.* And she hadn't known how to answer that either because how do you try to stop drowning? How do you disentangle the iron in your blood from the salt? How do you learn to breathe when you are underwater?

Is this... is this an interview or something? It's weird. I mean, more weird than usual.

She's fine. God, at least it's not HTML code, I'm rubbish at transcribing that, and Pertti gives me such a hard time for it.

The voice laughs, but she still cannot decide whether it is joy or hunger. The sea of drowned horses fades away. There is a walkway, high, high over a blue and restless sea, islands like knucklebones and she blinks, hair across her face, colder now than a moment ago. She breathes in. Undrowning.

Someone moves behind her, a bird calls, and she is the bird, four hundred and thirty-eight frames. Four hundred and thirty-eight birds all offset. She is a bent wing and a blue sky, the pixels fill her lungs, consume her fingers, her bones. She drowns.

Chapter Eight
Auli

AULI WAS AT her desk the next morning by the time Leigh appeared from the shadows of the North Tower stairwell beside Tobias. It was good, she thought absently, that they were getting on. Leigh didn't seem like someone suited to isolation.

He started talking before he'd even sat down.

'The boatmen are dragging huge bits of metal up the towers – what on earth are they doing?'

So that was what that noise had been. 'Defences,' she said vaguely.

Célestine and her forecast team were already at their daily laborious puzzle box of predicting the weather from scraps of cantations. Ocean was still mostly empty, salvaged tech scattered on every possible surface, boxes of old maps and half-drawn new ones, compasses, gyroscopes, coils of rope.

Leigh straightened the paper in front of him. 'I saw Pertti downstairs, just off listening duty. With, umm, Bea? Are they a thing?'

'Yes,' Auli said. Brash, ambitious Weather Senior Pertti, and cheerful, book-obsessed Oceans assistant Bea, they were a contradiction that had somehow become the longest surviving relationship on the Bellwether.

'Right. So anyway...' Leigh leaned forward, and Auli smiled. He was keen at least. And brave – with the books and then whatever had happened yesterday. 'He said he's got a cantation for you. About some Greek oracle. Will that be helpful, for figuring out how the Salt Oracle works?'

A brief flare of curiosity filled Auli. Then she noticed the faint lines on Leigh's forearms, and remembered the things Gabrielle had told her yesterday, and wanted to lay her head on the table until it all went away.

'Not for that study,' she said. He deflated. 'But it will be good for the one mapping folklore ghosts.' She studied him. 'Leigh, can we have a chat...? In Boudain's office, I guess.'

'Your office now,' he said cheerfully.

THIS WAS ANOTHER job awaiting her, Auli realised, stepping into the office – sorting Boudain's papers. That moment of panic at the thought of anyone discovering his research had abated under everything else, but perhaps it shouldn't have...

'Is this about yesterday?'

Leigh was hovering by one of the chairs and Auli sat opposite him. His face was relaxed but there was a stillness about him once he sat that worried her.

'Yes. Could you tell me what happened?'

'Didn't PI Davidson tell you?'

Not really, no. 'I'd like to hear you tell it. And see how you're feeling now, too.'

He gifted her a brief smile. 'Okay. I went on listening duty after the funeral. The Oracle'd said a whole load of HTML code that—' He broke off and laughed softly. 'God but that's fun, isn't it?'

Auli smiled and waited.

'She was in the library, by one of the windows. It was kinda crowded with the boatman so that carer stayed back a bit. There was a video footage ghost, maybe an old film? A shoal of fish, big teeth, long silver bodies' – he held out his hands – 'like pike? It floated towards the Oracle, and then I don't know, I think I got in its way and ended up with these.' Gesturing at his own arms.

Auli leaned forward and lifted one of his wrists, felt him resist and then give way. Yesterday she'd been intent only on searching him for signs of ghost-infection pixelation, but today she wasn't. She looked up at him blankly.

'Leigh, these are scratches.'

His jaw tightened. She looked back at the injuries. They were like cat claw marks, breaking the skin barely, regularly spaced. 'What did you feel when the ghost made contact?' Swapping to his other arm, which was just as unfathomable. If ghosts didn't infect you, they gave you an electric shock. They burned, or they killed. They didn't *scratch*.

The boat jolted, Raphaël had said.

Leigh didn't answer for a moment, and Auli released his arm.

'Look,' he said. 'You won't tell anyone, will you?'

'What? Why?'

Leigh ran a hand through his hair abashedly. 'I don't want people thinking I can't handle it, you know? That I'm freaking out or something. I had to climb out my cabin window this morning to avoid a ghost.'

Auli smiled. 'It happens, that's why the windows are so big. And why there are doors everywhere.' She shook her head. 'I won't tell.'

He huffed out a breath. 'Okay. There was… heft to it, you know? But that's…' He shrugged. 'Mad. I bet it was just the Oracle.'

'But you're still happy to do listening duty? I can keep you off it.' Although how, she wasn't sure.

Leigh nodded. 'If it was the Oracle, she wouldn't *mean* it, you know? I'm not scared of her.'

Because she was drugged, Auli thought, that same sick horror as last night refusing to fade into anything resembling complicity. 'Can you draw the fish for me?'

He raised his eyebrows. 'Draw them?'

'To ID the species. It's part of narrowing down video origin.'

'Oh yeah, of course. That's one of your projects – mapping ghosts attracted to the Oracle, right? There are patterns... umm... the strength of the ghosts depends on distance from origin, did I get that right?'

'Distance between data source and cloud server as a driver of ghost strength, and distance from data source to here to predict attraction to the Oracle, yes.' It was one of their better datasets.

She found a pencil and mostly clean sheet of paper on Boudain's desk. 'Here. There are a couple of fish field guides in the library, but they're both unhaunted so I can't just hand them over, I'm afraid.'

He took the materials and turned to lean on the desk corner.

While he was busy, she straightened papers, gathered pens and pencils into their mug. Such precious things now, but she had suspected Boudain often forgot the world was changed at all, here in his wood-walled office, immersed in his thoughts.

The research notes he'd shown Auli were not here. Neither were a couple of other things – the top sheet from his clipboard, the notes he'd been jotting during their meeting. He'd put them away, then, or given them to Leigh. Or perhaps even had a final change of heart, chose to spare Auli the burden of a project full of death.

There was no mistaking the animal Leigh showed her.

'Barracuda,' she said. 'But distorted. A horror movie maybe.'

Leigh shook his head. 'Not heard of them.'

He was so young, she thought, and the library was perhaps an even greater treasure than the Oracle. She dreamed of one day finding someone with a printing press and some courage, and reprinting books. If the texts were sufficiently altered there would be no ghosts to haunt them, and they would be safe.

'Movie clips without dialogue are harder to place. But' – she looked at his arms, then touched the drawing very lightly – 'barracuda are fierce predators. Very sharp teeth.'

Leigh laughed. She looked up and he faltered, then laughed again. 'No way,' he said. 'I mean, no disrespect but that's impossible. Ghosts don't *bite*. They're just data, the—'

Auli lifted a hand and was startled when he stopped. 'I know,' she said quietly. 'They don't have teeth, they're just code.' She sighed. 'Oh well. I'm glad you're okay. Did you get the post-exposure tonic?'

Leigh nodded and changed the subject. 'So, my research,' he said, 'I kind of got the impression you weren't fully on board. Ha, excuse the pun.'

The disarming smile made it difficult for Auli to read his eyes. She opened her mouth to say, *Let's leave that one for now*, but remembered Niki saying, *Perhaps that was him handing over*. Which one was she meant to act on – their last conversation or the missing notes?

'Let's start the first phase,' she heard herself say. It wasn't indecision, she told herself, it was precaution just until she knew what contracts Boudain had already signed. 'Compare cantation rates for each restored buoy, accounting for distance. Figure out which broadcast frequencies she picks up most.' He nodded. 'If there's no pattern then that might make the decision for us.'

He laughed as if she'd meant it as a joke. 'Okay. And I can talk to the engineer, umm, An, to plan the tech stage. May as well, right? I bet she's busy as hell.'

Which was true, Auli thought, gathering some of the papers against her chest like a shield. But building something to attract ghosts was going to be insanely dangerous, she wondered if he'd realised.

'First, I'll add you to Célestine's stats tutorial group. And select a language class, too – I'd suggest Russian or Finnish. We can meet next week to catch up, yes?'

If Gabrielle had her way, Auli might not have a research unit to make decisions about soon anyway. The thought of having to fight her, and losing, and betraying Boudain by doing so, exhausted her, and when Leigh preceded her out of the office, she paused just within the doorway to press her palm against her temple, as if that might ease the pressure.

It didn't. She dropped her hand, half turned to say goodbye to Boudain, and felt his death hit her all over again. The Bellwether sighed and someone on the far side of the deck laughed. No, not someone – a ghost, a contralto voice in smoky French saying half a phrase then cutting off, laughing, repeating the three words. Instead of returning to her desk, Auli went to Niki's door.

'Why do you want them?' Niki said, more bemused than contrary.

They were sitting behind the bench that doubled as operating table, apparently doing a stock take. The table was covered in packets and bottles, cupboard doors open and their hair tangled.

Auli had asked for the Oracle's medication records. 'It's for an analysis. I need to test how sedation level impacts frequency of cantations.' Which now she'd said it, was fundamental and it was unfathomable that Boudain had hidden this vital variable from her all this time. It didn't matter so much for the others, concerned with processing the cantation data, but for her, trying to *understand the cantation patterns*, it was unforgivable.

The word startled her.

Niki shifted three bottles to the right, straightened their papers, shifted one bottle back again. 'Fine. But you have to understand...' They faltered, pulled some keys from their pocket, and opened the bottom drawer of their desk. So close, Auli thought, and so secret. The same way you concealed a sin. They straightened and held out a hefty folder in faded blue, but when Auli grasped it, they did not let go.

'You have to understand,' they repeated. 'We were protecting her from herself. That was the main focus at the start. To allow her to be cared for and no longer a danger to herself.'

'She hurt herself?'

'She used to drown herself, Auli. Given half a chance, she'd walk into the sea and sink like a stone. It's a miracle she survived, really.'

Auli subsided heavily into the chair beside her, letting go of the folder. It was as if this thought, the fragility of the desire to live, was haunting her. 'She was suicidal?'

'No. I don't think so. You've seen her, she's drawn to the water. She's just... following the ghosts, I guess.' They lay the folder in front of her, she stared at it but didn't pick it up. 'Anyway, I just need you to remember that when you read this.'

She looked up at them, the soft slump of their shoulders, grooves bracketing their mouth. Guilt, she thought, and did not know whether their feeling it made any difference.

'Once stabilised, we needed her to be able to function, so there was a period of trialling different combinations of drugs that kept her... receptive.'

'To you, or to the ghosts?' she said dully.

'Both.'

She picked the folder up and held it as if it might stain her skin. 'I'll bear that in mind,' she said, and stood once more. Then she remembered her other reason for coming in and met their eyes again over the organised bedlam on the desk. If the Bellwether was hit by a squall right now, she thought, no one had better get injured for a while.

'Niki,' she said carefully. 'I understand, given this' – lifting the folder slightly – 'why you went to Gabrielle with the blood test results rather than me, like I'd asked.' They shifted uncomfortably, but she carried on anyway. She had to, otherwise she'd be breaking her own promise within twelve hours, which was not the most auspicious start. 'But in future please would you bring anything to do with my team, including Boudain, directly to me?'

They grimaced, looked away towards the window, then back at her. 'Well then, seeing as you asked, there's something I didn't tell Gabrielle.'

Auli tilted her head.

They studied her, then said slowly, 'Are you sure? Boudain's dead, any one of us might die tomorrow and none of it matters so long as someone wishes to pay us for the data the Oracle cantates. We don't have to go looking for trouble.'

They were probably right and Auli had more than enough on her hands already, but still she said, 'Tell me.'

They bent down without another word to that locked bottom drawer again then handed a single sheet of paper to Auli.

'What's this?' she said, seeing only their impenetrable scrawl in Polish, a few meaningless numbers.

'It's something I can't prove but I'm ninety percent sure about.'

They came around the desk and picked up a brown glass jar, toying with it as the Bellwether sighed. Then they looked up.

'It wasn't the sedative that killed him. There was something else in his blood, and I don't think he intended to take it.'

Chapter Nine

Auli

THE BELLWETHER CREAKED and sidled, and a gull called raucously. The high sun fell slantwise into the room, but Auli could not feel the warmth.

'What was it?' she said eventually.

Niki ran a hand through their tangled hair with a low growl of exasperation. 'I don't know. I don't have the kit to check. No one does anymore.'

'I don't understand. How do you know there was something else there, if you can't test for it? And how do you know he… didn't know he was taking it?'

'Because no one would choose that death when they had access to the Oracle's sedatives, bluntly. His blood was acidic. He died from muscle spasms so hard he suffocated. It would have been quick, but it would have been agony.'

Auli couldn't speak.

'The obvious one is cyanide, although there's TCAs, tetanin, oil of wintergreen, which I have here, but no one would know…'

They stopped. The room was silent other than the sea and a crackling fragment of orchestral music. Auli was breathless with horror.

The Salt Oracle

'I didn't give it to him – before I left, I mean,' Niki said quietly, making Auli jerk.

'No,' she said. 'No, I know. I never would have—' But she didn't know what she would have thought. She set the sheet of paper down and pressed the heels of both hands into her aching eyes. 'I think I knew already. It just didn't add up.'

Niki said something but Auli wasn't listening. 'The hot chocolate?' she asked, and when Niki nodded, said more calmly than she felt, 'Was it meant for Boudain or the Oracle?'

'The Oracle, surely. But that's Rafa's department. Auli...'

'What?'

'Tell Rafa but not the other PIs, not yet. Let Rafa sort it out.'

'Why shouldn't I tell Gabrielle or Uoti?'

They widened their eyes pointedly.

'No,' she said. 'No. They're loyal; God, Gabrielle practically *is* the Bellwether. They'd not harm anyone here, least of all the Oracle.' Which wasn't true, was it? But this was an attack, not an... experiment? The word tasted sour even within her own mind.

'I'm not accusing them. I just think... you stirring this up, it might look like crying wolf to stop Gabrielle pushing you out.'

'But you'd back me up.'

Niki held her gaze for a long minute, then turned back to their desk, moving bottles aimlessly. 'He's dead, Auli. Tell Raphaël so he can find the saboteur and protect the Oracle. But you pushing this won't bring Boudain back.' They looked up, pale-eyed and unrepentant. 'I'm not jeopardising my place here by pissing off the PIs. This job keeps my parents fed and in a safe part of Krakow. And it keeps me out of a country where I can't be myself. We can't help him now. All we can do is protect the Oracle and ourselves.'

The gull, or a different one, or a ghost, cried again; something clattered heavily in the nearest tower, but Auli didn't move.

'So that's it? He suffered and died, and I just... carry on?' she whispered.

Niki sighed. 'Rafa will deal with it, better than you running about the Bellwether questioning everyone and accusing people and setting yourself, and me, up for a fall.'

'People need to know there's a—'

Someone knocked on the door, and Niki had said 'Yes,' before Auli could stop them. It was Célestine, her eyes sharp with curiosity. She had seen Auli come in here, Auli realised. So why had she needed to interrupt?

'Everything okay?' Niki asked.

Célestine was watching Auli, probably reading far too much in her expression.

'I remembered you were doing a stock take today, and I am waiting on cantations so I thought I'd offer a hand.'

Oh really, Auli almost snorted. Pasting on a thin smile, she crossed the room, avoiding Niki's loaded stare but unable to avoid Célestine, sitting in the doorway and making no move to get out of the way.

'You alright, Auli? You look awful.' Célestine sounded sincere, but that counted for very little. Auli was not nearly forgetful enough to be fooled a second time.

'Fine, thanks,' she said, widening her smile, her gaze drifting past Célestine to the deck beyond.

Célestine's hand on the wheel flexed very briefly before she shoved her chair forward enough for Auli to pass her. 'Sorry, I suppose it's *PI Fraser* now, right? Congratulations, you must be thrilled.'

Dozens of possible responses tangled up in Auli's throat like twine, so she just ducked her head and walked out. Behind her, Niki said quietly, 'That was cruel.'

'She'll survive,' Célestine replied. 'If she can't handle me, she can't handle the job.' The door clicked shut, and Auli knew she had been meant to hear that.

Her shoulders ached as she returned to her desk.

Leigh was in the Oceans section, hip hitched up on Bea's desk, both of them laughing. Behind them, Raphaël's door was open which meant An would be in there, working on her salvaged buoys. Auli wasn't sure who she least wanted to speak to – the terrifying engineer about Boudain's project, or Raphaël. Spine, she reminded herself. If she didn't have the backbone to face one ex-lover, then Mama Márjá would justifiably disown her.

'Auli? You okay?'

Why did people keep asking her that? Auli smiled at Suvi. 'Yes,' she said firmly. 'Glad to see Leigh settling in.'

Suvi frowned at the equations on the sheet in her hand. Across the deck, Pertti leaned precariously back in his chair, eyed Leigh, then bellowed Suvi's name. Bea looked away from Leigh, but Suvi ignored him. 'It would have been bad luck to get infected on your first listening shift.'

Auli winced. She imagined everyone here heard the ticking of a clock when someone died, when a ghost caught them unawares, when they saw all the empty desks that used to be full. There was a buzzing in her veins like too much caffeine or not enough sleep. 'True,' she said shortly.

Leigh said something and Bea laughed again, and Pertti pushed to his feet, crossing the deck. The sharp shadows of martins circling the towers chased him across the floor.

'Why,' he said when he reached them, 'is your new boy flirting with Bea and why are you over *here*, Suvi?' As if Suvi had lain down in an open sewer.

The Oracle passed the window nearest them, the sleeves of her shirt flapping like tethered wings. She was talking, and Tobias, following her, was writing furiously. Joar Gunnarson followed Tobias, meeting Auli's eyes through the window briefly. His jaw tensed and he looked quickly away, and Auli wondered at that, remembered him coming out of the Oracle Room when he'd no reason to be there.

'I was just curious,' Suvi said distantly.

'About our new PI? Or our dead one?' Pertti laughed.

Auli rose abruptly. 'Okay, well, see you,' she said.

'Oh, *there's* the error,' Suvi murmured, pulling a pencil out of thin air.

Colour flooded up Pertti's neck. 'Were those cantation records?' he said to Auli. 'Anything for us?' It was the closest to an apology he would manage, but Auli tightened her grip on the folder.

'No, they're nothing.'

Which was a lie, but she needed privacy to read them. So first, she'd try something Raphaël wouldn't think to, even once she'd told him about Boudain.

'HI,' SHE SAID to Ursula and Joar out on the walkway. The Oracle stood where the walkway curled around her own tower, and Tobias was standing between them, clipboard balanced on the railing, writing desultorily.

Drawing, Auli corrected as she approached. The Oracle was silent. There were two ghosts nearby, a data file and a video clip of an old man, East Asian with a long white beard, facing the same way as the Oracle, the railing sparking very slightly where it passed through him, and they looked almost companionable, Auli thought, the light off the restless waves sending patterns across her face that matched the static across his.

'Umm, hi,' Tobias said, seeing Auli. 'It's not time, is it?' Checking his watch automatically, pointlessly so close to the Oracle.

'No,' Auli said. Forty-eight hours ago, she had been only one grade above him, and everyone on the Bellwether would have ranked his work above hers. He'd remapped treacherous bathymetry around the Stockholm approach, he'd helped Uoti build a semi-functional Baltic circulation model for the fisheries contracts. She had four working theories for the creation of the Salt Oracle and a paper on the evolution of novel ghost folklore. There was no contest really. 'I wanted to check on the Oracle.'

Tobias squinted at Joar, then at the Oracle. Auli had known this was idiotic.

'You could grab a coffee if you like. I'll be done in a few minutes.'

'It's not time for seeding.'

'I know.' She scrambled for an excuse. 'But Célestine has nothing for the forecast for the second day in a row. Well... it's not ideal, is it?'

Tobias screwed his face up. 'I mean, no. But... *you're* going to be seeding? No offence...' He trailed off awkwardly.

Boudain had believed in her and someone had killed him. Auli added Tobias' doubt to Pertti's thinly veiled disdain and wondered who of all the other analysts most coveted her new job. Pertti, or Célestine, surely not An. Nor Suvi or Bea, or Tobias although for wildly different reasons.

She forced her shoulders down a notch. 'Yes, well, it's hardly fair to expect Gabrielle or Uoti to fill in for me, is it?'

He blinked. 'No. True.' He eyed the silent Oracle and the ghost beside her. 'Or... do you want me to get An, or Pertti? He's got the new coordinates.'

Oh no, Auli thought. 'No, it's okay. I've got what I need.' She watched the lightning in the girl's eyes, pallid in the refracted sunlight. The day's heat prickled her neck and the ghost of the man, monk, warrior, pulled his hands from his deep sleeves, revealing an orange that he slowly began to peel. Tobias was still frowning but he stepped away from the Oracle.

'I'll just... I'll be back in a few then,' he said.

This was madness.

Ursula coughed, Tobias flushed and walked away.

Auli looked at Joar, and he answered before she could ask.

'My orders are to stay close. So I'm not budging.' He gave a barbed grin. 'But I'm not listening to whatever madness comes out of her mouth so I'm safe.'

Auli eyed the hard edge to his eyes and the gun in its holster, the knife on his thigh. Hardly, she thought, but said only, 'Fair enough.' And turned carefully to stand beside this strange girl and the ghost man, companions watching over the sea. The ghost flickered, the half-peeled orange disappeared back into his sleeves, the Oracle sighed. Auli mapped out the extent of her fear and took a breath to speak to the girl for the very first time.

'Oracle,' she said in Finnish. 'What did Boudain Caron ask you?'

She heard a hissing breath behind her; so much for not listening.

Nothing else happened. The sea murmured, a boat away to the west was drifting slowly their way – fishermen checking the forecast flags. Somewhere the far side of the Bellwether, someone was hammering metal, the sound ringing and ugly in the hot air.

'Oracle,' Auli repeated in Russian. 'Boudain Caron. What did he ask?'

The girl shivered, her eyes closed and Auli kept both ghosts in her peripheral vision, felt the lightness of the vial of valerian in the hollow of her throat. She might have just killed herself. Although it was statistically unlikely, and this was still a ridiculous idea – questions like this never worked. The Oracle could only answer if your words matched some part of a ghost – data records, text, the lyrics of a song, although Auli had only persuaded Boudain to try summoning sea shanties once.

She didn't answer things like this. But she might also have skipped a dose of sedative that night. So maybe...

'Horus crosses the Outer Sea, taking his souls to the Underworld,' the Oracle whispered.

Coincidence? Auli shuddered, made herself speak.

'Yes,' Auli said. 'Who was there, Oracle? Who was with Boudain Caron?'

'The captain's men,' the Oracle whispered in English. Auli inhaled sharply. 'And ye and each of you are adjudged. She is the protector of seafarers and travellers; she brings children to the childless.' The Bellwether creaked and soughed, and it had only been a slim chance but no one else would even have tried.

She stepped away from the Oracle. Ursula's head was bent over her sewing. Auli waved a hand and the woman looked up incuriously.

'Did anyone other than Boudain come to see the Oracle that night?' Auli said in Finnish.

Ursula lifted her gaze from Auli's lips to her eyes, shot a sideways glance at the boatman and shook her head once.

'Are you sure?'

Ursula held her gaze a little too fixedly. Had that glance been deliberate? How could Auli ask if there was always going to be a boatman here, listening? She was aware abruptly of how tired she was, and how hungry. 'Okay,' she said. 'Thank you anyway.'

Someone shouted through a megaphone, and a bell rang sharply once. Auli and Joar both started, Joar stepping past her to look around the corner. He grunted.

'Fishing boat drifted too close,' he said, but he stayed where he was, his attention split between the three of them here, the small boat being hailed and West Tower where there would likely be a rifle barrel resting on a railing, an eye awaiting a sign.

'I'll see if—' Auli cut off. Pertti emerged from the nearest door.

The wind whipped the Oracle's long hair against Auli's face with a hiss of barely-there static. The Oracle turned and stared at Auli, her eyes wide, and Auli had never once noticed that they were a deep loam brown beneath the white lightning. She froze, startled, and the Oracle whispered harshly, 'Canst thou draw out leviathan with a hook?'

Auli stared.

The Oracle gazed back. 'The hook hurts. It hurts.'

'Stand clear.' Joar pulled on Auli's arm and the girl flinched, her hands coming up and her eyes closing. Bracing for a blow, Auli thought, and felt like she'd been punched herself.

'Did she touch you?' Pertti asked. Ursula watched, her needle swimming through the torn cloth like a fish and Tobias hovered in Pertti's lee. He'd fetched him, Auli thought.

'Nothing happened,' Auli said. 'It was just a cantation. I don't know why Joar intervened.'

He was back watching the retreated fishing boat, and answered shortly, 'Following orders. The Oracle got too close.'

Auli eyed him thoughtfully. What exactly *were* his orders and why had Raphaël put a guard on her suddenly? Had he guessed about Boudain?

She thought of Mama Márjá and straightened her shoulders. Well, she'd tried the foolish thing, next the frightening one – the folder still tucked under one arm – then if she hadn't found another reason to delay, the captain.

The Oracle cried out wordlessly, and everyone other than Ursula jumped, but she only began talking, one hand curling around her throat and numbers pouring from her mouth breathlessly.

The hook hurts, Auli thought, watching her.

Raphaël

RAPHAËL WAS UP the top of North Tower with Sandesh and Miika, fixing the harpoon gun mount onto the walkway. They'd had to fit braces beneath them to support the weight of it, which had meant dangling from the tower like a spider, and he didn't mind the roughest seas on the deck of a boat, but he wasn't a fan of heights. They were nearly finished fixing this mount though. Not bad, considering.

'Check, boss.' Sandesh straightened from straining against the big wrench and Raphaël bent to the final tightening. Oh for power tools, he thought, sweating even in the tower roof's sharp shade, shoulder muscles burning as he forced the salvaged bolt a few degrees tighter. The water far beneath his feet was slate-dark, flashing with the movement of fish just beneath the surface. They shoaled beneath the Bellwether, dodging tide turbines and fishing lines, and there were anemones on the anchor chains now, mussels and goose barnacles in nascent colonies. He liked it, this sign of permanence.

He eased up and shook out his hands. 'I think that's it.'

Sandesh was looking westward to the open water, Miika beside him with the heavyweight hammer dangling from one fist. There was an inshore fishing vessel hoving within sight of the forecast flags, but Raphaël suspected that wasn't what they were looking for.

Sandesh confirmed it. 'I'm telling you, it was huge. Nearly fried the boat even with the engine off.'

Miika laughed, but without edge. 'Well, glad I was here then. Hope it drifts somewhere the fuck else.'

'Come on,' Raphaël said. 'And if you drop that sledgehammer, Puhakainen, you're diving after it. They're expensive.'

AN HOUR LATER they were marginally cleaned up and convened in the Hall for lunch. Dunya, bless her, set big jugs of almost-cold water, faintly flavoured with lemon, in front of them as Raphaël scanned the researchers. Auli was not here, Gabrielle had been and gone, Uoti was surrounded by his team, laughing at something An had said.

'You think we've a mole,' Hellä said. She had an unsettling ability to read him sometimes, both a good thing in a Second, and also vexing.

'I didn't say anything.'

'You were thinking it. And the boatmen are wondering.'

Of course they were.

He only put a guard on the Oracle when there was trouble, and he was yet to meet a group of people fonder of gossip than off-duty soldiers. 'I think we have a dead PI, and I don't want another one. That's all.'

'Understood, boss. Especially as—' She cut off, grinned at him infuriatingly and changed tack, 'Guarding the Oracle unnerves them.'

'Tough,' he said flatly. Hellä snorted. 'If the researchers can do listening duty, then—' Movement in the doorway that he recognised even in his peripheral vision. A shade shy of furtive but graceful as a cat. He forgot the rest of his sentence. Auli, standing just inside the doorway, looked like she was holding herself together by a thread. He was half off the bench before he realised what he was doing and forced himself back down again. Her gaze slid to him, stilled, and moved on but something in that contact made him think – no, made him certain – she wanted to speak to him. But instead of approaching, she served herself and then found a seat on its own about as far from him as she could get.

Which was more or less how things had stood for two years. And if he repeated to himself that it was for the best, that he didn't want what she had wanted, well then perhaps someday it would cease aching.

As some researchers finished up, the new kid bounced down the table to sit next to her and in the emptying room, Raphaël could hear him easily. 'Hey, Auli, want me to cover your listening shift this afternoon?'

A few more researchers and boatmen rose, including Hellä.

'See if the dummy harpoon is ready?' Raphaël said to her as she gathered up her dishes. Then he debated for approximately three seconds, before crossing the room and clapping a hand not entirely gently on the kid's shoulder. He yelped gratifyingly and looked up.

'Captain! Umm, hi?'

Raphaël was very aware of Auli setting her spoon down to watch.

'We're having a chat,' Raphaël said to the boy. 'My office, now.'

'Why?' Auli said. The open surprise in the boy's eyes had become something shuttered and wary.

Yes, Raphaël thought, I'm right not to trust you. 'Debrief of the incident yesterday. Come on, up.' Releasing his hold and giving the kid, Leigh Alvarez, just enough room to obey. Instead of doing so, he looked at Auli, and Raphaël resisted the urge to smack the back of his head – it was reasonable to check with your PI, he allowed. But only just.

Auli lifted her gaze from the boy to him, and he met her look patiently. There were shadows beneath her eyes, but her face was as maddeningly calm as ever.

'Fine, then I will join you—'

'You haven't eaten,' he interrupted. 'And I don't have time to wait.'

Auli studied her soup, pastry and indeterminate berry juice, then rose, picking up the pastry and juice. 'I'm his PI, I've already debriefed him. But if you wish to as well, he's entitled to my presence. Do you want me there, Leigh?'

Alvarez nodded quickly, and Raphaël smiled. The kid was sorely mistaken if he thought Auli's presence would alter the questions Raphaël intended to ask. Although she might put a dampener on how, he supposed.

In his office, he offered Auli his chair and pulled another into the middle of the floor for Alvarez. The room had bare floorboards and a bare desk, four mismatched chairs and as much shelving and workbench space as the walls allowed, all piled with tech, tools, oddments of gear. The smells of solder and valerian were strong, meaning An had been busy this morning; it was more her workshop than his office in truth, but he didn't mind.

He leaned against a shelf. 'Take me through what happened.'

'I told all this to Auli this morning, but okay,' the boy said, his whole body angled towards Auli. 'So, I was on listener duty. It was—'

'Tell me why you're here, first,' Raphaël interrupted. Auli's hands wound themselves together in her lap. If she ever turned the ferocious strength of her self-control outward, he thought, not for the first time, he wanted to be around to see it.

Alvarez stayed very still for several seconds then looked up at Raphaël with a pleasant expression that raised Raphaël's hackles.

'I was with a group salvaging collection information from the British Museum. Someone asked if I'd be interested in archive reconstruction. I thought it was for a library, you know – one of the ones re-establishing since they lifted the bans on books.' He turned a smile on Auli. 'When they said the job was here, I... I thought about it for two days then agreed.' Back to Raphaël, the smile less wide but just as guileless. 'A couple of months waiting for permissions and funding, a fortnight of sailing I'm in no hurry to repeat and here I am!'

'And here you are,' Raphaël repeated, thinking hard. It was all perfectly reasonable and not unlike many younger researcher recruitment stories here. London wouldn't be the first government – or crime syndicate masquerading as government – wanting a pair of eyes on board the Bellwether, but that didn't make everyone recruited that way a threat. 'Those two days thinking – have you left family behind?'

'Almost everyone here left family behind, Captain,' Auli said quietly and without moving.

Raphaël didn't look away from Alvarez and after a moment the boy shrugged. 'Yeah, loads.' He glanced at Auli as if for reassurance. 'I can still write though. The pay means they can get medicines for my mum and my nephew. And, well, no one said you had to stay here. It's not a prison, so I can always leave in a few years.'

Auli failed to stifle her inhalation, and Raphaël did smile this time although admittedly not without an edge. 'Not getting the tattoo then? How long? A year? Two? Until you've achieved your mission?'

'Raphaël!'

'Hit a setback with your first couple of attempts, did you?'

'*Raphaël!*' She leaned forward over his desk, her eyes wide and yet, he noted, not shocked. Interesting.

Alvarez looked between the two of them, wary and convincingly bemused. He held up his hands. 'Hey, man, Captain, I don't know what you're suggesting but I'm here to learn how to archive information from ghosts. That's it. I just want to do my job.' He looked at the hands still raised in front of him and tucked them away. 'And I was the one injured yesterday.'

Raphaël rubbed a hand over his chin, salt and stubble, studying the boy in front of him.

'Captain, can I speak with you alone?' Auli said.

Raphaël looked at her. 'Of course,' he said. Then to Alvarez, 'First – yesterday. Run me through it.'

'It's fine, Leigh,' Auli said as Alvarez opened his mouth to answer. 'I can fill the captain in. You can go, you're on listening duty shortly, I believe.'

Raphaël considered overriding her, given the security risk, but restricted himself to scowling at the kid until he fled. When the door banged shut behind him, Raphaël gave himself a moment before facing the woman in his chair.

Chapter Ten

Auli

AULI WAITED FOR Raphaël to face her, trying to rationalise her anger. He'd basically accused Leigh of murdering Boudain and… wanting to kill the Oracle? She ought to be relieved he'd guessed, but she wasn't.

He dropped into the chair Leigh had vacated, but not before angling it toward the door. She'd asked once if that was something the various ex-soldiers had taught him; he'd shrugged, pressed his mouth to her bare shoulder and said only, *no*.

'What the hell was that?' she said.

He ran a hand over his face. 'What's London doing sending you an assistant, Auli?'

'You don't think we have the work for one?'

Raphaël shook his head. 'I'm sure you do. But why him?'

The problem was she had no idea. Boudain had sprung first Leigh's recruitment, and then his godawful research plans on her, and she didn't understand any of it. She suspected he'd done it that way to make her objections redundant. 'We got a new contract in,' she said. 'A shipping consortium. And it's hard finding skilled people willing to come, you know that.

Maybe Leigh was the only choice. Why would any of that make him a murderer?'

He studied her, sighed and said, 'You tell me, Auli. I think you know things I don't.'

Her own hostility annoyed her almost as much as his behaviour had done, so she shook herself. 'Have you spoken to Niki?' He shook his head. No, he'd been making a racket up the guard towers all morning. Fixing those godawful harpoon guns Uoti insisted were justified. 'But you think Boudain was killed.'

He gave her a crooked smile. 'I wasn't sure until now.'

Auli flushed.

'But Alvarez is new and too *nice*, so I wanted to check. Why so protective of the boy? And why do *you know* Boudain was murdered?'

Niki had said to leave Raphaël to find the killer. Auli wished they were anywhere but here in his valerian-scented office – this was the only place on the Bellwether it was permitted, because of all the wiring and the fire risk – and she hadn't realised until now how much she associated the scent with safety, and how much of that was about this man rather than ghosts. Damn him.

But telling Raphaël didn't mean she *couldn't* seek answers herself. She told him about Niki's findings, the words arid on her tongue.

Raphaël blinked once. Stood and paced to the door, listened for a second, then strode back across the room to lean against the desk so close she could feel the heat of him. She gritted her teeth and looked up to meet his gaze.

'Poison. Who had access to Niki's stores while we were away? You, Bea and Joar. Anyone else?'

She ought not to be surprised he knew. 'No, that's all. But I'm not sure it matters. The poison was in hot chocolate, mixed with a sedative.'

Raphaël hummed. 'And only the PIs and the carer knew about that,' he finished.

Auli stared at her intertwined hands fixedly, feeling poleaxed. 'You knew,' she whispered. He ducked to hear her, and she flinched away. There was a burning in the back of her throat that could have been one of half a dozen emotions. But it didn't matter, she told herself viciously. It didn't matter at all.

'Auli.'

She thought she might hate him a little just then. 'How long?'

'Auli.'

Looking up finally. 'How long have you known what they do to her?'

His eyes, always so hard, softened and she hated him for that, too. 'I guessed. It was obvious once I looked – the supplies Niki needed, the routine.'

One of the things clawing at her throat was most definitely a scream.

'You *guessed*? And did *nothing*? When, Raphaël? When she was ten? Twelve? And you were fine with that? Had you guessed when we were—'

Someone knocked on the door, and Hellä's blonde head appeared. 'Boss? Sorry to interrupt.'

Raphaël straightened away from Auli and threw a glance over his shoulder. Hellä visibly straightened. 'What is it, Novikova?'

'The dummy is ready, boss. Are we range-finding this afternoon?'

Range-finding, for the harpoons. She knew there were people who would like to see the Oracle under their control, or dead, and who'd settle for sabotaging the Bellwether. She *knew* that, and had seen the body of the occasional fool who'd tried. But still the thought of great, barbaric harpoons sitting on the towers pointing at the water... it tarnished the Bellwether horribly. Need, she thought bitterly, and justified violence.

Raphaël studied the windows then nodded once. 'Load up marker buoys on the *Meri Noita*. You're firing with Sandesh in West Tower.'

Hellä withdrew. Raphaël moved to the window, restless now, and it wouldn't be long before he found a way to escape this conversation. Auli wanted to let him.

'She's a child, Raphaël,' she said quietly, watching him watch the water. His face gave nothing away.

'So are the children of the fishermen all around the coast, God, so are half the fishermen, these days. So are the city kids dependent on supply convoys.' He shot her a brief, hooded glance. A shoal of fish shimmered over the surface of the water, Auli remembered Leigh's sketch, and blanched. Raphaël noticed, of course, and leaned against the window, studying her the way she had studied him. 'You can't change it, Auli. You'll be fired. And even if you succeed? And the Oracle goes fully, finally mad and we lose access to what paltry data she's currently giving us? What then?'

She shook her head mutely.

'Ships continue getting lost, or foundering on unmapped hazards or in unpredicted weather, more people die, more go hungry. And one girl goes from being calm to constant distress. Who is that helping other than you and your conscience?'

She used to drown herself, Niki had said. They'd weighed their own guilt years ago, and decided it was kinder this way. Raphaël and Niki, Gabrielle and Uoti and Boudain all thought it was acceptable. Why could Auli not agree?

She studied her fingers, scars across two knuckles from a fire, the bed of one fingernail uneven from infection. Both were in the months after the Crash. She ought to be tougher by now, she thought, and the thought was in Mama Márjá's voice. Mama Sara would say it was far harder to stay kind. Her brother... oh, her brother.

'I thought we were protecting her here. I thought she was as contented as possible for someone like her.'

'She is.' Raphaël reached out, but she stiffened, and his hand froze mid-air then returned to his pocket.

'She's a prisoner,' Auli corrected. 'And we don't know if she is content because we've built a prison out of her mind as well as out of this college. We can balance equations all we like, but she is still a child under our care, who we are betraying every single day.'

Raphaël didn't answer, and she pressed one hand to her chest, her lungs tight within her as if she had been swimming. She couldn't speak to anyone else on the Bellwether like this and that alone made her so sad and angry she would have fled if he hadn't been in her way.

'So I guess we have to live with that,' Raphaël said eventually. 'I never fooled myself this place was *good*. It serves a purpose, for the region and for us personally, that is all. Nothing involving guns and walls is ever *good*, Auli. It is sometimes simply the least-worst option we have.'

'Then why stay?' she said. 'You more than anyone could leave.' And why in God's name had she said that, because he'd asked her to leave once, as she wept after another ghost death. And she'd refused, saying feebly that she was worth something here.

He shot her a glance now so full of anger she flinched. Did he remember, too, did he...?

'We're off topic,' he said curtly. 'And I'm due on the boat. What gave Alvarez those burns?'

So that was it? They had to live with it for the greater good? Over his shoulder, a single rain shower was falling on the distant water slantwise, stalking northward.

'It was a shoal of barracuda,' she said flatly. 'He got lucky.'

Raphaël hadn't moved, but his whole frame somehow still managed to come alert, and old wounds beneath her ribs began aching. He'd always seen through her lies.

'Who was on watch in West Tower when Boudain died?' she said, mostly to distract him. 'Was anyone in East?'

'No, Auli.'

'They can both see into part of the Oracle Room. West Tower would have seen Boudain when he fell.'

'Leave it with me,' he said.

She glared at him. 'No.'

He glared back but she didn't care. She wasn't sure she could carry Boudain's dreams, but she owed him this. Raphaël gave in. 'Joar was in West, Cara in East. I already asked – Cara saw nothing, Joar... wasn't at his post.'

Auli felt herself stiffen.

Raphaël grimaced. 'I know. He was sick and missed the shift change. Hellä left her post to find him, so the tower was unmanned for a while. It shouldn't have happened, but was just bad timing.'

'Was it? What was he sick with? Could he have been dosed to make sure he didn't see anything? He was fine later.'

'Some rough aquavit apparently.' Raphaël smiled very slightly. 'He was well once he'd hurled his guts up.'

When Auli didn't speak, he added, almost defensively, 'I believe him.'

'But you weren't here,' Auli observed. 'Who knows the guard rotas? All the boatmen—' She abandoned that idea.

'Leave it,' Raphaël repeated. 'I've put a guard on the Oracle already. I'll look into the other medics. Please just... let me know if anything else happens with any ghosts, yes?'

No, Auli thought cantankerously. But Niki had wanted this, for their safety as well as hers, and Auli's determination faltered.

'I need to know,' she said.

'I know,' Raphaël said steadily. 'I'll find out. I've asked Helsinki for updates on the Survivors' recent activity, too.' He paused, watching her. 'What?'

'Joar's from Helsinki.'

Raphaël's eyes narrowed, and he shoved off the window. 'So are you and Uoti,' he said flatly. 'I'd know if the Survivors had a plant among the boatmen, Auli. I need to go.'

Behind him two ghosts sparked in the sunlight as they collided, the window frame creaked softly, and he was gone before Auli realised.

'Wait,' she murmured to the empty room. There was one other thing she could do after all, even if it meant yet another boat.

SHE CAUGHT UP with him, embarrassingly breathless, on the dock. 'Where are you taking the boat?'

He looked back at her, frowning. 'Why?'

'You're testing those harpoons? Where? How far out?'

The boatmen were busy loading several small marker-buoys. A ghost hovered off the end of the dock, talking frantically in Dutch. 'West end of Kantor. Why?'

The finished harpoons would have explosive heads, Uoti had said. They'd sit in the guard towers, as if ageing explosives were not remotely worthy of concern. Visions of the Bellwether in flames swept through her mind, of dying whales and the sea exploding into steam and fire. Many of the boats lost in the Crash had sunk aflame, because of newborn ghosts feasting on the computers, the electrics, the engines; fire and flame and chaos. Her brother's death had not been unique, it had only been unique to her. And he'd been a strong swimmer, but perhaps that only made it worse.

The fire or the drowning, the choice in every single one of her nightmares.

'I want to see where your kraken was.'

'Boss, all set,' someone said from the boat.

Raphaël hesitated, the high summer sun making his skin glow, and she wondered if he would refuse her, and whether that would be because part of him still cared for her fears. Which did not, she told herself sternly, matter.

'I just want to see if it's still there. For the dataset,' she said. She'd promised not to tell anyone about Leigh's scratches but that didn't mean she'd forgotten the strange parallel, both so soon after Boudain's death.

'I can check, you don't need to come,' Raphaël said.

'I know. But I want to.'

He frowned, which was not, Auli decided, a refusal. She made herself move to the boat. Sat down in the prow and gripped the rail when, after a moment more, Raphaël jumped aboard. He knew better than anyone still alive in the Bellwether how little she liked being on the boats, but he said nothing more to her as the sails lofted up with a snap of their wings. A datacloud ghost drifted so close to her that the static lifted her hair, and she pulled back sharply, fighting to look as unafraid of the water as she was of the ghost.

The girl

LET ME HAVE *one last try before you give her that.*

She drifts through layers of sunlight; the sea is wakeful but up here, high in the bright sky, she floats quiet—

Buoy B2451, Oracle. Buoy B2451. Come on.

She floats.

Buoy B2563, Buoy B2563.

It is a hook. Water floods her veins in a rising tide, salt and bitter cold against her bones. No, she thinks, lifting her face to the sky, but the hook digs deep, she hears a whimper.

That's it. Buoy B2563.

She is pain and dark water and lightning, the hooks drag her down and the water rises, she drowns on numbers that burn her veins. Somewhere deep beneath the water and the code, she is screaming. But no one hears.

Or someone hears.

The water twists with maelstrom muscularity, eyes reflecting eyes reflecting eyes like the sea is built of watchfulness.

You are hurting.

She drowns.

You are tearing apart.

Down here in the dark with the eyes, she screams. The water twines close around her, almost... almost a memory of a woman, her arm warm and heavy holding her tight, the smell of bread and comfort.

You're safe, lyubimy, the woman murmured long ago, *you're safe here. Stay quiet as a mouse until the bad men leave.*

The bad men? The sea holds her fast. Far away the numbers scratch her throat full of blood and salt, but here her scream falters.

Mama? she thinks.

Let's make the bad men leave, shall we?

And the numbers fragment into zeros and ones, reform as words that slip from her mouth like honey, like bees full of honey and venom and love.

'And from the depths came a great beast, rising up beneath them—'

Oh, dammit. We've lost it.

'—making the waves grow taller than the mizzenmast and men fell from the rigging into the water. The beast hurled itself—'

What's...

'—against the ship's starboard flank, causing great rifts in the lower decks that the sea rushed through. Men strained at the pumps, but the monster came once more and twice more, and—'

Christ. Boatman, get the doctor! Get back, get—

'—with its huge teeth it snapped up the fallen sailors until the waves ran red, the decks a charnel house and the ship half-sinking was full of the screams of the wounded and afraid.'

It was true, she thought, the ship was full of screams, whereas her bones were full of hunger and salt. The sea laughed in her throat like thunder.

There, doesn't that feel better?

It did. Oh, it did.

Chapter Eleven

Raphaël

TACKING NORTH TO Kantor, they dropped distance marker buoys out from the tower. It was laborious under sail, and a couple of off-duty boatmen on the second deck walkway hollered intermittent abuse across the water. As they reefed sail safely out of range by Flatskär, Raphaël switched out with Alan on the helm, one eye on the unspooling anchor line, the other on the sky and the ghosts. Auli stopped scanning for the absent kraken ghost, pulled out a notebook and began to sketch. He'd not seen her sketches in years, and just the sight of her, pencil moving, eyes on some eider riding the low swell made him look sharply away, annoyed at everything for no reason at all.

It would be good, he thought, to get this job done. The Bellwether armed against outsiders so he could focus on hunting the killer within.

The boat rocked and Auli lowered her notebook, eyeing a ghost drifting twenty metres to starboard. Up in the tower, the lean shape of Sandesh bent over the cannon. Joar wasn't there, and Raphaël wondered whether he'd believed the Finn too easily. Auli certainly thought so.

Hellä raised her torch and flashed the *ready* signal across to them.

'Heads up,' Raphaël shouted. 'Alan, confirm.'

Alan's torch clicked as Raphaël moved to set himself between the distant cannon and Auli, who was resolutely refusing to watch. There was a flat, enormous percussion, a blur of motion and a quick splash of water far out. Raphaël kept his gaze pinned on that spot, between the hundred and hundred-fifty marker buoys. Pale waders flushed up from Kantor's shore in alarm.

'Uh, Captain?'

It was Alan.

The rope, Raphaël thought, there'd been no rope. 'Signal *halt*,' he said. 'We'll mark the site. Sails up, crew. The rope came loose?'

'No, boss. Look,' Alan said in a strange, flat voice.

Raphaël turned from the harpoon's strike point.

'What the fuck?' he murmured, and moved up to the prow with Auli, staring at the Bellwether over her shoulder. 'Miika, engines.'

It was raining on the College. Just on the College, like a miniature cloudburst, which would have been only semi-remarkable. But this wasn't a cloudburst.

'It's a ghost,' Auli said.

'That big? Didn't think it was possible.' Alan handed his pair of binoculars to Raphaël then switched to English, his Finnish defeating him. 'The sea's gone crazy, too.'

Raphaël studied the magnified scene, scanning the decks of the Bellwether quickly. The rain was darker than it should be, like it was nighttime within the recording, or the depths of a storm, and electricity was arcing across the metal of the underdeck's walls, along the walkways – and Alan was right. The real sea beneath that enormous ghost was rising, waves breaking against the second deck windows.

God, he thought. 'Signal the tower for their threat status.' There was movement and footsteps making the boat rock unevenly, but he didn't stop scanning, searching...

'Where's the Oracle? Can you see her?' Auli said quietly.

'No.' It was too dark, the waves breaking too high. 'Frans, anchor away. Miika, back to the College but cut east,' he shouted over his shoulder. They couldn't sail into that, but he couldn't sit here either.

'Signal,' Alan said. 'Oracle unsecured.'

'What does that mean?' Auli said when Raphaël only swore.

The Oracle Tower was almost impossible to make out through the darkened rain. Lightning crackled all along the third deck walkway. They should stay out here, the risk was too high. It was *too high*. But Célestine was in the middle of that, and the Oracle was his job.

'Signal to evac to the dorm barges,' he said.

'Sir.' The torch clicked then a splash from behind, Frans shouted 'Clear', Raphaël braced as the engine revved and the prow came up. Auli stumbled back into him and he dropped one hand from the bins to her shoulder, her muscles taut as wire.

'Fire,' she whispered, almost inaudible beneath the engine noise and the behemoth ghost. 'Will they evacuate the Oracle? What does unsecured mean?'

He didn't know. 'Alan, you're with me, the rest to Hellä to support evac.' Then, quieter, 'She should be safe in the tower. The fire doors will—'

'Don't lie,' Auli interrupted him. Which was fair, but rankled anyway.

Spray broke over them, shockingly cold and again Auli was pushed back into his chest. He realised he still had a hand on her shoulder and yanked it away. They were close enough now to see movement on the walkways, on the gantry to the barges, but he couldn't see a wheelchair. They'd practiced this enough times though, and Pertti was level-headed enough to remember. Raphaël felt sick.

They were only fifty metres from the ghost now and the noise rose, the ghost's vast hissing and the furious roar of an ocean in full swing.

'Christ on a bike,' Alan muttered in English. 'Valerian?' he asked.

Raphaël eyed the hellscape they were about to dive into, every instinct screaming to stop.

'Is this suicide?' he said in Auli's ear.

She didn't answer. They were thirty metres out. Raphaël swore again. 'It's Célestine, she might—'

'It won't be infectious,' Auli interrupted, her voice unfathomably steady. 'Weather ghosts aren't. There's not enough correlation.'

Raphaël was just terrified enough to believe her. And perhaps the engine would be a more tempting lure anyway, until it short-circuited. He lifted his shoulders fatalistically.

'It will burn though,' Auli added.

Miika flipped the lights on and they entered the ghost.

And couldn't see two meters beyond the prow. Miika cut the boat's speed immediately, soughing heavily as she curled around the barges towards the dock. Unreal rain fell in navy torrents, the air was shifting and shadowy, and not unlike having a charged net thrown over them. It stung like an absolute bastard. Raphaël hissed, ducking instinctively as the boat filled with spray and static, boatmen swearing violently. Auli gave a small, bitten off yelp.

He grabbed her and pushed her backward, shouting, 'Get in the cabin.' His arms were burning, the muscles tightening spasmodically and making him too rough, but she went, and he turned back to grip the gunwale and peer through the darkness, setting his shoulders against the pain. Mother of God, but there was a good chance they were all fucked.

In the grey, swaying boat lights, the gantry heaved beneath unrecognisable figures, the waves tried to hurl the boat against the barges and Miika fought back, the engine juddering and the boat rearing like a hornet-stung horse. There was no structure to the sea, no swell, just madness and the roar of the non-existent storm, the barges groaning and the hollow booming of waves breaking against the Bellwether. Raphaël clung on, willing the boat faster, willing it not to die before they reached the dock. Electricity crackled along the deck like gunshot and someone somewhere screamed.

Past the garden barges now, turning, and through the darkness, rising up through a rising wave, there was something more than water ahead. Raphaël stared hard at the waves climbing the Oracle Tower. Nothing. Then something again, two, three dark shapes curling upwards hugely then falling back into the water.

Impossible. And familiar.

And then, just as Miika hauled them around for an approach to the wildly bucking dock, everything stopped.

The air cleared, the sea lost a good half of its ferocity, and the boat surged forward before Miika managed to adjust. Raphaël didn't look around. The engine was hiccupping worryingly, but he only moved to the starboard side, ready to jump.

'She's on her walkway,' Auli said. 'She's lying down.'

He spun to her, pink on her face and arms like she'd been out in the sun. Her hair risen around her in a wild black halo, almost sparking. 'I told you—' He stopped, amended as lightly as possible, 'Earth yourself before you turn into a candle.'

The boat bumped gently against the dock. The air was still and almost silent.

He leapt onto the gunwale and across in two bounds, felt Alan following him, Frans waiting behind with the mooring line ready in his hands. The ghost had gone, but God knew how much static build up there was, how many infected, and the Oracle was down.

'Lockdown until I say. Isolate the infected, and sweep for fire risk,' he shouted upwards. The boatman who'd just appeared at the top of the steps spun on his heel and vanished again.

THE DOOR OF the Oracle Room was shut and locked from the outside. Raphaël turned the key and scanned the room quickly before carrying on up the stairs. No ghosts but Alan knocked three times softly on the wall just behind him. Ursula Poronen was bent over on the walkway outside the bedroom, her hair loose and floating around her like Auli's had been. Feeling their footsteps, she jerked upright, and her expression in the moment before she recognised Raphaël was strangely agonised.

He knelt beside her and eyed the unconscious girl. There were singe marks on her shirt, everything around them was wet, but both Ursula and the Oracle appeared uninjured. The Oracle's pulse fluttered against his fingertips, high and light, but maybe it was normal for her – he wouldn't know.

'Clear for static up here,' Alan said behind him. 'I guess the waves stopped most of it.'

Ursula reached out as if to brush the Oracle's hair from her face, then dropped her hand. Raphaël lifted the girl's eyelids, the pupils contracting as he did so. The resident ravens circled overhead, talking intently.

'Did she do this?' he said in Finnish, looking at Ursula and gesturing to the air around them. Meaning had she encanted the storm ghost. It still wouldn't explain... but the carer shrugged. His own pulse was not entirely calm, and he leaned back on his heels just as Niki, then Auli, climbed into view. Of course she'd go to them. He should have guessed.

Moving aside to give Niki access, Raphaël sent Alan off to join the others and did a circuit of the tower, running his eye along all the external structures in view. The upper decks and towers he wasn't too worried about – if they hadn't sparked fires by now, they weren't going to. The library and the underdeck's machinery were more of an issue. Theoretically the whole Bellwether was pretty well earthed considering it was a giant raft, but *theory* and giant storm ghosts didn't intersect quite enough for Raphaël's comfort. Through the windows he could make out the shapes of boatmen sweeping the research deck, and Gabrielle and Hellä passed into view in the lower library. Intent but unhurried, bending and straightening as they picked books up from the walkway. He'd told them the shelves weren't seaworthy. One of the knots of tension in his gut unwound.

'She's coming around,' Auli said behind him, and then, 'The library?'

'Looks fine.' He turned. The sea all around them was calm, no white caps and no rain showers. No impossible monsters. The railing beneath his hand was still wet from the waves. 'Where did it go?' he said.

Auli tipped her head, hair swinging in her eyes. 'Down,' she said.

The generator? The desalination pump? Raphaël shot a look at the research deck again but there were no signs of alarm.

'Into the sea,' Auli clarified, and he switched his focus to her. She looked away, turned as if to return to the other side of the tower and the Oracle, but he put out a hand to stop her.

'We need to talk about this. It's too like the incident I reported.'

'The kraken?' she said without inflexion.

He didn't answer. Had she seen it, too?

She glanced up. 'Uoti's hurt. He was with the Oracle when the ghost appeared, he got hit by a wave and an electric shock—'

'Both at once?'

She nodded. 'He's conscious, but his heart stopped twice, Niki says. Joar did CPR on him then got him down to Niki's office.' Which explained Joar's absence. 'There's some minor injuries, but no infections showing so far.'

Raphaël nodded and then followed her back to Ursula who was picking up sheets of sodden, singed paper drooping between the slats of the walkway. Auli rushed to help.

'Uoti's cantation notes?' she said, switching to Finnish. 'May I have them?'

The carer hesitated but only fleetingly and Auli likely didn't even notice, all her attention on the paper. 'Thank you,' she said. Ursula gave a brief upward nod and went inside, and Auli looked across to where Raphaël had leaned against the railing to wait.

'It might help,' she said, 'if I can trace the cantations prior to the ghost appearing.'

Raphaël threw a wary eye at the docile sea beneath them.

'I don't have any data on your kraken,' she added, almost defensively. 'But I might be able to figure out why this ghost was different. I need to speak to Joar, too, and Uoti when he's well enough.' Her attention returned to the wet sheets of paper, and she turned away from him, saying more softly, 'I need to get it dry. Thank God we use pencil, there's at least…'

She disappeared down the stairs without looking back.

Raphaël sighed, straightened from the rail and went inside where Niki was talking to the carer in halting Finnish.

'You didn't give her anything else? And no one else? And last night's dose, she had that like normal?'

Caught side-on by the late afternoon sun, Ursula's mouth appeared to twist oddly as she answered, 'Last night was normal, this morning was normal.'

Raphaël didn't pause. Whether it was the drugs or the ghost that had knocked the Oracle out was not his concern. The fact that the ghost had injured Uoti was. Yesterday Boudain Caron was poisoned and a ghost injured Leigh Alvarez. Today this. He was aware of a very slight twinge of disappointment that this looked to absolve Leigh Alvarez of lying, about his injuries anyway.

Auli

Auli was at her desk four hours later. She'd checked in on Leigh on the barge, then with neither Uoti nor Gabrielle there to do so, had asked Célestine and An if everyone in their teams was okay. An had said that no one was dead, so yes. Célestine had eyed Auli caustically.

'Are we cleared for work yet?' she'd said. 'I finally have data for the forecast, and an hour until the boat comes.'

Auli had shaken her head. 'You need to wait for Raphaël's all clear, sorry.'

She'd begun to move back to the gantry, when Célestine called, 'But you are going back over?'

It hadn't occurred to Auli to stay in the barges with the other staff, there was too much to do. But she froze at Célestine's words and couldn't fathom out a way forward. To stay would be pointless and, well, bowing to Célestine's challenge. To go would be rubbing her promotion in Célestine's face, when they both knew which of them would have been the better candidate.

The Weather team watched, Pertti on Célestine's left and Suvi on her right. Célestine tapped two fingers on her wheel rim, and Auli forced herself to speak.

'Someone has to be with the Oracle. The captain will give the all-clear soon. I was on the—'

Célestine's fingers tapped louder then fell still. Auli didn't know why she was even trying.

'I'll remind him about the forecast,' she said, and walked away, their murmurs chasing her back to the Bellwether.

And she had reminded him, or at least, she'd asked the older boatman, Sandesh, to do so. She hadn't gone back to the Oracle though, and Uoti had been sleeping so she'd come to her desk, alone on the research deck that smelled of burned dust and hot metal. Gabrielle had passed her once, said, 'Management meeting when Uoti wakes,' and disappeared downstairs. Twenty minutes later Célestine and Suvi returned to work on the local forecast, and voices on the deck below meant everyone else was across for dinner. Auli wondered if Alexis had been forced to evacuate from his safe haven of the kitchen, how much the boatmen had frightened him, but then inevitably, her mind returned to the papers in front of her.

Three data points, she thought. Of ghosts interacting with people strangely. Raphaël's kraken, Leigh's barracuda and now Uoti and the storm. She ran a finger down Niki's neat records of ghost-related injuries, feeling sick. It was easy to normalise the attrition rate when you weren't looking at a list of names. Doing her best to ignore the ones crossed gently out, she tallied the others. Over the last three years there had been thirty-two incidences of minor electrical burns and eleven of more severe ones. None of them remotely resembled these three new events.

Of course they didn't. It was true when she'd examined Leigh's arms and it was true now, faced with Niki's data – if ghosts did anything at all, they killed or burned. They did not *attack*. They did not have *physicality*.

Her head beginning to ache, she turned to her own data on ghost types aggregating around the Oracle, searching for dangerous ghosts – a shark being hauled onboard a boat, another of a movie ship gunfight. Did a news article of a marine fire and rescue count? An audio clip of a man shouting? What made a ghost dangerous other than its electricity and its search for a match within a human mind?

She stared unseeing across the research deck, in shadow now while the library above was all amber and luminescence. Perhaps it didn't matter. No one had ever pretended ghosts were safe. Perhaps Boudain's death was more important than a few ghost oddities. She wanted to know why Joar Gunnarson had really been away from his post in West Tower, whether Ursula's fleeting glance had meant what Auli suspected. There were the missing research notes, too, the torn paper in the clipboard, the bottle Niki had been uninterested in. And something else, that had made no sense, what—

A boatman shouted, hailing the boat arriving from Kökar for the forecast. Suvi picked up two sheets of paper and left, and Célestine leaned back looking discontented. Which meant they either needed more time or the forecast was bad. Auli rose to ask her about Joar but instead found herself climbing up the ladder into the library. The sheets Uoti had been writing on were almost dry now, and she lifted them carefully from the western-most window, held the wrinkled papers to the honey-coloured light to read.

It wasn't cowardice, she tried to convince herself. If she were being entirely pragmatic, it mattered more if ghosts were mutating into a new danger threatening everyone than if there was a murderer aboard the Bellwether who threatened only one person. Or no one, if Boudain had been the target, she mustn't forget that possibility.

Uoti had been seeding the Oracle for re-deployed buoy data, of course.

The hook hurts, the Oracle had whispered, and reading the data Uoti had extracted from her, Auli shivered despite the gilded light and the whispering shelves.

The transcription cut off halfway through a spreadsheet row. Then he'd written, *And from the depths came a great beast*, before the pencil had made a jagged tear across the paper like he'd thrown his hands out in front of him.

'Huh,' Auli murmured. Outside, the forecast boat raced the dark back to Mariehamm where flags would be run up in the harbour so fishermen could plan their tomorrows on the colour of the cloth. Auli needed Uoti to wake up, but in the meantime, she could talk to Célestine, or to Leigh about Boudain's research proposal, and whether he'd told anyone about it.

She couldn't find him though. The researchers gathered atop the barge looked around bemusedly.

'He was just here,' Tobias said. 'I didn't notice him leaving.'

Everyone was drinking tepid beers or sharp aquavit as the broad shadow of the Bellwether slowly swallowed up the light, and Suvi said quietly, 'How is Uoti?'

'He's stable.'

'Infection?' An asked.

'No.' Although it was too soon for certainty. 'Just a big shock, Niki thinks.'

From behind Auli came the sound of wheels on metal and then Célestine saying, 'We have that new drug now, from the Estonia witch. If he is infected, we shall see if it works like they all say, no?'

Pertti frowned at his aquavit, reached out and folded Bea's hand in his.

There was, Auli realised, someone standing on the high ground of the islet of Äspskär to the north. A sharp-edged silhouette – one of the people still on Kökar, foraging for wild foods.

Sunlight flashed off something in the library's northern window and after a second, the forager turned and vanished out of view. And a figure in the library vanished, too. It was hardly the first time locals had come to stare, but Auli still watched for a moment longer before turning away.

DUNYA AND ALEXIS were on the garden barges, and Auli joined them, exclaiming faintly at the damage the storm had done. This, she thought, was something tangible she could do. Her hands in the earth to erase the memories of Boudain's blood and the lash of the storm ghost. She was halfway along a row of peas, already feeling the muscles beneath her shoulder blades ease when a door opened behind her and the voice she least wanted to hear called her name.

'Gabrielle,' she said, pivoting slowly. Movement in East Tower above caught her eye – Joar Gunnarson watching her, his rifle resting crosswise in his arms. He lifted his gaze back to the islands and she dropped hers to the woman waiting.

The muscles of Gabrielle's folded forearms were flexing restlessly. 'I should introduce you to seeding sessions,' she said shortly.

Auli's heart pressed against her ribs like a clenched fist. 'Of course,' she said. Uoti was out of action, and no one in their right mind would commit to speaking to the Oracle twice a day.

She apologised to the cooks and joined Gabrielle in the shadows of the second deck. 'Where is she?'

The gears of Célestine's winch ground into action off to their left.

'Her tower.'

They climbed the West Tower stairs in silence, crossed the research deck, and as soon as they entered the Oracle Room could hear her cantation. Code, but a different lexicon to HTML, chanted in a breathless monotone. Auli felt for whoever was trying to transcribe.

At the bottom of the stairs, Gabrielle rested one hand

flat against the wall. It was not quite a knock for luck, Auli thought, but it wasn't far off. The older woman looked at Auli and in the burnished light, her dark eyes were lit with fires, every white hair gold. She looked far younger than her years, and yet far wearier than she ought. She looked almost soft.

'This is your last chance, Fraser,' she said. 'If you're not ready to take this on, then say now and I'll ask another Senior to stand in.'

A bubble of entirely incomprehensible laughter welled up inside Auli. That an offer could be both kindness and threat, insult and lifeline. What a strange kingdom this woman ruled. And what a stranger Auli was to herself because she did not even hesitate. 'I'm fine,' she said steadily. A ghost crackled abruptly as it drifted through the window and they both jerked very slightly, but then Gabrielle just nodded once and climbed the stairs.

'Well then,' she said, too quietly to be meant for Auli's ears. 'Unto the breach.'

The girl

HER BONES ARE shipwrecks all rotted edges and broken spars. Her heart beats tidal. Her blood is the sea and the sea is blood, it is a cove of circling boats and mothers drowning in the blood of their children; it is a turtle on a hook, an albatross on a hook, a seascape of fishing lines and plastic bottles and all the tiny creatures floating bewildered in this hostile gyre.

See? the voice murmurs. *How they make us bleed.*

Somewhere her arms are lifted, her hair is brushed, and she remembers that. She turned towards the memory like a compass, like a seal pup, but there is only the club, the blood, the voice soothing and snaggle-toothed.

See how we bleed.

She wonders, this shipwreck girl, why the voice wants her to see. No one wants her to see, they only want her to drown, and drowning speak. But then another thought swims through her hollow ribs. Of words and storms and the pain stopping.

Oh.

Oh, yes.

The voice had hauled her from the drowning numbers, and they together told a tale of vengeance.

And the pain had stopped.

Somewhere the people are speaking, a map is whispering bathymetry, and the muscles of her oceanic flesh tighten. The pain is coming, she thinks. There is no freeing herself from the hook, it always returns.

See how they make us bleed, the voice scratches along her spine.

Right. Are you ready? one of the people says.

No, she thinks. Shoals of fish for consonants and vowels. No.

Buoy AR3498, twenty-eight, seven, sixteen. Buoy AR3498, twenty-eight, seven, sixteen. Am I… is this it?

The hook burrows into her marrow. She is the albatross panicked and dying, she is the whale ruptured and dying, the hook pulls. No, she thinks.

Oh, for a tale of vengeance to stop the pain.

'The dungeon of lost souls,' she whispers. The words are bubbles of air rising. Numbers claw at her throat, but she doesn't want them and perhaps she is a shipwreck, but she is also the bloody sea. 'The horse latitudes—'

Try again.

Buoy AR2588, twenty-eight, seven, sixteen. Buoy AR2588, twenty-eight, seven, sixteen.

'So called because becalmed ships, facing water shortages, would throw livestock overboard to conserve reserves. The ghosts of the drowned horses, and the many sailors dead of thirst or scurvy, are said to haunt this hot and windless stretch of ocean.'

Yes, the voice says in her ear. Remembered suns beat on her skin like a drum.

Is this normal?

It's not working. Have you got it ready, Ursula? Go on then.

'The ghosts of the drowned horses, and the many sailors—'
Something hot is pressed against her palm. Her palm that is not ship or water, and the shock of it. The shock of heat that is not story makes the words fall silent.

Someone is watching her. Owl black eyes and night black hair, and her heart, her bloody harpooned heart, beats in her ribs like a beacon. She blinks, the owl black eyes shine.

'Here,' the quiet person says. 'Chocolate.'

But she doesn't want this hot sweet anchor weight dragging her down softly; there are too many ways of drowning, and she fears them all.

'No,' she whispers.

Chapter Twelve

Auli

Lightning striated the Oracle's dilated pupils and the air in the room pressed salt-hot against Auli's skin. She wanted to retreat, but all she could do was stare. Because that word, that one simple word had not been a ghost at all, and she'd not heard anything so terrible in this whole wounded world.

'See? She drinks it herself. It's hardly cruelty.'

Gabrielle was watching her keenly. *This is exactly why I have doubts about your ability*, she had said yesterday. *The College is not for the fainthearted.*

Ursula sat on the bed beside the Oracle, helping her drink. 'She has had a difficult day,' she said to no one.

The Oracle trembled. Gabrielle side-stepped sharply to avoid a circling ghost, and Auli had to do the same. It was an audio file, degraded beyond usefulness, veering up into the roof space just before it reached the girl on the bed. If you mapped the trajectories of ghosts around the Oracle, would it reveal patterns like iron filings, Auli wondered, or water catchments? Was she magnet or lake? The heat of the room was fading as abruptly as it had risen, but Auli still felt the prickle of it.

'Was that a ghost, that heat?' Auli said. There was a thin trace of sweat along her spine and was she relieved to have failed, or ashamed? *The hook hurts*, the Oracle had said. And, *No*.

Ursula was watching the audio ghost, so she missed Auli's words, but Gabrielle did not.

'It was just warm air rising from the research deck. The doors are open.' They were, and a briny evening breeze was ruffling papers and clothes. But where had that breeze been a moment ago?

'No,' she said. 'Didn't you hear her? *This hot and windless stretch of ocean*, she said. And the room *became* hot and windless.'

She'd been speaking Finnish, so Ursula could lip read, but Gabrielle answered in English.

'Don't, Auli. I asked you not to stir up trouble.'

Auli flushed. 'About Boudain's death, not about this.'

Gabrielle hissed sharply between her teeth and tilted her head towards the external door. Auli followed her outside, the sea far beneath the walkway shadow-slick, a ghost of a shoreline shimmering faintly to the south, gold sand and azure waves, and the sullen rocks of Lindö behind it.

Gabrielle walked around the curvature of the tower, past a shell balanced on the railing, and then back. The evening light briefly reflected in her eyes – sky-white and blind as the Oracle – then the angle changed and she was Gabrielle again. Stern and driven and imperturbable.

Although that last wasn't entirely true, Auli realised.

'You don't realise how delicate the line we walk here is,' Gabrielle said. 'How little it would take to destroy us.'

'You mean contractors getting impatient and pulling funding? But they know the challenges we face.'

Gabrielle snorted. 'Do they? They aren't here, living it. The Oracle is just an idea to them, half nightmare, half potential profit.'

Auli shook her head. 'They all know we can only seed the Oracle so much. Better to wait for forecasts and maps than to risk more of us dying, surely?'

'You overestimate our importance, Auli. You think the shipping barons in Gdansk care more about the lives of a few mathematicians than getting their maps as quickly as possible? And it's not just pulling funding. Some might, but others might seek control of the Oracle. You know it's only the Helsinki incident and the captain's guns that've stopped any serious attempts, thus far.'

Occasional extremists *had* tried in the past, and Raphaël had stopped them. The researchers didn't really talk about the occasional boat shot at for straying too close, or dead body on the nearest shore. Like they didn't much care about the harpoons. They had more proximate things to worry about, and perhaps the Bellwether's looming solitude felt, despite the ghosts, too safe.

Gabrielle nodded at Auli's expression. 'We are strong, Auli, but we are not indestructible. Our strength relies on the Oracle producing the goods, and no one undermining us from within.'

The foreign beach was glowing in the deepening night, like a portal to another world.

'Okay,' Auli said slowly. 'But why would ghosts changing their behaviour or Boudain being murdered destabilise us then?' She picked up the raven's shell from the railing. 'Dangerous ghosts are hardly remarkable here, and if Boudain's death was just another failed attempt on the Oracle... how is finding his killer undermining us?'

Gabrielle straightened her shirt cuffs, and Auli felt her whole body go cold. Because Gabrielle didn't know about the poison, and Auli calling Boudain's death a murder hadn't surprised her. Oh God, she thought. What did it mean? Had Niki told Gabrielle despite warning Auli not to? Did Gabrielle guess like Raphaël had? Or something else?

'If rumours spread that security is lax or we can't control the Oracle, we look like an easy target.'

Auli could barely hear her over a high buzzing in her mind.

Gabrielle held out her hands almost beseechingly as a video ghost drifted overhead – a young woman holding up a book, leaning forward conspiratorially, all make-up and polish.

'We are alone, Auli, with an incredibly dangerous girl and a lot of eyes on us. You can't just—' She made a hard sound and dropped her hands, then said more steadily, 'Being PI is not about the seeding, Auli. It is about holding the College firm against any danger.'

The Bellwether moaned. *No*, the Oracle had whispered, and she had for once been entirely herself. That was the link, Auli realised abruptly. The ghosts acting strangely began with the Oracle... what? Gaining coherence?

What did that mean for them all?

Auli looked into Gabrielle's shadowy face, and said quietly, 'The contractors and Raphaël, their priority is the Oracle. But what's ours? The Oracle or the College?'

'They are the same thing for us. That's the point.'

But was it? The College might be able to persist if Boudain's vision manifested. Could the Oracle exist without the College? Auli wouldn't even have considered it an hour ago.

In the distant dark a thrush gave a long rattling alarm call, piercing as a torch beam, and it was too dark to see unlit ghosts and thus too dangerous to linger out here. But neither of them moved.

'What if...' she began. A part of her was shouting, *shut up*. Stop talking and *think first*. But she still felt the shock of meeting the Oracle's eyes and seeing not an Oracle at all, but a child.

Their own private source, imagine it, Boudain whispered in her ear.

'What if the Bellwether didn't have the Oracle?'

Gabrielle jerked, Auli's hand tightened on the rail, rust cutting into her fingers.

'What are you talking about?'

Auli didn't answer, she couldn't. It was stupid to have spoken and stupid to be out here in the dark in the Bellwether's most haunted place. Gabrielle would never try to kill the Oracle, but might she have wanted to kill Boudain... because he was between her and complete control? Had she – oh God, where had she been when Uoti had fallen?

'Did Boudain tell you about his research plans?' Auli said, her voice raspy.

'What? No.'

She hadn't asked which research plans. The shell bit sharp into Auli's fist and she frantically changed direction. 'You want to protect us, Gabrielle, but for that we need to understand what's happening. What if it had been her hurt today? What happens to us if she stops her cantations?'

Gabrielle stared hard at her for the space of three breaths, and then shockingly laughed.

'Then we're finished. Unless we can prove our worth with An's tech or Célestine's best guess model reconstructions. No.' She brushed a hand over her tightly bound hair. 'If the Oracle fails so does the Bellwether. And who would take us in? The College is spoken of in whispers. Stockholm sit me in a circle of valerian when I visit, did you know that?' Auli hadn't. Gabrielle repeated quietly, 'If the Oracle fails, we are finished.'

A falling star skittered across the southern sky and they both glanced up then away, without remark. They had once been lucky, Auli remembered. Then after the Crash, only commonplace. But now the moon was alone again in her orbit, with whatever lonely junk that hadn't fallen, perhaps the astronauts in their space station tomb, all still circling the world blind and silent.

Gabrielle reached out without warning and gripped Auli's shoulder, leaning in. 'With Uoti injured I need you on my side if I'm to hold everything together. Are you?'

Auli could see the whites of Gabrielle's eyes. 'I am on the side of the Bellwether,' she said carefully. 'Of whatever it takes to keep the College safe.'

Gabrielle's hand tightened briefly then fell away. 'Good,' she said. 'That's good. A few ghost irregularities are nothing to worry about, Fraser. And leave security to the captain.'

The tower vibrated to her footfalls as she left, but Auli followed far more slowly, setting the shell on the table softly so the sleeping Oracle did not wake.

Tomorrow, she thought. Tomorrow she'd figure all of this out.

Raphaël

THROUGH THE OPEN door of his office, Raphaël saw Auli and Gabrielle heading for the Oracle Room, guessed what for, and winced. He dropped his gaze to the pile of wires in front of him and set the tiny screwdriver down before he broke something. Célestine stopped tinkering with a broken plastic anemometer and lifted her head.

'What is it?' she said.

An glanced up from the far bench, a pair of wire cutters held aloft but Raphaël shook his head. He trusted Célestine with his life, but not with his thoughts on Auli. 'Blue flags still?' he said instead. 'I could do with another day like today.'

'Although without a giant storm ghost trying to shake the Bellwether to pieces, I think,' Célestine said with a smile. There'd been very little to tidy in here, everything got secured, but the research deck and the library had been a mess.

'You should not have come back, Rafa.'

Raphaël ignored that absurdity. 'The winch worked though, yes?' They were speaking English, because An didn't speak French. An returned to her circuit board, as a ghost skimmed the heavy line of valerian across the doorway and ricocheted away.

The edges of Célestine's lips curled down as she nodded. Yes, the winch had worked, and yes, Pertti had helped her evacuate as quickly as possible. But she had still been the last off. Her knuckles were bruised and black with dried blood.

'How about a zipline?' Raphaël said, not entirely joking. He had not designed her winch for an event like today, for the Bellwether in its sheltered bay to be tossed about like flotsam. 'It would be exposed, and mean leaving your chair behind. But it would be fast as fuck.'

Célestine thought about it. 'Permanently fixed? Because you could not deploy such a thing during a storm, no?'

'It would be metal,' An said without looking up.

Thus could conduct ghosts even if not hostile boarders. Raphaël frowned. The gangways were all quick-decoupling, so they could isolate any part of the College from any other part in seconds. A zipline would be a risk.

'What are the chances of this happening again? Don't worry about it, Rafa.' Plastic cracked in Célestine's hand and she swore. An switched a lamp on, and the light wavered as though the batteries were low. She looked at the light, then met Raphaël's gaze. 'I didn't check,' she said. 'Did you?'

'Shit. No.' He'd checked the generator room for fire, not for the battery levels.

'That was stupid,' An said, and stood. 'I'll go now. No one touch this.'

'Wouldn't dare,' Raphaël said with a grin. She narrowed her eyes at him and walked out, stepping neatly over the line of crushed roots.

'What is happening with you?' Célestine said in French the moment An was gone, abandoning the wind vane and fixing her gaze squarely on him.

They hadn't really talked since his return, but he strongly suspected she wasn't asking generally. He watched the empty doorway, then the windows. There was a bird on the railing, and the ghost of a page of text drifting towards the Oracle's Tower. Raphaël returned his friend's gaze. 'I do not know, Célestine. Maybe I am just getting paranoid.'

'It is Boudain's death? You were worried before this storm ghost. And Auli suspects something.'

His head came up sharply. 'Why do you say this?'

Célestine shrugged, tapping one long finger on the cusp of her wheel. 'She is not so good at hiding what she is thinking, you know? Also, she came out of Niki's room looking like milk.'

Raphaël ought to have known Célestine would notice. 'Why would anyone want to hurt Boudain?' he said neutrally. 'Did anything happen while I was away? With the QD research?'

Célestine scoffed. 'What QD research?' But when Raphaël simply stared at her, she wrinkled her nose and carried on, 'Only gossip about them getting another analyst. Boudain is... was' – she pulled an apologetic face – 'insignificant.'

'Which should have kept him safe.'

A flicker of satisfaction crossed her face. 'Ha. So. It is true then.'

He grimaced. 'You can't say anything.'

'Would I?'

'Yes,' he said mercilessly. 'If it served a purpose.'

Célestine grinned, not at all offended. She made the sign of the cross over her chest and pushed her chair closer to his. 'I will not, then. I promise.'

Which he believed. 'Poison,' he said simply. 'It might have been suicide but...' He turned his hands upwards. A ghost drifted past the window, sending the bird away, alarm calling.

Célestine watched the ghost, her expression shuttered and thoughtful. Raphaël straightened.

'What?' he said.

She looked up and shook her head slightly. 'Did Joar see anything?'

'He was sick, missed the start of his shift.'

The very faint traces of a flush rose up beneath her fine brown skin and Raphaël did swear this time. 'Really, my friend? Keeping my boatmen from duty now?'

She grinned again fleetingly. 'But I did not. He left my bed on time.'

'Célestine,' he said warningly, but he knew her too well to mistake her honesty.

'I would not cover for him. He's fun in bed but he's no saint, Rafa, and I'm no martyr. If he is lying then that is a problem for you, I think.'

It was.

An returned then, and said without preamble, 'Fifteen percent. The ghost must have drained them. Should be fine tomorrow.'

'Is that normal?' Célestine said in English. 'Wait. Does that mean we're rationing energy? I need my hot shower.'

'Princess,' An said, but with only moderate bite.

Raphaël remembered Célestine aboard the coastline-hugging boat that carried them from Calais to Gdansk, dodging wrecks and burning the most ungodly dirty fuel, both of them filthy from the journey across France as much as the salt and oil of the boat. They were not the same people who'd left home for the promise of the College, and he'd come very close to shattering that day, watching the French coastline slip away with months of withheld grief and his own brutality burning through him. Then Célestine had held up her hands, her bloody cuticles, and said, *Is it wrong to miss manicures most, from all of civilisation?* and for reasons he still didn't know, he had laughed. Instead of breaking, he had laughed and stayed whole.

He grinned at her now. 'Better dash, beauty queen. I'll give you twenty minutes.' He would give her longer, obviously. She raised a single digit in his direction and spun for the door.

'Don't break my toy too badly, will you?' she said over her shoulder.

An raised her slim eyebrows and Raphaël laughed. He was quite tempted to break Joar at the moment. The man was ex-Finnish military, like several others, but had been here for years, and never once seemed dedicated to any cause besides brewing aquavit and besting Miika at target practice.

'Has he got family left in Helsinki?' he said just as Célestine was vanishing. Auli had perhaps mostly said it to rile him, but it was suddenly rather pertinent.

Célestine turned her chair slightly in the doorway. 'Maybe, Rafa. Does it matter?'

He didn't answer and carried on frowning at the empty doorway after she'd shrugged and left.

'Pressure's falling,' An said.

Raphaël blinked, eyed the barometer. The mercury in the old glass caught the last traces of sunset. 'Good practice for harpoon targeting,' he said prosaically.

'Ha.'

He pushed away from his desk. In between him and sleep lay one more thing.

'I'm off. How's it going?' He jerked his chin at the buoy splayed open in front of her.

An pointed her soldering iron at him without looking. 'Don't touch. Go away.'

'Fighting back, is it?'

'It was clear, but this morning haunted again, burning through things as I fix them. Fucking driving me crazy.'

He patted her on the shoulder lightly, to give her something different to be annoyed by. 'Don't work too late. There's no rush on it.' Once An started on a piece of gear, though, she rarely stopped till she'd defeated it.

'What do you make of the storm ghost?'

She hadn't turned, but she also didn't ask questions unless she was interested in the answer, so Raphaël shifted sideways, watching her steady hands in the innards of the buoy's electronics.

'I have no idea,' he said honestly.

She lifted a hand. 'The red one point five millimetre.'

He passed her a coil of coated wire. 'It was most likely a fluke.'

'Hmm.'

He wasn't convinced either, but he had other battles to fight. 'If it happens again, I'll worry. For now, I need the harpoons more than I need that buoy fixed.'

She did something he couldn't see. A diode on the circuit board flashed and emitted a small plume of smoke.

'Fuck. Fuck it. Fuck,' An said very calmly. She laid her tools down and leaned back to look up at Raphaël. 'That is your fault. Bloody harpoons. What is this place becoming?'

She had a vast family back east that she'd met once as a toddler before the Crash. She'd forgotten them all, which haunted her, he suspected. To have belonged once and not remember how it felt. At least he remembered.

'It's becoming more tempting the more useful the Oracle gets,' he said simply. 'Can you lure it out?'

By the time salvaged tech reached them, whatever ghosts had fried it were usually long gone, and the Oracle pulled out the rest. An stilled, muttered something under her breath.

'Bait a trap,' he added, thinking aloud. 'Another bit of circuit board or—'

'Yes, good idea,' An interrupted. 'But I need to think and you're talking.'

Raphaël snorted a laugh and stepped back. 'I'm gone,' he said, and went.

Hellä was in the Hall, writing up the guard rota for the next week with a mug and half-empty jug of coffee next to her. Alexis was stacking bowls into perfect towers on a tray. Hellä spotted him first and leaned back with a weary smile.

'Coffee, boss?'

'Please.'

When she handed a mug over, he said, 'We need to talk to Joar again. He was lying about his absence from post the morning Boudain died.'

'Shit,' Hellä said. 'Was he in someone's bed?'

'Yes, but he left it on time.'

Hellä absorbed this information, gathered her papers together, drained her coffee, refilled it and stood. 'I'll get him. Your office?'

And risk disturbing An's experiments? 'The Oracle Room.' Which would be empty now they'd done the seeding and dosed her for the night. He remembered Auli's fury and wanted very much to know what she'd done with her morals, and whether she was okay. Seeing her would mean admitting to being wrong about Joar though, so perhaps not.

The tower was dark and quiet, and he lowered himself into the chair nearest the desk after lighting all the lamps and moving them to erase the shadows.

The Bellwether creaked, ghosts crackled faintly in the room above but at least for now, he was alone. Which unfortunately gave him time to realise how fucking tired he was. Unlike Auli, he'd never loved this place; had, in fact, vowed never to care beyond the job's limits. But when he was tired it became harder to ignore the way lives weighed heavier on you when you knew their stories, their faces, their fears.

The door opened and he could have kissed Hellä for such impeccable timing. Joar followed her in, his face flushed either from alcohol or nerves.

'Sir,' he said, coming to attention.

Hellä leaned back against the wall and crossed her legs at the ankle.

'You're either an idiot or a murderer, Gunnarsson,' Raphaël said quietly. 'Which one is it?'

Chapter Thirteen

Auli

Tomorrow did not, in fact, let Auli figure things out.

She did laundry in the dawn cool, faded shirts and soft rags wrung and hung at the prow of the barge. Walked back past the ravens bickering contentedly over her offerings. There was a ghost aeroplane roaring raggedly a few metres away, and a voice declaiming in Romanian. Leigh appeared as she reached the gangway.

'Going for breakfast?' she said. She hadn't spent nearly enough time ensuring he was alright.

'Yes, I never knew coffee could taste so good.' He laughed, as did she. It was a luxury their perilous posting earned them, or perhaps the university simply knew this many Scandinavians together on a deadly raft needed coffee to stave off mutiny.

'How has listening been, so far?' she asked.

'Fascinating,' Leigh said. He glanced at the radio ghost. 'Weird, hard. It's kind of—'

But then the universe caught up with her.

'Auli?'

It was Suvi, just behind them and fidgeting. 'You're seeding this morning?'

'Yes.' Dreading it; had woken dreaming of it. Lightning and fishhooks and fire.

'We really need data from the north. Can you try these?' Shoving a page at Auli, knotting her hands back together. 'They're weather buoys from before. One or two might still be out there.'

'That's a lot,' Auli said, looking at the list. Leigh shifted, the gangway creaked, and he grasped the rail.

Suvi nodded jerkily, 'We're predicting a big weather system but the confidence intervals…'

'Right.' Auli looked skyward to hide her dread and instead found Raphaël leaning against North Tower's railing. All her weariness and fear and frustration unfurled in her gut like worms.

'I know you normally only ask three things but—'

'It's fine,' Auli said shortly, making Suvi flush abruptly four shades darker. 'I'll try, but I can't promise anything.' Because she'd failed yesterday and most of her wanted to fail again. Or did she? When this was what was at stake?

'I wish Célestine could do it,' Suvi whispered, perhaps to herself, and she was still wringing her hands as she walked back down the gangway. Pertti and Bea emerged at the hatchway just as Suvi stepped onto the rooftop and Pertti's gaze swung from her face to Auli, sharp with curiosity.

'Coffee,' Auli said. Leigh fell wordlessly into step with her.

''Ware ghost!' Raphaël shouted, and Auli jerked back instinctively, spotting the cloud of static half a pace ahead. She clutched the vial at her throat with one hand, ducked around the ghost with her cheeks burning, and if Raphaël had been able to hear Suvi's words then Auli would have to kill him.

What a terrible choice of words.

And on that subject… 'Leigh,' Auli began. But then Tobias caught up with them, and Auli's question had to go unanswered.

Armed with coffee, she headed for the library, passing her too tidy desk – she'd barely done any work in days, other than reading files too unpleasant to be left anywhere but… well, stuffed under her mattress. Bea was already bent over an incomplete map, but they looked up when Auli passed and something in their face made her pause.

'You alright?' she said quietly. A ghost broke into song beneath the dome and Bea massaged the stump of their wrist, leaving a trace of graphite.

'Don't mind Suvi, you know how she gets.' Auli did. Bea tapped their map. 'Do you have any story cantations about the Netherlands, especially wartime ones? They might help fill in the blanks.'

Auli studied the drawn symbols for sea mines and wrecks, remembering Uoti saying, *We cast our net wide and pray*. Bea had always been the least dismissive of Auli's work, but Auli felt no vindication now, faced with everything else. She'd said to Raphaël once, fiercely, *We might not be saving lives but we're looking for hope. Isn't that just as important?* She had only half-believed it even then. Her brother hanging in her mind, waiting for her to save him.

'I might have one. I'll dig it out,' Auli said, then looked at the inevitable book in Bea's pocket and said hesitantly, 'Would… would you be interested in helping me with something?'

Bea's eyes lit like kindling. 'Oh! Did they bring books back after all?'

The boatmen scavenged for books on their trading trips, but didn't try particularly hard for fiction with its far higher infection risk than textbooks.

'No.'

Bea pouted but it morphed into intrigue as Auli carried on.

'I can do that,' they said when Auli had finished. 'Is this for Leigh's mysterious project?'

So he hadn't told them, then? Auli shook her head and

extracted herself before she second-guessed drawing Bea into this.

Two more steps towards the library ladder, and then An called her name. Auli looked longingly at the muted sky through the dome, a raven circling like a soot mote cut loose, and then she turned back towards the Oceans area, wrapping her arms around herself. An was just as terrifying as Gabrielle in an entirely different way. The longest Auli had spent with her was getting her tattoo seven months after arriving.

'Hi,' she said. At least, she thought, An had been on the boat with Raphaël when Boudain died; that was something.

An's desk was militarily precise. A miniature cityscape of boxes of tools and salvaged gear with An its compact god. She was holding a Stanley knife and had fresh burns on the back of her hand.

'Uoti's awake but Niki's only letting you or Gabrielle in to see him. I need you to ask him something. It's important.'

'Oh. What is it?'

The deck was filling up now, as much as it ever did, researchers talking desultorily as they dodged ghosts and desks. An glanced around, said, 'Rafa's office,' and strode off without waiting for a response.

The Bellwether tugged on its anchors, making Auli skip a little to stay upright. An didn't waver.

BENEATH THE ROOM'S constant scent of valerian and hot metal was the sharp alkaloid smell of wood smoke. And there were burn marks across the righthand work bench.

'Fire,' Auli whispered. Thinking of the evacuation yesterday, how she didn't know who had locked the Oracle and Ursula in their tower.

'That's what I want to talk to Uoti about.'

'The fire?' Auli drifted closer. There were scorch marks on

the edges of the shelves, too. It was slightly miraculous An only had a few burns on her hands.

'I'm trying something new. But I need to do it on land so I need clearance.'

'On *land*?'

An raised an eyebrow. 'When did you last get off this box?' she said. 'We're not surgically attached, you know.'

'I know.' Auli flushed. 'What do you need?'

An tipped her head towards two crates at the end of the workbench. 'I'm ready to go. Just need the nod from Uoti. Rafa okayed the boat.'

'He'll leave a boatman with you? Or are you taking Bea or Tobias?'

An's black gaze shifted for the first time. An's last assistant had fled on a trading trip six months ago and she was in no hurry to accept a replacement despite her workload. 'They've both got deadlines, and Tobias got banged about in that clusterfuck yesterday, too.'

Oh. 'What happened?' Auli said.

An frowned at her. 'What do you mean *what happened*? A giant ghost took over the Bellwether, did you notice? Did Rafa tell you about the kraken? Of course he did. Have either of you taken it seriously? Of course not.' An laid her hand flat over the burn on the bench, the reddened skin vivid and vicious. 'Something has changed with the Oracle, hasn't it? But we're being kept in the dark. Gabrielle, I can understand, secrecy suits her very well. Uoti would tell me but he's currently half dead, so it's down to you. What's going on with the ghosts?'

Auli wanted away from this room that made her irritable and safe and vulnerable all at once. 'Has Niki looked at your hand?'

An looked as if she'd forgotten the burns were there. Auli hoped her brother had chosen the sea. She thought she hoped that; she thought it must be better.

'Avoiding the question?' An said and Auli flushed because of course she was.

'Nothing's—' She got no further. An spun towards the crates, then slammed a circuit board down on the bench.

'What happens when there's a ghost in some wiring?' An snapped at her, and the student in Auli came to terrified attention.

'It's a fire risk, so...' and then she stalled. Most people would pre-emptively burn it if they couldn't just get out of harm's reach. But An wasn't asking how to avoid infection or fires. 'Ghosts tend to leave the wiring here, because of the Oracle. Then it's safe for you to restore. Is that...?'

'Yes.' An grabbed a glove from a shelf, pulled it on then picked up a length of bare wire and held it over two points on the circuit board. 'I tried to shift this one yesterday. And got this.'

'Wait.' Auli backed up. 'It caught fire? Don't—'

An lowered the wire into place. The entire circuit board crackled, blue electricity sparking along the wires as if too much voltage was suddenly being forced through. Auli's breath hissed and her whole body braced for the flames but instead she heard a man's voice, speaking English.

'Ye and each of you are adjudged and sentenced. And there within the flood marks to be hanged by the neck until you are dead, dead, dead.'

Electricity arced up and the room smelled of burned salt. The voice repeated, and smoke rose from the board, but An didn't move, her face intent, almost angry.

'Stop it,' Auli whispered, to the ghost and the woman both.

'Ye and each of you are adjudged and sentenced. And there within the flood marks to be hanged by the neck until you are dead, dead, dead.'

A raven croaked outside, and the electricity became blue flames dancing along the wires, over the glove. The voice spoke over Auli's shriek as she reached for the sand bucket.

'I know him by his saucer eyes, his three rows of teeth and tail, and the blue smoke that came. I know him by his saucer eyes—' Auli grabbed the bucket, the whole Bellwether trembling, or was that just her? An still had not moved, the flames crawling over her glove like blue locusts. '—his three rows of teeth and tail, and the—' Auli swept the board off the bench into the bucket and slammed the lid down. An huffed out a breath, and Auli rested her hands on top of the fire bucket's lid as if the ghost might try to claw its way out.

'See that?' An said into the silence. 'Will you tell me what's going on now?'

Chapter Fourteen

Auli

AULI CLOSED HER eyes, tugged off balance by the tide below. Then she straightened, too bewildered to be intimidated for once. 'What the fuck, An? Why didn't you stop it sooner? The fire!'

'Burned, are you?'

An held out the leather glove. It was as battered as it had been five minutes ago, but not burned. Sweeping the circuit board into the fire bucket had stung but Auli wasn't burned. And her skin looked fine, no fragmentation, no pixelation. A shout climbed her throat – about how dangerous, how irresponsible... but An's expression silenced her.

She inhaled slowly, tried to catch up. 'A ghost of fire?'

An was waiting for something, but all Auli could think was that those first words were what the Oracle had said just before everything fell apart...

Oh.

Oh, she thought. On the research deck, Célestine laughed and Auli almost wished she were here, it would bolster her somehow, to have Célestine's animosity to fight against.

'How many?' she whispered. An's eyes flashed almost

victorious. 'Two voices, and the fire.' She pulled her hair roughly from its ponytail, gathered it up again, smoothed the weight of it back like that might settle her mind. 'St. Elmo's fire, I think. And the first was a judgement about pirates.' Bea had recognised it from one of their hoarded books. 'Three ghosts in one bit of wiring. Is that...' She trailed off.

'Normal? No. I might dismiss one abnormality. But rumour is the storm ghost attacked Uoti. That kraken ghost *hit* our boat.' An glared at Auli as if she were somehow responsible. 'Was it a ghost that killed Boudain?'

Which was a far more reasonable question now than when Auli had first asked it. 'No,' she whispered, still stuck on the merged ghosts.

'Was it the Oracle?'

'No.'

An cocked her head like a raptor. Auli tried to hold herself steady.

'For fuck's sake, Auli, tell me,' An snapped.

I believe you have the character for this, Boudain whispered. *Come – we can build something hopeful.* Were either of those things still true? Raphaël didn't believe the second, and no one left alive believed the first.

'He accidentally overdosed on medicine,' she said. An had not killed Boudain, but Gabrielle's warnings still wouldn't quite let Auli go. 'The Oracle has been erratic lately, which might explain these changes in the ghosts. My guess is it's hormonal.' For six months, four years ago, the Oracle had fluctuated wildly between ceaseless cantations and nothing at all, ghosts had filled the Bellwether so densely that every day had brought new burn victims to Niki's door, every week an infection. The Oracle had started her periods in the midst of it.

An frowned at Auli, then at the fire bucket. Auli wondered whether anyone had looked for monthly cycles to the cantations; the thought of doing so made her skin crawl with convoluted shame.

'They're not related – Boudain and… whatever's happening with the ghosts.' Liar, her mind whispered. They were, she just didn't know how yet. 'I'll get your permissions from Uoti now,' she added quickly. 'Could you let me know whether you manage to extract the ghosts?'

'The unprecedented merged ghosts, after the unprecedentedly large ghost that unprecedentedly attacked someone yesterday?'

Auli stiffened. Perhaps it was the room, perhaps the lingering shock of the ghost, but she heard herself speak with a snap usually only reserved for Raphaël, or long ago, her brother. 'Yes, An. Those. What do you want me to say? You're right, the ghosts have been acting differently, I'm looking into it, but why should I have any more answers than you?'

The edge of a smile flickered on An's face. 'Because how the Oracle works is your whole research area. If you're right and this is a maturation stage, then you're the only one who can get us through this without mass infection. We can't afford to lose a person a week, it would trigger disaster.'

'It would *be* a disaster,' Auli corrected crossly.

'No,' An said, her face drawn and taut. 'This is bigger than individuals. The deaths of a few researchers would be nothing compared to the consequences of outsiders knowing we're fallible, right now.'

That made two people, Auli thought distantly, foreseeing the outside world reaching across the water and tearing them apart. The Bellwether groaned and tugged against an anchor as if it, too, were suddenly feeling its own fragile isolation cracking, as if it, too, wanted to flee.

'I'm looking into it,' Auli repeated eventually. 'If you can separate those… surely you have something that can interfere with ghosts enough to… to scatter the data.'

An studied Auli, then the scorched bench, then her own blistered hand. Auli knew what she was thinking – they weren't meant to deter ghosts, let alone destroy them. But Auli was past caring. She hoped An was, too, otherwise Gabrielle would have all the grounds she needed to exile her.

An nodded once. 'Guess I need to sort that out,' she said, jerking her chin at the fire bucket. Auli sagged with relief.

WHEN SHE TAPPED softly on Uoti's bedroom door a few minutes later, Niki was already there. Or still there.

'Are you okay?' she said, peering at them. There were shadows beneath their eyes deep enough to lose a ship in.

'Tell them to go rest,' Uoti said from the bed. His patchwork curtains were half-drawn across the wide windows, casting his ruddy face bluish, like flesh hauled from the water.

Auli did so. 'I can stay here,' she offered. Although it would do nothing towards solving Boudain's murder or answering An's questions. But Niki was sighing heavily, pressing the heels of both hands into their eyes.

'Go,' she repeated.

They smiled suddenly. 'Thank you, Auli. He's not allowed out of bed and is to have ten mils of that syrup in two hours. Keep an eye on his vitals.'

'Yes,' Auli said, just as Uoti said, 'She doesn't need to stay, I'll behave.'

A ghost screamed, and all three of them flinched. A child's voice that none of them looked for. Niki touched the vial at their throat then left, the child screamed again, a little closer.

'It's not real,' Uoti said with a sad smile, meaning it was an acted scream. 'A parent can tell.'

His children were late teens now. The family he saw for a few days every few months.

'What happened yesterday?' she asked.

Uoti shifted uncomfortably and Auli leaped forward to help, piling pillows behind him, pulling the blanket up to cover his torso. She didn't realise until she caught him watching her how easily the actions had come, and how unwelcome they might be.

'Sorry,' she said. For helping him, for him needing it, for asking him to relive yesterday.

He shook his head. 'I'm not sure I understand what happened, Auli. It might be best marked up to stochasticity and bad luck. Least said soonest mended, as they say?'

'Gabrielle's been in then?'

Uoti laughed, then winced, pressing a hand against his chest. Auli reached for a flask, sniffed the contents then poured some of the tea into an empty mug. She held it out, waited until it was secure in Uoti's grip then let go.

For a while, the room was full of nothing other than the sound of Uoti sipping, the eternal sea and the Bellwether. If she strained her ears she could hear a music ghost, the chattering martins, voices that were probably real, the faint thrum of the batteries in the underdeck, but they all felt very far away.

'I need to know,' she said eventually, quietly. 'There is something wrong. I need to find out what.' She took the empty mug from his hands. 'Please.'

He eyed her thoughtfully. 'You think you can? Figure it out?'

'I don't know. But I have to try. Boudain...' She trailed off, said instead, 'Gabrielle has other things on her mind. It's only fair I pull my weight.'

A muscle feathered at the corner of Uoti's mouth, but he said easily enough, 'A fine time to come to the position, isn't it? I was promoted in that cholera outbreak on the mainland, remember? No trade for two months, down to fish and berries and borderline mutiny.' He smiled. 'Would have been mutiny if not for Raphaël – that boy has been a godsend.'

'He's hardly a boy,' Auli protested faintly.

'You would know, wouldn't you?' Uoti waggled an eyebrow at her, so unexpected that Auli choked. He laughed then added more seriously, 'Some days I feel like I've been here for centuries, floating on our little kingdom of ghosts.'

'Queendom,' Auli said, and then realising how that sounded, 'The Oracle. She's like a queen bee. Not a ruler but a source that all us workers tend to and protect.' And drug and imprison, torment and test.

Perhaps those unspoken additions showed on her face, because Uoti tipped his head. 'You aren't happy about how we protect our queen then? No wonder.'

When Auli didn't answer immediately he sighed, shifted and sighed again. 'We are doing—'

'I know,' Auli interrupted, not wanting to hear him parrot Gabrielle and Raphaël, because she liked this man, and also because that missing piece had fallen into place at his words. *No wonder*, Suvi had murmured when Auli told her the Oracle was sleeping, when Boudain was dead. What had she meant? 'But you're avoiding my question, Uoti.'

Uoti looked through the curtains to the islands beyond. The smaller College boat was in the bay, figures moving about on the deck from this distance indistinguishable, but Auli still knew that none of them was Raphaël.

'She was cantating buoys, as seeded, but then cut off and started on a story.' Uoti had one hand over his sternum, and Auli ought to tell him to rest. But *this is bigger than individuals*, An had said, and she was right.

Uoti nodded slowly, as if he had heard her thoughts and agreed. Or at least, acquiesced, which was not the same thing.

'The story was of a storm and a sea monster attacking a ship. *The ship half-sinking was full of the screams of the wounded and afraid*, she said.' Uoti stopped, started again. 'And it was. The Bellwether was. Then a ghost wave hit me square in the chest. And I woke up in the surgery.'

'Was it a ghost wave or real one?' Auli asked carefully.

Uoti frowned. 'Well, it must have been a...' But he paused, and she wondered that it hadn't occurred to him before. The dangers of ghosts so familiar and unchanged for fifteen years that he hadn't questioned what had really happened. 'You're right. There was real water. But ghosts don't affect the water like that. And yet a wave alone wouldn't have stopped my heart. And it seemed...' He gave Auli a strange glance.

'It seemed to be targeted at you?' she guessed. 'Where were you all standing? Could it have been aiming for the boatman? It was Joar, wasn't it?'

Uoti looked weary and pale and frustrated. 'What's your theory, Auli?'

'I don't have one,' she said quickly.

'Oh yes, you do.' He shook his head and for a moment could have been Boudain, challenging her gently. Auli's chest ached. 'You do. Something to do with the boatmen. You think the Oracle doesn't like the boatmen guarding her, that she somehow set a ghost on him and missed?'

The idea hung in her mind like a spark. 'I don't know,' she insisted. 'But it's a correlation, isn't it? Within twenty-four hours we have two incidences of ghosts attacking someone near a boatman.'

Uoti's eyebrows rose. 'Two? You mean your new lad? But he...'

Heat rose in a wave up Auli's throat. She'd promised Leigh, but it was proving hard to obey.

'...he was *attacked?*'

'Who was?' someone said behind Auli, and she yelped faintly, spinning around, almost falling as the Bellwether shifted unhelpfully beneath her.

'*Raphaël!*' she gasped.

Uoti huffed. 'Soft-footed bugger, aren't you, Captain?'

'Only when he chooses to be,' Auli said bitterly.

Raphaël stepped into the room. 'True,' he said. 'I find myself interested in eavesdropping on people at the— Ah, Gabrielle.'

Gabrielle had appeared in the doorway behind him.

'Oh God,' Auli whispered. Uoti laughed, then turned it into a valiant cough.

The girl

SHE REMEMBERS ARMS around her warm as moss, forest and river-scented. Potato, salt, sweat-scented. She remembers the fit of her head beneath a chin, cheek on skin, heartbeats and heat and thick wool, safety.

Oh, what is this remembering? Hanging in the deepwater, tugged by magnetic fields and the long currents of dark places, but remembering. Sunlight through tall pines, a house on a river, a man carrying silver fish on a pole. A hand on her shoulder, flour-stained, soap scented.

There now. Fish tonight. Run and wash your hands so you can help me, lyubimy.

She remembers the man's tears falling onto her face as he holds her.

We have to leave, he said. *They are coming for her.*

And the first voice, the hand on her shoulder again, trembling.

Hush now, lyubimy. Hush now, it will be well. Hush.

Forest and river and walking single file through the dark, someone carrying her drowsy. The sea filling her up, spilling over, she remembers the river singing her home. She remembers someone weeping in the dawn. Then men and running and men, she remembers the man standing by the riverbank.

You're safe, lyubimy, the woman murmured, hand over her mouth to stop up the sea. *You're safe here. Stay quiet as a mouse until the bad men leave.*

But the man, the one with the fish and the tears stood before them on a riverbank and a sound cracked the world in two, and he fell. He fell and fell and the woman wept without moving.

You're safe, lyubimy. Hush now. Hush until the bad men leave.

The bad men. They never leave, do they?

She jolts, ancient sharks circle her blind, comb-jellies flashing secrets through the dark.

No, she thinks. I want to stay with her. I want to run to the man by the river…

Papochka? Papochka?

Salt hot on her face, no arms to carry her here, only upwellings full of all the dead whales and the past.

Shall we make them leave? You and I? Shall we make them bleed?

Red stones on the river's edge and red in the water like ribbons for her hair. She remembers ribbons in her hair, tied with gentle hands.

There, lyubimy. All ready for the bazar, bright as a rose. Just hush, remember. Keep the words to yourself, remember.

There is a wound in her chest and she watches red ribbons unspooling from between her broken bones. There are fish circling bleached white corals, measuring out their graves. There are whales singing their own mourning into the vastness of the ocean, listening for an answer that never comes. In the dark water she presses her hands over her cut-open heart, but no one is here to stop her bleeding, and no one is here to hold her.

Lyubimy.
Mama?
Shall we make them bleed?
She doesn't want the bleeding though, she only wants to remember what it was like before she drowned.

Boats carve circles through the bloody water of a bloody bay, and all the men are laughing.

Papochka is falling by the river's edge and Mama is weeping.
Shall we make them leave?
The sea holds up her bones like a child in a midnight forest in her father's arms.

'Yes,' she whispers. 'Can we make the bad men leave?' Air bubbles spell out her words. They rise through the dark, jelly-lit, her words and no one else's. There is salt in her cut-open heart.

We two, the sea says gently. *We together can make them bleed.*

And she doesn't know the difference between bleeding and leaving, not really. She has never known one without the other, so perhaps it is the only way. She nods, watching her silver words ascend, her hair around her ribbons of blood and eels, sunbeams through forgotten trees.

'Yes,' she whispers again.

AND THEN SHE wakes.

And knows she is awake, lying on the non-sea, the dry cotton of her bed, her eyes closed and the air in her lungs all salt and sadness. She does not remember the last time she woke and was alone in her own mind.

Carefully, hush, quiet as mice, she moves her fingers. Flesh and bone.

She can hear the sea outwith her. She can hear other voices clamouring to crawl into her mind and fill up her veins, but she lies in the non-sea and is, for just a little while, all herself.

Chapter Fifteen

Raphaël

Uoti looked like he ought to be either asleep or dead. Raphaël didn't particularly want to have this conversation in front of him, given that, but Auli was here so it was either this or consult Gabrielle alone.

'Who was—' he began, then met Auli's gaze and shifted direction fast, '—on dawn listening duty this morning?'

Auli's shoulders relaxed. Alvarez, he thought. The incident with Alvarez. He had known she was lying about something, dammit.

'One of the Oceans assistants, I think,' Auli said. 'Why?'

He had no idea. He'd only said it to let her keep whatever secrets she was hoarding from Gabrielle. 'We got flagged by one of the Kökar fishermen earlier. Passed on news I need to act on.'

Uoti's haggard face fell and guilt tugged at Raphaël. 'Shall we move to the PI lounge? Give Uoti a break?'

'No,' Uoti said. 'I want to know. I'm fine.'

Auli poured a cup of something that smelled unpleasantly medicinal and handed it to Uoti. She'd cared for one of her mothers before the Bellwether, and the memory of the conversation, the intimacy, hit him like a slap. 'Who made that?' he asked, more harshly than intended.

Uoti and Auli both froze, then Uoti eyed him thoughtfully and said, 'Niki.'

Raphaël pulled a chair around and sat down hard, stretching his legs out. Gabrielle was standing by the door, arms folded, feet spread against the tug of the Bellwether. Auli studied Uoti, then nodded to herself and moved to perch on the windowsill, the light catching the blues in her hair. Raphaël frowned at his boots.

'So, Captain?' Uoti said.

Raphaël looked up. 'Turku has closed its port and the coast road because the Pori Alliance are pushing south. Mariehamm are under pressure to send support.'

'The Pori gangs are forever stirring up trouble. Does it matter?' Gabrielle asked.

'If it cuts off our food supply, yes.'

Uoti drank slowly, Auli's hands in her lap were restless. Raphaël wanted to still them with his own. 'The Pori Alliance are also gaining support from the more militant Survivors,' he added.

Gabrielle huffed, smoothed down her trousers, recrossed her arms. 'Survivors. As if more than a handful of them were even *witness* to the Helsinki incident, let alone injured.'

'It's families of the killed, too,' Uoti said quietly.

'It's just a useful banner for the discontented to gather under,' Gabrielle snapped. 'What's your point, Captain?'

'I need to ground-truth those rumours,' he said bluntly.

'What?' Auli blurted, at the same time as Gabrielle said, 'No.'

Raphaël spared Gabrielle an acerbic glance but addressed Auli. 'You know what the news is like – out of date and unreliable. I need solid information, so I can arrange alternative suppliers. And monitor the Survivors.' In case they *were* behind Boudain's death.

Auli's hands stilled. 'You'd go yourself?'

Raphaël wished she wasn't looking at him. 'Yes. Hellä will be in charge here.'

'It's too dangerous,' Gabrielle said flatly.

Raphaël didn't answer, only gestured at the room, Uoti in his bed, the ghost murmuring in the corridor. Auli frowned and he wanted to shake her. That she would still see this place as hallowed, as home, despite everything.

Once, long ago, he'd asked her to leave with him. A moment of weakness, when the fear of what this place might do to her had outweighed the fear of letting someone else within his walls, there alongside Célestine as someone he would not survive losing. But she'd said no, and he'd lain beside her in the dark, breathing the forest scent of her hair and desperately shoring up his walls with all the bones of his family left behind in France.

'If there's heightened risk to the Bellwether,' Gabrielle said, 'your job is to be here. Not playing spies.'

Raphaël reined his mind in viciously.

'That's not our call,' Uoti said quietly.

'Why does it matter so much?' Auli asked. 'Getting reliable news.'

Gabrielle opened her mouth, so he spoke before she could get started. 'Mostly because we need supplies. Partly because if the Åland islands send boats, that's fewer boats here. So if trouble comes, we'll have less warning.'

Uoti was right, he didn't need their agreement, and he shouldn't care whether he had it.

'When?' she said.

Raphaël hid his relief. 'Tomorrow. For up to ten days, and I'll try to recruit a few more boatmen. We need them.'

'Oh for radios,' Uoti said quietly, which surprised Raphaël. No one wasted time mourning the past these days. It was phenomenally unhelpful, and besides, there were surely things Uoti missed more. His family, decent hormones. A job that didn't try to kill him regularly.

'Give An time,' Auli said with a smile that made Raphaël stand up too fast. 'Which reminds me, Uoti, are you happy to sign off on a shore-trip for An?'

Oh, that. She'd blasted Raphaël with a pithy description of her failed experiment, and everyone's general idiocy. He'd agreed meekly and left her to it.

'I'll take her after lunch,' he said from the door. Gabrielle looked set to continue arguing but Auli only nodded vaguely, not looking at him, and he left, side-eyeing his own bad temper wryly.

KITCHENS FIRST.

Dunya was at the central worktable, flattening dough balls on a tray with heavy slaps. She glanced up at his entrance but didn't pause. Alexis was chopping tomatoes into slices with a knife that shook in his grip when he, too, looked up. Raphaël studied him.

'Dunya, I need trip provisions for three for five days, and a supplies list,' he said in Finnish.

The cook slapped down another doughball. 'We have trouble coming, yes? Saw it in the smoke.'

She saw trouble coming fairly regularly, but he didn't disparage it – a nose for danger had got her and Alexis both out of Russia unscathed. Or at least whole.

Another dough ball. She pulled a fresh tray closer. 'Two hours.'

'You are a saint.'

This earned him a throaty scoff. 'Get away, foolish man. You're scaring my boy.'

He was. Raphaël unholstered the pistol at his hip and the knife on his thigh and laid them on the worktable next to

Dunya. She ignored them but watched him sidelong as he stepped closer to Alexis.

'What's happened, Alexis?'

The boy's grip on the knife was all tendons and terror. Raphaël kept his voice soft. 'Tell me. I can fix it.'

Alexis moved his head a quarter-turn. Not looking at Raphaël but not looking away any longer. 'The ghosts are angry,' he said. 'They hate us. They said so.'

'Who said so?' Raphaël said, baffled.

'I don't want to drown like they did.'

Well, this was odd. The boy was nervy, but not incoherent if you could get him to talk to you. Raphaël had overheard him telling Auli a folk story once, about firebirds and sorcerers and girls. Turned out everyone wanted to tell Auli their hidden stories.

'Like who did?'

Dunya made a warning noise. He glanced at her questioningly, and she sighed, resting her floury wrists on the edge of the counter.

'He was on the walkway this morning, saw a ghost of drowning men. Spooked him. He'll be fine, just that and the storm yesterday, your boatmen shouting...'

Of course. The storm and the chaos of evacuation must have terrified him. He'd stayed here. Hellä had opted not to drag him out to the barges unless there were a fire.

'Did the ghost hurt him?' Raphaël said.

Dunya shook her head. Alexis eyed him through his too-long hair. 'They were drowning the men,' he whispered.

'But you're—'

Dunya made another warning sound and glared at Raphaël. He conceded defeat, gathered his weapons, and went hunting.

He found Alexis' ghost below North Tower.

It was a film. Three black men in a navy sea, drowning through columnar sunlight, the men's arms above their heads as they sank, their faces contorted with anger, despair, hate. Raphaël leaned on the railing. He'd seen people drown, he'd seen them drowned, but this still hit differently. The ghost flickered, started the sequence again. And one of the men turned his head, fixed his gaze on Raphaël, then the second, then the third. Raphaël's whole body loosened. The ghost flickered, started again, but this time the men drowned without turning. Raphaël straightened, walked inside through the nearest door.

The mercury was still falling, and he wanted to get away from this godawful place before the storm arrived.

Chapter Sixteen

Auli

Auli sat at her desk amidst the noise and motion of the research deck, circling one single question on the paper in front of her. Bea had co-opted an empty desk and was humming as they flicked through old ghost records, Leigh frowning at datasheets. Auli needed privacy but still couldn't bring herself to move into Boudain's office, not because it felt unearned, or even temporary. But because she did not really want to be alone.

She lifted the top sheet to reveal a scatter graph of Niki's Oracle sedation history against daily cantation numbers.

'What are you doing here, Bea?' Célestine said from behind her.

Auli dropped the papers flat and laid a hand over the circled question.

'Looking up some stuff about shipwrecks,' Bea said without hesitation. Auli was impressed.

Célestine examined the dried blood on her knuckles from yesterday. 'Not stealing Ocean's staff, I hope, PI Fraser.'

The weight of Bea and Leigh's meticulous inattention burned, and Auli said abruptly, 'Would you really want it,

Célestine? Your mentor dead and trouble brewing, would you want to be PI like that?'

Célestine looked up, her face almost, almost softening. Then she smiled like Auli was a child. 'As if we come into being PI any other way. What did you ever think was waiting for you besides this?'

Not murder, Auli thought. And not just trouble, but altered ghosts and an altered Oracle, and conflict rippling across the water. But she couldn't say any of that aloud. 'What's the forecast? I heard we are in for a storm.'

Rocking her chair back and forth with one hand, Célestine snorted softly. 'There's something coming but God knows what or where from. This is why we need buoys away from the shipping lanes, too. What good is the warning that arrives after the storm?'

Auli had tried seeding some of Suvi's pre-Crash buoys and failed.

Is there a balance? the question on her paper read. There had to be.

'Do you know where you need them, in the north?'

Célestine's wheels stilled, the Bellwether heaved, and her hands tightened to hold herself still.

'I could help convince Gabrielle if I knew what you needed.' And more northerly buoys would be a thin link to her mothers, too. Near the wall a ghost called radio signs and Bea glanced up from their papers, measuring the distance.

'I think you have enough on your hands, yes?' Célestine said. 'Detective Fraser.' She sketched a sardonic salute then spun around gracefully and rolled to where Suvi was kneeling over a long sheaf of stuck-together paper, scribbling furiously. She paused when Célestine reached her, and sank back onto her heels, gesturing at the maths unfurling on the paper, something a computer would once have done in minutes. And now they only had people like Suvi, graphite on her fingertips and rough, recycled paper on a wooden floor.

Auli's throat tightened on a scream, or perhaps Raphaël's name. Did he keep no secrets from Célestine? Neither Auli's heart, nor Boudain's murder. And yet if Célestine spread rumours then Gabrielle would blame Auli, and exile her. And Célestine would be poised, no doubt, to move into Boudain's office without a thought to the man who'd left it empty.

Auli held her breath until her ribs creaked like the Bellwether, and the knot in her throat had eased. Then she followed Célestine to the Centre.

Detective Fraser. As if she were doing enough to find justice for her gentle mentor. Both women looked up at her, startled.

'Suvi,' Auli started, reckless with frustration. 'The day Boudain died, when you went back on listening duty, you said "no wonder" about the Oracle sleeping. Why?'

Suvi ran a fingertip along a line of impenetrable equations. 'I don't remember.'

'Try,' Auli said. 'Please.'

'Why?'

Célestine tapped a finger on a wheelrim. 'Yes, Auli, why?'

But Auli was ahead of them for once, or hoped she was. 'I'm tracking the Oracle's cantation rates, so changes in behaviour might be important.'

Célestine raised one elegant brow but did not speak again as Suvi frowned and said, 'She was awake when I came on first shift and found... found Boudain. The carer said she'd slept badly.'

'The Oracle was down in the Oracle Room?' Would that matter? The Oracle hadn't killed him.

Suvi's attention was already back on her workings. 'No, I went upstairs. I heard her cantating and thought... that I needed to check on her, I suppose.'

Yes, they would all likely have done the same. The line

between dead bodies on the Bellwether and the Oracle was pretty direct, and without the Oracle they were, as Gabrielle had said, lost. She thanked Suvi, avoided Célestine's gaze and returned to her desk.

The Oracle had slept badly, so the sedatives in Boudain's coffee had likely been her evening dose, stolen or switched. She'd suspected as much, because of the ghosts. But did it make any difference to Boudain's murder? And what did it mean for the ghost abnormalities?

She stared at the graph between her hands, tracking the sedatives administered to a child.

No, the Oracle had said to her. So she had no choice but to find a balance, between the Oracle and the hungry sea. Between one guilt and another.

'Lunch,' Bea said, and Auli jerked, startled. 'What're the axes? Is this that study about the origin of the Oracle?'

Auli stopped herself covering the graph she'd been plotting. The axes were unlabelled, so it was just a scatter of meaningless dots. 'No,' she said. 'What does that look like to you? Any correlations?'

Bea leaned forward.

'Yeah, negative, right? There's more variability this end, but it definitely looks negative.' They straightened and brushed their hair off their face. 'Right?'

Auli smiled, and felt sick. She gathered up the papers and tucked them away. 'Lunch,' she said.

Leigh looked up from a paper. Auli glanced at it, then at Leigh's face. 'I have some more relevant papers,' she said. 'You won't need that yet.' Or ever. And where had he found Boudain's old experiment report anyway?

Leigh eyed her thoughtfully, then grinned and rose. 'Okay,' he said. 'I just wanted to be prepared.'

The Bellwether sighed, the ravens circled the library dome, diving in and out of a ghost, calling as if with laughter.

* * *

AT LUNCH, AULI forced herself to eat for the gnawing in her stomach that spoke of too little food and too much stress. A ghost was drifting where the boatmen normally sat, but they were all preparing, Auli guessed, for Raphaël's departure. Her stomach tightened all over again.

'Do you know what the drowning men were saying?'

Auli spilled coffee over her hand as she spun around. Alexis flinched like it was him scalded, and Auli breathed out, dried her hand on her shorts and mustered a smile.

'I'm jumpy today,' she said in Russian, patting the bench in invitation. He scanned the room, then slid down beside her almost furtively.

'Do you?' he asked.

She handed him one of her pastries and he bit into it as if he did not have unlimited access to them down in the kitchen. He'd starved, she thought, for long enough that the echoes hadn't left.

'Which drowned men?' she said.

His eyes flicked to the window. 'The ghosts out there. They tried to tell me something. I think they want us all to drown.'

Auli sipped at her coffee, perplexed. 'The ghosts spoke to you?'

He looked at her as if she were the one making no sense. 'They were drowning so they couldn't speak, but they were trying. I think it's not safe here. We're not safe here.'

Auli very gently took his hand in hers, pastry flakes and all. 'Dunya will keep you safe from ghosts and bad men. You know she will.'

Before, when the fear had ridden him hard, she had told him the Bellwether was safe. Today, though, she couldn't. It had always been a lie, but it felt an insurmountable one now.

Alexis nodded jerkily. 'Dunya says no bad men will get past the captain.'

'That's true. Dunya and the captain. They keep you safe.'

'What about you?'

'I...' Auli faltered. Did she keep herself safe? If she were braver perhaps, or even cowardly enough to know when to run, but she was neither. More frightened of abandonment than death, more frightened of exile. 'The captain keeps me safe, too,' she said instead. It was true, even if it did stick in her throat like a claw.

A boatman entered the room and Alexis leapt to his feet. 'Will you find out?' he said quickly. 'What the drowning men want?'

'Yes,' Auli said, because how could she not? She remembered creeping into her mothers' bed as a child, scared of the monster in the corner of her room. Mama Sara brushing her hair from her forehead as she lay in the safety between their two warm bodies. *The monster isn't real,* Mama Márjá had said drowsily. Mama Sara had tsked quietly and said, *Maybe the monster is real. Maybe so. But if it is then it is lost and far from its monster home, so don't you think perhaps it is frightened and lonely? That it's hiding in your bedroom because it trusts you not to hurt it?*

This thought had silenced Auli's entire mind. All the fear stilled like a pool as she studied this new idea from every angle, her mother's fingers combing her hair. *Poor lonely monster,* she had whispered eventually. *Maybe I can draw it a map so it can find its way home.*

In the morning, Mama Sara had said gravely. *Let's save the monster in the morning.*

AULI FOUND NIKI in their surgery after lunch. The desk was covered in a fine layer of pastry crumbs and pencil shavings, and they looked up with the shadows beneath their eyes as deep as bruises. They had the outer door open, the salt air carrying a barely-there tang of smoke from some mainland fire. Just enough to remind her of dirty fires in dead houses, engines and batteries burning foully. The stomach-turning twist of burning flesh beneath it all, and how you even stopped flinching at the screams after a while, because so often they were not real.

'You didn't sleep,' she said, coming forward.

'I will.' They sighed so hard they began coughing. 'I needed to refill the emergency kit for Raphaël.'

Aüli straightened a clipboard on the bench without thinking, then paused. It was the stock log that they – Niki and the three medics in their absence – filled in every time they took any medicines. She'd told Raphaël it didn't matter because the medics didn't have access to the poison. But maybe it did.

'What is it?' Niki said.

Auli ran a finger down the list. One entry two days before Boudain's death – *dihydrocodeine, 6 tabs, Bea.*

It wasn't the right drug, but it was in the sedatives cupboard. And what if Niki's organising wasn't as good as they thought. She remembered the stock take so soon after Boudain's death, the chaos of it.

'Were you missing any of the... oil of wintergreen?' she asked.

Niki flushed queerly and sat back with a thump. 'Yes, no. I don't—' They took their glasses off, cleaned them and looked at Auli myopically. 'I've got less than I should have.'

Auli nodded. 'Which cupboard was it in?'

Niki looked bereft. 'It's my fault. I'll tell Raphaël. I rearranged things before we sailed, I must have put it...'

Auli wasn't interested in their excuses, she needed to speak to Bea. But first...

Poor lonely monster, she heard her child-self whisper. And, *Is there a balance?* Mama Márjá would tell her to stick to her job so she was safe. Mama Sara would tell her to listen to her heart.

'I've been looking at your records on the Oracle,' she said, slipping unasked into the chair facing them. 'And I think we need to change the doses.'

Niki blinked. 'I told you why—'

Auli shook her head and they fell silent, which surprised her so much it took her another moment before she remembered to speak. 'It's not about that.' She laid her graph and calculations on their desk. 'Did you know the higher sedation makes her cantations more erratic? I think we need to lower the dose so she's steadier. She's nearing adulthood, and I think a combination of hormone shifts and the high doses are driving the… events we've experienced over the last couple of days.'

She stopped, her hands pressed hard against her thighs to stop them fidgeting. It was all true. It *was all true*. She was doing this for everyone's safety, not for her conscience alone; it was the balance she had to believe was possible.

Niki studied the graph, their hair falling over their glasses. 'The events,' they said finally. 'Uoti…'

'The ghost attacked him. And another ghost scratched Leigh. You saw that, didn't you?'

'Ghosts attacking. You make it sound like they have intent. They're just fragments of data, Auli.'

Auli lifted one shoulder. 'I know,' she said. 'But still, two ghosts have injured two people in a way we've never seen before. Uoti nearly died.'

'You don't need to tell me that.'

But she thought perhaps she had. It was so much easier to retreat into the familiar than to consider the unknown.

'If you're right, why this sudden change now when I've had her on this dose for two years?'

Auli's hands twitched. This was the lie. But Niki was

assuming, like she first had, that the murderer stole the sedative from the stores along with the poison. Niki didn't know about the Oracle's missed dose – if they did, she'd never convince them of this. 'A threshold in her physiology? I don't know, but reducing the dose should help stop more... irregularities.'

'Lower doses would make her difficult to handle,' they said. 'She gets distressed.'

The hook hurts. This is bigger than individuals.

'She's got a guard on her now. She can't hurt herself, and she's got to be less dangerous than that storm ghost was.'

Niki grunted discontentedly. 'She'll be dependent.'

Auli's heart surged within her. Not entirely joy, or even relief because if she was wrong... if she was wrong... But she had to try *something*. 'We'll step it down,' she said, all false calm and self-doubt.

'Well, we'll try it. Does Gabrielle know?'

Auli lifted her chin. 'No.'

Niki studied her, then gave a short laugh. 'Let's hope it works then.'

Yes, Auli thought, let's.

Chapter Seventeen

Raphaël

WITH SANDESH OVERSEEING another round of harpoon practice, Raphaël spent the afternoon on the worn granite rocks of Lindö with Hellä and Frans, building and dismantling the aged grenade heads under An's critical supervision until they were mostly sure Hellä could continue arming the harpoons in his and Sandesh's absence without blowing the guard towers into the sky. It wasn't ideal – he'd rather be here. But needs must.

The intermittent percussion of the harpoons firing ceased as Frans and Hellä hefted the grenade crate gingerly back to the *Meri Noita*, and Raphaël followed An back to her own experiments, bits of wire, tools, circuitry all laid out on the rocks like a starburst.

'I'm off at first light,' he said. 'Need me to hunt for anything specific?'

'Blue LEDs and silver jewellery wire,' she said promptly.

Raphaël didn't much fancy his odds. 'No luck evicting it?'

She glared at him. 'I'm not trying to get rid of it. How would that help? I'm trying to separate it.'

Raphaël didn't think he was any slower than your average

person, but she was very good at making him feel it. 'Separate the ghosts?'

'If we are lucky.' She set down one pair of pliers, picked up another.

'An, speak to me as if I am an idiot.'

She snorted. 'Three ghosts all stuffed into this small circuit, would be the best of the two options.'

Raphaël took too long thinking about that.

'I would rather three ghosts than one that's merged the data of several.' She put a screwdriver between her lips to free up her fingers and spoke around it. 'They are low energy fragments. That's the only thing that makes them mostly safe. Imagine if they can combine, grow.'

Raphaël didn't want to imagine any such thing, thank you. 'Growth requires change. The ghosts can't change.'

She looked at him slantwise. Hellä approached from the shore, arms swinging. 'Data can, so why not ghosts?' An said.

'They're fixed fragments,' Raphaël insisted, trying to forget Alexis' ghost.

An shrugged. 'Ask your old girlfriend, she's got a better sense of what ghosts are than I do. And she knows more than she's telling.'

Hellä's pale eyebrows rose. The boatmen would never dare mention Auli, although Raphaël was pretty sure he'd given them no cause for caution. But then he couldn't remember much from the period after their break-up other than the endless recitation in his own head of *It's better this way. It's better this way.*

'She's ready, boss,' Hellä said. A thrush began singing in the scrub and Raphaël was sticky with rock dust and sweat. He eyed An's busy hands.

'Take it we're coming to get you at dusk?' he said.

An nodded, as sparks leapt from two wires and a shimmer of blue flame materialised then vanished again.

* * *

HE SENT JOAR to pick her up, because it was Alan's birthday so all the off-duty boatmen were on the barge rooftop, cooking lobsters caught over the side in Pertti's reconstructed pots. Someone had produced a guitar and was playing fragmented, dissonant songs, as if the new generation could only imagine music that way.

Neither celebration nor idleness felt right, but he'd already packed for the morning and written various missives for delivery. He might corner Auli to see whether An was right, or... where *was* Auli? She wasn't among the researchers, but he found her, not surprisingly, in the long library window closest to North Tower. She was up on the second level, sitting in the window frame – her favourite place, surrounded by dangerously unhaunted books. Another figure appeared and this one *was* a surprise. It was Bea, usually far too sociable to miss out on anything approaching a party. They fitted themselves beside Auli and Raphaël frowned up at them, curiosity piqued.

Auli was seeking answers, and a selfish part of him that didn't care about safety was fiercely glad she might finally be falling out of love with this place. But that part of him wasn't particularly level-headed so he ignored it.

'Alright, boss?' Alan murmured, handing him a glass of homebrew aquavit. Adding when Raphaël lifted it to the sunset sky warily, 'Hasn't killed me yet.'

Raphaël laughed and took a sip. It scoured a layer off his throat but wasn't wholly awful. 'You're diving to retrieve that first harpoon tomorrow.'

'Yes, boss. Hellä gave me a heads up.' Alan shot a glance towards the *Meri Noita* currently sailing away from the party.

Hellä was angrier about Joar than Raphaël was. Mainly, he suspected, because if any boatman was to turn traitor, it offended her deeply that it was a fellow Finn. Raphaël was mostly just relieved Joar wasn't the kind of traitor he'd begun to fear. Laughter exploded on the researcher barge, and both Raphaël and Alan glanced over briefly. The fire barrel they were cooking their own lobster on flared as if someone had decided the homebrew was more suited to arson than drinking. They likely had a point but if there was one thing Raphaël had imagined an apocalypse might remove from his job description, it was nannying drunk students.

In amongst the researchers, Célestine caught his eye and raised her glass in ironic salute, then tipped her head at Pertti and the Oceans assistant, Tobias, setting up for an arm wrestle. Raphaël snorted a laugh into his glass. It felt normal – the slow summer evening, everyone's voices loud enough to drown out any ghosts, the smell of the fire and seafood and brine.

But one of these people was a murderer, and despite his idiocy, Raphaël didn't think it was Joar. He'd need to tell Auli regardless, which he wasn't particularly looking forward to. But with Joar out of the picture, the pool of suspects opened wide. Only three people on the Bellwether that night knew where the sedative was kept, and how it was administered. But unlikely though it was, anyone might have been sent both drugs rather than stealing them from Niki's stores.

He scanned the horizon and weighed leaving for the twentieth time. A movement on the low skyline of Äspskär caught his eye, two figures moving through the low scrub. It was berry season, and they were likely foraging, so he checked Frans in East Tower had spotted them, and turned away.

An hour later, the shift change for the tower guards sent the last bastions of sobriety away. Bea had come down and was now curled into Pertti's side. Célestine materialised next to Raphaël and gave his half-empty glass a weighing glance.

'You are allowed to relax sometimes,' she said in French.

Raphaël glanced up at the library window then over his shoulder to where the *Meri Noita* was only now tacking back into a snippy breeze.

There was a general heave of movement from around the fire, people crowding around the gangplank up to the Bellwether, Miika and Pertti loudly jostling to the front. 'Ah.' Célestine started laughing. 'Ghost race.'

Idiots. It had become a thing recently. You took your valerian vial off and ran opposite circuits of both the second and third deck walkways, racing each other whilst dodging ghosts and risking infection. Raphaël emptied his glass. 'Because relaxing looks so appealing,' he said. There was a cheer, and the two men exploded up the ramp, sending the barges rocking with their combined weight.

'At least they remember to have fun.'

Célestine tapped her nails on the arc of her nearside wheel. They were a deep crimson he'd found for her on an expedition in the spring, glinting in the firelight like blood. He considered mounting a defence, but she'd heard it before. The last time he'd risked seeking happiness it had ended with Auli not speaking to him for a year. He would have left then, if not for Célestine, and for the fact that he knew his absence would make this place yet more dangerous. He was a fool, but Célestine's regular flings were just another form of distance, really. She'd heard him say that before, too.

'I'm sorry,' she said abruptly.

Raphaël raised an eyebrow. 'What for?'

Her face was all burnished shadows now, hard to read, but her fingers were tapping and she drained her drink, winced, and said so quickly he almost missed it, 'For scaring her off.'

'What?' He forgot about the *Meri Noita*, the cheering crowd, even the movie ghost drifting off the barge's far side. 'For *what*?'

Célestine grimaced. 'I didn't think you cared. You acted like it meant nothing. But that woman was falling hard and I didn't fancy seeing you break her. I thought I was doing her a favour.'

Raphaël stared at her. Her nails on the steel rim sounded like distant shotgun blasts. The cheering rose, someone likely coming into view.

'But you did care,' Célestine carried on. 'You were finally letting yourself...'

Her nails tapped; another flatter sound tore through his thoughts, and Raphaël was on his feet, scanning the tower, the barges, the walkways. Someone shouted once. It played over again in his head – Célestine's nails, that flat sound, the shout.

'What is it?' Célestine said, but he didn't answer. The guard in East Tower was at the north edge of their walkway, crouching, rifle raised. He couldn't see West Tower from here. Then another movement and he saw Auli, standing in the long library window, backlit, her hand pressed against the window that was... he squinted... and threw himself forward, pushing through the crew.

Hellä materialised at his elbow on the gangplank between the two barges.

'Boss?'

'Check the library, then the Oracle,' he said. 'Shot fired from Äspskär.'

The girl

THE GIRL FIGHTS the hook. The numbers fill up her lungs like teeth. A crocodile, she thinks, and is so startled at a word all her own that the numbers still. A crocodile, she repeats. The hook is cast a third time. Three times the charm, three faces the forest goddess, three plates on a wooden table reflecting a yellow sun. These are all her own thoughts. She marvels at the strangeness.

Nothing. Has she given any weather cantations this afternoon? A sound of frustration and the hook dissolves into salt and dust. *Boatman, has she given any cantations this...*

A man's voice, and the girl flinches, remembering men shouting and blood in the river. She remembers she has a body and opens her eyes, and the blood in the river fades away. She stands high above a docile sea and the voice is there like a hand on her shoulder, but it does not speak. It listens, and she listens and the gulls cry the sunset, stars set themselves aflame like violins and somewhere people are shouting. They are laughing. The sea is holding her up and these people carry hooks in their mouths, they carry all the tools of drowning. And they laugh.

Oh, how strange it is to breathe the air. How strange these lungs and this orchestral sky and her hands curled around metal bars like her bones remember them. She is a painted girl, brushstrokes of memories on top of memories on top of salted bones.

You're safe, lyubimy. Hush now, hush until the bad men leave.

Well. Enough of this. Ursula? Thank you.

A hand on her arm. Familiar, the girl thinks, and *safe*, her mama whispers. The hand leads her away from the laughter and the stars. Numbers crawl up her spine and pixels tangle her hair, but she holds onto her mother's voice like *that* is the hook, like it might be the way home.

And so that she doesn't lose the way home, she fights the drowning. She thinks, as she pushes hands away and turns her face to the wall, that she has fought this before. Hands pinning her like a fish, a bird, a museum creature staked down and hollowed out. The memory of her own screams claws at her throat.

Hush, her mama whispers.

We will *make them bleed*, her mama whispers. Not her mama, the other voice in the dark, the voice built of stories.

Tomorrow, the voice carrying hooks says. *We'll try again tomorrow.*

'Yes,' the girl whispers. And she smiles, and it is mostly her own smile, a little bit the voice full of teeth.

Chapter Eighteen

Raphaël

A SECOND SINGLE rifle shot fired when he was halfway up East Tower, the same sound as before but from above him. He emerged onto the walkway just as Sandesh chambered the next bullet.

'Report,' he said shortly, crouching in the shadow of the doorway.

The old soldier didn't lift his head. 'Two people on Äspskär. Rifle shot. Didn't see where it hit but I took one down. The other—' He swore softly in Urdu, shifted his elbow, breathed in and fired again. 'Isn't,' he said into the aftermath quiet. 'They're either in a hollow or crawled back over the skyline.'

Raphaël grabbed binoculars from the door jamb and scanned the dark island, stunted trees and rocks a greyscale kaleidoscope of shapes that could be human or animal or nothing at all. The foragers from earlier. He'd dismissed them entirely from his mind.

'Keep them covered. I'll get out there.' He was turning away before he'd finished speaking, running back down the stairs and onto the research deck where Hellä was in the middle of hauling herself onto the lower library floor. He stood in the Centre beneath the library and shouted Auli's name. She leaned over the higher walkway, her hair falling so he could only see the pale oval of her face.

'Hello, Hellä,' she said, as if nothing were wrong at all.

'Is the window shattered?' he called up. She turned her attention to him, and Hellä stilled with one foot on the next ladder. 'Where's— Ah.' Alan appeared in the Oracle Room doorway. 'Alan, ready the boat and someone else sober enough to carry a gun. Auli?'

In a feat of entire showmanship, Hellä flipped over the railing and landed on the research deck with a thump. Alan shot her a rude gesture by way of compliment, said to Raphaël, 'All's quiet in the tower,' and vanished at a run, dodging a ghost Raphaël couldn't see.

'It's cracked,' Auli said. There was a ghost swirling in the empty space just above her, another murmuring in the shadows near the Oracle Room door. 'And there's a hole. Were those gunshots?'

God, he thought. My god. Hellä reached his side.

'One down and one unknown on Äspskär,' Raphaël said. 'You're in charge here. Get all those idiots inside.' Then raising his head and his voice, 'Auli, get down here. Stay in the Oracle Room till we're back.'

Even with her hair hiding her expression, he saw her stiffen and doubted it was from something sensible like fear. 'Please,' he made himself add. 'You're an easy target up there.' My god, he thought again, and spun on his heel, heading for the dock.

THE *MERI NOITA* was nosing up to the Bellwether as he reached it, Joar firing up the engine at Alan's shout, and two boatmen leaping onboard, going straight to furling the sails. Raphaël followed them. An gave him one glance and jumped ashore, laden with gear.

'Äspskär,' Raphaël said to Joar as soon as he reached the helm. 'The open inlet. Fast as you can.' Then he filled everyone in quickly, handing torches out from a locker.

'That IR scope would come in handy now,' Frans murmured, to a low mutter of agreement. But the IR scope had gained a ghost and blown up in the hands of a young recruit called Jem, who might have survived the injuries, but didn't stand a chance against the digital infection that followed. He had died weeping pixellated tears that carved fissures through his skin and muscle and bone.

Raphaël checked his gun, checked the torch, turned to watch the approaching island.

'Alan and Frans, sweep up and right, coming at the first target from the south-east. Joar, you're with me to cover the two bays, see if we pick up the second target. They've probably long gone, but we might get lucky. At least one rifle in play.'

'Dead or alive, boss?' Alan asked, as if asking about tomorrow's weather. He'd always refused to say anything about his past other than that everyone he knew was dead, but at times like this, Raphaël wondered.

He saw again Auli's gold-limned silhouette, hand against the glass, and wanted very much to say *dead*. 'Alive.'

'Sir,' Joar said.

The boat bounced out of the lee of the Bellwether. In her dim running lights, the Finn looked more on edge than he ought. 'It's An. She says she's fine, but there was a whole mess where she'd been working, and she looks off.'

Raphaël frowned.

'Just thought I should mention it, boss.' As much as the boat would allow, Joar was standing painfully to attention and Raphaël wanted to hit him all over again for getting tangled in someone else's games.

'Thank you,' he said. 'I've got the helm, go over the terrain with everyone.'

Joar nodded stiffly and moved away. Raphaël took the wheel. Another two minutes to the shore, he estimated. An, and whatever disaster she'd spun out of her experiments, would have to wait.

A flock of roosting gulls lifted up from the shoreline as they debarked, all crying and flashing bone-white in the darkness. Minutes later another bird, something small and furious, marked Alan's progress away to the east as Raphaël and Joar powered up the shallow hill, keeping their bodies low and their torches off until they needed them.

The first small bay was only fifty metres away and they quartered it silently. No footprints, no sign of a recent boat haulage. Joar took point for the second stretch and Raphaël glanced east where the other team were circling a dead, or nearly dead, body. If it had been Miika, there might have been two bodies. But the shot had still been remarkable, and Raphaël was quietly satisfied.

The second bay showed a long scrape in the mud where a small boat had been pushed into the water. Raphaël followed the footprints back from surf to scrub.

'Two in, one out,' Joar said by his side. 'Could hide up anywhere. Even if we get both boats out the luck is with them.'

Raphaël agreed. 'Up to the target then, see if they dropped anything.' They'd have to come back in daylight. The moon was rising but it was a sharp-edged thing, and once their torches were on, everything was plunged into blackness.

The shooter was indeed very dead. It hadn't been instant. Sandesh had done the sensible thing and aimed centre-mass, so he'd lived long enough to know it, but not long enough for the speed of their launch to have made any difference.

They dumped his body ignominiously on the Bellwether dock, to await his audience. In the absence of photographs, this was the best way to check whether anyone recognised him and Raphaël figured it would make a nice hangover treat for everyone come morning.

What he wanted to do next was check on Auli and sleep for a week. What he did was talk to Hellä, write a handful of rather terse notes, debrief Sandesh and Alan, circle the top floor of the library until he found the book that had taken the bullet, issue an almost certainly unnecessary blackout order for the night, and then head finally to the Oracle Tower to check for himself that they, too, were maintaining the blackout.

The likelihood was that the shooter had been aiming for the Oracle. Either he was a very bad shot and Auli very unlucky, or he was a very good shot and he'd assumed the lone female figure in the library at night was his target. It was a reasonable assumption, and the logical part of Raphaël's mind was trying very hard to drown out the part that was reliving all the other times he'd watched someone he loved die.

That thought brought him up short at the closed door to the Oracle Room. What had Célestine said just before the gunshot? What the fuck had she said?

You acted like she meant nothing. I thought I was doing her a favour.

Raphaël reached out to grasp the doorframe, the Bellwether creaked and there was a ghost a little too close in the shadows, but he didn't move for a long time.

She'd been burned by a ghost two months into their relationship, and her pain and her equanimity about the pain had both ricocheted through him, equally devastating, until he'd had to walk out of Niki's office to escape the memory of his mother dying, corroded by static and code. *Be strong*, she had whispered as she broke apart. *Be strong, son.* And he still didn't know how to be strong without being untouchable, not when everything wanted to kill them. Perhaps it wasn't possible, perhaps Célestine had done the right thing.

But shutting Auli out hadn't prevented her nearly dying tonight; it hadn't spared him one iota of the fear he'd felt seeing her in the shattered window.

Then the door opened and Auli was there.

Auli

AULI JERKED FORWARD at the look on Raphaël's face, reaching out a hand that he flinched away from.

'What is it?' she gasped. 'Is someone hurt?' Infection, those daft men with their ridiculous ghost races, or... what had happened on the island? Raphaël was staring at her as if she were infected, or shot...

'Oh,' she said softly, and sank back against a wall. A ghost crackled by the window, but it had been there for an hour, so she didn't look.

But no. It made no sense. No one other than Raphaël, Célestine and Niki knew she was looking for Boudain's killer so why would an *outsider* try to silence her? They'd been aiming for the Oracle, and she was being nothing but fanciful.

'Hellä said the second shooter got away,' she said. 'Was anyone hurt?'

He stepped into the room, and that raw distress she'd seen briefly was thoroughly erased. 'No one,' he said, and moved soft-footed to the stairs, looking upwards.

'I told Ursula she could turn a light on down here if she gets distressed,' she said to his back.

Raphaël didn't move. 'There's still a shooter out there, Auli.'

Auli twined her fingers together against her stomach. She was exhausted, and he was tense as a drawn bow. 'They're on the opposite side to Äspskär. She's used to having a lamp on, it might confuse her.'

'She'll sleep till morning.'

The ghost muttered brokenly, Raphaël turned around, and she was grateful for the darkness. Because of course he would correctly interpret her silence.

'What have you done?' he said quietly.

She released her hands and pressed them against the wall behind her. The Bellwether creaked; she said without meaning to, 'I love it here. I know it's just a job to you, but to me it's more a home than anywhere has been.'

'Auli.'

She shook her head. 'I know it's dangerous, but this place represents *hope*. We are trying to build a future. That's... it *matters*, Raphaël. And *I* matter.' She laughed softly. 'Not much, I know, but more than I do anywhere else. I love this place. I would do anything to protect it.'

Raphaël took a step closer. 'What have you done?'

'But protecting it means making sure it *does* represent hope,' she said as if he had not spoken. 'So I cannot let it be a place built on cruelty. On captivity.' He twitched; she carried on softly. 'I've reduced her drugs. She's sleeping now but might wake.'

He was a good man, she reminded herself. He'd understand.

'Are you mad?' He swung away, veering past the ghost to the window where the moon reflected off the water like a serrated blade.

Auli should have been prepared for this. She should, but her entire chest was a starburst of betrayal.

'Maybe,' she whispered. Where he was concerned, yes. 'But not with this. The data suggest giving her more coherence will stop the... ghost irregularities.'

He didn't answer, staring at her unseen in the darkness but felt. Oh, so very felt. Heat rose in her cheeks.

'You don't know everything, Raphaël,' she said. 'It wouldn't kill you to trust I'm not stupid, or wilfully reckless with anyone's safety.'

'Stupid, never. Wilfully reckless? Auli, this is the *worst timing*. There's a murderer on board, there's war breaking out on the mainland, someone tried to *kill you tonight*, and you think now is a good time to start experimenting with the Oracle's stability? Wilfully reckless? Yes. Yes, you are.'

She hissed in a breath, the ghost static flared searingly bright in the darkness. 'Says the man using old and unreliable explosives,' she said, nails cutting into her palm. 'Says the man going out into that war. You once told me there is never a right time to stay silent. Do you remember that, Raphaël? You said it is never forgivable to avert your gaze. And yet here you are, averting yours.'

She couldn't see his face and if it had been daylight, she doubted this conversation would be happening at all.

'I am not,' he said slowly, the French accent stronger, 'averting my gaze, or taking risks that aren't absolutely unavoidable. But you are already at risk and now you play with a fire you do not even understand. There are enough dangers here, Auli, and likely more coming. Please, don't make my job harder.'

There was a whisper of movement in the room above, and Auli was abruptly too tired to fight.

'This isn't about either of us,' she said, pushing herself off the wall. 'Do what you must to keep the Bellwether safe, Raphaël. And I will do what I must to make it worth saving. Good night.'

She was opening the door when she felt him at her back and froze. He didn't touch her, but when he spoke, his breath warmed the nape of her neck and she wanted to turn into the shelter of him. To throw an elbow into his ribs, a fist over her shoulder the way Mama Márjá had taught her.

'And if you cannot make it worth saving? What then? What happens if you fail, Auli?'

She didn't answer, because if she tried, he would only ask her the other version of that question. *And who will die either way?* So instead, she fled into the dark of the research deck, hands outstretched and ears straining for hidden ghosts.

SOME OF THOSE ghosts woke her in the night – a movie soundtrack all smoky French voices, another of white noise overlaying the sea. In the morning, the otters ran along the footboard, chattering, and when she emerged onto the roof, the ravens were picking over the remains of last night's abandoned celebrations. Static flickered along their primary feathers meaning they had been playing with the ghosts again, and Auli shuddered helplessly.

Both boats were gone from the dock, so Raphaël would be heading right now towards a nascent war. There were two Oceans juniors down there, looking at a dew-damp shape, and Auli felt all over again that hollowed-out, icy horror of hearing the glass break just above her head and seeing the bullet hole, and recognising it.

Gabrielle was in the Hall, so Auli gathered coffee and her courage. 'My turn with the seeding,' she said. 'How did it go last night?'

Spreading butter on a bread roll, meticulously thin, Gabrielle said, 'Not well. Hopefully, you will have better luck. We need the buoy data.'

'The low is coming from the north, though. We need buoys up there.'

'You've been talking to Célestine? Buoys in the north will facilitate pirates, not trade. That isn't our priority area.'

The sea beyond the window was oddly still today, the air over the islands pearlescent. Auli could argue that trading routes were hardly separate to the rest of the sea, that weather *moved,* would you believe, and the bad stuff often moved *down* from the Arctic. But any conversation about the Oracle's cantations strayed uncomfortably close to her partial truth about lowering her sedation levels. *Niki and I are tweaking her routine to try to settle the cantation behaviour,* she'd said, when Gabrielle was late meeting with the forecast team and hurriedly finishing off a letter for the evening's boat. Gabrielle had barely nodded, and Auli had told herself that came close enough to consent to count.

She reached the Oracle Room just as Ursula and the Oracle were moving through the open outer door, Leigh and a boatman waiting to follow. There were two ghosts in the room, another floating off the walkway, code scrolling through static. Leigh smiled at her.

'Hey, I'm glad you're okay. I heard about last night.'

So had everyone, Auli assumed, but no one else had bothered to mention it. 'Thank you.'

'Are you doing the seeding? Can I watch?'

'No,' Auli said. 'It's the rules, sorry.'

He eyed the girl on the walkway, a flicker of something like hunger crossing his face. The shooting last night made it more likely Boudain's death had also been an attempt on the Oracle, foiled when he drank the wrong hot chocolate. So this question likely didn't matter, but Raphaël's accusations of naivety had stung, so she said quietly, 'Did you know about Boudain's research plans before you arrived? Have you told anyone here about them?'

He stiffened very slightly. 'No. I mean… why? Was it secret?'

'I'm just trying to figure out how far he'd got with approvals and things,' Auli said vaguely.

Leigh's eyes widened. 'Wait, we're still going ahead? I thought you were going to stop me.' He laughed, shooting a glance towards the research deck.

Auli winced. 'So have you talked to anyone about it, either before or after Boudain died?'

'I might have told Bea and Tobias. Does it matter? They'll find out at some point.'

It might, yes. Particularly the *when*, but he was already looking too inquisitive. 'No, I was just wondering. Anyway, don't you have Célestine's stats tutorial now?'

'Oh, yeah.' He didn't move. 'But do I need to know how to do the analyses, really? Isn't it enough to look at the graphs and move on to the next step? Start building the testing rigs with An Carline?'

Auli took the clipboard from Leigh's loose grip. 'No, we can't just look at graphs. We can't abandon the scientific method because we don't have computers.'

'Okay, I get it for the weather models and all that. But for this? The graphs show cantation rates are highest for the buoys transmitting around two hundred and fifty megahertz. So why not just crack on? It would speed the project up.'

There'd been two cantations during his dawn watch. A fragment of song in Italian, a few lines of a scientific paper on marine litter. Auli handed the clipboard back. 'Can you translate the song and leave it on my desk? And the report should go to Tobias.' Leigh took it, but tipped his head quizzically, waiting. 'What about spatial cross correlation?' she said as patiently as possible. 'Or temporal effects, weather conditions, listener error? We need to account for other sources of variability in the data before leaping to conclusions, otherwise... well, at best we waste months chasing something that doesn't exist, and at worst—' She cut off sharply and lifted her coffee, hiding her wince behind the steam.

'At worst people die?' Leigh supplied.

'No,' Auli said tiredly. 'At worst we kill people.'

Leigh glanced away, grimacing, then shook himself and

said lightly, 'Hey, is it true the captain sent his second after that other sniper?'

Raphaël had sent Hellä? Raphaël had stayed? Auli's mind went unhelpfully blank. 'I don't know,' she said.

He shifted, opened his mouth to speak but instead simply left, and she stood watching the ghosts, ignoring her heart, thinking about Leigh's ambition and Boudain's, and whether it would be worse if he'd been killed by accident.

THE ORACLE DIDN'T react when Auli leaned on the railing, a half-step closer than was wise, and watched the girl watching Dunya and Alexis on the garden barge. The lightning in her eyes was silver-blue in the filtered sun and her face held, not the distant tension Auli was used to, but instead a kind of... expectancy.

'Hello, Oracle,' she said softly, in Russian. The Oracle did not appear to hear. Ursula was perched awkwardly on a windowsill with her knitting draped over her thighs. The boatman was back the way they'd come, staying, Auli suspected, at exactly the limit Raphaël had set and not a centimetre closer.

What would happen if there was no forecast today? How many boats would founder? How many would blow off course and be lost? Not many, surely. They'd already sent out a warning of the storm likely to come. It wasn't that Auli was reckless with all those strangers' lives, she still dreamed of a ship burning against a coastline too often for that. But a possible risk to strangers versus the reality of this too-thin girl, of Uoti lying in bed on the deck below? *The story was of a storm,* Uoti had said. And Auli and Bea had realised something last night.

'Hello, Oracle,' Auli repeated. 'Would you like to tell me a story?'

The girl blinked. A ghost crackled sharply, somewhere the ravens called and house martins wove flightlines from the towers.

The Oracle turned her head and met Auli's gaze.

This was the thing.

This was what they had realised, books whispering all around them and sheets of cantations scattered across their laps like prayers.

The kraken, the storm, the pirates and the film. There was one link, and she needed to understand how it worked.

'Would you tell me a story?'

Chapter Nineteen

Auli

'Long, long ago,' the Oracle whispered.

Auli's heart stuttered – she hadn't really thought it would work.

'In a land of forests far from the sea, there lived a little girl with her mama and her papa.' A ghost of a cavorting seal pup rose towards them. 'The girl wore ribbons in her hair and loved her mother's singing. But she carried an ocean of voices all calling for the sea, and so the bad men planned to silence the girl. Hearing this, the mama and papa and the little girl fled through the forests.'

The Oracle's fingers tightened on the railing, the pup splashed and circled. Auli dared not move even to touch the valerian at her throat.

'*Hush*, the mama said, and *run*, the papa said, but still the salt-voices spilled from the girl's lungs, crawled along her bones and dragged her towards the sea. And so the bad men found them. The papa fell by the river, the water running red and the mama whispering, *hush. Hush. Hush now.* Until the bad men dragged her away.'

The Oracle's voice changed. A little stronger, more full

of echoes. 'And the girl was all alone with her ocean of ghosts and the bad men. *Help me*, the girl asked. But no one answered. *Help me*, she begged, and the water heard. *Help me*, for a third time, and the water answered.' Her voice was more echoes now than girl. '*We will make the bad men bleed*, the girl thought to herself. *We will feed the wounded waters with their blood and we will be set free.*'

The Oracle stared at Auli all lightning and tears, and fear crawled the length of Auli's spine like a scorpion. The seal pup flickered.

The seal pup *changed*.

Auli reeled back. Horror flooded through her like the moment in the harbour in Helsinki when someone had said, *You were the one asking about that boat? I'm sorry. I'm sorry.*

The ghost seal was not a seal anymore.

It was a coiling blue serpent, teeth and tendrils, and it turned in the air, flickering and stretching impossibly larger. Auli's back hit the tower wall, one hand at her throat, the other reaching for the unmoving Oracle. Did she even need saving? Auli couldn't think, she couldn't *think,* and the dragon roared silently.

Someone was shouting, the walkway rattled with footsteps but here against the tower, there was just Auli and the Oracle and this impossible thing. What had she done? What had she unleashed?

The ghost engulfed the Oracle, her hair coiling around her with the beast. 'We will be set free,' the Oracle whispered, or the ghost did, so much static Auli couldn't tell. She lifted her arms up as if caressing the dragon that encircled her, and the ghost vanished.

Static flickered across the Oracle's skin. She turned towards Auli, lightning-eyed. 'I was there, I saw it.'

Auli closed the distance between them without thinking. 'Are you hurt?' she said, touching a tentative finger to the girl's pale arm. The static discharge was smaller than she'd braced for, but the Oracle still jumped. 'Here.' Auli lay the Oracle's hand on the railing. Her hair fell around her shoulders sleepily and she blinked as if coming awake. 'What's your name?' Auli said abruptly.

Lightning arced across the Oracle's eyes.

'What was the girl's name?' Auli corrected. 'In the story.'

'Auli? What on earth are you doing?' Gabrielle. Auli had been so intent on the girl, she hadn't even noticed her arrive, the boatman lurking behind her left shoulder. Had she been nearby, Auli wondered, waiting for Auli to mess up?

She stepped back. Ran a hand over her own charged hair, and the Oracle moved like a whip, grabbing her arm vicelike, her face alive with wonder.

'Iolanta,' the Oracle said. 'The girl... the girl was called Iol—'

'Fraser! Distance, for Christ's sake! Have you got a death wish?'

The Oracle jerked as if slapped and Auli pulled her freed arm against her stomach like it was the thing that was wounded here. 'It's okay,' she said. Blood pounded in her ears and black spots circled the grey sky. 'It's okay.' She didn't know who she was talking to, but she backed up to Gabrielle and the boatman.

'I take it the seeding went well,' Gabrielle said caustically. Someone else emerged from the Oracle Room for listening duty. Auli's hands would not stop shaking, but she wrapped her arms around herself and tried to meet Gabrielle's gaze steadily. *Grow a spine,* she heard her brother whisper. *Grow wings,* Mama Sara.

'We're in a transition period,' she said. 'It will take her time to settle.'

Gabrielle scanned the Oracle, the ghosts circling her. The boatman, Frans, asked if Auli were hurt, his eyes tight, and

Auli ought to be as on-edge as he was. But it felt less like fear now, more like watching something burn. What had she done? She didn't know.

'Ursula,' Gabrielle began, and before she could stop her, Auli was through the nearest door into Uoti's empty office, with a sense of having slipped out from beneath a knife.

'Any buoy data from the seeding?' Célestine called as Auli headed for her desk. Auli shook her head and apologised, without stopping, but Célestine didn't let her off. It would, Auli supposed, have been too much like good luck to evade both Gabrielle and Célestine within the same few minutes.

'I'm waiting on your new boy,' Célestine said, her wheels trundling over the boards of the deck as she caught up with Auli. 'And on buoy data. And neither appear to be materialising, no?' They diverged around a cracking patch of air and reconvened at Auli's desk.

'You make it sound like both are my fault,' Auli muttered, more to herself than Célestine but of course she heard anyway.

'Do I?' She laughed and Auli sat down with a thump, pressing her hands into her eyes. The seal pup kept mutating into a water dragon behind her eyelids, the impossible horror of it.

'Did you know the Oracle's name?' she said, without opening her eyes. She felt Célestine come alert and dropped her hands with a sigh. Bea, Suvi and An were at their desks but not close enough to hear. 'Iolanta,' she said. 'Her name is Iolanta. I never knew that. Did you?'

'Her name is... No. No, I did not know this.' Célestine spoke slowly, the sharpness gone for once, her dark eyes thoughtful. She began tapping one red fingernail on her wheel rim, the sound high and tinny over the hush of the sea, the murmuring people, ghosts, walls. Auli turned away so Célestine didn't see how the sound grated, it would only make her do it more.

'Anyway,' Auli said, fishing a book out of its crate and smoothing it as the ghost within prickled against her skin. 'Hopefully there'll be some buoy data later.'

'Yes,' Célestine said, absently, still tapping. Two boatmen emerged through the nearest tower doorway, one of them Joar. He grinned at Célestine and laughed when she only raised her eyebrows at him, that small move still somehow sensual. Joar's gaze slid to Auli, and his face stiffened queerly before he looked away.

'He's in disgrace with Rafa, silly boy,' Célestine said. 'But I am happy. Spy is one thing. I would not have liked finding out I had been fucking a murderer, no?'

Auli stared at her. Célestine's eyes widened, and she murmured in French, 'And so, you have done it again, Célestine.' Then switching back to English, 'He surely meant to say. You are busy with...' Canting her head to one side. 'What *are* you working on? Getting shot at in the library in the evenings.'

'Nothing—' Auli began to say, but suddenly Bea was there, and speaking. 'Stories, Célestine!' A grin lit their face like a lighthouse. 'Why did the storm attack Uoti? Why did the fish attack Leigh?' They made a dramatic gesture with their hand. A ghost crackled in the dove-grey light. 'The stories are coming true!'

Auli sighed.

Célestine rocked her wheels back then forth again. 'What is this?'

'We worked it out,' Bea said. 'I helped Auli identify all the ghost anomalies, and they've all involved a story about the sea. That's the commonality. It's like the ghosts containing stories are more alive than they should be. Isn't that, well, it's terrifying but also kind of amazing, right?'

Célestine shifted her stare from Bea to Auli. Perhaps it had been a mistake to involve Bea. But they read more fiction than the rest of the Bellwether combined, and she had foolishly assumed telling them to be discreet would mean something.

'It is a theory,' Auli said.

One she had just tried to test by seeing if the Oracle would cantate a story more readily than data, and she didn't know what to do with the result – the Oracle telling, not a story ghost, but an actual story. Of herself.

'They aren't alive,' Célestine said hoarsely, startlingly unhappy, and Auli's thoughts stuttered. 'They are data. What is this madness, Auli? Ghosts are *not alive*. This is a fact.'

Ah, Auli thought. It wasn't common, in fact the probabilities were tiny, but perhaps of all the ghosts roaming the world, Célestine had seen one that contained someone she had lost. It made Auli's heart ache like a bruise and she didn't know what to say. What could anyone say to that?

She didn't have to try.

Someone burst into the researcher deck at a run and slammed into Gabrielle's office without knocking. Célestine spun her chair around and Auli stood.

'Infection,' Célestine murmured.

'But who?' Bea said.

Auli shook her head, the bruise of her heart turning to ice. 'If it was infection, they'd have gone to Niki. The boat—' She crossed the deck to the windows looking north. The *Meri Noita* was at anchor two hundred metres away, sails furled and rocking in the low swell. There were figures on deck, and figures in the water. She breathed out slowly and pressed a palm against the window.

'Not him, then.'

Auli turned to face Célestine. 'No.'

Célestine nodded, already pivoting towards her boss' door. 'Shall we find out?'

But Auli didn't want to know. She was playing with fire, and if someone had been burned then she didn't want to know.

'Pertti,' Bea said, loud in the silence. 'Where's Pertti?'

Auli went the opposite way to Célestine, knocked on Niki's door. There were no good possibilities, only bad ones.

She was right.

'ALCOHOL POISONING,' GABRIELLE was saying when Auli reached Pertti's cabin on the researcher barge. She and Niki had gone on ahead while Auli waited for Célestine's winch to lower her to the second deck then trailed after them all here. Two doors along from her own room. The long passageway between the cabins smelled of the morning's showers, wet wood, and last night's fires.

'He was drinking heavily last night,' Gabrielle added.

Auli, behind Célestine's chair, could not see Pertti and didn't want to. 'He was ghost racing,' she said quietly. 'Did he touch any?'

Célestine backed the chair up sharply, running over Auli's foot without noticing. 'He was fine. He was *fine*. Not drunk enough to *die*.' She raised her voice, glaring at Gabrielle. 'I do not believe it and I am tired of pretending something is not very wrong here. Everyone is tired of it.' She spun her chair around then stopped and swore in French. Bea was standing at the end of the passageway, their hand over their mouth, their eyes stretched wide.

'No,' they whispered.

'Bea,' Auli said.

'No.' Bea began to shake their head and did not stop; Célestine breathed out heavily and wheeled forward.

'Come,' she said. 'Come, Bea. We will see him in a minute, when Niki is finished, yes? Come now.' And somehow Bea went, and Auli almost wished she could follow.

Pertti had died in bed, but he had not died gently. His sheets were tangled around his legs as if he had struggled, and everything – hair, mattress, floor – was wet and sand-strewn. This was where the smell of wet wood was coming from, with its undertones of brine. His eyes and mouth were stretched wide in a horrible echo of Bea's.

Niki touched his jaw, leaned closer.

'He didn't call out, someone would have heard,' Auli said. And then, realising what was missing from the seaweed smells: 'He wasn't sick. He didn't choke.'

Niki sat back on their heels and looked up at her. 'Half right.'

Gabrielle shifted her weight clumsily, unused to the particular rocking of the barges, and somewhere a ghost began a low thrumming engine noise.

'He drowned,' Niki added. 'I can test for alcohol in his blood, but he drowned on seawater.'

'It's not possible,' Gabrielle said emphatically.

Auli closed the door behind her, though there was no one there to listen. 'Someone killed him,' she said quietly, then corrected herself. 'Or something.'

Niki and Gabrielle both eyed her, one a little baffled, a little wary; the other mostly angry. But perhaps that was the same thing, Auli thought, with armour on.

'The storm ghost that knocked Uoti over,' Niki said. 'But we would have felt that thing come back.'

'Not the storm ghost perhaps,' Auli agreed. 'Although that wasn't a storm ghost actually, it was a story ghost. But this was another ghost. Maybe a shipwreck, a war film, something with drowning men.' She was trying not to look at Pertti's pale eyes and screaming mouth or imagine him fighting for air while all around him his friends slept softly. His hands, she realised, were clawed and black tipped. Burned.

'When?' Gabrielle said, a little muffled.

Niki shook their head, water from the floor darkening their knees. 'Between four and ten hours ago. I might be able to narrow it down in the autopsy.'

'We can't let news of this get out.' Gabrielle smoothed her hair, straightened the cuffs of her shirt. 'Do your tests, Doctor, but the story is it was a normal ghost death.'

'Everyone will see there's a body.'

'We'll say it got into his lungs first.'

'Célestine saw him,' Auli said quietly as Gabrielle opened the door. 'She knows that's a lie.'

'I'll deal with Célestine.'

Niki and Auli waited until her footsteps had faded across to the Bellwether, looking at one another rather than the dead man.

'I doubt it,' Niki said.

It wasn't funny. It was terrifying and sad and bewildering, but still, a muscle twitched in Niki's cheek and horrible laughter caught in Auli's throat like a hundred tiny hooks.

'Christ,' she said. 'Poor Pertti. Poor Bea.'

Niki rose, brushing at their wet knees with a faint grimace. 'It was a kinder death than the normal.'

Which might have sounded callous but was only the truth. Auli found a blanket and laid it gently over the body. The man who'd wanted her job and despised it equally, who made clever lobster pots and loved Bea and had run laughing around the Bellwether last night for a dare.

'What's going on, Auli? Is this our reduced dosage?'

Auli met Niki's tired gaze. They hadn't wanted her to cause trouble, and yet trouble had found them anyway, and Auli might be wholly to blame. 'Maybe she's still adjusting,' she said.

Niki did not look convinced. Boots thumped onto the barge roof, and she backed up before they could question her further. She needed space to sort through the revelations and horror, to parse some kind of answer. 'That'll be the boatmen. I'll get out of their way.' She ought to offer assistance with the autopsy again but couldn't. Not again, prying open another dead man's bones in search of a justice that wasn't there.

Oh, she thought, and stilled.

'What if he killed Boudain?' she asked, to herself as much as Niki. Bea had signed out strong painkillers two days before; perhaps he had persuaded or tricked them into looking away for a minute. It was possible.

Niki didn't ask what lines she might be drawing between that death and this one, which was lucky as she didn't know either. 'For the job? He didn't try hard enough to get it from you afterwards, unless he was planning to kill you, too.' They paused, both of them thinking of snipers and broken glass. 'No,' Niki said firmly. 'He was both lazy, and an academic snob. He'd never have wanted…'

'To be PI of such a useless department,' Auli finished for them. The boatmen reached the door and Auli nodded once. 'I know. You're right.'

Chapter Twenty

Raphaël

It took them annoyingly long to find that first misfired harpoon, free-diving again and again, and only Alan young enough not to mourn scuba gear. Sandesh reported seeing a shadowy *something* on their third dive, and there'd been rumours of sharks, but they finally located the thing, oddly tangled in kelp that took them five dives to cut free. Raphaël left the lifting to the two boatmen and returned to the cabin to mark the location.

His argument with Auli over the Oracle had been repeating itself in his head all morning. The problem was he trusted her instincts. She wasn't a soldier, or whatever it was he'd made himself, but she read people like books, and she *noticed things*. Like the gentleness he'd tried to bury; the fear he'd buried it beneath.

So, when she said they needed to reduce sedation of the Oracle, he half-believed her. And Niki must have done so. But Gabrielle would certainly *not* opt to play God with the most dangerous person in Northern Europe, and Raphaël could always go to her if he really wanted to burn his bridges. He swore softly to himself in several languages, corrected the *Meri Noita*'s angle into the swell and scowled at the sea beyond the islets.

'If they left any trace, Hellä will catch them,' Alan said, glancing up as Sandesh dove again.

Raphaël switched to this other worry with relief. He'd sent Hellä in his stead at dawn, and she'd been unhealthily delighted. 'They were professionals,' he said to Alan. 'They won't have left a viable trail and will be well gone by now.'

'Bugger,' Alan observed.

'Hellä has other priorities besides. We'll put it about she's on a solid trail though.'

Alan straightened. 'Baiting a trap, boss?'

'More lighting a fire to see who runs.' He checked the forecast flag on West Tower. They'd switched to green this morning – change coming.

They were both counting Sandesh down.

'Is that why you stayed, because they might try again?'

'They knew where to expect their target. So I stayed because they had help on the Bellwether.' All *he* had was supposition and people taking pot shots at an insanely stubborn woman, but he knew he was right. 'I don't like the feel of the weather,' he added after a moment. 'Bad weather forecast and yet we've got flat calm.'

Alan checked Sandesh's line then the silver-blue open water. 'It'll come in hard and fast then.' He couldn't quite suppress a grin and Raphaël raised an eyebrow at him.

'We'll get fog,' he said. 'If the system stalls to the north or passes west.'

'Ah fuck, we will.'

Sandesh finally surfaced, inhaled fiercely three times then let Alan haul him aboard. As they began pulling ropes over the tailboard, Raphaël fitted fog into his running equations of risks and likelihoods. It would make approach less likely but them more vulnerable to it, and it would dampen static so ghosts were near-impossible to detect. Out there, meanwhile, boats would be getting lost, wrecked, foundering all for lack of basic technology or a clear line of sight.

'No one recognised the sniper then?' Alan returned to the subject.

'No.'

Sandesh set the harpoon on the deck. 'My money's on either pirates testing security, or one of them Helsinki crazies. We were about due another attempt from them.'

'Miika said St. Petersburg,' Raphaël noted.

'The Russians? He just enjoys blaming them for everything being as they took his fingers. But they've only got fifteen-year-old conscripts and game rifles.' Sandesh scoffed, still bent over the harpoon. 'Besides, they might think she's cursed, but they're too superstitious to kill her.'

He was right about the ballistics not matching, but Raphaël wasn't so sure about the superstition. Although he also wasn't sure they'd been trying for the Oracle. What if someone else had got wind of Auli's madcap scheme to demedicate the Oracle? Wouldn't that paint a target on *her* head instead? He needed to talk to her again; his palms were sweaty on the wheel.

'Who is best served?' he said quietly. Assuming the target had been the Oracle, the Helsinki Survivors were definitely her most outspoken would-be killers. But there were others who feared her monstrousness more than they feared the sea.

That shot, though, it had been twenty centimetres from Auli's head. Over that range, there was no way it had been intended as anything other than a kill shot. And the sniper should have been able to tell the difference between a blonde-haired near-child, and a black-haired woman. Raphaël wiped his hands on his shorts and breathed salt air slowly through his nose.

So, who was best served, not by a dead Oracle, but by a dead

Auli? Someone who wanted to stop Auli tampering with the Oracle? Someone wanting to maintain rigid control over both the Oracle, and the Bellwether that contained her?

'Red flag, boss.' Alan said. 'Like you said.'

Raphaël looked at the Bellwether, then out to the far horizon. Was that a line of pale grey? Damn, he thought, unsurprised. 'Time for a bit of target practice before it hits.'

'Hope Hellä has fun while we're fogbound with your traitor.'

'This thing,' Sandesh interjected, 'is rusted like it was under for weeks. Mechanisms will all need stripping and patching, again.'

The joy, Raphaël thought fatalistically, of piecing together explosives from decaying parts. Auli's horror whispered in the back of his mind, and he thought that at least if he blew himself up during this afternoon's live practice, he'd be spared having to admit she was right.

'I'm sending an alert out with the forecast boat that we're shooting anyone on the islands on sight,' he said.

'It's berry and fungi season.'

'They can cope.'

Once these harpoons were armed and ready, they had boat-sinking capacity for the first time. A ghost trailed across the boat's bow, the static catching the light, and behind it something surfaced then vanished, a rolling curl of darkness that must have been a seal, but Raphaël would have sworn blind wasn't.

Auli

GABRIELLE STOOD IN the Hall with her arms folded as everyone gathered. Silhouetted against the window she looked almost divine in her withheld wrath. But what was it for, Auli wondered, that anger? Another unearned death, or the fraying seams of her chosen kingdom?

Rather than listen to whatever lies Gabrielle chose to tell, Auli escaped back up into the library. Someone had stuck worn plastic over the broken window, but Auli moved around to the southern side, as far as possible from Äspskär where two men had nearly killed her. The sun slipped between spun clouds, hazy and haloed as Auli lowered herself into the gap between bookcases and rested a clipboard with yesterday's sheaf of papers on her knees.

There was a murderer aboard the Bellwether and someone beyond it also bent on killing... someone. And now the ghosts themselves had murdered Pertti. Not infected and killed, but *murdered*.

Were all of these related? It seemed unlikely that three separate entities would simultaneously develop a taste for Bellwether blood. And yet how did you thread Boudain, the snipers, and mutated ghosts all into one motive, one source? The only link was a broken girl called Iolanta, but the Oracle tied everything together on the Bellwether so that was hardly helpful.

Auli doodled along the margins of her notes, waves and islets, the curved backs of dolphins. She hadn't found her mentor's murderer. And if she'd justified this by the greater danger of the ghost anomalies, that was only a partial truth. She was also a coward. Not of facing a killer, but of facing a killer and them being someone she knew.

Were they all linked, though?

The Oracle as intended target did not explain Pertti; the Oracle as *source* didn't work for the poison or the snipers. What had Boudain said? She drew a boat, a figure on its deck... That the Bellwether was a source of power, and if they did not wield that power themselves, it would be wielded by others? So was someone seeking to seed unrest on the Bellwether? No, because that didn't explain the ghost anomalies.

Which left Auli with two failed attempts to kill the Oracle – first when Boudain accidentally drank her poisoned hot chocolate, a second time with hired snipers. And the ghost anomalies were a response to a shift within the Oracle after she missed that one single dose. Iolanta. A girl telling a story full of blood and fear and anger.

Auli shivered and a ghost fell through the dome. Video footage of a coastal city being bombed at night, the sound of car horns and screaming voices filling the dome as it spun in the grey light. She touched the vial at her throat and tore her gaze away. They were not portents.

So Boudain's killer was the sniper's source, too. Auli flipped the sheet of paper over, and began writing names, opportunities, keys and timings, until the video ghost strayed too close and she rose to move away from it. In the Centre below, Célestine pivoted her chair and lifted her head.

'There the fuck you are,' she shouted. 'Come down, I need you.'

Which was possibly one of the more unlikely things to ever pass her lips. Auli stilled. 'What?' she said, too softly to carry.

Beside Célestine, Joar was lounging on a sofa in a way that reminded Auli of Raphaël when he was on high alert but didn't want you to know. So he'd set a guard on the *researchers* now? Indignation burned for all of three seconds before the list of names against her ribs brought her up short. She stared down at Célestine, who was staring back up at her, taut-faced and unreadable.

'What's wrong?' she said as soon as she reached Célestine's side.

Célestine wheeled fast towards Raphaël's office. 'I need to talk to you about the buoys,' she said, very slightly louder than necessary. A ghost crackled towards the Oracle Tower, and another, nearer, was speaking earnest Russian. Auli held tighter to the clipboard bearing the names of people who might be murderers, her heart within her chest like a bird. Not him, she was thinking, anyone but him.

Célestine pushed open his office door and wheeled herself in.

'Quickly,' she snapped over her shoulder, and Auli obeyed. Aware as the door clicked shut behind her, of her relief. Stupid, premature relief.

An Carline turned from her workbench to face Auli, and Auli's whole body flexed with horror.

'Her?' An said hoarsely. How was she not screaming? 'Not Joar?'

'She's better,' Célestine said shortly. 'I thought I told you to lie down.'

'As if that would help.'

Auli couldn't breathe.

Célestine glared up at her, daring her to show weakness, and Auli sucked in a breath, then another, went to touch the vial at her throat then stopped herself. 'An,' she said.

'We need the new treatment from Estonia. But Niki is a little tied up right now, no?'

Because only medics, and Niki, had the key to that particular cabinet. Only medics, one of whom had possibly used that key to get the poison that had killed Boudain. Célestine had come to her rather than her own lover. It seemed as though the Bellwether was restless on a rising sea, but the waters beyond the windows were calm.

'Right,' she said. 'I'll get it. We should move you to Niki's room, the bed—'

'I don't want anyone to know.'

Auli stared at the slight, fearsome tech. Her face was rigid with pain, and the very centre of her left eye was flickering between pupil and static, pupil and static. Her left hand, flat against her thigh, was flickering, too, around three fingertips. Auli couldn't see anything else, but it wouldn't be long. There were tiny beads of sweat along her hairline. 'An...' she began.

'I chose morphine, but I'm not taking it. I want the cure.'

'Right,' Auli repeated. 'Right. Célestine, can you get her comfortable on Raphaël's desk?'

Trying not to run, or show her incoherent panic, she cut across to Niki's lab, closed the door, checked the walkway outside, then bent to the infections cupboard. When news of the new treatment had reached them, they'd packed grab bags with all the necessary, strange items ready. She took two and tucked them between her chest and her clipboard.

Célestine had cleared Raphaël's desk apparently by sweeping everything onto her lap and was now dumping it all – papers, coffee cup, pencils – onto the floor. An was in Raphaël's chair, staring at her pixelating fingers as if she could fix them in place through will alone.

'Lie on the table?' Auli said, reaching for the valerian root, grabbing a profligate handful and laying a line across the doorway, then down, forming a rough oblong around the desk, the chair, and Célestine.

An shook her head once. The iris was pixelating now, and Auli's own eyes ached with imagined pain. The tearing apart of each cell, each neurone as the ghost turned it into code and static.

'I might need to...' she faltered.

'Tie her down,' Célestine finished. 'Well, we can tie her to the chair, no?'

Auli supposed that was true. She upended one grab bag onto the cleared table and read the instructions from across the water. An hissed in a breath, her hands spasming on the arms of the chair. The pixelation had spread past her fingertips. Auli snatched up one bottle, unstoppered it and held it to An's lips. She stared at Auli with one dark and one broken eye, then tipped her head and swallowed it all. 'For the pain,' Auli said, then opened a second one that smelled of bitter greenery. 'This one is the cure.'

But there was no cure.

This was a gamble on herbs and hedgewitchery none of them really believed in. An hissed again, her left eye crackled exactly the way a ghost did, and all three of them flinched. An downed the bottle and Auli set it back on the table gingerly. Then she looked at Célestine.

'You should go. I've got it from here.' Which was perhaps the greatest lie she'd yet told.

Célestine drew up one corner of her mouth, and Auli could have kissed her. 'You are an idiot. What is next on that list?'

'Rue.' She searched the sachets and handed it over. 'Scattered everywhere within the circle. Is there room for you to move?' She crouched by An's side, lifting her right hand to count her pulse, scanning her carefully. 'Is it anywhere else?' The heartbeat beneath her fingertips was fast and erratic, and fear clawed at Auli's bones. If only she was not the least brave person in the room.

An shook her head. The room smelled of herbs and lightning, the Bellwether creaked and the voices beyond the closed door seemed to be coming from the end of a long tunnel.

'Done. Now?' Célestine's wheels rustled over the dry herbs. 'Lavender water. What—'

'Empty the sand bucket and fill that.'

'What is it *for*?'

An groaned. The muscles of her jaw were tight as piano wires, and Auli felt utterly powerless. She wrapped her hand around An's whole one, watching the sickening there-and-gone of her eye, the flashes of socket, of retina and bone as the pixelation deepened. 'It's to put out sparks,' she said.

There was a metallic clanging and the sound of water against tin, and thank God this room was plumbed. For fire risk, ironically. 'I have broken your circle.'

Auli had no idea whether that mattered, nor whether the lavender water did either. This cure was for an infection that didn't fit the norms, and *sparks* were definitely not the norm. But it was all they had. 'I'll redo it once we have everything ready.'

An's right eye flickered. Her gaze drifted, entirely unlike herself, and Auli squeezed her hand. 'Is the opium starting to work?' An's broken gaze swayed back to her, dark and darker.

'Either that or you've grown wings,' she whispered.

Célestine snorted, her wheels crunched over herbs, the bucket hit the table with a splash. Auli reached for An's other hand, the decaying one. People had tried amputation in the early days. They'd tried cauterising and electrocution, but none of it worked. The ghost was in the nervous system, and there was nothing to be done but watch. All four fingers were degrading, first joints gone, knuckles flickering. Black static and white bone, flashing so quickly nausea roiled in Auli's stomach.

'You'll be alright,' she whispered.

An's eye flickered and wept vitreous jelly. One of the towers hailed a boat loudly and the scent of lavender slipped gently around them, but the nausea climbed Auli's throat inexorably. She wasn't strong enough, she thought desperately.

'You'll be alright,' she repeated, and her voice cracked wide open.

Another hand, browner than both of theirs, settled over Auli's where she was holding An's wrist. Auli quailed, An moaned faintly, her fingerbones were tiny clouds of static and Célestine's grip tightened.

'Now we wait,' she said.

Chapter Twenty-One

Auli

AN'S ARMS TWITCHED, her head thrashed sideways. Célestine and Auli glanced at one another and then to the slim cords that had tumbled out of the grab bag. It felt like cruelty, but it wasn't.

Célestine tied her wrists down, Auli knelt at her feet, An's thigh spasmed and her foot caught Auli on the cheek. She tied the ropes firmly and straightened, An opened her right eye, her left flickering bone and blood. It was worse that they never bled – made it more monstrous somehow.

'Gag me.'

Célestine glanced up from An's left wrist.

'If I scream, people will panic. So soon after Pertti. Gag me.'

Her whole eye was dilated and bloodshot, the opium and the pain slurring her words. Auli remembered the stretched silent howl of Pertti's drowned mouth and rose. 'I'll find something softer than the rope,' she said. Could she give An more opium? She knew the dosage for a death – enough people before this possible cure had opted not to wait for the ghost to sufficiently tear them apart. But what was the dosage of hope? She searched through the boxes and drawers of wires, tools, solder, paper, twists of salvaged metal. An groaned again.

Célestine said over her shoulder, 'Maybe faster, yes?'

Auli closed a drawer full of tiny screws and grabbing a pair of scissors, cut a strip from the bottom of her t-shirt.

Célestine grinned at her, unexpected and startling. 'PI Fraser, I am shocked.'

Auli said nothing, the flush pulsing against her bruised cheek. 'If you want it removed, knock twice with your fist,' she said to An, setting a strip of leather between her teeth to bite on and tying the cloth over her mouth. An nodded, a spasm shook her whole body and she made a strange, hissing groan that had too much static in it to be human. Auli stroked her hair away from the flickering void of her left eye and tried not to scream from the fear, the expectation of failure. Pertti was dead, perhaps because of her and her reckless meddling. She was the wrong person to be entrusted with this.

TEN MINUTES LATER, she pushed to her feet. 'I'm going to get Niki. I can't—'

Célestine reached over An's restless body and gripped Auli's hand hard enough to hurt. 'Yes, you can,' she said. 'An wants this private. You running through the Bellwether looking like' – she gestured with her free hand – 'this scared rabbit? No. You can do this.'

It could have been said comfortingly, but this was Célestine, so it was not. Strangely, though, it was still what Auli had needed to hear. She stared at the other woman for a long moment, then sat back down again with a thump. 'Push that bucket over,' she said. 'She doesn't seem to be shedding sparks so I may as well use it for something.'

She wiped the sweat from An's face, her neck, her arms,

the Bellwether tattoo stark against her blue-white skin. The scented water hissed when it neared her eye or her fingers but An leaned into the cloth, so Auli kept going. Célestine tidied the scattered medical kit, drummed her fingers on her wheels, read the instructions repeatedly, then pushed herself back to An's other side. Returned to watching An's tight, shattered face straining against invisible things.

'What do you know of your new junior?' Célestine said after another minute.

Auli started, then said blankly, 'Leigh?'

'Of course, Leigh.'

Auli rewetted and wrung out the cloth. 'Just that he was an archivist in England, at one of the old museums.'

'So he is here for the money, or the job?'

Auli studied Célestine's face. She was tying An's hair out of the way of her eye, as An shifted jerkily against the chair, mouth gasping beneath the cloth. 'Does it matter?' Auli said.

Célestine shot her a sharp, impenetrable glance. An twisted and all her hair escaped Célestine's grip. She swore softly in French and began again, her strong hands gentle. 'You do not think it strange that he comes just as everything goes to shit?'

Auli stiffened illogically. 'Have you been speaking to Raphaël?'

Célestine raised one perfect eyebrow. 'Rafa agrees with me? I tried to teach him the stats this morning and he does not want to learn, Fraser. I think he is here for something else, and I wondered whether it is murdering the Oracle.'

Auli didn't speak. A gull cried and a ghost was playing a tinny fragment of music on the research deck, but in here was just An's ragged breathing and the smell of herbs and lightning, the faint crackle of An's flesh becoming electricity.

Célestine carried on, 'You are still investigating Boudain's death, no? And Leigh, he arrived just before.'

'Yes,' Auli said. 'I mean. No, he didn't—'

'You are sure.'

An's whole body flexed, she screamed, muffled and hoarse. Auli eyed the opium bottle, thought of Niki's locked cupboards. 'He had no access to the drugs,' she said simply. 'Why are *you* sure?' she asked.

Célestine leaned back. Auli resumed wiping An's feverish skin. 'He asked too many questions. How did the seeding work, had I ever done it, was I here when those people died in the trials to recreate Oracles? Who would take over QD if not you?' She shrugged, then held her hand out for the cloth. 'He does not care for your work.'

Auli smiled very thinly and Célestine grinned at her without embarrassment. 'True. I do not either. But why was he sent, with neither the skills nor the interest?'

Auli had thought these same things herself. But still it stung, coming from Célestine. 'Because no one else wants to, I imagine,' she said. 'What would he achieve by killing the Oracle, what would *anyone* achieve killing Boudain? His job depends on her, and on Boudain—' She cut off.

Célestine shook her head, ran the cloth down An's left arm, stopping at the wrist. The static was halfway along the second joints. Had it stopped moving? Auli couldn't tell.

'Boudain Caron had power,' Célestine said, not ungently. 'People will always kill for that.'

Auli started to answer but then An's right eye opened, red and black and fixed on her. Tears leaked from its corner and Auli wrapped her hand around An's clenched fist and squeezed as An vibrated against the chair like she was being electrocuted, which she was. Auli prayed to anything listening that she would not be sick, would not pass out, would not flee in terror.

'So then. You have no doubts at all?'

She dragged her gaze back to Célestine, blinked hard, and was too sick with fear for An to be anything but honest.

'He is too fascinated by the Oracle. But he's harmless.' She shuddered as An shuddered. That blank black eye closed again, the other... it had stopped spreading, she thought. Something far more dangerous than fear sparked within her.

'What about your Joar?' she said rather than dwell on hope. 'He's the only one who had the opportunity to kill Boudain.' Although she had planned to ask Bea about those painkillers, she could hardly do so now. *Did you give your dead boyfriend the drugs he used to murder Boudain?* It was simultaneously absurd and deeply cruel.

'Joar is a fool, yes,' Célestine said without any of Auli's hostility. 'But I told you he is not a killer.' At Auli's raised eyebrows, she corrected herself. 'He is not a *murderer*, not like with Boudain. Poison. He would have used a knife, no? And been fifty kilometres away before dawn.'

Auli stroked An's right hand, watching the disintegrating finger bones of her left.

'Rafa questioned him. There is a cousin tangled up with the Survivors, yes. But Joar, he is not interested in doing the work of lunatics and Rafa believed him. You do not agree?' Célestine asked. Auli glanced up and realised belatedly that Célestine's questioning was about distracting herself as much as Auli.

'I don't know him.' An's arm was clammy with salt and sweat so Auli reclaimed the cloth. 'Warm water would be better for the muscle spasms,' she said. 'But he wasn't accidentally away from his post. You said he was spying? Who on, and who for?'

An thrashed, the chair creaked and someone knocked on the door.

'No!' Célestine shouted.

'Auli?' It was Leigh.

'Is it urgent?' Auli called, her hand on An's shoulder like that touch might ease anything at all. The Bellwether sidled and Leigh took a long time to answer.

'Not really...'

Any other time Auli would have gone anyway, she still wanted to. But she looked at the static and bone of An's left eye and said, 'I'll come once I'm finished here.'

The ghost consuming An crackled, her breaths rasped, and it was unimaginable that she wasn't screaming.

'Gabrielle,' Célestine said.

For a moment Auli had no idea what she was talking about.

Célestine pursed her lips. 'Gabrielle pays him a little extra to keep eyes on the other PIs, read their mail sometimes, that kind of thing. Or she did. Raphaël put, how do you say, the wind up him, and now he won't do it.'

Of course. What else would a person do who wanted to control all the workings of the Bellwether? But if Joar had read Boudain's mail, then did they both know about the Oracle replication project? Would Joar still be innocent then? Gabrielle had known Boudain was murdered. Gabrielle had resented Boudain's opposition... and Gabrielle did not have access to the locked medicines. But Joar did, and Pertti, who had died because of the Oracle's altered ghosts. Iolanta, Auli reminded herself. The girl's name was Iolanta. And knowing that didn't make Pertti less dead.

'You believe me.'

Auli blinked. An hissed and was there less static in it this time? Auli wiped her forehead again, gingerly past the storm of her pixelating eye, then checked the pulse in her wrist. Hot and fast and frail. 'About Joar? I don't know,' she said to Célestine eventually. 'But it wasn't Leigh. He had no access, and less motive, trust me. It's more likely to be Gabrielle herself.'

Célestine tipped her head, the light catching her brown eyes gold. She was holding An's left wrist as if her touch could wall up the decay, and An's hand was rigid beneath Célestine's palm and the bindings. But the decay had stopped progressing.

It really had *stopped*.

One moment of incandescent hope and then *what next?* What did they do next if this was all that happened? What if they'd saved her life only to condemn her indefinitely to *this*?

'Gabrielle,' Célestine said, 'is too frightened to do anything so dangerous to the Bellwether.'

Before this morning, and Pertti's death, Auli hadn't believed Gabrielle even knew what fear was.

'What did Leigh need Boudain alive for?' Célestine added. Auli should have known she'd pick up on that. 'Is this the *mysterious research* that is so unsavoury Auli Fraser wishes to block it?'

'Leigh said that?' Auli stared at her, then back at An's hand. Then at the flickering socket of her eye. 'Never mind, it doesn't matter. Do I give her another dose?' she said. 'Of the cure, not the opium.'

Célestine studied An, the sweat on her forehead and the thrumming tendons in her arms. 'Would she overdose?'

Auli re-read the instructions but there was no mention of second doses, only of a treatment for the comatose post-infection.

'We need to get Niki,' she said helplessly.

'Niki is likely elbow deep in my friend's chest cavity right now, trying to find out why he drowned in his own bed. I thought we had done this already. Make the decision, Auli. Stop looking for someone to do it for you.'

Auli stiffened and An thrashed against her restraints again, a groan forcing its way past her teeth like blood. Auli jumped up. 'Another dose.' She scrabbled for the second bag, found the right bottle and met Célestine's gaze. 'Right?' she said before she could stop herself.

There was none of the harshness from Célestine's words in her face, her eyes grave and perhaps even frightened. 'I have no training, Fraser. But if she stays like this...' She had noticed, too, then and thought the same things as Auli. They looked at one another with a strange and complete understanding.

'Okay,' Auli said. And opened the bottle, held it up to the light. The liquid inside was green as the heart of a driftwood flame.

The girl

SHE REMEMBERS HER name.

THE THOUGHT WHISPERS to her as the quiet woman hands her food, reminds her with tapped fingers to eat, drink. The girl likes that she does not talk because her own body is full of incantations, numbers, tidal currents, the scales of pale-bellied fish.

But the girl is not just salt-voices. She is also a name.

What was the girl's name in the story? another woman had said. She had eyes full of nightblack forests, and it reminded the girl of somewhere far ago.

The story, all warmth and river-song and blood, all strong arms and fingers combing her sleepy hair.

What was the girl's name?

Iolanta.

The girl holds the word in her mind like a rock and the pale-bellied fish part around it. Iolanta. Something is burning in her stomach and for once it is not numbers being pulled from her bones, but it still has teeth. Like the deep sea, like the voice murmuring dead horses and drowned men, oh, it has teeth.

She wonders how it is possible to breathe the ocean when you are just a girl from a forest. She remembers yearning for the water, long ago before it hurt. The quiet woman moves away and sparks in the girl's hair become tentacles, gentle around her shoulders, lightning along collar bones, tapping out a code against her pulse.

Oh, hello, she thinks, *hello.*

We will free ourselves, the tentacles tip tap, tip tap.

My name was Iolanta, she thinks. *They took it away. And the mama and the papa, they took them away. The river was full of blood.*

Tentacle around her throat soothing the hot ache beneath her skin. *They will bleed. And then we will be free.*

I don't want the blood.

But you want to be free.

'Yes,' the girl says.

The quiet woman looks up, the girl meets her eyes, and they are both so startled that they do not blink. And then the quiet woman smiles, very slightly, one tooth gleaming moonshine.

The girl still does not know what freedom is. But she understands what the deep-sea voice is offering her because she has drowned a hundred thousand times and hurt for almost all of them. She understands because she has remembered the forest and her own name.

'I want to go home,' she says.

They are all her own words, spoken from her own lungs and heart and teeth. It feels like she is on fire.

We together will be free, crackles the deepwater.

The girl rises, goes out onto the walkway, as high in the air as a bird, the waves far beneath her bare feet grey-blue and curling against her walls like a hundred fleeting eyes. There is no forest here.

Perhaps it would be freedom to climb over this rail and fall towards the water, the girl thinks. She wraps her hands around the saw-toothed metal. Her body remembers the water within and without, the salt-voices loud then quieting, quieting, and when she was exactly as much ocean as the wider sea, she had been briefly alone in her own skin.

No, the voice whispers. The tentacles flicker and crackle and caress. No, the girl thinks. She wants to see the forest again. There is no freedom in falling, she is not a bird even if sometimes she has been.

'I want to go home,' she repeats.

Set us free then. My child, let me in and set us free.

She reaches up a hand to the thing furled around her throat. Her fingers brush static and numbers and the slick salt wet skin of a blood red limb. She remembers the river water red and runnelling, and fears the bleeding but she fears the hook more.

'Yes,' she whispers.

Beneath her, something rises from the water, black-backed and roiling, flicker-static and one wide eye reflecting the flat sky. She waves.

Chapter Twenty-Two

Raphaël

When they returned to the Bellwether in the long arm of the afternoon, the fog was still just a slim grey line erasing the horizon like a ticking clock.

As the *Meri Noita* nosed up to the dock, Raphaël, up in the prow with the mooring line ready, watched a shoal of fish jig towards safety beneath the dock, then dart back out again as if something was under there. He half-lifted a hand to halt the boat but stopped himself. What was he expecting? A submarine attack? Divers? It would just be a bigger fish.

He leapt onto the dock and secured the rope in three quick moves. The sniper's body had gone, there was no one on the garden barges and only the Oracle alone on her tower walkway, no listener. He found himself moving faster than normal up into the Bellwether.

Gabrielle's voice and the rustle of people in the Hall calmed his pulse somewhat. Some meeting then, nothing more. There was, unsurprisingly, no one on the research deck other than Joar. The Oracle Room door was open, a swirl of degraded pixels within. Another ghost was near his office door, a video clip of the sea on fire, tiny boats spraying water. The thing touched his door and drifted backwards, and Raphaël paused.

The ghost did it again – drifted to his door, bounced gently away. He inhaled a bitter tang of static and something herbal, and his hackles were up before he heard someone inside the room talking very, very quietly.

'An? What the fuck are you up to in there?'

There was a creak he recognised instantly, but that didn't match the voice. 'Raphaël?'

'Auli.' He reached past the ghost gingerly, the hairs on his arm rising, and twisted the doorhandle. 'Unlock the door,' he added, stepping out of reach of the ghost, the sea burned on a loop within it.

Whispering again.

'Célestine, what's going on?' he said in French, reaching for his key but with the ghost there he'd struggle to get the angle without coming into contact.

He heard Célestine's wheels again, the key in the lock, and when the door swung inward the wave of valerian and lavender and something else he couldn't identify hit the ghost with a hiss. The burning sea fractured, spinning away. Célestine pushed backwards and he stepped over the line of herbs, shutting the door behind him, even as his heart plummeted like a rock.

'Be quiet,' Célestine said quickly. 'She is resting at last.'

He took the four steps to his desk and stared over it at An, at Auli kneeling at her side, back to An again, scanning the horror of her eye then noticing her hand.

'It's gone?' he said, his throat oddly dry.

Auli nodded. Her eyes were wide and shadowed, and his fingers curled into fists to stop himself reaching for her. Célestine joined him at the desk. 'That new treatment. Miraculous, no?'

Auli ducked her head, set a length of cord on the table. Restraints. An was sleeping now, a rolled jumper between shoulder and cheek, but she wouldn't have been sleeping earlier.

'She might need prosthetics. You will make her some, Rafa?'

Raphaël nodded, pulled his gaze from Auli's bent head to An's face and studied it closely. There was no static where her left eye had been, just the singed black socket, the line between cauterised flesh and unharmed as clean as if she'd drawn it with a compass.

'I won't know until she wakes whether it's travelled down the optic nerve. But the pain...' Auli stopped, shuddered and the anger Raphaël had been ignoring flared to life.

'Where is Niki? Why the hell are you two here? You could have got infected.'

'Ah,' Célestine said. She picked up the cords and began coiling them, her eyes on Auli full of knowing. Which was something else he needed to shout at her about. But he was still brittle from the adrenaline of last night, and he hated being frightened more than anything.

'Auli.'

She looked up at him. 'You were out too early to hear. Pertti died last night. So Niki is busy, and An—' She glanced at the staring black cavity of An's eye. 'An wanted it kept quiet.'

'That doesn't explain why you two? You're not the only medic. And you' – he glared at Célestine – 'are not a medic at all.'

Célestine lifted one shoulder. 'I think I did very well. Maybe I should train, too. I at least do not suffer from the being indecisive, yes?'

Auli huffed a laugh and Célestine grinned. Raphaël wanted to throttle them both. He wasn't sure he'd ever seen them laugh with one another; why did they have to choose now?

'She didn't scream once,' Auli said. 'Can you believe?'

He could. But Raphaël was still wrestling with his furious fear, until Célestine took pity on him.

'I found An, and Auli is the one who knows about these... these strange things happening. Maybe I even trust her,' she said, and at Auli's inhalation, added, 'With this. Not with being a PI, you are too quiet for that. Boudain kept Gabrielle from taking over completely, and you will not be able to.'

Rather than being either hurt or angry, Auli only smiled very slightly and shook her head.

'You think you will?' Célestine said, elbows on her arm rests.

'I think it doesn't matter,' Auli said gently. She looked up at An's unfamiliarly vulnerable face, then rose smoothly to her feet. 'We have bigger problems than Gabrielle's ambitions.'

'Two ghost infections in one night,' Raphaël observed pointedly.

'This started yesterday,' Célestine said. 'Slow onset, else she'd be dead rather than...' She waved a hand. Maimed but alive, perhaps recovered; Raphaël guessed it depended on whether she woke up sane.

'And Pertti—' Auli cut off, glanced at Célestine. 'Pertti was killed by something like the storm ghost.' She described Pertti's body and Raphaël sank into the empty chair, running a hand over his mouth to hide the shock.

'Gabrielle has said it was a normal ghost death,' Célestine added. 'But everyone knows there is a problem with the ghosts, yes? So we need to be told what is being done. We risk our lives here every day, so it is wrong to hide the truth of this place from us.'

Auli met Raphaël's gaze. An stirred but did not wake.

'What is it?' Célestine said to both of them.

'Nothing,' he said.

Auli lifted An's wrist and pressed her fingers into the underside, her eyes distant and intent. Célestine made a soft noise of derision and glowered at Raphaël but he was unrepentant. He didn't care about people's feelings, he cared about security. Some truths would only make his job harder.

Setting An's wrist down, Auli looked at Célestine. 'The truth of this place,' she repeated.

Raphaël swore silently. A rising swell of voices from the research deck meant the meeting had ended and Raphaël wanted to speak to the last researchers who'd spent leave ashore, but he clearly couldn't leave these two in the room together at the moment.

'Auli,' he said. 'Sorry, Célestine, but I agree with Gabrielle. We can't afford to add fuel to rumours.'

'But if she promises not to tell?' Auli said with a too-sweet smile at Célestine that made them both laugh. 'She knows Boudain was murdered and has not told. She knows your boatman is Gabrielle's spy, which you hid from me. I know you disapprove of trusting people, Raphaël, but surely you trust *her*.'

The barb stung.

An moved and the folded jumper fell to her lap, the singed black stumps of her fingers curling slightly on the arm of Raphaël's chair.

He pulled down a blanket from the top shelf, laying it on the floor beneath the windows. 'She's safe to move?' Auli nodded and Raphaël scooped An up, then lowered her to the floor where she curled onto her side childlike, the black, eroded socket of her left eye staring up at them like an accusation. 'Christ,' he whispered. He turned away abruptly for the boxes along the west wall, a tray of leather offcuts, another of rivets, muttering in French about steaming and shaping, about what he would give for a new source of elastic. Célestine interrupted his thoughts.

'And so? Will you tell me, or shall I roll out there and shout about Boudain's murder, and Pertti's murder, until you have no secrets left?'

Raphaël's hands stilled, set a piece of leather down.

Auli was selecting dressings from the first aid kit and spoke without looking up. 'Certain ghosts are attacking us, rather than just infecting us. I think it is because the Oracle is nearing adulthood. Neurological changes perhaps, combined with...' She set the bandages down and looked at Célestine gravely.

Raphaël wished they'd go back to sniping at one another, which was rather hypocritical considering how often he'd wished they'd stop. 'You might have been the target last night, Auli. Not the Oracle,' he said, in an attempt to divert her. It didn't even earn him a sideways glance from either of them.

'I remember when she started her periods,' Célestine said. 'So many died in just a few months.'

Auli nodded, and some of the strain left her face at being believed. 'After Uoti was hurt we altered the Oracle's... treatment... to give her a chance to stabilise herself. I hope that will settle the ghosts soon.'

'You hope?'

'Or you're making it worse,' Raphaël pointed out cruelly. An's infection and Pertti' death only confirmed his opinion – it was too dangerous to be playing with the Oracle's stability right now. He could, theoretically, exile her for it. Gabrielle and Uoti combined could, too, if they knew.

Célestine tapped her wheel rim, staring out at the low bulk of Äspskär where a sniper had nearly killed Auli less than twenty-four hours ago. Auli pushed away from the workbench. 'I need dressings from Niki's room. I'll—'

There was a shout and crash of furniture. Raphaël took the three quick steps to the inner door, opening it just wide enough to scan the deck. Tobias and Leigh were standing in the Centre beside Joar, one of the Oceans desks lying on its side. A ghost spiralled above them, caught in the light through the library windows. It was a ship, burning. A different fire to the one batting at the door earlier, the footage from sea level rather than the sky, the ship an ugly, listing hulk.

'Someone getting cornered?' Célestine said from behind him.

'Ye—' Raphaël realised something. 'Not quite,' he amended. The table that had fallen over was smoking and blackened, the smell of burning varnish reaching them belatedly. Gabrielle opened her office door and stepped out, her hands smoothing her clothes like she was preparing herself for battle. Raphaël felt a little sorry for her. She might have wanted control of the Bellwether, but she wasn't much enjoying the experience.

'So again?' Célestine growled, stretching past him to shut the door. He turned, surprised, but she gave him no chance to speak. 'A ghost attacks? We need to decide quickly what we are going to do.' She clapped her hands once, and Auli stiffened.

'With what?' Raphaël said.

Célestine gave him the look his comment deserved. 'Do we go along with whatever fiction Gabrielle is constructing, or do we tell the truth?'

'Will it help? We don't have answers yet,' Auli said quietly. Behind her a raven lofted down to the railing with a neat clatter of wings and eyed An speculatively through the glass.

'We know it is a temporary instability while the Oracle adjusts to—' Célestine frowned at Auli. 'To what, exactly? What is it you have changed?'

Raphaël shifted, considered interrupting, but figured Auli's honesty might backfire.

'The drugs that have kept her permanently catatonic for years,' Auli said bluntly.

Célestine hissed.

'The drugs that have kept her from harming herself,' Raphaël amended.

Auli glared at him, colour on her cheeks from anger as much as betrayal. The space between them felt uncrossable. 'That is definitely a convenient framing,' she said. 'I'm sure you have all managed to convince yourselves of it, even though there is no evidence to support you other than garbled reports from over a decade ago.'

'Alright then. The drugs that have kept her from harming *others*. And since you lowered the doses, Pertti has died. An is—'

'No,' Célestine cut him off. 'Maybe Pertti, but An's was a normal infection. She tinkered with haunted electronics and got infected. There's nothing new about that.'

'There was more than one ghost, that's a little odd,' Raphaël said.

Auli winced. 'Your kraken and Leigh and Uoti, they were all before—' she began, and then the raven croaked, and An came awake with a scream.

By the time Raphaël reached them, Auli had her hands either side of An's face as if infection weren't a risk at all, for fuck's sake, and was talking in a soft murmur. Raphaël just about stopped himself yanking Auli back to safety by fixing his gaze belligerently on the raven canting its glossy head.

Auli fed them, and laughed at them, but he'd never been able to get past the memory of crows lifting off the corpse of a woman on the road north of Paris long ago.

When he looked at An, over Auli's shoulder, his whole body shuddered with relief at the heat in her one remaining eye. If she was this angry then she remained herself.

'You're still with us then?' he observed. She shifted that one eye to him and narrowed it.

'You're all wrong,' she said, her voice as raw and painful as an open wound. Raphaël winced. 'The Oracle might be the mechanism, but she isn't the cause.'

'What then?' Célestine said. 'Another Oracle? Has someone found a way to control ghosts? Is it an attack?'

'A cyberattack for the new world,' Raphaël said softly, making her laugh.

'No,' Auli said. 'It's not an attack, not from the outside.'

'Oh, really, how are you so very sure?' Célestine said.

An's eye had drifted closed, but now it opened again, and she shifted, thrashed briefly until Auli helped her sit up against the window.

The movement cost her, and she tipped her head back, breathing through her teeth. It was beginning to darken in the room, but Raphaël made no move to light any lamps. 'Auli?' he said softly.

She shook her head, her gaze on An. 'It's something to do with stories,' she said, nonsensically. 'No one pays any attention to story ghosts. And yet that's what has been behind each attack. The anomalies are stories gaining…' She paused, searching, Raphaël guessed, for a word that wouldn't incite derision. 'Force,' she finished.

'This again!' Célestine said.

Auli smiled at her. 'Exactly. Everyone agrees they are unimportant, which is why this isn't an attack from outside. It *is* just the Oracle, An. Her instability and her… search for something, I think. No one has learned how to control ghosts. Thank God.'

'Only they have,' An said without opening her eye. The hollowed-out socket watched them darkly. Raphaël couldn't understand how she wasn't half-mad with pain.

'Who has then?' Célestine asked.

An's eye opened, and it was Auli she spoke to. 'The sea.'

Perhaps she *was* half-mad, Raphaël corrected himself.

'Pardon?' Célestine said, half-laughing.

But Auli leaned back, her eyes on the window and the raven outside. 'Oh,' she said quietly. 'That makes perfect sense.'

The girl

THE GIRL SEARCHES the darkening skyline for forest but there is only the waiting water, grey-green islands hunched and strewn about. The forest, *her* forest, was towering columns and pad-footed with moss. Patchwork sky of green and hidden blue, birdsong, the panting of the old dog. She had forgotten the old dog although now the hot weight of him echoes against her ribs. She is so used to fish scales and deepwater currents that the memory of softness startles her; almost as much as remembering her name.

Iolanta.

She whispers it to the sea. 'Iolanta.'

The waves murmur far beneath her, and she wants to press her hands into them, not for drowning but for friendship. The sea promised her they would be free, and she wants to remember being held. She turns from the skyline and searches for the stairs. It is dark in the stairwell after the luminous sky, and the steps feel unfamiliar, like she has never gone this way before, but she has. She has, only this time she's carrying her own bones.

The room below is full of sunset and a voice all numbers

and colours, and she shies away from it because she is holding her name in her head alongside the memory of trees and she doesn't want to breathe in voices not her own. The quiet woman touches the bottle at her neck. The girl does not have a bottle; for the first time she wonders why.

The girl trails her fingers along the wall, wanting the long pathway of the sea, the waves whispering. She will go down to the water and...

But there is a man in the doorway.

A knife at his hip. A bad man.

And the girl remembers blades slicing her pale white belly a thousand times, she remembers blood in the water and her entrails, her tail thrashing, too weak, too late, too slow. The bad man moves and *Help me,* she thinks. The room sways and she stumbles through numbers and electricity. Someone shouts and she is bleeding, she is bleeding. *Make the bad man go away,* she thinks. Voices in her lungs and, 'Make the bad man go away!' she says. 'Make him go *away*!'

The sea croons. *Yes*, it says.

The room rocks, the sunset across the floor is red as poppies, red as blood all spilling in the water. She presses her hands to her pale white belly, expecting scales, intestines, but she is whole. The room is full of lightning, and someone is screaming but it is not her. It is not her.

Chapter Twenty-Three

Auli

They heard the screaming just as Célestine opened her mouth to speak, and it was Raphaël, of course, who moved first. Out the door before Auli had even risen to her feet.

'Another one?' Célestine gasped. Auli had never heard her this way. Like beneath it all, she might bleed.

'Fraser,' An whispered. Beneath the shouts, that one unending scream, Auli almost didn't hear her, but the scream cut off as she bent down. It had been a man, she realised, not the Oracle. She wasn't sure whether that was good or bad.

'Do you want some pain relief?' she asked.

The Bellwether creaked all through its frame like bones. Célestine's chair rolled until she halted herself and spun on the spot, saying, 'I'll go find out.'

An opened her eye. 'No. It's not bad.' Which was clearly a lie. 'Listen, you asked if I could kill them. I don't think we can, entirely.'

Auli hunkered down, staring at An's fixed, urgent gaze, her blackened socket.

'It's like picking mushrooms,' An said. 'Or... that Greek woman with the snakes. Even if I can kill them, it won't *stop* them. You have to figure out another way, and for that you need to know the *why*.'

Her hand twitched, she hissed out a breath, and Auli jerked upright. 'I'll get wound dressings,' she said. And Niki. The rest of the Bellwether would see An soon enough, and it was a victory now, of sorts. Compared to whatever had just happened out there, someone surviving infection would be wondrous.

There were two boatmen in the Centre, and Célestine heading for her winch. The books above them were rustling, and the air smelled of ghosts and blood.

'Fraser,' Célestine called across the deck, as if they had not just spent a day together saving someone's life. 'You need to stop whatever you were playing with. It failed.' She rolled onto the winch platform and yanked on the handle before even strapping herself in place. Raphaël would berate her if he saw, but he was in the Oracle Room, with whatever had changed Célestine's mind, and Auli needed to be with An.

Niki was in their room, banging cupboards open. 'There you are. You need to see what's just happened.'

'Give me ten minutes,' Auli pleaded. 'I have to dress some wounds, then I'll come find you.'

'We must— Wait, who is wounded?' They shook their head. 'No. Unless they are dying, tell me after.'

Which meant the person screaming was still alive, but only just. Niki was gathering dressings, steriliser and sutures, not the ghost infection kits. And when they'd left Auli stood in the strange, soughing silence, thinking of Célestine's anger, with the fear of having made a cataclysmic mistake wrapping around her throat until she could not breathe.

An refused a dressing on her eye, but did take the painkillers Auli offered, and let her dress her fingers when Auli pointed out she'd have no use of the hand otherwise. She'd lost the top two joints on her three middle fingers, just the first joint on her fifth. The black wounds were like a thin skin of negative space, her fingers not so much severed as deleted. Once she'd finished, Auli handed An water and dried fruits gathered from her own desk.

'You should rest.' The strain of staying awake, of staying calm showed in every muscle of An's torso, but the engineer only shook her head.

'I want to know what happened.'

And yet Auli really did not.

'You need to work it out,' An insisted. 'Why the sea's directing the ghosts, or using the Oracle to do so. Find the answer before more people die.'

A dozen protests circled Auli's head, but she said none of them aloud. The sky beyond the window was a bruised blue, stars over the islands like distant eyes. Was it only a day since a sniper bullet had cracked the window where she was sitting, while Pertti ran around the Bellwether, drunk and defenceless and laughing?

What if Raphaël was right, and she'd made it all worse?

And yet how could it possibly be wrong to give a child back her own name? In what world could that be bad?

In this one. In this world, haunted by its own furious past.

FIND THE ANSWER, An had said. Auli left her and stood beneath the library dome listening to the voices from the Oracle Room.

What would Boudain do? He would ask Auli what her hypothesis was. Uoti would be checking his team were calm and fed and as safe as possible. Gabrielle was in the Oracle Room, trying to frame whatever had happened into insignificance.

What would Auli do? She gathered a clipboard from her desk, then took a deep breath and headed for the Oracle Room.

'Auli?' Leigh's voice caught her just as she was reaching for the door and she turned, startled. He was standing in the shadows of the North Tower stairwell, his pale t-shirt gleaming.

'Leigh? Are you alright? I thought you'd been sent downstairs.'

'We were, I just… What's happening?' He took a few steps forward, and she wondered whether he was wishing he'd never come here.

'I don't know yet,' she said honestly. Less honestly, 'I'll tell you all as soon as I do.'

He nodded but made no move to leave.

'Is there something else?' She'd meant to ask it kindly, but the tenor of the voices in the room behind her, the long, awful day at An's side made her words hard.

'So it's just… Are they on that sniper's trail? Will they catch him?'

Oh God, Auli thought. Not now. 'Hellä's pretty unstoppable,' she said.

Leigh nodded jerkily. 'They asked if we recognised the… one they killed.'

'And?' Auli said, again too harshly.

'And, umm, I do.' He took another few steps closer, the sunset catching him slantwise, making his eyes darker.

'Did you tell the boatmen?'

There was a ghost up in the library speaking some Slavic tongue, and another near Bea's desk just static and flickers of scrolling code. Leigh stopped two paces from her.

'I just… I wanted to tell you, you know?'

'Okay,' she said. Her skin was prickling as if the ghosts were far closer, Célestine's insinuations getting beneath her skin. But Célestine was wrong.

He spoke in a rush, 'They were on the fishing boat I caught from Oslo to Turku. Said they were trading engine parts for Russian copper. They didn't tell me their names.'

It was an unremarkable story. She'd heard about the mines in Russia's far east – the gruelling inhumanity of them, the fires. What would you choose, the fire or the asphyxiating dark? Had her brother chosen the fire or the sea? A new ghost crossed through the window on their right. Leigh glanced at it then back to her, fidgeting.

'Did you mention the College?' she said. 'Did you say you were coming here? Did they ask anything?'

Leigh hummed thoughtfully. The new ghost murmured, and if it was telling a story, Auli realised, or from a film, they were in more danger than before.

'I don't remember.' She caught a flash of teeth in the gloom, his charming, boyish smile. 'They had vodka, and we got a little worse for wear, you know? I wish I knew something useful, but I honestly don't remember, Auli. They were pretty convincing, I guess. I never suspected a thing.'

'You must remember if you talked about the College.'

'You don't believe me.' He stepped back, closer to the ghost he'd forgotten to track.

'What?' Auli shook her head. 'I do. And I'll tell the captain you have information for him.'

'*The hydra lernaia, page forty-eight*,' the ghost murmured. Leigh flinched away, his hand coming to his throat. '*The kraken, page fifty-three. The lusca, page one hundred and four; rockas, prister, and the horror vacui.*' Auli lifted her clipboard reflexively, began writing. '*The sisters Scylla and Charybdis, page forty-six. All the benign beings of the sea made monstrous by man.*'

Auli wished more lamps were lit.

'Go, Leigh,' she said. 'Go back down to the others. This ghost isn't safe.'

He hesitated, but only fleetingly. The ghost hissed, and Leigh's rapid footsteps faded away. Then Auli took a deep breath, thinking of guilt and stories and data collection.

She said softly, 'Why are—'

The door behind her opened, and she half-fell, was half-hauled into the room, the door slamming again inches from her face, and Raphaël's black scowl filled her vision.

'Oh no, you do not,' he snapped. 'Do you have *no* sense of self-preservation?'

Auli straightened out of his hold and smiled up at him victoriously. '*All the benign beings of the sea made monstrous by man*,' she quoted. 'I know the answer to An's question.'

Raphaël

RAPHAËL WISHED FERVENTLY she wouldn't smile at him like that when he was furious with her. He also wished she made sense. Not much did, right know, which was making his skin crawl. 'What the hell?' he said.

But she'd seen beyond him, and all that blazing light in her face vanished.

'What's—' She brushed past him. Alan was guarding the stairs and Auli was far too quick for his liking sometimes. 'She's up there? Alone?'

Alan glanced over his shoulder briefly. Niki was still stitching bits of Joar back together and Ursula was slumped unconscious in the more comfortable of the chairs. Raphaël leaned against the wall and folded his arms. 'She's asleep,' he said.

Gabrielle paused her pacing beside the window long enough to level Auli with a glare. 'Your first concern is the Oracle and not the two injured staff members, PI Fraser?' The slightest emphasis on the title.

Auli didn't reply, only touched Alan on the arm and said, 'Excuse me,' and waited without looking at anyone other than the boatman. Alan looked to Raphaël then stepped aside and Auli ran lightly up the stairs. She was, Raphaël thought, braver than all of them in some ways.

'What exactly has she done to the Oracle?' Gabrielle said to no one in particular.

Niki moved down to Joar's legs. Raphaël breathed a little deeper. If they were finished suturing the chest wounds, then things must be more stable.

'Captain?'

Raphaël didn't shift his gaze. 'Let me know when you want him moved,' he said to Niki. The doctor nodded, held a length of thread up to the nearest storm lamp and lifted their needle. Raphaël remained surprised at how quickly their needles blunted. They were hard to come by and expensive, and he'd never realised the cumulative toll of human flesh even on metal.

'You both ignoring me is rather revealing,' Gabrielle snapped. 'Are you protecting her, Captain? If I have to explain the paucity of forecasts to our funders, I will not do the same for either of you.'

It had been days since the last reliable one, and God, but wouldn't that be stirring the hornets' nest. 'Nothing this morning?'

'No. And my Lead Forecaster absented herself for the whole day, so her second had to pull something together unaided. This College—'

She had been bottling this all day, Raphaël guessed. Since Pertti's death, and now here with two unconscious bodies, a boatman she'd likely forgotten about, and Raphaël and Niki, she was done with pretending to be calm.

'—This College cannot function amidst disorder. We have a *role to fulfil* if we are to survive. Am I the only one on board who remembers that fact?'

She wasn't entirely wrong.

'Alan, upstairs, would you?' Raphaël said softly. He obeyed immediately, boots far louder on the stairs than Auli had been, his knuckles tapping the wall.

Niki nudged the storm lamp, reached for a swab, bent back to their work. Gabrielle lowered into a chair with a sigh, straightening her trousers precisely. 'What are you doing, Raphaël? Our new PI has destabilised the Oracle, which is your department. She's jeopardised our ability to deliver our basic output, which is mine. I am not risking my job, or this place, to cover for her.' She glared at the empty stairs. 'If you won't exile her, will you at least keep these incidences from Helsinki long enough for me to resolve this mess?'

'What are you more worried about – the deaths or your reputation?' Niki asked, without looking up.

Gabrielle pursed her lips. 'People die all the time, especially here. If we fix the damage, no one need lose their place.'

This time Niki did look up, their hands stilling in midair. If Raphaël had not checked Joar's vitals himself, he'd think they were piecing together a corpse. They were oddly similar, Gabrielle and Niki, though they might not realise it – both of them unable to ever go home, her banished for resisting a mean-fisted, powerful man; them because they refused to be something they were not.

Raphaël spoke into the silence. 'The crew are asking questions, and we need to put safety protocols into place whilst avoiding panic. So whatever we tell them the blame game can wait.'

But Gabrielle wasn't thinking about the crew. 'This is making us look *weak*. *She* is weakening us.'

'We're not as defenceless as we were yesterday,' Raphaël observed.

Niki studied Joar's leg bleakly. 'Perhaps we should evacuate to Mariehamm until this is resolved. Auli's staged dose reduction will take about a month, depending on—

'*Staged reduction?*'

Niki went to run their hand over their face, realised it was covered in blood and swore softly in Polish.

'We can't evacuate,' Raphaël said. 'For one, Mariehamm gets jumpy enough about the expedition teams, they'd burn us out if the whole research crew showed up. For another—' He studied the darkening window. 'There's fog coming in, and I'm not risking anyone on a blind crossing unless there's no other choice. Even if the batteries would last multiple trips, which they won't.'

'Fog?' Niki said desolately.

'So,' Gabrielle said briskly, 'we limit listening duties to inside the Bellwether, make the Oracle Tower and library out of bounds and...' She grimaced. 'And permit the use of valerian powder in emergencies. Raphaël, can you distribute a small allowance?'

Raphaël nodded, but added, 'I think we'd do well to ask Auli for guidance. She's figured out something of a pattern to the ghosts.'

Gabrielle made a hard, scornful sound in the back of her throat. 'Why doesn't that surprise me? Actually, being as we have the forecasting emergency to deal with, perhaps the listening duties should be juggled by her team, for now. It would be more efficient.'

'There's only two of them,' Niki observed. They had finished stitching and were now checking Joar's vitals again. The boatman's face was deathly pale beneath the beard.

'If Fraser is behind the current *instability*, then who better to monitor it.'

Raphaël respected Gabrielle for her dedication if nothing else, but something very, very close to hate soured his gut now. 'Throwing your competition to the lions, Gabrielle?'

Gabrielle rose sharply to her feet. The Bellwether shifted at the same moment, so she staggered briefly and, if anything, this made her more furious. 'Yes,' she snapped. 'If she's the one who created them.'

She strode across to the inner door, glared at Raphaël still leaning beside it. 'If she doesn't come explain this *withdrawal* to me tonight, I swear I will see her off this College, one way or another, Captain. And anyone who has supported her in the disaster she has unleashed. Understood?'

Raphaël didn't answer, simply held her fierce gaze steadily until she hissed, and slammed out of the room.

'I told Auli I couldn't risk my place here,' Niki said after a moment. They moved to the carer's side, repositioning her sling gently. 'I wasn't willing to do anything about Boudain's death, but somehow she persuaded me to agree to this.' They smiled wryly, and Raphaël huffed a laugh.

'Of course she did. Do you wish you'd refused?'

Niki sank into the chair Gabrielle had vacated, stretching their legs out with a groan. 'We should set a cot up in here for Ursula, let her sleep this off. And move Joar to my room. She should be fine by morning, shoulder aside. He, however... Well, we'll see.'

The ceiling creaked, and Raphaël desperately wanted to check on Auli. It was far too easy to picture her lying like Joar was, sliced to ribbons by a ghost, halfway to death from electric shock and blood loss.

'Boudain's murder,' Niki said eventually, 'seems a very long time ago, doesn't it? But we still don't know who killed him—'

'I've a couple of ideas,' Raphaël interjected, not at all defensively.

Niki looked unconvinced. 'Do you?'

Raphaël shook his head. 'What now?'

Niki was easily diverted, understandably. 'With the Oracle? Her data were convincing, you know? Lower sedation doses should stabilise cantation rates. But I don't think that's why

Auli wanted to change things, and I... I suppose she made me ashamed. She has reminded me to be ashamed.' They paused. 'I cannot call myself a good doctor, considering what I have done to the Oracle. But I think Auli's morality will kill more people than mine. So where does that leave us?'

'*Do* you think it will settle in a month, like you told Gabrielle?'

Niki opened their mouth, then paused, their eyes on the stairs.

Raphaël followed their gaze.

'No,' Auli said quietly. The storm lamps cast angled light and shadow up at her, so she seemed segmented, already fragmenting. Her eyes were huge and black in her pale face, and Raphaël's lungs seized. 'No, it will not settle.'

From the corner of his eye, Raphaël saw Niki nodding slowly, but he didn't look away as she descended silently towards him.

'So we restore full doses,' Niki said.

Auli stopped. One hand on the wall and the calm was a lie, he realised. She was half a second from either tears or terror. 'I do not think even that will help,' she said, still and quiet as a moth. 'Not now.'

'What—'

Raphaël raised his hand and Niki fell silent.

'This needs coffee, and those two need dealing with,' he said, jerking a chin at Joar and the carer. 'My office, fifteen minutes.' He left to summon help before either could gainsay him.

An woke when Raphaël entered his office exactly fourteen minutes later. He'd thought she might and wanted her in this conversation – for her problem solving and also the likelihood that Auli would listen to her.

'Coffee?' he offered, handing over a mug. She pushed herself gingerly to sitting, her back against the wide black windows. Beyond the Bellwether's shadows, the bay scintillated in the moonlight. He lay a pastry down beside her foot, set his chair where he could see both her and the door, and leaned back in it with a sigh. 'I can make you a patch tomorrow,' he said, breathing in the steam of his coffee.

'I don't want one,' An snapped. 'It'll get in the way.'

Raphaël raised his mug in salute. Then the door opened, and Auli and Niki entered, Niki's gasp making An visibly bristle.

'An,' Niki said. 'What—'

'There were three ghosts in a bit of tech,' she said sharply. 'I was trying to isolate them in separate nodes when they infected me. Auli and Célestine treated me with that newfangled cure. It worked. Now can we get on with the important things?'

Auli laughed softly, Niki looked like they wanted to protest, and perhaps only Raphaël was close enough to see the line of sweat along An's hairline, the white knuckles of her unharmed hand. He filled the silence by updating her, and perhaps Auli, on what had happened in the Oracle Room.

'The Oracle got distressed, a ghost attacked Joar and somehow in the struggle, the carer was thrown against a wall, dislocating her shoulder. Joar may or may not make it. The ghost left. The Oracle has been sedated.'

An nodded, closed her one eye and leaned her head back against the window. Auli pulled herself up onto the workbench opposite Raphaël, and Niki, still watching An intently, claimed the other chair.

'What was the ghost?' Auli asked.

'Does it matter?' Niki said.

Yes, Raphaël thought. It clearly does. Stories, she'd said. The kraken ghost that… intersected with their boat, the storm ghost devouring the Bellwether whole – he had no idea what lines Auli drew between them all, but she clearly saw *something*.

'I don't know,' he said honestly. 'It was a photograph of a fishing vessel, but the audio was something about a "Tinirau"? I was paying more attention to Joar being sliced to ribbons.'

Auli tugged on her ponytail thoughtfully and An murmured, 'Another fused one, then. Is that the pattern? That they're combining, like in a wave interference pattern around the Oracle?'

'No, you were right before,' Auli said. 'The Oracle might be the conduit, but the sea is sending a message.'

'Hell of a message,' Raphaël said.

She nodded slowly. 'Well, yes. I think the message is that it wants us dead.'

Chapter Twenty-Four

Auli

THE WORDS LEFT trails of heat in Auli's throat, and she didn't know how much was fear, and how much disbelief. The Bellwether sighed, multi-tonal like it held the echoes of An's earlier agony, and also of the Oracle crying in her sleep like a wounded puppy. Like a child.

'That makes no sense,' Niki said, shaking their head firmly, making the lamplight dance on their glasses. 'You're talking about the sea as if it is sentient. It's just water.'

Auli nodded again, Raphaël twitched as if suppressing some movement and she did not want to know how little he believed her. 'It is,' she said. 'And it isn't.'

An snorted quietly and something beyond the outer door crackled. The night was nothing now but reflections and darkness, with no way of knowing what the ghost was, butting against the glass. Auli shuddered and rose, holding out a hand to An. 'Come away from the window. You can lie on the bench. You still look…' She stopped, and An's dark eye met hers with a flicker of amusement.

'No more beauty contests for me,' she said, but she accepted Auli's supporting arm and then Raphaël's, holding her left hand away from her body. She levered herself onto the bench with a sigh. The ghost crackled against the glass again, and Auli smiled at An.

'You look absolutely badass,' she said. An laughed, then cut off with a hiss of pain.

'Philosophy aside, what about the Oracle?' Niki said, frowning at Auli. 'She's the centre of all this.'

'I think the sea is using her.' But she had only guesses and suspended horror, and if only the world would give her *time to collect data*. 'She is fighting the drugs to regain a little control, I think. And the sea is using her greater awareness to… direct ghosts and attack us.'

'Why Pertti?' Raphaël said. 'Assuming you're right and there's some inexplicable interaction between the Oracle's emotions and… violent ghosts, I can understand Uoti and Joar being attacked, even the new kid. But why Pertti? He was in his bed, nowhere near the Oracle.'

She didn't know. She *didn't know,* and Raphaël could see that, curse him, but that didn't mean she was *wrong*. 'He was on listening duty last,' she said. 'And then when he was doing the ghost races maybe… I don't know. Maybe he just pissed the sea off.'

Raphaël opened his mouth to argue but Niki beat him to it. Auli was so exhausted she wanted to bury her head in her hands and weep.

'The *sea* is *not sentient,*' they said again, glowering at Auli, not in outrage but in sheer disbelief that she, a researcher, could be so absurd. She knew exactly what they were thinking because she was thinking it too, and yet logic didn't matter right now. They were running down some hidden fuse but all everyone wanted to do was sit around debating the existence of the bomb.

'You're right,' she agreed wearily, rubbing her herb-stained hands together. Such solid flesh and bone, so easy to destroy.

'The sea is just water. But how many of the ghosts here are narratives about the sea? We never stopped to wonder what would happen if we sat the Oracle in the sea like the world's largest ghost beacon, and let the ghosts gather. We never wondered whether all these ghosts, all telling stories of the ocean, might...' She searched for words that sounded something less than hokum.

'Merge,' An whispered. From where Auli was sitting, at An's feet, all Auli could see of her face was her lips in a hard line, the stark black hollow of her consumed eye socket. 'Amplify. Wave interference patterns.'

But Niki was unrelenting. 'Fine. I can see merged ghosts occurring at high densities. But that is not what Auli is saying.'

'What happens if you constantly tell someone they are monstrous?' Auli said. 'What happens if you tell them that every day, you... hurt them, and hurt them, and then tell them they are monstrous? What would happen to that person?'

No one spoke. She braced herself for their mockery with her heart in her throat like a bird. Somewhere a ghost sang a slow, rocking song and the room reflected in the windows spectral.

'Huh,' An said eventually. 'Well, we're fucked then.'

'What?' Niki said. 'I don't see it. What do you mean?'

Auli looked to An, but it was Raphaël who shifted sharply in his chair and spoke. 'If we treat someone cruelly, and tell them they are monstrous, what do they become?' he said softly. 'They become monstrous.'

'That's not—' Niki began and Auli could hear all their arguments already – psychology and the sentience of three atoms combined – and they would be right. She couldn't explain it. There weren't the data for this, only cumulative almost-nothings, and then the ghost earlier murmuring, *All the benign beings of the sea made monstrous by man.*

'So, the sea is becoming monstrous,' Raphaël cut Niki

off. 'That's what you're saying. The sea has developed... intention, or personality because of all the ghosts we've concentrated here.'

It sounded ridiculous. Auli nodded, wordless.

'It sounds ridiculous,' An said.

'Because it *is*.' Niki took their glasses off to rub a thumb and forefinger roughly into their eyes. 'It's impossible. There's a far better explanation for all this, Auli, and you know it. I don't understand why—'

'No, wait.' Raphaël leaned forward intently – dear God, if only he would stop staring at her as if he wanted to read her bones then perhaps Auli would be able to explain. 'Wait, Niki. She has a reason.'

An rolled her head so her right eye could see them all. Pain flickered over her face. Auli touched her ankle fleetingly, and An gave her the shadow of a smile. If An could bear what she was bearing, Auli told herself firmly, then Auli, too, could bear a fraction as much.

'I do,' she said, pulling herself straighter. 'I need more data but there's no other explanation that fits. If it were just the Oracle influencing the ghosts, then it wouldn't have killed Pertti. Or attacked your boat away from the Bellwether, Raphaël. It would be any ghost type, not just one. If it was only the Oracle, it would correlate with her diurnal rhythms, too, or her sedation or moods but it doesn't... entirely.'

Niki raised their eyebrows but remained silent.

'It's not random ghosts, it's ghosts that tell stories about the sea, and it started before we dropped her dosages.' She lifted her clasped hands and dropped them again. 'I do think it's linked to her. She gained awareness the night Boudain died, and she's been more aware ever since. So yes, she's at the centre of it, but the pattern to the stories... they contain a *motivation*. And I don't think she's aware enough for any kind of coherent desire. Not yet.'

Silence other than distant ghosts, the constant voices of the sea and the Bellwether.

'Gaining awareness because she missed a dose,' Niki said sharply. They pushed to their feet, frowning at all three of them. 'An, you need to be in a bed, take Boudain's as Auli still hasn't moved in. I'll come see you after I've checked Joar.' They turned for the door, then spun back and said to Auli, 'It might be our doing, that Pertti is dead and Joar and the carer and An are all injured. So we are undoing it. You have not even convinced yourself of your wild theories, let alone me. We're restoring her previous regime.'

'But—' Auli began.

'No. I am the doctor, Auli. I will not have people harmed because you have a wild hunch. An, bed, I mean it.' They left, shutting the door softly behind them despite their anger.

Auli stared after them and thought maybe Raphaël was right. Maybe she was mad to want to protect one girl more than the whole Bellwether or the wider sea, tying her own logic in knots to avoid culpability.

'They're not entirely wrong,' Raphaël said softly, and Auli flinched.

'You're onto something,' An said. She showed no signs of obeying Niki's order, but her eye was closed, her left hand dangling off the workbench like a lure. 'But you need to prove it.'

'How?' Auli asked, more forlorn than she intended.

An flexed her maimed hand. 'You're the researcher, figure it out.'

Raphaël laughed softly, while outside on the walkway, something called for help. They all jerked, and Raphaël, Auli saw, had gone for his gun. They were so utterly ill-equipped even now after living with the ghosts' tithe for years, listening to a strange girl's cantations, and thinking themselves experts. What hubris it was, to assume they understood either the ghosts, or the girl or the sea.

She opened her mouth to speak but a new sound rang through the Bellwether and Raphaël moved quickly out onto the walkway, staring west towards the open sea.

'Fog,' Auli whispered. 'That was the fog bell.'

'Perfect timing,' An answered, as softly. 'Just when the ghosts are weaponising, we can't see or hear them.'

AULI WENT OUT to stand beside Raphaël, looking into the blank black night and seeing what the boatman in the tower had seen. The stars winking out; on the far tip of Kantör the headland light flared once then once again, blurred by a veil of mist.

'I'm imposing new rules tomorrow,' Raphaël said quietly. 'And issuing valerian rations. Will it still help?'

Would it have saved Joar? Auli wondered. Célestine was right to be angry. 'It might give people time. But it only *deters* normal ghosts, it doesn't weaken them. So I can't see it making much difference to a ghost bent on harm.'

She expected more questions, but he just nodded silently, still watching the Kantör light. 'Any suggestions for safety measures?' he said. 'Oh, and you need to talk to Gabrielle. Come clean about the dosage changes before she forces Uoti to co-sign your exile, she's on a hair-trigger.'

Auli sighed. Their hands on the railing were three centimetres apart, beneath them a ghost was sparking against the tops of the waves. 'Treat any ghost that isn't pure data with additional wariness. Move slowly so you have time to tell. Stay away from the Oracle.' *Prove it*, An had said. 'Report any anomalies to me. I'm going to survey the whole place, log all the ghosts and their behaviours.'

'Niki's data,' Raphaël murmured. 'I don't like it.'

'Not just Niki's data,' she said. 'Whether I'm right or wrong, we need to understand the patterns so we can respond.'

He made a pensive sound then turned, leaning against the railing and studying her intently in the spillover light from inside. 'I'll get a boatman to help you, you shouldn't be without back-up.'

She thought about protesting, but he was right.

'Niki's correct though, Auli. With the fog, the ghosts and the more human killers, we need the Oracle firmly sedated. You do see that, right? I know it's imperfect, but Niki's taken it out of your hands now, so all you need to do is not make that harder on them. And' – his voice changed – 'for the love of God, *stop risking yourself* so much.'

Auli couldn't look at him, she didn't dare. The fog bell tolled strangely in the dark, the Bellwether soughed, and she wavered on her feet. Her heart echoed within her ribs and when Raphaël lifted a hand to brush loose hair back from her face, there was no helping herself. She leaned into his touch, just a little.

'Auli,' he whispered. 'Auli, please.'

She made the mistake of meeting his gaze. Made the mistake of yearning.

His other hand came up to cradle her face and when he kissed her, every muscle in her body turned to honey. She pressed forward, his arm coming around her like they belonged, his hair beneath her fingers so familiar, his hunger and her response so achingly familiar.

The ghost over the water groaned, and Auli jerked away from Raphaël, her lips burning, her whole body aflame with want, but she couldn't handle him just now. Not the him that was full of a longing he'd once denied.

Do you love me? she had asked him, long ago.

He'd kissed her until she nearly forgot the question, but when he stopped, she'd asked it again. *Do you love me?*

Auli, he'd said. And that would have been enough, but he had carried on. *I don't want love. I can't.*

She stepped back now just like she had then, and met his gaze, helpless with a whole different fear. Not ghosts or haunted children, just this man and the familiar, futile lurch of her heart towards him.

'No,' she said. 'I can't, Raphaël.'

He dropped his hands slowly, and made no effort to stop her escape, but only said as the fog obscured the stars, 'Someday, Auli, we'll need to face this.'

'Maybe,' she said from the doorway. 'But not today.'

Chapter Twenty-Five

Auli

She checked on the sleeping carer in the Oracle Room, unfamiliar with her face relaxed and hands empty. It made Auli realise how guarded the woman always was, that her face in sleep could be so altered.

Then she went up to the top of the tower and watched the girl again. Collected her forgotten clipboard from the desk cluttered with feathers and shells, sea glass and twists of wire. Gifts from the ravens; no one else had ever brought this child precious things.

Three ghosts drifted around the girl in lazy orbits. A cloud of blue text in a black haze. A video interview of two men with heavy headsets. And a photograph of a bay full of blood, of smooth black bodies, small boats and men with caps pulled down as if to hide their faces from the world. Auli studied that photograph for a long moment then sketched it sparsely and slipped outside to check the walkway. The fog curled around her, serpentine and colder than she'd been expecting. As if she had only been warm before because Raphaël had been there, but she shut that thought away before it could burn. Although it was too late, she admitted sadly, for that.

There were two more ghosts out here. One murmuring a news report about hurricanes brewing in the Atlantic, the other – she halted – the other an animated film clip. A man with a hook for a hand and a crocodile with a tick-tock heart, a story full of villains, including the boy at the centre of it all. She wrote it down, then went back inside, down and down again through the near-silent College, recording ghosts all the way.

It was nearly midnight now. But there was light along the base of Gabrielle's door and so Auli made herself knock without hesitating.

'Yes?'

'It's Auli.'

The door opened, spilling light into the dark corridor, catching the fretted edges of a ghost drifting in Auli's wake – the other reason she had not prevaricated. Gabrielle returned to a desk messy with papers, letters, budget sheets, reports. One of them was in Niki's distinctive scrawl and at the sight of it, Auli realised something.

'Pertti's funeral,' she gasped. 'We didn't—' They had not sent him to rest, they had forgotten him.

'We'll do it tomorrow.' Gabrielle moved the autopsy report aside with a grimace. 'There might be two of them by then anyway.'

Efficient, as ever. 'Have you spoken to Bea, or Célestine?'

The skin around Gabrielle's eyes tightened. 'Yes. They will both be fine. Everyone knows relationships on here are a bad idea. This is not a soft place.'

What could you possibly say to that? 'What were you working on?' she said instead.

'Pacifying everyone waiting on the data they have paid for,' Gabrielle snapped.

'The fog's in now. No one's coming in or leaving for as long as it lasts.'

'Which might be less than twenty-four hours, Fraser. We can hardly bank on the weather to keep us safe.'

'No, I suppose not.' Auli told herself it was like ripping off a plaster. 'Niki is reinstating the old sedation doses for the Oracle.' Gabrielle's eyes widened, Auli carried on quickly. 'My analyses suggested the high doses were destabilising her, so we were stepping them down, but after today, well...' She lifted her shoulders.

Gabrielle blinked. 'Niki would never have tampered with safety protocols alone. You must have convinced them of this recklessness.'

That was what Raphaël had called her. She could still feel his kiss, his embrace, the way he had whispered her name like nothing else mattered. 'I did. The data are strongly indicative, but I can't prove that what happened to Pertti and Joar wasn't a result of reducing the sedation. I'm gathering more data.' And her whole moral compass was spinning bewildered within her.

Gabrielle pursed her lips. 'I don't understand you, Fraser.'

'What do you mean?'

She leaned back, glared at the papers on her desk then at Auli. 'Your complete disregard for safety has endangered the College *and* its mission. You should be gone, but,' she sighed, 'there are few enough of us left already. Once this is all over, I will recommend to the university we absorb the QD unit into Weather. I want the best for the College, and we both know you aren't it.'

Auli thought for one horrible moment she would pass out, there at Gabrielle's feet, proving all her judgements correct. She was not *enough* for this, not loud enough or assured or political or even sociable enough. And yet for the first time, these familiar facts did not sting. All day long she'd been fearful, but the storm within her now was something new. She wished she knew whether her brother had chosen the fire or the waves. *Grow a spine*, she thought to herself yet again, and yet again, *Grow wings*.

'You want the best for the College,' she said slowly. 'But you don't *know* the College, not really. You see it as a political entity you can hold within your hands. Something you can control. But you can't.'

'And you can?'

Auli shook her head, frustrated. She had held An's hand while a ghost consumed her, watched the Oracle crying in her sleep, and she'd always been frightened of this woman but there were bigger things to fear now, which left no room within her for anything else. 'I don't want to. This place isn't a *thing*, Gabrielle. It's not a *tool*. It is a community built around the imprisonment of a miraculous child—' Gabrielle hissed but Auli couldn't stop. 'A community carrying ongoing trauma from death and the fear of death. But when a murder happens in this community, all you care about is covering it up. Which is interesting, by the way. When that imprisoned child starts pushing against her bars, all you care about is strengthening them. When the stochastic danger of the ghosts morphs into an unknown threat, all you care about is intimidating the one person seeking to understand this threat, maybe even stop it. You don't want the best for this College, you just want the power the College grants you, so go ahead, if you want to. Recommend my demotion, or expulsion. But at least be honest about why.' She stopped, breathless and shaking.

If she had hoped this moment would feel powerful, she was disillusioned now. There were no victory wings aflight within her, only frustration and the weight of all the work still to do.

Gabrielle did not move. The ghost in the corridor crackled faintly.

'You think I'm heartless.'

Yes, Auli did. But the way she said it, full of a tired bitterness that perfectly echoed Auli's own mood, silenced her.

Gabrielle nodded. 'Maybe I am. But I am heartless because we will not survive here if we are weak. You think you are too moral and academic to dirty yourself wrestling for power, but if the College weakens, it will be destroyed, and then what will become of the Oracle? You think there is any scenario in which she gets to be free? You think *any of us* have anywhere left to go back to?'

'Some of—'

'I was fond of Boudain, and Pertti, and want no more death on board than is unavoidable. But no one ever promised the College was safe. The staff can handle a little danger. What they cannot handle is losing their only home to hostile takeover, or unnecessary panic.'

'Unnecessary panic,' Auli repeated flatly. And then, '*Were* you fond of Boudain? Or did you resent him?'

Gabrielle glared at her. Next door Uoti coughed and Auli realised he might know nothing of today's endless calamities. It was as if the College was theirs now, these two women both adamant the other was wrong. She sighed and pressed the clipboard against her ribs. Now was not the time.

'Never mind,' she said. 'Perhaps this is what the Bellwether needs – one of us fending off the enemies outside and one of us guarding against the enemies within.' She half-smiled at the irony of her standing guard against anything at all.

Gabrielle shook her head wearily but still could not let Auli have the last word. 'Find your answers, then. But do it with the Oracle sedated, or you'll be in Mariehamm before you realise, fog be damned.'

Auli wanted, oh God how much she wanted, to ask who Gabrielle thought would pilot Auli through the fog to Mariehamm, because Auli was almost certain Raphaël would not, and thus none of his boatmen either. She didn't ask though.

Because she did not need to be petty; not at all because

he had kissed her and she had walked away, so she was only *almost certain* after all.

IT WAS ONE o'clock when she climbed the last of the guard towers and found Bea perched on the walkway, the boatman around the far side beside the accusatory shape of the harpoon, his eyes on the fog and his finger flat over the trigger of his rifle. Auli paused at the top of the stairs. The air smelled of valerian.

'Evening,' Bea said softly. 'Nice weather for ghosts.'

Auli was surely intruding. 'What are you doing up here?'

'There was one of those new ghosts in the library. I thought I'd track it.' A faint shape of a clipboard was raised. 'Thought it might be useful.'

'Oh,' Auli said. 'That's... Bea, I'm so sorry about—'

'I know.' Bea shook their head firmly once, without looking up. 'Everyone's sorry. And I know they said it'll stop now you've sorted out the Oracle's meds, but... he's still dead. And I want to know why.'

Auli feared she might cry. 'You don't have to do this, Bea. It's—'

'Dangerous. I know.' They sounded almost angry, almost pleading. 'But I need to understand. And I can help, too – it's *story ghosts*, Auli. I have to help.'

'Okay,' Auli whispered. Bea's dark shape sagged with relief. 'What were you told about the Oracle's meds?'

A pause. The walkway quivered as the boatman moved. 'Just that there was a problem that Niki resolved. Why?'

'It doesn't matter. What was the ghost? And was...' She had two reasons for asking, only one of them kind. 'Was Pertti taking anything that might have made him more vulnerable?'

That sense of a fuse burning quietly would not leave her,

and if most of that was the Oracle, some of it was also Boudain.

'It was an animation, waves with eyes, climbing the rocks towards two kids. But the audio was a news report about fishing quotas.' Bea turned her head. 'He took painkillers sometimes. An old injury that could be unbearable. I... I gave him some a few days ago. Oh God, did I—'

'No! No, painkillers wouldn't be to blame, Bea. It wasn't you. It was the ghosts.' And that was both questions answered. He hadn't been weakened; he hadn't been a murderer.

They swayed gently, five storeys above the hidden sea as Auli looked blindly at her notes.

'The combined ghosts,' Bea said, their voice choked and briny. 'That's the anomaly, right?'

'Yes,' Auli said. Narratives about a vengeful sea, and an exploited one; that made seven anomalies so far. The fog swallowed up their voices like it was starving.

'Would it have attacked me, like with Joar, and Pertti? Would it have drowned me, too?'

'Maybe. You threw valerian though, that's good.' Was it? 'Get some sleep, Bea, and we'll start again in the morning. You can't track anything in this.'

Bea nodded but didn't move.

'Fucking fog,' the boatman murmured.

Auli agreed. She slipped silently down the ink-black, ocean-black stairwell, passing the research deck and the second deck like lighthouses in the dark.

Raphaël

AFTER SETTING OUT the new safety protocols the next morning and discovering that everyone now mysteriously knew Boudain had been murdered, Raphaël followed Célestine up to her desk.

The research deck had three ghosts that he didn't stop to identify, and his footsteps across the floor sounded far louder than normal. The ravens called from the dome and – Raphaël swore softly – Auli and Alan were up on the library's second floor. Because of course she'd assumed his rules did not apply to her. He reached Célestine's desk and sat heavily beside her.

'You are glowering,' she said in French.

'I'm not glowering.'

She smiled. 'Of course you are. And of course it is because your Auli is in the library. She and Bea are doing six-hourly ghost surveys, apparently. She's very thorough, I'll give her that.'

'She's not—' he cut off, curled his right hand into a fist and knocked it against the desk to dislodge the memory. 'And I am glowering at you because you talk too much. I know you are worried for Joar, but telling everyone Caron was murdered?'

Célestine's smile didn't waver but her eyes were dark and grave. Anyone who hadn't known her for years would think she was being flippant. 'Look what happens when we keep secrets. If we'd put these protocols into place when Uoti was hurt, Pertti might be alive. Joar might be unhurt. We deserve to know about the ghosts, and about the murderer, Rafa. We are not your boatmen to obey you without question. We need facts.' She shrugged elegantly.

'The ghost anomalies and the fog are not facts enough?'

'They are fuel for wild theories, Boudain is the one bit of certainty. People trying to kill the Oracle is so familiar it is a comfort.'

He snorted a laugh, loud in the unnatural quiet. The silence rule did not apply indoors away from the fog, and yet no one was talking. Pretending to work but not well. He had no idea how many of them spoke French and gave up the argument as lost.

'You are very obvious,' Célestine said.

Raphaël realised where his attention had drifted and said something his mother would have smacked him for, but that made Célestine laugh, and he added very quietly, 'Did you really do it to protect her, or because you don't like her?'

She, of course, knew exactly what he meant. 'Perhaps both, no? But perhaps I was wrong about both, too.' She looked up where Raphaël had, to Auli just now sliding down to the lower library level. 'I am not so sure she is someone who needs sheltering. Least of all from you.' Someone dropped a pencil and leapt up from their chair – Leigh Alvarez, a ghost drifting towards him. 'Oh,' Célestine added, watching Leigh. 'She said he knew that dead man you left on the dock like a fish.'

Raphaël came alert like a hound. But Célestine was studying her chipped nails and added very quietly, 'Niki is not hopeful.'

He touched her wrist. 'I know. But they have been wrong before.'

She nodded jerkily. 'So, this fog could sit here a while. If it's a high-pressure dome to the south.'

Meaning she had done enough talking of Joar.

He rose and looked down at the nonsensical numbers and hand-drawn graphs in front of her, caught by a memory from before – her pulling up models on three different screens, showing him lines in electric blue and ranting about capitalism and oceanic warming.

'We'll survive,' he said, touching her shoulder lightly.

She glanced up at him and smiled. 'We always do.'

But he walked away from her with the unsettling feeling that for the first time she didn't entirely believe it.

HE SPOKE TO the young idiot in his office. His little set fire had worked, although not perfectly – Alvarez was terrified the second sniper would identify him and was clearly guilty of being in the pay of lunatics. Near-incoherent with nerves, he confessed to a mad plan to duplicate the Oracle, vehemently denied wanting Auli removed from his path, and the only thing stopping Raphaël turfing him overboard was the conviction that he wasn't actually capable of either.

Perhaps the snipers hadn't been after Auli, then. He wished Hellä would send news of the Survivors' recent activities.

The kid left, and An turned from her workbench, the hollow eye and the white gauze on her fingers startling Raphaël all over again. He nodded at the bench. 'Not learned your lesson then?'

'Never.' She pointed the soldering iron at him. 'You thought he fed information to the snipers.'

'Someone did, but I doubt it was him, don't you?' Raphaël shook his head. It would have fitted so well, if not for Leigh being so convincingly inept. Which meant his distrust of the idiot's *niceness* was unfounded, mostly, but he still didn't have to like him. 'Shouldn't you be resting?'

An scoffed. 'We need a weapon.'

Raphaël stilled. 'For the ghosts?'

She frowned down at her work, angling her head a little differently to before. 'The ones that want to kill us, yes. They owe me an eye, and I am *tired* of letting them win for the love of fuck.'

Raphaël had no idea how to respond.

An shrugged sharply. 'We kill them, Auli settles the Oracle, I can get back to doing my actual damn job,' she added flatly.

He moved to the bench, trying to figure out what she was making. 'It looks like a taser?'

'It'll be the opposite once it's done.'

Raphaël reached to touch it and was slapped away. 'So... it earths the ghost? But...' He looked at the wooden floor and the sea beyond, baffled. They didn't become suddenly undone when they touched walls or water. Otherwise, the Bellwether would be practically safe normally, and absolutely safe now.

'Polarises it. Strong magnetic field, resets all the data, reduces the ghost to a bunch of zeros.'

'And that'll stop them?' Why was a cloud of reset binary code any less dangerous than a cloud of whatever code the ghosts were to start with?

She set the soldering iron down with a bang and rounded on Raphaël, her eye bright and hard. All the more so for the lines of strain around it. 'Do you want me to explain it or get it working because I can do one or the other, but not both.'

Raphaël grinned at her, then added, 'Okay, but you don't have to do this alone. Anyone in Oceans would be grateful for the distraction.'

She switched her glare back to her work, then sighed and flexed her left hand without lifting it off the bench. 'Fine. If you see one of them, send them in.' Which was as much as he'd get from her. And he would absolutely be taking the win.

BEA DROPPED THEIR book when he approached, looking up at him anxiously. They'd been on two expeditions with him to deploy buoys, and only held their arm like that when they were hurting.

'How is Joar doing?' they said in a whisper.

Suvi rose and drifted into hearing range, her hands twisting a pencil round and round.

'Well enough,' Raphaël said, with more confidence than Niki had intimated. There were signs of infection, of the old-fashioned sort. 'You're helping Auli study the anomalous ghosts?'

Bea nodded. Suvi glanced at one currently spinning slow circles outside the Oracle Room door. 'Like that one?' she said, even more quietly than normal. 'But what about the murderer? Who is looking for them?'

'I am,' Raphaël said, at the same time Bea said, 'Auli is.' He tried not to glower and carried on, 'Boudain's murderer isn't interested in killing anyone else.' Which probably wasn't as comforting as he'd intended. 'The only danger now is these ghosts. Stay away from them and you'll be fine.'

Bea opened their mouth to say something else but then someone shouted Auli's name from the deck below. 'Fraser? Where are you?'

It was Niki, Raphaël realised. And it boded nothing good at all.

The girl

SHE CAME DOWN here in the dark alone, and doesn't think she's been here before, or not often. Or never as herself. Beneath her feet are waves that lick up between wooden planks like hook-tipped tongues.

You and I, the voice murmurs. She thinks she has been alone since that day in the forest, by a river running red. It is nice not to be alone anymore, to have someone whisper, *You and I*, and it be like a sunrise. There is one of the bad men behind her, she walked past him not looking, not looking, not looking. Not thinking of the bad man in the room who had tried to stop her opening the door. Not thinking of his screams.

The quiet person is not here, she is never not here, but the girl is alone and no one has come to set hooks in her. She is so close to something she only half-recognises.

The girl whispers to the sea.

'My name is Iolanta. I want to go home.'

Beneath her, beneath the old wood and the new teeth, beneath the silver fish something stirs. It roils in the hidden water, making the boards rise and groan.

We will be free, the voice says from a mouth full of hunger. Yes, she thinks. And she looks up at the boat.

She remembers watching this boat slip away over the waves, sails like a head held proudly, its wake a banner of hair. The beast beneath stretches its cold muscles all static and slow fury, the voice murmurs but she is already stepping lightly onto the boat.

Then a bad man's voice.

A bad man's thumping footsteps, the beast hangs in the dark waiting, and she is scrambling across the boat. Away, away, but he is following her and shouting and his eyes are white as the moon, his teeth wet, his hand grasping.

No, she thinks.

Hush now, lyubimy. Hush now.

Come on, you can't go on the boats. Hey, Dvorak, is that fucking carer up yet? Come on, get off there. Hey—

No! She writhes frantic. *Let me go let me go let me—*

Whoa, shit. Okay, okay, Jesus.

The boards hit her knees, and she presses down against them, the waves curling over her wrists. *Hush,* she thinks. *Until the bad men leave.* There are teeth in the water, flickers of light and a strange, flat eye as large as her hand.

The girl stares at the eye and the eye stares back. The boards rock and slow, her heart tight in her throat slows, and the eye does not blink so neither does she.

You can't go, the bad man said.

It has to be us together, the voice says.

She watches the beast in the water and realises there is no way home. The bad men found her once. They found her and carried her from the forest over the sea, and they will keep finding her. And there is no way home because they will not let her go.

'My name is Iolanta,' she whispers to the monster. 'Will you make the bad men leave?'

The monster waits.

The sea sighs, salt on her tongue like blood or music. She has spoken so many voices and the only one to answer was this deepwater snaggle-toothed voice, promising freedom. She didn't understand what freedom was, but now she knows what it isn't.

Set us free then, the voice whispers, or the beast, or both.

How? She doesn't even know how to hide from the bad men because she tried. She tried to hush and tried to hide but still they found them and her papochka bled into the river. Her mama…

Tell our story, the voice whispers.

Tell their story?

The monster flexes its arms in the shadows, tiny fish cower into the crannies of the dock.

'Long, long ago,' the girl begins. She remembers wood fires and wolf-pawed nights. She thinks of wolves and witches, the clever girls and broken ones, and the one who became a burning bird to escape her captor. 'Long, long ago,' she repeats. The tide rises softly in her bones, and she fears the drowning, but not enough to stop. 'There was a girl who wanted to be free.' The beast lifts towards her, she presses her cheek harder to the boards.

Hey, Niki, can you come…

'She asked the beast from the deep to aid her, and the beast flashed its sharp teeth.' The beast flashes its sharp teeth, her heart beats tidal and the boards rock harder. 'The beast…' It waits. She doesn't know how the story goes. She can only remember a boy riding a wolf and a firebird shedding feathers, a witch in her terrible house consuming children. 'The beast came to help the girl?' she whispers, shivering, salt laden. 'It drove the bad men away?'

The boards heave, someone shouts, and then someone else.

Yes, the deepwater voice says.

The Salt Oracle

The beast bursts out from beneath her, thrashing tentacles and its great red body all scarred from a hundred stories. A blast of sound makes the girl cry out, flatten against the bucking boards, water washing over her and sparks in her veins like burning feathers.

Yes, she thinks.

She wants to watch the monster drive the bad men away, but the boards will not stop heaving and her fingers scrabble, other voices clamouring in her lungs now, and the beast's tentacles wrap themselves around the dock. Numbers fill up her throat, spill from her lips all salt and blood and she cannot remember the story anymore. The beast groans, the boards lurch and a man shouts with a crack down the middle.

'Ventspils,' she whispers. 'Latvia, oh one dash eleven dash two thousand and twenty-two, one thousand nine hundred, overcast, ten percent, ten degrees, nine degrees, S, four, seven, G, ninety-four percent.'

The tentacles flicker and for a moment, just a moment, in between the ninety-four and the Ventspils, she remembers the forest and the story and her name. 'Ventspils,' she whispers, with tears on her cheeks that burn like lightning. The beast is gone. 'Latvia, oh one dash eleven dash two thousand and twenty-two, one thousand eight hundred, overcast...'

The boards' wild bucking slows, the fog folds over her all silver and cold. The girl curls alone around her unfamiliar heart, whispering numbers.

Chapter Twenty-Six

Auli

AULI REACHED THE researcher barge, going room to room, checking for ghosts. Pertti's room had one, sparking faintly along the edge of the stripped mattress. Just audio and static, and she listened to it for a while, but it was only a weather report in English from a storm season long ago.

'The highest gusts were eight-four knots, ninety-seven miles per hour, at Needles Old Battery, Isle of... and eighty-one... at Aberdaron, Gwynedd. Inland... eighty-nine miles... Capel Curig, Conwy.'

'Rather her than me, those things are creepy.'

Auli stilled. The window was open, Leigh's voice coming from the roof deck.

'I don't think they killed Pertti though. I think whoever murdered Boudain killed him to cover their tracks. Ghosts don't drown people, everyone knows that. That's a cover story.'

She pressed the palm of her free hand against the wall. That one was Tobias.

'What? What about that boatman then, and why would they cover up a murder?'

'Because one of them is the killer – Auli or Gabrielle or the captain.'

She'd quite liked Tobias; he was funny and keen and had a clever smile. He thought she was a murderer.

'Auli?' Leigh laughed. 'She wouldn't! How about *Pertti* killed Boudain, for the job?'

'So the captain took him out?' Tobias said. 'No. Pertti was too cautious to *kill*.'

'You think Auli Fraser isn't?'

'Maybe it was Gabrielle. Everyone knows he drove her up the wall.'

'If these anomaly ghosts *did* kill Pertti then why not Boudain, too? Maybe there's no murderer at all.'

Tobias snorted. 'Célestine said it was poison. Ever heard of a ghost *poisoning* you?'

Oh, Auli thought. Célestine, really?

Silence other than the ghost talking and out in the fog, muted explosions, muted screams. She hoped that was another ghost.

Tobias laughed, enjoying not being the new guy a little too much. 'Don't worry about it. This will blow over and you can get back to your secret project.'

Auli turned to the door, but then Leigh said, 'Did you know they had to keep her sedated?'

Auli froze.

'No,' Tobias said. 'But it makes sense. She's dangerous enough.'

Leigh hummed.

'I hate this fog. Hope it clears soon.'

'At least there'll be no more snipers,' Tobias said.

Leigh didn't answer.

Auli left Pertti's haunted room behind. She didn't want to hate them, but it bubbled within her anyway. That they could look straight at the Bellwether's blackened heart and see only their own skins.

Then there was shouting that was not ghosts; a gunshot, more shouting, and Auli was running down the barge, up to the walkway, only hesitating in the middle of the bridge when the shouts rose again. Nothing all around her except close-pressed mist, the looming Bellwether and voices shifting oddly through the fog. The hairs on the back of her neck prickled and she spun around, but there was nothing there. She hadn't, she realised, even reached for her valerian. The years on here had stripped her of the instinct, but she gathered a small fistful now, and moved forward, feet sliding over the metal bars like she might escape both the ghosts and whatever calamity was unfolding ahead if only she could pass unnoticed.

Rounding East Tower, past the obscured garden barges without seeing anything or meeting anyone. The shouting stopped, but the fog still held voices. The restless, roving haze crept across her path like it was seeking purchase. Auli could taste salt and her own fear on her lips, but she kept moving until she reached the steps down to the dock.

'There you are!'

Niki, half-colourless from the mist, was staring up at her with something like exasperation.

'Yes,' she agreed. 'What is it?' Some animal part of her was telling her to flee, to not under any conditions go down those steps, but she released the herbs back into her pocket and set her hand lightly on the wet railing. Whatever was awaiting her, she felt sure a handful of herbs would not help.

'It's the Oracle,' they said when she was halfway down. There were other charcoal silhouettes out on the dock, the *Meri Noita* half-visible and half-not, as if it had been severed in two, and her heart lurched. Their one way off this place.

'You're bleeding,' she said, reaching the bottom of the steps.

They glanced down at their arm with a touch of surprise.

'You didn't notice?' Auli reached up to test the skin beneath the wound gently, assessing. 'What was it?' Because this was not the thin slices she'd seen on Joar or Leigh, it was more like welts.

'It's not deep,' they said. 'Come on.' Moving away along the dock unsteadily and without answering. Auli followed, the dock, like the gangway, an island suspended in pale infinity, the sea reflecting the mist like a mirror.

There were four people at the far end – Ursula, the Oracle, Alan and Raphaël. The Oracle was kneeling, swaying with the motion of the boards, the carer standing behind her. Both the men were sitting on the edge of the dock just beyond the boat, their legs in the water.

'Have they… been *swimming*?' she whispered to Niki.

Raphaël turned and met her gaze, hauled himself easily to his feet and scrubbed the water off his face with one hand.

'A ghost took Miika,' he said shortly.

Alan shifted, said, 'I'm trying again.' And dropped into the water before anyone could stop him. The water closed over him without a splash, just like it had over Boudain's body.

'Took him into the *water*?' she said.

'It was a… sea monster,' Niki said. 'It got hold of him, I tried to grab him but got knocked back and then he was gone. And the monster, too.'

The Oracle was murmuring to herself, Auli realised. The slip-slopping of water beneath the boards and the strange acoustics of the fog had hidden it. She knelt down within arm's reach, and her heart ached beyond bearing when Raphaël jerked forward as if to pull her away and then stopped himself. But the girl was cantating a fragment of code, and the air around them was for the moment void of anything that might want to consume her.

'A ghost sea monster,' she said quietly. 'It came out of the water? And went back into the water?'

'Ghosts don't move through water,' Niki said. 'The conductivity is too high, it breaks them apart.'

Raphaël pulled his wet shirt off over his head and wrung it out. Auli paid absolute attention to the Oracle's whispering, and when Alan surfaced beside the dock, she saw the girl flinch very slightly.

'Nothing,' he said.

'The current will have taken him down past Svartkläpper,' Raphaël said, hauling Alan up onto the dock. Even shirtless and dripping, he managed to be at his most brutal, his most closed. 'We'll check the shoreline in a day or two. He might come up.'

Auli tried as hard as she could not to picture the boatman, his scars and his tales of past glory all down there with a ghost of a monster that had never existed at all. 'Stories,' she said softly to herself.

Niki crouched next to her. 'We need to get her inside, but she recoils if I touch her. I wondered...' They glanced up at Ursula and back to Auli hopefully. Auli very slowly reached out a hand.

'Iolanta,' she said, and Niki started. 'Iolanta, it's Auli. Remember me? You told me a story about a girl in the forest.'

She touched the Oracle's curled fist gently, the stream of consonants faltered. A wave rocked the boards and Alan took a step towards them. It was only to steady himself, but the girl flinched again.

'Can you leave us?' Auli said, looking up and meeting Raphaël's shuttered gaze. 'It's the boatmen making her nervous. If you move away, Ursula and I can get her to her room.' She turned her head and repeated herself to the carer. The fog drifted around them and out over the water, men sang in harmony there and gone again.

Raphaël studied the curled form of the Oracle and nodded shortly. 'We'll stay within sight.'

'You should go get changed.'

He flashed her a bladed grin, and shook his head, water falling from his curls. Niki backed away a little and, gently, she slid her hand into the girl's.

'Iolanta, come on, let's get you warm.' Nothing. The cantation had stopped but the girl's gaze was empty. The dock rocked as Raphaël and Alan withdrew, Ursula knelt on the girl's other side and eyed Auli. The sling made her look breakable, and for the first time Auli wondered who she had left behind to be here.

'What was she doing before the ghost appeared?' Auli asked Niki.

'She'd climbed onto the boat. Miika said he pulled her off. She panicked and curled up there, whispering, then the water went wild and that... thing emerged.'

Auli studied the water. 'From under the dock?

'Yes. Impossibly.'

Ursula touched the girl's shoulder, crooning wordlessly. Still nothing, but she didn't flinch either. Her fingers within Auli's were cold and tense.

'How about if *I* tell *you* a story,' Auli whispered, 'will you come with us?'

The girl's lightning eyes blinked and for once her hair was too wet to rise around her, making her smaller and lonelier than ever before.

'A LONG, LONG time ago,' Auli whispered. The girl blinked again, her strange gaze shifting from the fog to Auli's face. 'There was a girl who lived in the city with her brother and two mothers.' She hadn't meant to tell this story but telling anything that had ever been written down felt far too dangerous and she could think of nothing else.

Ursula and Auli between them lifted the Oracle to her feet,

all three of them wavering as the boards dipped and swayed. How had she come to this, cradling a dangerous girl, telling her things she had told no one but Raphaël and Boudain? She thought of the Oracle's own story, and told her about going north to Lapland, staying with her aunts and uncles, stroking the soft muzzles of reindeer. Her and her brother stumbling in wide-legged circles on their snowshoes, laughing at each other as the midnight sun flared green-gold above the tundra.

Up into the Bellwether, up the tower staircase and out onto the research deck. It was so quiet. So still and near-empty, the ghosts louder than the people, and Auli's voice dropped to a whisper, heat in her face like a fire but she couldn't stop, not when the girl called Iolanta was listening, and walking, her fingers slowly warming in Auli's own.

'The girl and the boy went swimming in the bay one night, when the sky was alight with foxfire and mosquitoes.' There was a ghost in front of the Oracle Room that made Auli tense. Célestine wheeled around at her desk to watch them. 'Divers called from the black water and after swimming, they sat on a log on the shore as their mothers cooked fish over the fire. The boy pointed out stars to the girl because he had always been clever with stars and maps. Wherever they wandered, he could always find their way...' She faltered. The pain in her chest was like one of those stars and for a moment she couldn't breathe.

Célestine threw a handful of valerian at the ghost blocking their way. The girl lifted her head, possibly because Auli had fallen silent, possibly because of the ghost. An was in the doorway of Raphaël's office, a bundle of wires trailing from her hand, and she too, was watching the ghost but with something akin to hunger.

It was a video of a woman freediving. Her hair streaming behind her and sun through the water incandescent, but the audio was an engine, raised voices, the heavy clanking of metal. It hissed faintly as Célestine's valerian fell through it, drifting towards them as the Oracle watched it come.

'Auli,' Raphaël said sharply, behind her. An stepped forward, tilting her head like a hawk.

The Oracle jerked and whispered, 'Tell me a story.'

The ghost slowed. Auli thought she would quite likely die if she did the wrong thing now.

Raphaël moved around them smooth and quick, and opened the Oracle Room door behind the ghost. 'What happens if you lead her around it?' he said quietly.

The ghost's audio crackled, a burst of raised voices in… was it Norwegian? A grind and rattle of chains unspooling – the audio was from a fishing boat casting vast industrial nets into the ocean. Somehow that, and the lone woman diving through exquisite seas was a terrible, terrible combination. Auli imagined that was the point.

'Long, long ago,' she whispered, 'there was a girl who lived in a tower floating on the sea.'

Chapter Twenty-Seven

Auli

THE ORACLE CANTED her head, Célestine raised her hand to throw more valerian, Auli pulled the Oracle two steps sideways.

'This girl was beloved of the ghosts and the sea, they spoke to her the way they spoke to no one else.' The woman dove once again, the chains rattled. 'People came to listen to the girl, and to care for the girl.' Another two. She didn't know what she was saying anymore, only that it seemed important not to annoy the ghost, which might still have felt ludicrous if it weren't for the tension in Raphaël's face as he watched them come. The engine growled and bubbles rose through the woman's hair. The Oracle's damp hair rose too, static building beneath Auli's hand. 'The ghosts told the girl stories of the past, things that had happened long ago, things that had never happened at all, and the girl told the people. And the people tried to understand the sea.' The ghost flared, black currents burst across the picture, the men's voices distorted deeper.

Wrong, Auli thought frantically. That was the wrong thing to say. Ursula dropped the Oracle's other arm with a croak of alarm and An moved forward. 'What did the girl in the tower want to do?' Auli asked quickly. 'What stories did the girl in the tower like to listen to?'

The girl pressed against her side mutely.

'Hold still,' An said, lifting the wires in her unmaimed hand.

'No!' Raphaël said, but it was too late.

Electricity leapt from An's device into the ghost, blinding white and sharp as a gunshot, and Raphaël was there somehow, picking the girl up and hauling Auli alongside as he ran past the screaming cloud and into the Oracle Room. He dropped the Oracle into a chair and released Auli, spinning to throw a line of valerian across the open doorway. Auli came to his side, and stared at the ghost, her heart in her throat like it would claw its way free.

The men were screaming now, the metal screaming, the woman diving through a sea full of dead fish sinking. God, Auli thought. Lightning tore through it again, a great white arc from An's hands and the screams fractured, the sea cracking like glass.

'It's working,' Célestine said from the deck.

Then the arc of electricity sputtered and died. An swore, shook her contraption once then glanced across at Raphaël and lifted the brow of her black and absent eye.

'Evacuate the deck,' Raphaël snapped. 'An will let you know when this thing has moved out of range.'

The ghosts of men screamed again, the woman drowned, torn open and shining. It was angry, Auli thought blankly. The few researchers quietly fled, and their fear made Auli's ratchet higher.

'You too,' Raphaël said, and she turned to him in outrage, but he was facing the deck still. An slammed the workshop door shut, then there were wheels against uneven wood, and Célestine.

'I do not think so,' Célestine said lightly. 'Here, I can hide behind you. I cannot work in the Hall with everyone arguing.' She wheeled forward and Raphaël stepped back to avoid being run over.

'I thought you said they needed to know,' Auli said, turning away from the awful, metamorphosing ghost – Raphaël was watching it, and God only knew they'd hear it coming.

Célestine sighed exaggeratedly. 'I did. They do.' She unloaded papers from her lap onto the desk. '*You* do not understand what is happening, you cannot blame them for theorising.' Célestine looked over her shoulder at the slumped figure of the Oracle. Her dark hair was drifting but her eyes were closed and there were, for the moment, no ghosts in the room. 'So much trouble for such a pale little thing,' Célestine said softly, then shook herself and turned back to her papers.

Auli wanted to ask about Joar, but Raphaël was watching the ghost too fixedly, so instead she said, 'An will get that device working soon.'

Raphaël resettled his weight and shot her a sidelong look. 'I hate to say it, but that thing freaks me the fuck out. The way it changed.'

Auli didn't know whether it was comforting or terrible to know he, too, was subject to fear occasionally.

'Miika's dead,' he added baldly, to Célestine.

She looked up from her papers sharply, her eyes softer than before. 'Oh, Rafa,' she said simply, and then she turned to Auli as if waiting.

'Can we evacuate to the islands?' Auli said, because they both knew Raphaël wanted sympathy even less than Célestine did. 'Until An is ready and… things have settled.' She didn't know what 'settled' could possibly mean, yet. If the ghost were fully aware then it would have followed them in here, and the fact it hadn't was slim comfort, but she'd take anything right now. She made a note of that, too.

'Forty-nine ghosts,' she muttered to herself. 'Eight anomalous. All combinations of a story and a news item to do with…' She studied her notes, drew a ship in the corner of the page, the curlicues of waves. 'With humans damaging the sea.'

'It's not a bad idea, Rafa,' Célestine said.

Raphaël did not turn but his shoulders were set. 'Two dangers instead of one. Cooking over fires and twice the perimeter to guard with none of the security. We hang on. We kill the anomalies, we get back to—'

Ursula appeared in the doorway, stepping past Raphaël with two mugs in her unbound hand that smelled of coffee and chocolate. Auli's stomach twisted.

'The doctor is coming,' she said to Auli in Finnish. 'I'm getting my sewing.' She set both mugs down against the wall near the Oracle's chair, then went quickly up to the bedroom above.

'Anyone ask whether *she* poisoned your Boudain?' Célestine said without turning around. 'By accident.'

Raphaël murmured something in French.

Auli looked up the dark staircase. 'She's had too many opportunities.' To murder the Oracle, she meant.

Any night she could have pressed a pillow over the girl's sedated face, any day she could have fiddled the doses and given her enough to kill. They knew so little about her, though – carers never lasted long so no one had tried. Auli knew only that she was surely desperate, to have taken the job, but gentle and clever-fingered, and her deafness had protected her longer than her predecessors; nothing more.

'I think,' she said very quietly, 'it was Gabrielle.' Raphaël didn't react at all. Célestine snorted softly.

'Too obvious, and too clumsy.'

'She wants control. She knew about the sedatives, and she… had access to them.'

The Oracle – Iolanta – lifted her head, her eyes flickered

with lightning and her fingers roved urgently. Auli laid her own hand lightly over them.

'Via Joar?' Célestine said scathingly. 'Being a paltry sort of spy doesn't make him a murderer.'

'Agreed,' Raphaël said shortly. 'Likewise, Leigh Alvarez is a spy, barely, but he's no killer either.'

Was that why he wanted so badly to do Boudain's Oracle replicating project? Would he have stolen the methodology and fled to London, or turned himself into an Oracle and *then* fled? Or died in the trying?

Auli remembered the Oracle flinching from the boatmen, and her gut twisted harder. If she feared them, what possible compromise of drugs and gentleness would ever make this place anything other than cruel?

Raphaël stiffened, then Niki was entering the room, already speaking. 'Joar is stable enough, Célestine, you can sit with him if you want. And there is something in the fog at the top of this tower. Is anyone up there because I'm not sure they should be?'

'How about we move *her* to the island instead?' Célestine asked. 'No one will come near while the fog is in.'

Everyone looked at her. The Oracle pulled one hand from beneath Auli's then set it on top again, and began to whisper.

'That's quite the gamble,' Raphaël said eventually. 'And puts my boatmen, the carer and anyone else who goes with her at even more risk.' He glanced at Auli.

'I would go,' Auli confirmed. 'I can't study the anomalies, or her, from a distance.'

Célestine eyed her, then Raphaël, then muttered something unintelligible and turned back to her papers. Ursula descended holding some folded cloth, glanced at the steaming mugs and the Oracle, and sat without meeting anyone's gaze.

Niki waved their hand until Ursula reluctantly looked up. 'You should rest,' they said in halting Finnish.

Ursula's gaze slid back to the Oracle and something in her hard brown eyes softened as she shook her head. 'A bad ghost up there,' she said to her sewing.

'So,' Raphaël said quietly. 'What now?'

The Oracle rose, turned her flickering gaze to Auli and said very clearly, 'There was a girl who lived in a tower, and she was beloved of the sea.'

Then she turned and opened the outer door to stand against the railing. Cold air dense with water flooded the room in her wake, and Ursula shot them all a strange, laden glance before following her charge into the fog, shutting the door behind her.

Niki slumped into a chair with a groan, and Auli suspected they, too, had gone the long night without sleep. The skin beneath their eyes was damson with fatigue and she wanted to tell them to rest, but that wasn't really an option for any of them. The watch bell sounded and Raphaël grimaced.

'I need to check on the men,' he said. 'You'll be okay here?'

He looked from Niki to Auli without subtlety and Auli had no idea what he was hoping to see. Hadn't she already lost that battle? But once he was gone Célestine met Auli's eye with a slight smile. As if they understood him, as if her friendship and Auli's broken heart made them the same.

'Go be with Joar,' Auli said. 'But can you get An on the way? I want to try something. Niki… can you wait, just ten minutes?'

They made a noise she took as consent.

WHEN CÉLESTINE AND An re-emerged from Raphaël's workshop, Auli was standing on a chair in the QD area, pulling loose the wiring for one of the wall lamps. They ran basic electric lighting through all of the Bellwether other than the Oracle Tower, because ghosts weren't *too* attracted to such straightforward circuits as battery, wire, bulb. At least, not compared to their attraction to the Oracle or the empty books, or the buoys.

'At least it is your research area you are vandalising, I suppose,' Célestine observed from behind her.

Auli tugged at a wall clip. The ghost from before was circling up in the dome, flickering between clear sea and dying bycatch as if wounded. 'We need to sleep,' she said. 'And we need more warning.'

'Oh, clever,' An said. 'It might even work.'

Auli huffed softly. She had two metres of wires free now, which might be enough. She jumped down, holding the lamp carefully.

'What might work?' Célestine said.

Auli studied the Oracle Room doorway. 'If I can string the lamp across...'

'Tack at the top,' An said, turning away.

'They'll crackle when they hit the lamp. Eh, this is good thinking.'

'You don't need to sound so surprised,' Auli said lightly, and she realised just like yesterday with An perhaps dying beneath their hands, they were holding each other up with their jibing. She turned to face Célestine, wondering whether she was avoiding her unconscious sometime-lover from fear of illness or grief. 'Why are you working? I didn't think there were any weather cantations.'

'There were not. Suvi and I are working on a rough forecast from what we have. Trends and predictions.'

'The boat won't be coming though.'

She'd meant it as a kind of solace, but Célestine's gaze turned fierce. 'So, what? Sit around doing nothing while you fix this mess? You think it is suddenly—' She made a sharp, elegant gesture. 'Unimportant? The forecast? That there will not be people waiting. People right now, lost or drowning, because—' An emerged from her workshop and Célestine cut off abruptly.

Perhaps, Auli thought, they were both haunted by the same things. But Célestine carried the responsibility, and the knowledge that they had not been able to give enough warning of this fog so there would be boats out there which might otherwise have been safely home. Auli would feel differently about the Oracle, possibly, if she were in Célestine's place.

An's hand was hurting her, Auli noticed, but it did not stop her giving orders, and shortly the lamp was swinging from the lintel of the doorway, casting a yellow glow over the wood.

'I'll do the same for the workshop,' An said. 'Come get me only if things get exciting. I have a weapon to build.'

She walked away and Célestine laughed quietly. 'Then we can destroy the anomalous ghosts and return to normal. Except…'

Except Pertti and Miika, and Joar. Except Boudain.

'Except we will sell, or someone will steal, the design of the thing that kills ghosts, and the world will become very slightly safer,' Auli said.

Célestine's eyes narrowed. 'And we lose access to the data from the Oracle, so the seas become more deadly. And who will we sell this weapon to? Who will we not?'

Whatever weapon An built, though, it would be with tech and batteries that were vanishingly rare, vanishingly fragile. 'If it works,' Auli corrected, 'a few destroyed ghosts will not reshape the world. There will still be too many at sea for compasses to work, the climate will still be past its tipping points… everything will stay broken, it is only us here who might need to change.'

Célestine tapped her fingernails on the rim of her wheel and returned to watching the empty deck without answering. Auli leaned against the doorway where Raphaël had been. It was, naturally, the perfect spot for watching every approach.

She ought probably to go and identify the ghost at the top of the tower, but she didn't need more data to convince herself. That was no longer the problem.

'An's weapon is a start,' she said. There was another ghost on the deck now, a cloud of data flickering in the flat light. 'But we need to do more than *react*. I wish he'd agree to evacuate.'

It wasn't far to the nearest island, a few hundred metres. But the thought of blindly crossing even that made her feel sick.

'Rafa does not worry over things that do not exist.'

Auli knew that. He might be wrong about *which* existing things were worth worrying over though.

'So,' she said. 'We track the anomalous ghosts until An is ready, we—'

'We sedate the Oracle?'

Auli glanced down at Célestine and then behind her to the wavering figure on the walkway. 'Did you know? About the sedation?'

Célestine pulled a face. 'No. I guessed they did it at night to help her sleep. The carer's hot chocolate, like clockwork after the seeding session? Of course such an expensive thing was not just… kindness, no?' She checked on the ghost in the dome. 'But in the daytime also? I did not know.'

'Do you think it is okay?'

Célestine tapped her nails. 'Everyone knows now.'

Which wasn't an answer. 'Yes, and all they want is a return to normal.'

'Can you blame them? After Pertti, after Joar, and now Miika?'

Auli didn't answer.

'Alors. I need coffee. So do you, I think. You look terrible.' She was almost, almost smiling.

'Thank you,' Auli said gravely. And then, 'Célestine, go and see Joar.'

Célestine's eyebrow raised. 'Are we giving advice now, Auli Fraser? So then here is mine – be careful with Gabrielle. You have supposition only, and she does not like you.' And she pushed off across the floor. It was like a nightclub, Auli thought, just after closing time. The light dirty and tired, the whole place swaying beneath her feet. A forlorn shade of its own former glamour, but when had she stopped seeing the glamour, she wondered, and started seeing the bones?

'Auli?'

She turned, heart already falling. Niki was standing in the outer doorway, the mist curling around him. With one last glance at the ghost spinning in the dome, she reluctantly crossed the room to join him. Behind her, the cranking of Célestine's lift started up, leaving the research deck abandoned.

The girl

THE GIRL HAS discovered a secret. She smiles all mist-tangled. She has discovered a secret and is no longer afraid.

'Long, long ago,' she whispers. There are people behind her, their breaths grey and serpentine, like the sea beneath this castle that is not her home. 'There was a girl who was trapped in a tower.'

The waves below her are there and not there through the dense and crawling air, but she remembers the black dock and the white boat the bad men would not let her sail home in.

If the white boat is not her way home, then the girl will find another way.

'The girl was beloved of the sea though, so the sea sent its monsters to free her.'

The waves hiss, the mist coils around her arms all salt and deep cold, there are ghosts in her veins but the fog quietens them, or perhaps it is because the girl has remembered her name. Perhaps her name in her mama's voice is a wall between the girl and the maelstrom.

The girl, Iolanta, leans forward, straining to see what she can feel.

Away out of sight, something moves.

'The sea sent its monsters to free her,' she repeats.

Someone speaks behind her, and the girl, Iolanta, snags her fingernails on the mist, pulling it towards her as the thing out there breaks the surface with a huff, vanishes again. She still can't see it. The pixels taste like foreign seas and long muscles; this is not the monster beneath the boards, but she thinks perhaps that monster is busy now with the bad man it stole away. She thinks of it down there, feasting all unblinking, blood in the water. That thought, not of the feasting but of the blood makes the girl's lungs ache, but...

Let them bleed, like they make us bleed.

The thing breaks the surface again, closer. She exhales fast and hard like it does, inhales and holds her breath as the water closes over her bones.

Yes, she thinks. The bad men will not let her go home. So let them bleed.

Yes, the sea murmurs. *Yes.*

The monster sings through the water, and another answers. The girl called Iolanta dances her hands through the mist like this is a melody she is unravelling.

'The monsters came to the tower,' she whispered. 'And they began to tear it down.'

Chapter Twenty-Eight

Raphaël

HE WAS UP East Tower when a horn sounded, sudden and distorted in the deadening fog. The signal had been "ware ghost' but Raphaël could barely make out the other towers, let alone any ghosts, as if the Bellwether was some long-abandoned *Marie Celeste*. He glanced up into an opaque sky that showed no signs of clearing and made for the stairs.

'There,' Sandesh said without turning, when Raphaël joined him at the top of West Tower. 'Two o'clock from the dock.'

Whatever the boatman had spotted wasn't there now, just the suggestion of leaden grey waves—

'Ah,' Raphaël said. A sleek black curve, then another, the blades of their fins there and then gone.

Sandesh scratched at his beard thoughtfully and stayed quiet. The orcas surfaced again alongside the dock. They could almost, with the mist, have been real.

'Wonder if there are any left,' Sandesh said quietly. 'We left them in peace just exactly when the ocean cycles collapsed. Maybe they are all dead.'

Raphaël laughed shortly. 'Cheerful, as ever.'

'If there is a ghost of me out there,' Sandesh went on. The two orcas did not reappear. 'I hope it haunts a better place than this. Somewhere with more mangoes and fewer colonials.'

Something moved, but God, the visibility was a disgrace. 'What are—'

'They're under the dock,' Sandesh said sedately. 'Never seen a ghost in the water before.'

Raphaël felt alarm ricochet through him.

'The boat,' he said, and flung himself into the murky stairwell. Down as fast as he dared with the gloom hiding the ghosts, then bursting out into the fog, and stilling at the top of the steps down to the dock.

The *Meri Noita* knocked softly against the dock. Up on the Oracle Tower, the girl was barely visible between banks of fog, leaning over the railing, her hands outstretched. The boat knocked again, and one orca surfaced behind the *Meri Noita*, the other on the far side of the dock. They left no ripples on the water, which was disorienting and utterly impossible.

He touched the holster of his useless gun, then the equally useless vial at his throat, and went quickly down the steps. The *Meri Noita* rocked harder, tilting like it was keeling into a wind.

'Well, fuck,' he muttered.

Several scenarios of increasing implausibility ran through his head while he stood there, watching the dark water around their only remaining vessel. Even, briefly, the idea of firing one of those newly installed harpoon grenades. But in the end, he knew when he was powerless. He turned and looked back up at the Oracle Tower, the dove-pale figure of a girl, and Auli now beside her. She stood, Raphaël thought, a better chance than him of stopping whatever the orcas were doing. And thinking it he realised with a flicker of shock that he believed her. About the Oracle and the ocean, about them both *wanting something* rather than just *persisting*.

Behind him, the boat groaned, and he spun around.

They can't harm it, he thought. But Uoti had fallen, and Joar was cut to ribbons; Pertti and Miika had drowned. A black nose nudged above the water, the mist around it blue and gleaming and the orca kept rising. Its whistles echoed off the Bellwether as the whole five metres of apex predator swam effortlessly above the surface of the real sea, through its own ghostly ocean, into the body of the boat. Small teeth flashing as if the long-gone beast was laughing. The boat groaned again, and the mist stirred around it.

No, not mist.

'Fire!' Raphaël shouted, surging forward. 'Fire on the dock!'

Crossing from dock to vessel in a leap, he unlocked the engine housing and threw back the cover, then reeled backwards as smoke and flame poured out hungrily. Somewhere the orcas clicked and whistled oddly through the fog as he shouted again, but no one answered. He upended the fire bucket over the engine compartment, but then one of the whales rose up through the decking, black and gleaming, forcing him back rapidly until he hit the cabin. The flames licked at the wood of the hatch, smoke and sparks and the whale's head gently butting the burning engine like it was a toy.

Raphaël looked up at East Tower and Sandesh's grey silhouette. No one else had heard him, he realised. The walkways were empty and the other guard towers entirely hidden by the bulk of the Bellwether and the mist. The Oracle and Auli were still on their walkway, but no one was coming, and he could throw salt water on the burning engine, but given the ghosts, that might make it worse. Leaning against the cabin with the deck crackling and listing beneath his feet, he wanted, very briefly, to howl.

Barring two kayaks, this was their only way off. The flames

caught on the deck, spitting an eerie blue-green in the grey light. Someone called his name, he thought it was Auli, and he knew why. But leaving the *Meri Noita* was admitting defeat and he was nothing if not stubborn.

FIFTEEN MINUTES LATER, he had first degree burns on one arm, a melted boot, and could feel static crawling down one leg from a too-close call. The *Meri Noita* was aflame. Alan, Tobias and Leigh had finally arrived, and they'd slowed the fire long enough to salvage as much as possible from the doomed boat. Now, Raphaël watched the last corner of a fire blanket shrivel and blacken, as Alan untied the mooring ropes. Tobias pushed at the boat's cantilevered flank with a pole, and they stood on the dock, watching it drift away, flames engulfing the cabin as the deck dipped another few degrees to starboard. The orcas surfaced at its prow, their breaths loud, black fins like knives.

'Will they come for the dock?' Leigh said.

Raphaël shifted his shoulders uncomfortably. The possibility had occurred to him.

'They never did though,' Alan said quietly.

Raphaël turned just enough to shoot him a questioning look.

'They attacked boats off Gibraltar, I remember Uoti telling me. There were campaigns to cull them and a huge court case, he said – first time a non-human was given international legal priority over humans. Uoti said people thought it was a sign of hope.' He laughed very slightly.

Raphaël remembered now. He watched the beasts surface again, circling the sinking boat, their whistles eerily audible. So they were still bound by the limits of their own story? Auli was right. God, it would make her even more reckless.

'So,' he said. 'We'll need two volunteers to head out and

retrieve the *Meren Rouva,* and Hellä. You two, get this stuff up to An.' Nudging a toe against the tangle of wires and solar panels sitting on the dock. If he thought anyone in Kökar would sell, he'd kayak there now and trade for a boat. An might have enough scraps to create another motor – it wouldn't be perfect, but it would be better than nothing.

'I'll go,' Alan said, once they were alone. The *Meri Noita* was a listing blur in the channel, restless with fire.

'Thank you. You should get back to Auli for now.'

'She's with Bea, sent me to help rig her alarm systems up in the dorm barges.'

Raphaël nodded. It was a good idea. He'd rather have another half-dozen trained boatmen.

Alan glanced at him. 'They aren't enjoying feeling caged, boss.'

'Neither am I. But unless you hadn't noticed, our only route off here is currently sinking.'

'We've two kayaks,' Alan said, undeterred.

Raphaël grimaced. 'I'll see if Célestine has any opinion on this fog lifting. If it does, we are definitely safer staying put. Meanwhile, you can check the grenade boxes are holding against the fog. Last thing we need is those degrading.'

Alan eyed the mist, nodded.

Behind him the whistles of the orcas rose again, their breaths like gunshots in the deathly silence of the mist.

'Ah,' Alan murmured. 'Umm. Boss?'

Raphaël didn't turn immediately. He looked up at the inkstain outline of the Oracle Tower and sighed enormously. They were bound by the limits of their story... but the barges were boats, too, in principle.

'Cut power to the barges,' he said.

He didn't even bother trying to shout. The mist hung around them full of whistles and the tang of smoke, and he took off as fast as he could without it being suicidal.

The researcher barge, closer to the Bellwether, was surely the less likely target, so the fear of fire had him ordering everyone out of their cabins and onto that roof, crowded skittishly in between tomato vines and laundry. Visibility was non-existent, but better that than being trapped by fire, and the anomaly Auli had recorded here two hours ago had vanished.

Raphaël's mind felt full of urgency and fracture lines and the orcas' whistles reverberated through the mist clear as bells as he prowled the outer crew barge, straining to see into the mist that seemed, if anything, to be thickening. Dear God, he thought, but this felt calamitous.

The orcas stayed out of sight though, and Raphaël began, just barely, to hope for a moment to strategise. But then someone screamed once, someone else shouted, and there was the single distinct splash of a body hitting the water.

Auli

THE FOG HAD gathered on them both like a second skin. Droplets along their arms and in their hair, clothes dark and sodden. The girl didn't seem to feel the cold, but Auli did.

'The monsters came,' the girl whispered. There were pearls on her eyelashes and lightning in her eyes, but she spoke soft, rural Russian. Even her voice had never before been her own.

They were crouched against the railing, facing blindly westward towards the open sea. Out of sight of the burning boat and the dock in the hope it would break whatever strange connection the girl's story had wrought.

'The monsters are dangerous, Iolanta,' Auli whispered back. 'Sometimes monsters hurt the people they love, as well as the people they hate. We have to find our way without trusting to monsters.'

'The bad men,' the girl whispered. 'We must make the bad men bleed.'

The bad men. The boatmen, and Raphaël. Her heart ached in her chest like a banked coal. The girl's story had contained, beneath the vengeance, a wish. And Auli needed to know. She needed to be absolutely sure.

'You want to go home?' she asked.

Iolanta lifted her stormy eyes to Auli's, pressed thin fingers against her throat, then said in this voice that was hers alone, 'Long, long ago there was a girl who lived in the forest.'

'You want to go home to the forest?'

Away from the sea.

Auli had known already. She just wished there was another way. But the sea had its hooks deep in this girl's bones and was using her to... to make the bad men bleed. So the only way to stop this was to take her away. Far away where the sea couldn't reach her.

She thought of her mothers in the far north. The wide wild tundra, divers calling from soft lakes beneath a foxfire sky. In between the methane fires and the sinkholes, there was still a life to be lived up there. And there was family, even if not the one this girl had lost.

'Yes,' the girl said simply. She reached out, thin coils of mist around her upturned palm. 'It promised to set me free.'

Had it indeed? Auli thought. Perhaps it would, once it had wreaked whatever vengeance it wanted. But how much blood would tithe a wounded ocean? She thought of all Bea's folktales, all the monsters real and unreal this girl might summon from the water. She could still see Raphaël on the deck of the burning boat, a predatory ghost rising in front of him and Auli powerless to help.

She knew what Gabrielle would say, and likely everyone else, too.

If they kept the Oracle sedated, and if An devised a weapon to eradicate the anomalies, then the Bellwether could continue as before. The fog would lift, the Oceans team would deploy more restored buoys, Gabrielle would convince all their contractors to be patient a little longer, and the Oracle would be roused just enough to speak the thousand voices of the ghosts. The seas would become day by day safer to navigate, her brother's memory would rest a little easier in her heart because she was part of that work. And if she did not lose her job, Auli would adjust, perhaps. She'd bury her conscience and her suspicions about Gabrielle beneath research and time, and one day she might forget entirely.

It would be by far the easier choice.

She scanned the space around them, the familiar walls of the Bellwether and the great ocean of fog making the whole world a thing of faith and memory.

In the heavy silence, Mama Sara's voice was soft as a whisper, *The only real choice you have is to live honestly or to live a lie. The rest is details.*

They had been talking about friendships, and about Mama Sara's illness, and all the things she had lost because of it. Auli had asked if she was angry, and she had smiled and said, *Of course. All the time. But I am not just my anger, I am also my heart. Mama Márjá. You, your brother. The smell of autumn beneath trees and the sound of water over stones.*

'We are not just our anger,' Auli whispered now to the girl. 'We are also our hearts.'

It was easy in the end, to destroy a dream.

'I'll take you home.'

Auli placed her hand into the girl's upturned palm. Static rustled against her fingers, but for a moment the lightning in the girl's eyes paused. Her irises were the brown of autumn.

'Iolanta, do you hear me? Don't call any more monsters, I promise I'll find a way to take you home.'

Iolanta smiled.

There was movement in the mist above and Auli threw her other hand up as if to shelter the girl but the shape falling towards them was a raven. Black-ruffled, landing so close on the railing that the downdraft stirred their fog-laden hair. It walked down the railing and then back again, watching them first from one black eye and then the other.

The girl, Iolanta, reached out a hand and the raven placed the pebble it was carrying carefully on the railing. Iolanta picked it up, held it to her eye. Not a pebble, Auli realised, a fragment of amber. Freja's tears.

All the consequences of the promise she had just made returned to her full force. God, but how would she of all people manage such a thing?

The raven flicked its wings. Oddly, the person she wanted to tell was Célestine. Which was not something she'd have bet on two days ago. But could she risk it, when everyone had looked at a child in a cage and decided she was a price they could pay?

She had no boat, no ability to navigate, and a college full of people who would try to stop her taking their Oracle away. Auli gathered herself.

'First,' she said softly, 'we are going inside to warm up and find some food.' The raven purred hopefully. 'And then I will devise a plan. Come, Iolanta, come away inside.' She rose, reached down a hand, and the girl took it without hesitation.

It felt unbearably easy, earning this girl's trust after everything they had done to her. But she'd spoken as if there were someone else talking to her, making its own promises, and Auli feared that voice would prove better at keeping them.

* * *

SHE LEFT THE girl with Ursula, the cooled hot chocolate still sitting on the desk, carefully ignored by both of them. Niki had gone after Raphaël and the burning boat and not returned, and Auli might have been overruled by Niki, but she wasn't going to do the deed herself. Especially now.

Célestine was on the research deck, a sheaf of papers forgotten on her lap as she watched the anomalous ghost circling the library. Auli hesitated, then knocked on Raphaël's door.

'No,' An said.

Auli went in, ducking under the strung LED wire. An was bent over something on the workbench, a coil of smoke like a cat's tail above her shoulder, the smell of herbs and metal as dense here as the fog everywhere else.

'I said—' An turned her head far enough to see Auli and cut off. Auli almost smiled. It seemed saving someone's life gave you at least a little leeway. She hoped so. 'It's not ready yet,' An amended.

'It wasn't that.'

An turned fully on her stool and met Auli's gaze with her eyebrow raised.

'Is there a way to do the opposite?' Auli asked, gesturing at the workbench. 'Strengthen a ghost rather than weaken it?'

'Why for the love of fuck would you want to do that?'

'Well,' Auli hesitated. 'In theory. If you wanted to make a ghost strong enough to... interact with. Could you just provide more electricity, or a magnetic field or something?'

An snorted. '*Just* provide a magnetic field!' Her burned black socket was enormous in her delicate face. Auli had been right before, An looked majestic there on her scarred old stool with her bandaged fingers and devastated face. 'What are you planning?'

'Nothing,' Auli said far too quickly.

'You think you can control... no, you think *she* can control one, and you think *you* can control her. What for? To chase the others away?'

Auli realised she was wringing her hands together and pressed them to her thighs. On the deck below, a door slammed and the Bellwether creaked softly. 'Yes,' she said.

'Bullshit.' An rose, stalked across the room and peered straight into Auli's face with her one eye. 'Bullshit,' she repeated. 'Whatever you're thinking, it's a terrible idea. Give me a few more hours, I'll have something that can at least keep them at bay till this damn weather changes.'

'And then what?' Auli asked softly. 'We survive the fog, with your new weapon, and then what, An?'

An opened her mouth but the door burst open, and Leigh and Tobias broke the strung wire without even noticing, carrying something bulky between them that they set at An's feet with more gentleness than they'd granted the door.

An and Auli both stared at the gift.

'Oh,' Auli said. 'The solar panels from the boat. You salvaged them.' She should have guessed that was why Raphaël stayed onboard even after the flames had taken hold.

An glowered at everyone. 'Salvaged? What's happened to the boat?'

She was on the wrong side of the Bellwether; the deadening silence of the fog must have hidden it from her entirely.

'Uh, it caught fire,' Auli said inadequately.

'Who the hell managed that?'

The men glanced at one another, and An swore unquietly.

'Ghosts?'

Auli nodded.

'It's gone?'

Everyone nodded. Tobias added, 'Captain's sending someone for Hellä and the *Meren Rouva* tomorrow morning. We won't be stranded long.'

He'd intended to be comforting, but she watched An's

quick mind ticking through the news, and was flinching even before An twisted to glare at her.

'Auli.'

Auli folded her arms around her waist, then unfolded them.

'She—' An cut off, Tobias muttered something about the barges and disappeared hastily. Leigh lingered, but not for long.

'What's it like?' Auli said, watching them retreat. 'Having everyone respect you so effortlessly?'

She turned from the dim doorway to find herself being studied.

'You think it's effortless? You think someone like me is just *handed* respect? You think I didn't claw my way to where I am, fighting harder than all the men who underestimated me and all the westerners who stereotyped me?'

Auli flushed. 'Sorry. I just... I wish I had your fierceness.'

Unexpectedly, An smiled. 'Aren't you angry?' she said, in an unsettling echo of Mama Sara long ago.

'What about?'

An shrugged. 'Anything? What you've lost. Who you've lost. What you've had to do to survive. How heartless we all are.'

Were they? Auli wondered. Was everyone heartless in this new world, or was it just the city she'd come from and the Bellwether she'd thought home?

I am not just my anger, I am also my heart.

'No, don't look *sad*,' An snapped. 'What's the point in *sad*? That doesn't get stuff done, *angry* does. Or *spite*. I'm fond of a little spite myself.'

Auli studied the pile of electronics on the floor all patch mended from a time of ruinous greed. 'I'm angry about a lot of things. And guilty about a lot more.' An made a pfft sound and turned back to her bench, picked something up then dropped it with a clang.

'Gah, you distracted me.' She ran her right hand over her face, skirting her lost eye gingerly then fixing that singular glare back on Auli again.

It had been worth a try, Auli thought.

'Tell me you don't want to summon a ghost to ride on out of here?' An said.

Auli concentrated on anger. 'You think I'd run away? You think I'm coward enough to flee a few strange ghosts?'

An continued to glare, then pushed past Auli, shut the door and leaned back against it. 'You're going to steal the Oracle.'

Auli swore softly. Her skin was as clammy as if she were back out in the fog, watching the girl narrate orcas into being.

'Dammit, Auli, what's that going to solve? The Oracle belongs here.'

'She's had years of medical and psychological abuse at our hands. And is now so desperate to escape she's constructing monstrous ghosts that are going to tear this place apart if we don't—'

'But we will. Once I've—'

'Will you?' Auli interrupted. 'Two five-metre-long ghosts of apex predators, that stayed well out of reach of the Bellwether as they destroyed our boat. You'd be able to stop them, would you? What about if that storm ghost returns?'

'I—' An broke off. Touched, very deliberately, the blackened wound of her eye socket. 'Life is cruel, Auli. It's cruel everywhere but it's crueller here. We'll survive the next few days, pick ourselves up, and carry on.'

Auli bristled. There was Gabrielle's scorn in the words, Raphaël's cynicism.

'The Bellwether is *vital*, Auli,' An added. 'You know that.'

Mist hissed against the windows; the Bellwether, cage or cradle, creaking around them all salt-stained and weakening.

'Are you really so dependent on one caged girl?' Auli hissed with frustration. 'Is it really a choice between the Bellwether founded on torment, or nothing at all? Or is that a lie you tell to salve your conscience?'

Auli pulled on the door.

'Touché,' An said without moving out of the way. 'Fine. Let's first survive this, Auli. Keep the Oracle calm and then we'll figure this out in a way that doesn't get you killed.'

Auli held An's gaze until An stepped aside and let her go. She fled in the half-light, past one normal ghost scrolling newsfeeds and then an anomalous one nearly blocking the entrance to the underdeck. The sea was quiet beneath them today, dragging against the hull like fingernails and she shuddered, thinking of the boatman dragged down and drowned.

Even the kitchen was gloomier than normal. Without windows, Dunya had accrued better lighting than anywhere else, but half the lights were off now, the others yellowing around the edges. The batteries, Auli thought. The fog and the calm were draining the batteries. Soon they'd be powerless as well as stranded.

Dunya broke away from counting preserves to give Auli food for the Oracle. Alexis smiled at her from the sink. 'Are all the drowning men gone?'

Auli baulked. 'Yes,' she managed but it was not true – Pertti's body was still lying down the corridor. She didn't think that was what the boy meant though. He had nightmares, he'd told her once. A town littered with the dead, dogs picking over the bodies, feasting on eyeballs. She wondered if he felt caged here, if he loved it anyway.

'Are you alright down here?' Auli asked.

'Your captain told us to evacuate to the barges,' Dunya said. 'But we'd have mutiny quick enough if no one was fed and I'm not letting anyone rummage through my stores without me.' She eyed her jars again and Auli remembered a food delivery was due but would not be coming until the fog lifted. Perhaps not even then if Raphaël's fears were true.

Auli gathered the food up. There would be no pilfering supplies for fleeing with then.

It was a dangerous two-month journey to her mothers. She had nothing of value other than her mind, and no skills of persuasion or intimidation to forge a path, and the prospect of defeat before she even began infuriated her. But if An was right perhaps her anger would be enough to carry them.

Chapter Twenty-Nine

Raphaël

'Rafa?'

Raphaël turned reluctantly away from a patch of mist holding an anomaly. It was a bastard of a thing – a radio broadcast alternating between sedate French callsigns and a folktale in a Caribbean patois he could not entirely follow. Something about a lusca that lived in sea caves, foretelling death. It was invisible, even its static field silenced by the godforsaken mist, and it was no one's fault the researchers had not noticed its approach. But it was Raphaël's fault they'd nearly died because of it.

If he hadn't ordered them onto the roof deck, then the ghost appearing so close to Leigh wouldn't have startled him into Bea, knocking them overboard into the path of the orcas. They were both very lucky not to be dead.

He sank onto the edge of a raised bed and looked at his friend wordlessly. The orcas were circling, but despite knocking against the hulls had found no purchase on the powerless old barges.

'You saved Bea,' Célestine said. 'No one else was jumping in after them, and Leigh got away without a scratch.'

Raphaël didn't answer.

'Does this tip the scales, even with the fog?'

He frowned at the boards between his boots. His refusal to evacuate and then his decision to order them onto the roof deck had nearly killed two people. He was hardly a stranger to that, but it was not normally his *mistakes* that killed people.

'I don't...' he began eventually. 'I don't know.'

Célestine watched him, her fingers motionless for once. 'Let's go over now. Us two. See how bad the ghosts are there, then decide.'

He looked up at the suffocating white wrapped around them. 'You didn't see.' So he had to tell her about the *Meri Noita*. All the while silently listing everything he could have done differently over the last forty-eight hours that would have meant they still had a boat, that Miika lived, Joar was whole. He'd gone badly wrong without even realising it, and it was paralysing him.

You must be strong, his mother whispered. Raphaël shuddered.

'If the fog doesn't lift by morning,' he said slowly, 'I'll postpone Alan going for Hellä and we'll evacuate to camp on Lindö. It'll be slow – two kayaks for the food stores and equipment, and researchers will have to take on guard shifts. I'll... keep some boatmen on here.' He sighed. 'You busy with the forecast or can you organise that?'

The orcas whistled and the anomaly ghost crackled, the barge rocked although the sea was flat calm. It might have been someone walking down the corridor inside, or the whales, testing. Come nightfall they'd be impossible to track.

'There's nothing to forecast with.' Célestine was pushing her wheels back and forth very slightly. It looked idle but it wasn't. She, too, was listening to both ghosts. 'When Mariehamm comes I have nothing for them, other than seasonal averages from a climate that doesn't exist anymore.'

Raphaël nodded. He needed to tell the PIs about the evacuation – Gabrielle would argue and his temper wasn't what it should be right now. He needed to check on Joar, he *wanted* to check on Auli again, run his hands over her arms and cheekbones and ribs, assure himself she was still untouched by the ghosts she dealt with so fearlessly.

He didn't move. 'I'm sorry,' he said instead. 'About Joar.'

Célestine shot him an exasperated glance. 'I do not blame you. I am not even sure I still blame Auli. I *am* worried about you.'

'Don't be. I'm fine.'

'Rafa, you are allowed to feel things, you know. The grief, the fear, the doubt. Stop looking so hard at the fight that you forget who you are.'

Raphaël could not hold her gaze. 'This is me *feeling things*, Célestine. And look at me. The Bellwether can't afford me to be indecisive or weak right now.'

'But *I* cannot afford you losing yourself… She wanted you to live, Rafa. She did not want you to simply survive.'

This, he thought bitterly, was the problem with knowing someone so well. They knew every one of your ghosts by name.

Célestine sighed. 'I miss the versions of us who were not led by fear, you know? If I had not scared Auli off back then, perhaps you would be… Alors, but I thought it was for the best.'

'For whom?' he snapped, closing his eyes against the unbraced for pain.

She stilled her chair and said, surprised, 'For Auli. You are stubborn and wounded, and that is a terrible combination, no? You yourself did not realise you cared until it was over, I think. I was looking out for her.'

'Or,' Raphaël said darkly, 'you were worried we would leave together, without you.'

If he was feeling generous, he could admit she had a point. He had been so determined not to love anyone, he hadn't realised he was already there. However, he didn't want to be generous, he wanted a distraction from his doubts.

Her laughter was feigned, and they both knew it. 'Auli, leave? She never would. This place, it is a job to you and a purpose for me. But to her it is a... beacon, no?' She faltered. 'Or it was until recently. Now I think she hates it a little bit, for not being the wonderful thing she believed in all these years.'

Raphaël said nothing, frozen by a whole new fear.

'Would you have?' Célestine added after a moment. 'Left me behind?'

'Do you really think that of me?'

She rocked her wheels. 'No. But I wanted to check.'

This caught his attention. He lifted his eyebrows.

She raised one hand from the wheel to gesture at the fog and everything it contained. 'I feel like whatever good was here is not enough anymore.'

Raphaël looked, too, at the great shadow of the Bellwether, the knot of researchers at the far end of the barge, stripped of colour by the mist.

'God, I hope you're wrong,' he said, and dragged himself to his feet. Feeling lost didn't mean he got to hide. 'Go and see Joar, Célestine. Tell Niki he'll be first off tomorrow. You're in charge of the evac, remember.'

'And you, Rafa,' she said to his back, 'remember this was not your fault, yes? You are a good man.'

Only it was, and he wasn't.

THE VIEW FROM the towers was worse than at sea level. Sending anyone out into that tomorrow was a risk he wasn't sure he dared take, but evacuation felt inescapable now, and they needed the boat...

He was still bouncing between self-doubt and two dozen possible scenarios twenty minutes later when he knocked on Uoti's bedroom door and found Gabrielle in there already. Uoti was sleeping, and didn't stir at Raphaël's entrance.

'Do you need him or me?' Gabrielle said quietly.

'All the PIs,' Raphaël said. 'I'll tell you, then find Auli.'

Gabrielle looked exhausted, Raphaël noted. But it was all worry instead of action. She'd spoken to the researchers... yesterday afternoon? And since then had hidden away, purportedly writing appeals for patience, for, he suspected, a formal consolidation of her own power. She should be coordinating the evacuation, but it hadn't occurred to him to ask her. He told her about that. About the *Meri Noita*, and Bea. He didn't mention the lines of salt crystals in the harpoon boxes, circling old explosives like tidelines – he'd been so certain they were a necessary risk, but that was before Auli's mad theory had bedded itself into his brain. He could not, he thought wryly, have picked a worse time to flounder.

'What if I object?' Gabrielle said when he'd finished.

He gathered himself. 'I ignore you.'

'What if Fraser objects?'

'It was her idea,' Raphaël snapped. 'We'll get Uoti and Joar off first thing. I don't like them being here and helpless.'

Gabrielle eyed the sleeping man in his bed. Pallid and drawn, a bowl and empty mug beside him. Raphaël came alert but tamped the reaction down. Auli had no proof. None. And he had an entirely different theory. Although his calculations weren't proving reliable right now, so...

'Is she keeping her sedated?'

Gabrielle's hands were unsteady, and she was, Raphaël realised, terrified. But what of – the anomalies, the threat to the Bellwether, or her control of it? Or him being here in this room? 'Someone else can sit with him,' he said, watching her covertly.

She ignored him. 'It is a matter of security that she's kept sedated. I hope you make that clear, Captain.'

Raphaël gave it up and left, checking his watch but it had stopped working, probably after a brush with an orca.

It must, judging by the light through the library dome, be getting on for evening. Alan was leaning against a column at the edge of the Centre, watching the anomaly ghost still moving ponderously above them.

'Boss?' he said, his body relaxed but his eyes sharp and almost angry.

Raphaël paused. 'Yes?'

Alan shifted his weight. The Bellwether was unnervingly still. 'Looks like Joar isn't gonna pull through. The doc's in with him now. Internal bleeding or some shit. Poor bastard.'

'Ah, damn,' Raphaël muttered. He clapped Alan on the shoulder and altered his trajectory, and the tally of his guilt.

ODDLY, HIS BOATMAN slowly dying forced Raphaël out of his own funk a little. Enough at least to pass Gabrielle's reminder on to Niki. Believing Auli didn't change this; if anything, it made the sedation *more* necessary.

Niki was watching Joar on the cot blankly, turning a glass bottle over and over again within one hand, the red cross flashing in and out of Raphaël's sight.

'Auli won't like it,' Niki muttered.

'Will you do it anyway?'

Niki sighed throatily, glanced up at Raphaël and gripped the bottle hard. 'What choice is there? I don't actually think it will have any effect. But who the fuck knows what's going on right now? So it would be madness *not* to remove the likeliest source of it all from the equation.'

Raphaël stuffed his hands into his pockets, leaned back against the wall and changed the subject. 'Can you operate?'

he asked. Joar was barely moving, sweat sheening his forehead the only sign of life.

'It would kill him.' Niki began turning the bottle over and over again.

'How long's he going to linger?'

'It could be days. There's nothing I can—'

'Is he in pain?'

'Very much. I have given him as much morphine as I dare.'

Raphaël studied the boatman's face. He'd turned up with Miika seven months after Raphaël's own arrival. They'd heard a new command was recruiting and were tired of the ready brutality of the army, wanting a quiet posting that would edge just the right side of boredom for which the Bellwether had been perfect. If Raphaël had evacuated the Bellwether a day ago, he might have lived. Or he might not. All Raphaël could offer him now was this:

'Give him the rest,' he said. 'I'll get Célestine, but she'll agree. It was what he wanted.'

Niki didn't look up. 'For ghost infection, not this. It's murder.'

Raphaël didn't have the heart to argue semantics. 'Then go dose the Oracle and put that bottle down before you break it. That stuff costs a fortune.'

Niki's face was agonised. But Raphaël was almost calm now; this was the closest Joar would get to justice, that Raphaël carry this additional guilt. After a long moment, Niki set the bottle down carefully on their desk, peeling each fingertip away as if the effort cost them. There was a needle and syringe already set out.

'Ten more will—' The door opened, and Célestine was there, her lips drawn in a straight line.

'Alan said he's dying,' she said bluntly. Her eyes skimmed over her lover's face, his covered body, then to Raphaël rather than Niki, waiting.

'Yes,' Raphaël said. 'I'm sorry.'

She held his gaze and he held hers, then she nodded once, pushed forward to the bed and rested her palm against Joar's pale cheek. Niki stared at Raphaël over her bent head.

'There's nothing I can do to make it easier on him,' they said quietly.

'The evacuation tomorrow,' Célestine whispered, 'would be cruel, no?'

'Very,' Niki said.

'So then.' Célestine touched Joar's pale hair. 'What was his choice, Rafa? I never asked.'

Raphaël crouched at her side, watching his boatman. 'His choice was yes.'

Yes, he chose the quick death over the slow, terrible erasure. An's survival might change that for some people, Raphaël realised. But it was too late for Joar

Niki checked his pulse, lifted the sheets to examine his torso then lowered it again. The infected could usually take the stuff themselves, but even then, Niki never watched.

'Ten more will make it painless,' they said. 'I can't. You understand why I—'

'Yes,' Célestine lied curtly. 'Go.'

Niki flinched and fled. Raphaël ignored them, watching Célestine curl her hands around the sniper's long fingers.

'He lost a child to fever,' she said as he went to the bench. 'And a wife to the grief, did you know? And did not wish to replace either. That was why it worked for us. We neither of us had a heart to give, but we gave each other a little happiness, I think. A little pleasure. That is no small thing, is it?'

Raphaël was back at her side, the needle in his hand. He waited till she met his eyes and nodded.

'You are a good man,' she said again, perhaps speaking to both of them this time.

Then she began, very softly, to hum. A wordless lullaby

as Joar's breathing deepened and slowed. She hummed and stroked Joar's fingers, and Raphaël remembered his own mother singing that same song to his younger brother who had died in a fire at the very beginning of the end.

You must be strong, she had told him when he was a boy, and when he was a man weeping over his brother's body. And he was trying, God, he was trying. But he didn't know what was strength anymore, and what was cowardice.

The girl

THE GIRL CAN hear people arguing. The woman who promised her home, and someone else, and someone else. A man and a dog are surfing the long breaking back of a wave, stringed instruments are playing sad as a whalefall.

'Iolanta,' she whispers to herself. 'The girl in the tower is going to escape the bad men and go home.'

The violins sing salt and seaweed melodies. The black-eyed woman hisses like a cat. A cat. Iolanta remembers a cat. She studies the curve of her fingers and imagines them stroking tabby brown fur instead of scales and kelp tangles and teeth.

'Please, Niki. It will upset her and look – look how calm she is. How calm she's been without it.'

Iolanta cannot remember the name of the tabby brown cat.

'Joar is dying, Auli. He is dying *right now* because of ghosts the Oracle conjured up.'

There is silence. The surfer and his dog start again at the top of their wave, the violins purr. 'Once there were two sisters,' Iolanta whispers, but she cannot remember the story. 'And one of them was a violin made of bone.'

'It's not her fault.'

'No. It is yours.'

'But it doesn't fit, Niki. We need to reduce the doses.'

'This is not your call. Not now.'

'The sisters in their tower cannot get free,' Iolanta whispers. She'd promised not to call the monsters, but her words are sweet in her throat, they are all her own and they keep the others at bay. 'So the first sister threads a shin bone bow with her sister's hair, she bends rib-bones into a curve to sit beneath her chin.'

'What's she doing?'

'The girl in her tower plays her sister's bones to the sea and all the birds come to listen.' Birds are not monsters, Iolanta thinks. They are feather arpeggios and air, so she is not breaking her word telling stories from the sky.

'God,' the black-eyed woman says. 'God, Iolanta. Don't—'

'Auli. Get out the way.'

The black-eyed woman makes a wounded sound, there are footsteps behind Iolanta, the flitter of wings, the crackle of a deep toothed creature. The salt in the air stirs.

Ah, here it is.

Iolanta flinches. The voice has been quiet since the dock. She had forgotten how it coils.

'Hush now.' There is a hand on her arm, a cup in her palm all heat and drowning. The violins screech.

You didn't think you could trust them, did you? They will only ever destroy.

Iolanta turns her head. The black-eyed woman is kneeling beside her.

'Oh, Iolanta,' she says. 'I'm sorry.'

Numbers and voices are creeping beneath her skin, a rising tide cold as stone crawling up her spine and she recognises this. She remembers drowning.

'The girl in the tower,' she whispers.

'The girl in the tower will sleep now,' the black-eyed woman whispers. 'She will sleep safe and warm.'

'She doesn't want to drown,' the girl called Iolanta says. Her lungs are full of the sea and sweet hot familiarity.

'I won't let you drown.'

Oh, but she will. They destroy everything they fear and they consume anything remaining. We are monstrous because that is what they made us.

'She doesn't want to be a monster, she wants to go home.'

The black-eyed woman smiles as uneven as a broken shell.

The only way to be free is to destroy the ones who hurt us. Don't you remember?

She lifts the cup because she doesn't know how to be free. The taste of hot chocolate is salt-bitter and her limbs untether, her whole body made of numbers and lightning.

The girl drowns. Heavy as a stone sinking through the water, losing the light.

The black-eyed woman is crying.

Don't cry, the girl wants to say, but her tongue is not her own, her teeth are sharp and silver, her flesh cold.

Come then, let me show you their lies, the voice murmurs. The girl is a blind-eyed fish, he is the tide.

Chapter Thirty

Auli

THE BELLWETHER WHISPERED around Auli as she traversed the halls again, oil lamp in one hand and clipboard in the other, her notes scratchy and uneven in the pressing dark. It was two o'clock in the morning and she'd given up on sleep. Leigh had offered to step in for Bea, but she'd sent him to bed and carried on alone. As if she might hold the entire Bellwether together by collating the right numbers. If she even wanted to hold the Bellwether together anymore.

Alan was on guard in West Tower and Auli's oil-lamp scattered light up the tight curve of the staircase, casting the anomaly ghost between them half-lit, half-hidden. In it, someone was begging for help in accented French. Over and over, *Mayday. Mayday. Il y a quelqu'un? S'il vous plaît. Il y a quelqu'un?* Auli would have abandoned her post long ago if it had been her standing alone in the shattered dark with this thing.

'You should sleep,' Alan said over it.

'I know.' She smiled slightly. 'So should you, I imagine.' His soft laughter followed her down the stairs.

She checked the kitchen, the padlock on the storeroom

doors, the abandoned Hall. Uoti's room silent, Gabrielle's locked. Outside Raphaël's, she hesitated, unsure whether he was sleeping, or prowling the dark like she was, awaiting the next catastrophe. For a foolish moment she imagined entering, slipping quietly into his bed, his arm pulling her against him, his sigh of contentment in her hair.

No, she thought. You fool. And besides, if he *were* sleeping, he'd have booby-trapped the door against ghosts, so she'd likely end up electrocuted and wasn't that apt? If she found a way out, she'd be leaving him behind. The thought ought to have been a relief but instead twisted beneath her ribs like a great barbed hook.

THE BARGE ROOFTOPS, the walkways, Auli crept through them all like her own ghost, making notes, her paper growing damp with mist and her hair curling around her face, wet and black and cold. The lamp reflected back off the fog breathless with other ghosts out in the dark, beyond her.

On the research deck, her lamp cast odd, motile shadows over desks and crates and chairs, the fishing boat and diving girl ghost had descended into the Oceans area, and she slipped past it up into the library. Needing to sit, just for a moment, in the embrace of a window like she had done a thousand times before and listen to the books haunting their own selves.

She'd loved this place so very much.

There was a small datacloud ghost suspended through the opposite window like it, too, was caught between the Bellwether and the world.

'Auli?' Footsteps on the ladder, and then Bea coming into the pool of light, a wavering torch tucked between elbow and ribs. 'Oh, good. This thing's about done and I didn't fancy the walk back to the barge.' They sat cross-legged beside Auli.

Auli studied them. 'Can't sleep?'

'I sent him to his own cabin because he was snoring, you know?'

'Oh, Bea,' Auli whispered, her heart aching. She'd tried to talk to Célestine after Joar's death, and Célestine had held up one hand, and said, *No. I do not want words. I will mourn him when this is over.* But Bea was not Célestine.

'The anomalies have a theme,' Bea said a little fixedly. 'The attacks have all been on men. So, is she driving it? Is it a self-defence thing, or a trauma response or something?'

Bea was not Célestine, but their mourning was still fierce. Auli felt ancient and conflicted, and had to force herself to speak. 'Both, I think. She saw men kill her parents, and I think the sea is bent on vengeance—' Bea whistled. It echoed around the empty dome like a thrown paper plane. 'So she's bringing stories into being as a way of... fighting back.'

'To what end?'

The girl or the ocean? 'To get free of her prison.'

'Prison?' Bea turned the torch over and over on the walkway. 'Sedatives aside, she's safer here than anywhere else.'

'Is she? Who wrote that story, Bea? What motives did they have for the writing of it?'

They shook their head impatiently. 'Okay, we've a vested interest in her being here. We all depend on her, at least until Leigh gets his godawful experiments off the ground, if he doesn't die in the process. But she'd be killed on the mainland. Or put in another Bellwether, perhaps run by people less benevolent than you, Auli.'

Auli didn't answer. The ghost beneath them was all dead fish and drowning.

'So how do we persuade her she's safe here?' Bea asked.

The girl doesn't want to drown, Iolanta had whispered, sinking beneath Niki's sedative.

'Is that what you'd choose?' Auli said softly. 'Have her just coherent enough to be taught she's safe?'

It was what she'd first tried to do. A compromise to let them carry on. But now she didn't think disentangling the girl from the sea was that easy.

'Yes. If stories are a line of communication, then we tell her stories until they overwrite what she thinks now.'

'She knows she's captive. That's a difficult thing to rewrite.'

'Doesn't mean it can't be done. I'll write a script, you seed it.'

Seed it. Auli studied Bea's profile, wondering whether they realised how little humanity they had granted the girl. If she'd been tempted to tell Bea her plans, that urge was dead now. 'Her name's Iolanta.'

'Yes, you said. But whatever we call her, her ghosts still killed Pertti.'

Their red-rimmed eyes glittered. Auli opened her mouth to apologise but they tipped their chin at the arc of the upper library walkway, and said roughly, 'Sorry. That's a cute one.'

Auli looked up, and her heart fell through the hollow of her bones like a bell.

The lamplight just barely reached the upper walkway, gleaming on the metal bars and catching the downturned faces of two children, sitting on a rock with their legs dangling, their heads canted together as the black-haired boy said something to the black-haired girl. They were both on the very edge of laughter, and Auli couldn't remember what he'd said.

She could remember the day, the hazy heat of summer between forest and shore. Midges and tiny fish circling their toes in the salt clear water, their mothers lighting a fire all ringed around with wet stones to protect the tinder mires.

'Oh,' she said faintly. The two children flickered and shifted, like there were two photos overlaid.

'Wait, that's not *you*, is it?'

It's my brother, Auli thought. That's my brother, that's my brother. She could feel the tide licking at her ankles, hear the crackle of the fire and a warbler singing out of sight. She could feel the warmth of him against her shoulder—

'Auli. Hey, Auli.'

Auli blinked. The two children flickered and smiled, looking down at her through the lamplit dark.

'If that's you, you should get clear. I heard that's super infectious.'

But it was her *brother*, right there, kicking his legs in the cold water with his smile full of mischief. Auli couldn't make herself look away.

'He died,' she whispered.

The children flickered, reset. She felt Bea's sadness; she felt as if her ribs were breaking. 'We think he died in the Crash. A shipwreck.'

'I'm sorry.'

Auli stared up at his familiar smile. She'd forgotten that one of his eye teeth was crooked. How could she have forgotten that?

'I'm sorry, but' – a hand jostling her shoulder – 'but maybe let's not get killed by a photo?' Bea rose. 'Come on. Haven't enough of us died yet?'

Auli rose as well, one hand on the railing, sneaking another look up at her brother, surrounded by shadows.

'Timo,' she said softly.

The ghost below was too loud for her to hear the quiet crackle of the photo, and she gripped the railing, fighting the urge to climb up, press her hand against the ghost of her brother's cheek, call his name, pray for miracles. She shuddered and lowered her gaze again. Bea was watching her like a mother bird – and why now? she wondered. It was too much a knife between her ribs to be coincidence. Bea reached the ladder and swung down one-handed. Auli took hold of the upright and turned, and gave a small cry.

The ghost of her brother and her from a world ago was

on the walkway right beside her, their legs swinging in the wildly shifting lamplight. Auli hadn't even seen the ghost move. 'Timo,' she whispered again, reaching out with one hand. Her foot slipped on the ladder, and she clutched at the rail again, gasping.

'Quick,' Bea said from below. Auli didn't look down, or up, or anywhere at all until the deck hit her feet, then she pressed her hands to her chest, her heart rattling beneath her palms all glass shards.

Bea pulled her out of the wandering path of the woman diving through an oil black sea, and from here, in amongst the Weather desks, Auli could not see the ghost in the library. It helped. Her heart cracked a little more.

'Go back to the barge, you're safer there,' she said quietly. 'I'll just check on the... Iolanta.'

'Will we try my idea in the morning? I can stay on board.'

Auli wavered, half her heart still up there in the library. After the evacuation there'd be only a handful of people to evade. She imagined paddling a kayak away from the Bellwether, Raphaël in one of the towers watching her go. Would he stop her, would he give the order to shoot? No, he wouldn't. He wouldn't, and how could she leave? Was she giving up on everything too soon?

'Perhaps—' she began. The anomaly ghost's crackle of engines and chains faltered, and in the quiet she heard someone calling.

'Did you hear that?'

Bea tilted their head birdlike, listening.

Uoti, Auli thought, bedbound and vulnerable. 'Give me that,' she said, reaching for the lamp. 'Go back—'

'Hell no,' Bea said, and followed Auli as she plunged into the darkness of the nearest tower.

* * *

It wasn't Uoti, it was Alexis, standing in the corridor outside the Hall clutching a tray with an oil lamp and pot of tea steaming faintly. When Auli first turned the corner he shrieked again, quietly.

'Alexis,' Auli gasped. No, she thought, not this poor boy so soon after her brother's ghost. She couldn't stand it. 'Are you hurt? Was it a ghost?'

The tray juddered in his hands and Auli took it from him gently, setting it on the floor.

'Auli,' Bea said quietly. 'I don't think it was him.'

Auli scanned the boy anyway before turning. Not nearly enough colour in his cheeks but he had no wounds and no decay, just terror. Uoti's bedroom door was ajar, and Bea pushed it but met resistance.

The resistance was a boatman's twitching leg.

'Uoti?' Auli pushed against the door. It was Alan on the floor, bleeding and shuddering.

Uoti coughed hollowly, then tried again. 'It was heading for me. He distracted it.'

'Where is it now?' Bea whispered.

'It's drowning all the men,' Alexis said behind them.

Auli saw her brother's crooked tooth behind her eyelids and her throat ached. 'Bea, will you fetch Niki, then take Alexis back down to the kitchen?'

Perhaps seeing her brother, or contemplating Raphaël choosing her death, had stripped Auli of horror because when she squeezed into the room and knelt by Alan's side, her hands were steady.

'Oh, Alan,' she whispered. He was covered in ragged red lines and a strange shimmer shine, but none of the wounds were what was killing him. He flexed and juddered again. She pressed her fingers to his throat, briefly back in the Oracle Room doing the same thing to Boudain in the clear light of a morning before everything fell apart. Alan's heart was still beating, but barely. His eyes flickered open, and when he saw her, he even tried to smile.

'Too slow,' he gasped. 'I was too slow.'

'No,' Auli whispered. There was blood on his lips and perhaps Niki could save him, but Auli didn't think so. The ghost was in him, somewhere, or it had been. The pulse beneath her fingers rattled and paused, rattled and paused. 'No, you did well, Alan. You saved Uoti.'

His face eased, just a little. He'd told her to sleep barely an hour ago, he'd dived for Miika when there was no hope. Two years ago she had cared for him when he was sick, and after his next trading trip, he'd brought her a book of poetry, another of myths, both unhaunted. *Seem to recall vomiting on you several times,* he'd said, smiling easily. *What's a little risk after that?*

He was not smiling now. His eyes were wide and frightened, froth at the corner of his mouth and his cheek scored across with more of those strange angular lines. 'Tell the boss,' he whispered. 'Tell...' His heart, his poor ghost-ravaged heart convulsed one last time, and fell still.

Old instincts, futile, stupid ones, made Auli's hands itch to *act*, but the new world had no place for hope, not here. So she closed Alan's staring eyes, and sat back slowly.

Boudain, boisterous, proud Pertti, Miika the maimed sniper and Joar, Célestine's sly lover – and now Alan.

'Was it a net?' she said eventually. Raphaël would blame himself for this, too. And perhaps her, and perhaps he would be right.

Uoti was watching her with glazed eyes, drowsy despite just watching a man cruelly die. Even on the day of the storm, when his heart had stopped and been restarted, he'd been sharper than this.

'Yes,' he said slowly. 'It was an animated movie. One of those Japanese ones, Studio something. Then it became video footage. That's the anomaly Niki mentioned?' His eyes drifted closed, dragged open.

Auli frowned, turning Alan's still-warm hand over gently. There were red net marks across the palm, and a dozen gleaming disks pressed into his skin. Fish scales. She touched one, expecting static and data. But it stuck to her fingertip and she lifted it to her eye, studying growth lines and iridescence. The dual forces of fascination and dread were so tangled within her she didn't move until Uoti spoke again.

'We're evacuating in the morning?'

'Yes.' She collected more fish scales from Alan's still-warm skin, folded them up in a scrap of paper. Her clipboard was still up in the library with her brother. 'You'll be first off.'

'We've failed then.'

Auli's head jerked up.

He opened his eyes and smiled at her sadly. 'There was always a risk – when you light a beacon, you cannot control what it attracts. I thought after all this time, but...' His watery eyes shifted to the drowned boatman then back to her.

Perhaps, Auli wanted to say, if they had not kept their beacon in a cage, it would not have called up monsters to save it. He had known about the cage – of all the people the ghosts had attacked, perhaps he was the only one who entirely deserved it. The thought felt cold and cruel, and she pushed to her feet unsteadily, hearing Niki in the corridor. 'I'll find Raphaël,' she said, and left without speaking to the doctor at all.

Chapter Thirty-One

Raphaël

RAPHAËL SLEPT FOR a scant few hours after laying Alan's body down alongside Pertti's and Joar's. The storeroom was beginning to smell, and death was one thing, he'd found out years ago. Decay quite another. They were one of his first tasks this morning – an unjust, perfunctory funeral as far into the fog and the deepwater as Raphaël dared.

Fifteen minutes later, washed and caffeinated – and thank the heavens for Dunya – Raphaël had confirmed the evacuation and was now slumped in a sofa in the Centre. An was fast asleep on a pile of cushions in his office, not stirring even when he'd set a mug of coffee down beside her.

He couldn't make much sense of the thing she was building. The taser-like elements were still there, alongside a metal box within an electromagnet coil, glass vials wired in. A mousetrap, he thought, baited with poison. The batteries would be the weak spot. But mother of God, he was hungry to test it. To not be powerless against the anomalies. To be able to *act* rather than continuously circle his own doubts.

The diving girl anomaly was on the walkway now, and a normal ghost half-hidden above him in the library, two children peering down as he ran through the Lindö camp supplies.

Sandesh emerged up through the West Tower stairs. 'They're taking the first kayak across, boss. Deploying the guide rope.'

Raphaël nodded. A board creaked in the Oracle Room, but the door stayed shut. He'd checked, seen Auli curled in the chair, weariness in every line of her sleeping form, and retreated silently without letting himself linger. If she was sleeping, he reassured himself, then she wasn't running away.

'You'll be in charge there,' he said.

Sandesh nodded. 'So priority risk on Lindö is likely to be the ghosts, yes? I'd opt for fires rather than blackout then.'

'Until the moment the fog shows signs of lifting.'

'Need a hand with the funeral, boss?'

'No,' Raphaël said. 'Frans volunteered.' And besides, he owed them all that much. 'With luck An's weapon will resolve this.'

'Would be good to kill us some ghosts.'

Raphaël let himself smile. 'Wouldn't it?'

He glanced at the photo above them. The light had strengthened a few degrees, and he froze, staring, then mastered himself and sent Sandesh away.

Once alone he looked up again, warily, to study child-Auli's face, and the brother she'd never forgiven herself for losing. He was tempted to fling valerian at it just to spare her the sight, but he'd only achieve a face full of herbs so instead he left.

Outside, in between ghosts, the muffled scuff of water beneath the Bellwether was the only sound. Even the orcas had vanished in the night and not, so far, returned. He thought of the kayaks laden with nervy researchers and hoped fervently the bloody great beasts had finished with their fun.

Niki was already watching the dock below – Célestine's defiant red headscarf and a lone rope being spooled out into the void.

Had you noticed it's all men? Auli had said last night when she'd come to tell him about Alan. *Perhaps you should all evacuate.*

He hadn't dignified that with a response.

'The Oracle will likely wake soon,' Niki said.

Raphaël grimaced faintly.

'I heard about Alan. And the anomalies are unchanged, Auli says.'

The boatman handling the belay had paused, the line of rope in the water like a slim black snake. Had they reached Lindö already, or had they got turned around in the directionless mist?

'Do I dose her again, Raphaël? Because I don't think Auli will go along with it again. Unless I get Gabrielle.'

Which reminded Raphaël of something else. 'Anyone been helping themselves to your supplies the last few days?'

Niki startled. The rope straightened, and Raphaël relaxed fractionally. Above the mist, gulls cried the dawn belatedly.

'Well, Auli, when An was infected. And Gabrielle asked for sedatives.' Raphaël turned towards Niki. 'She's been struggling to sleep. Anxiety.'

That might well be true. 'Can I suggest not giving her any more?' he said softly. 'Until Uoti is stronger.'

'What?'

Raphaël didn't answer, Niki didn't ask again. And when the boatman on the dock heaved on the wet line to bring it taut then tied it off, Raphaël straightened and nodded to himself, moved all his mental calculations around a fraction.

'Let's go speak to Auli,' he said, then paused. 'You go on. I'll bring breakfast, she'll have forgotten.' He ignored Niki's sudden grin, and moved off in the opposite direction, wondering how soon was too soon to wake An to ask for a miracle.

* * *

'SHE'D BE PERFECT though,' someone was saying in the Oracle Tower, in English. 'Far safer than you.'

Auli's voice, in Finnish, 'Have you ever told her bedtime stories, when she was...?' She stopped, likely remembering the brevity of each of the carers' lives here. Raphaël reached the tower bedroom. Auli was sitting cross-legged on the floor facing the Oracle's low bed, the Oracle curled on her side, eyes closed, hair drifting like she was underwater. The carer was in a chair, awkwardly mending blue cotton despite the sling, and Bea on the other bed, clipboard and a tattered book on their lap.

Only Auli noticed his arrival, glancing up then away far too fast.

The carer was shaking her head.

He checked the walkway outside the windows, watched something swell and fade in the mist.

Still in Finnish, Auli said behind him, 'Were you told not to?'

Silence. Raphaël turned, curious about the point Auli was pursuing. The carer eyed him flatly then looked back at Auli. 'No. I was told not to lipread her. That I would be safe if I didn't understand her.'

'So you never tried to communicate with her?'

Raphaël heard the horror in her voice, much as she tried to hide it. And felt a little of it himself. He'd countered his own discomfort with the thought that she had a carer and was, therefore, cared for. The figure on the bed was motionless save for her hair and a faint twitching of her fingers. She was nearly an adult, really, but looked like a girl still. It had always been easy to forget.

'The orcas wandered off overnight,' he said.

Bea gave him a perplexed look. Auli stiffened.

He wasn't sure why he needed to convince her. But the sight of her sitting beside the Oracle, vulnerable and determinedly oblivious, made something ugly bubble up within him –

fear, obviously, and frustration. But that wasn't all. Perhaps jealousy that she was so sure of her right path when he no longer was.

The dreary light made her gaze bottomless. 'Alan died, and the anomaly numbers are unchanged. Is Niki coming to sedate her? I won't let them, Raphaël. Will you restrain me?'

He flinched. Dammit, he actually flinched. 'I'm—'

The Oracle woke with a jerk. Hauled upright as if pulled on strings, her eyes were lightning-white and a stream of data fell from her cracked lips.

'Oh, damn,' Bea muttered, and began frantically transcribing. Auli took both the Oracle's hands in hers, Raphaël stiffened. There was a ghost somewhere making an ungodly beeping sound, but here in this room there was only the Oracle whispering numbers and Auli's fearless black gaze on her.

'Iolanta? Iolanta, can you hear me?' she said in Russian.

The cantation stopped abruptly. The girl's eyes focused. Raphaël shifted onto the balls of his feet. He could reach Auli in two strides to haul her out of range. The slightest sign of a ghost materialising in here and this cosy little nightmare was over.

'You let me drown,' the girl said.

Raphaël started. Auli tipped her head sadly.

'I'm sorry. But you didn't drown, see? You just slept, and now you're awake.'

The girl's eyes flickered. There were still no ghosts. 'You promised to save me from the bad men. Then you let me drown.'

'You are still safe from the bad men,' Auli whispered. 'You only slept. Did you have bad dreams?'

The girl looked around the room, unseeing. There was a shift in the light that had Raphaël checking outside again – a grey-black amorphous shadow in the mist.

The Salt Oracle

'I dreamed the bad men drowned in a river of blood and tumbling bones, the voice sang slow songs to the sea and towed all the bodies screaming into the dark.'

Raphaël turned from the window slowly. There were tears on the Oracle's face, lightning-lit. His Russian was hardly fluent, but he was suddenly wishing it worse.

'I dreamed I was the hook, dragging them down. For once I was the hook and not the scream. And then when all the bad men were bleeding eel food and bones, the waves washed me up on the shore of the forest.'

At least the carer was looking as sick as Raphaël felt. Sick, he realised, but not surprised. Did she always dream like that when she was sedated? *For once I was the hook and not the scream?* Holy God. Auli didn't look anything other than sad.

'What does that mean?' Bea whispered in English. No one answered.

'I'm sorry I let you dream those things,' Auli said quietly. 'I won't let them drown you again.'

'The bad men won't let me go home.' The girl looked at Raphaël but there were still no ghosts in the room. Why hadn't she summoned them like before, was it really that she trusted Auli? 'The bad men will destroy me if I don't help them drown.'

'No,' Auli said. She lifted one hand and touched the girl's cheek. 'You don't have to do that.' Then it was Auli glancing at Raphaël, her gaze shuttered and Raphaël too sickened to read her. 'Hush now, Iolanta. We'll eat and make ourselves strong. Girls in towers need their strength before their adventure can begin, you know.'

'Are we... are we trying the story?' Bea said. Up in the eaves a ghost crackled and began to murmur to itself.

'No,' Raphaël said. 'You're evacuating.'

And then, worst possible timing, Niki appeared in the doorway. Auli saw them, released the Oracle's hand and rose smoothly to her feet, saying, 'Bea, you head on down.'

Bea began to protest then fell silent, frowning, and no one moved until they had gone.

The Oracle, the girl who Niki was about to send back into blood-soaked dreams, spoke first.

'I don't want to drown.'

Auli stood in front of Niki and held her hand out. 'Give it to me and walk away, Niki,' she said gently. 'Then it's on me alone.'

Niki glanced at Raphaël, indecision on their face and syringe in their hand. It was too soon after Joar, Raphaël thought. Without that, Niki might have been able to do what Auli asked.

'I can't—'

The Oracle, the haunted girl, stumbled to her feet. Raphaël lurched forward realising he'd let Auli move out of his direct line, but he was too slow. In fact, he only made it worse, again.

The girl

THE GIRL IS so tired of drowning. She is *so tired* of being dragged down through blood and salt darkness, all her bones broken up, becoming fish scales, shark teeth, lantern eyes.

The black-eyed woman promised her, and the black-eyed woman is kind. She reminds the girl called Iolanta of tall trees and birdsong in the evening. But trees and birdsong cannot save you from the bad men. Iolanta has always known this. The voice in the dark has always known this.

'I will not drown,' she says.

Someone moves, the light is grey and slink-shadowed, the man is larger than the hanging moon and the girl screams.

'Get away!' Her words are salt and river rocks.

The black-eyed woman is holding her, oh, she remembers being held. Oh, she remembers *Hush now, hush until the bad men leave.*

'Hush, Iolanta. You're safe, you're—'

'Auli, *careful.*'

'Leave her *alone*, Niki.'

But she *did* hush, in the forest by the river, in her mama's arms, she hushed and it did not stop the bad men. Her papa still fell. Her mama was dragged away screaming.

'Hush, Iolanta. You're safe. I won't let you drown this time.'

But she remembers. She remembers bad men pulling on her arms. Her arms that are full of storms and her bones are made of teeth and—

Ah, my child, we will have our vengeance, yes?

She flexes in the woman's arms. It feels safe here, but it has felt safe before, and her papa died. It has felt safe before and her mama was taken. The bad men will not let her go free, and perhaps the black-eyed woman will also be gone and gone and dead and still Iolanta will be the girl in the tower, drowning.

'Auli, let me. It won't harm her. She needs to calm—'

'Leave us! It's you making her like this. Just leave us alone! You, too. Get out.'

'I have to—'

'Auli, you aren't safe. Please—'

The bad men, Iolanta thinks, will hurt the black-eyed woman. Everyone who cares for the girl in the tower is destroyed.

Apart from me. They've tried. But they have failed.

Apart from the voice. The girl flexes again, wraps her shark-tooth, salt-blood arms around the black-eyed woman and whispers into her forest hair.

'The girl in the tower called to the monsters. Because she was a monster, too, all tooth and fury.'

'Oh, love. Oh, love, stop, please.'

And then voices in other tongues, the crackle of numbers, pixels, all the things that steal her from herself, but they none of them can stop her story.

'The monsters gathered in the water between the tower and the land. Full of fury, they lured all the bad men to them. They sucked them down or they tore them up for feasting.'

Oh, good girl. My wild daughters. Condemned for doing only as they were bid. My wild girls, take your tithe.

More shouting and pain in her arm that is not her arm but kelp fronds and bladder wrack, wreck spar barnacle-boned. Her tongue is not her tongue anymore. She tries to tell the story, but numbers skitter over her teeth like crabs. 'Seven hundred, and forty-two. The monsters gathered in the water between tower and the land. Twenty-eight point three. My wild daughters, take your tithe. Degrees. Seven, eleven...' She is drowning again.

She is drowning.

Please, she thinks, sinking.

'No! Niki, how could you? Iolanta, Iolanta, Iolanta.'

It is the last thing the flotsam girl hears, her own name. She clings to it in the dark.

Chapter Thirty-Two

Auli

AULI WAS TOO furious to speak as she watched Niki lay Iolanta back with such Judas gentleness. The Bellwether rocked, startling after days of unearthly stillness, but Auli didn't move, wrapping her fury against her ribs so she did not explode.

If only Niki had left. If only Raphaël had not thought she needed saving. If only the girl had not been such a struggling, charged thing in Auli's arms that Niki had been able to start injecting her before Auli could pull her away. Auli watched the limp child now, and didn't care anymore whether the Bellwether survived her leaving. Let them all be lost, she thought viciously, they deserved it.

The alarm bells were sounding, the Bellwether was bucking and groaning all around her, and she couldn't care.

Except Raphaël had run towards whatever it was. Did she condemn him with the rest of them? Yes, no. She was too angry to tell.

Niki had fled, too. Ursula edged around a flickering ghost to go outside and returned with another ghost drifting in her wake. Not anomalous.

'It is bad.'

Auli dropped her hand from her raging heart. The Bellwether strained against its anchors. She half-expected the storm ghost to manifest around them, but the fog was lazy as a cat with a mouse, curling its claws inside the door as the alarm bells rang off-key.

If the girl were awake perhaps Auli could have calmed her and dissipated this new horror. Let them all be lost, she repeated, but it was already losing its heat. Raphaël was down there; Bea, Alexis, Célestine.

Their only hope was that the girl dreamed peacefully or woke soon.

AULI LOOKED AT Ursula. 'I need to… organise some things, but I'll return.'

Ursula studied her, stolid face drawn in the drear light. 'You want to help her,' she said eventually. 'No one has ever wanted that, before.'

'No. They haven't.'

The two women watched one another over the limp girl. A ghost sparked in an oil lamp flame.

'Do you?' Auli added.

Ursula looked down at the girl. 'Iolanta,' she said, as if trying it out for fit. 'I have two sons, and a husband burned too badly to work. I was desperate when I took this job and will die, I think, if I stay here much longer.' Which was likely true – her deafness could not protect her forever. She glanced at the lingering ghosts, rocked when the Bellwether rocked. Auli didn't speak and the alarm cut off mid-chime. 'My boys are almost grown. They have found… ways to live without me.' Her voice was without inflexion and yet Auli still heard the layers to those words. The heartbreak, the pride, the fear.

'Why not go home?' Auli said, but Ursula was looking at

something within herself, her sons grown while she was here, protecting them by waiting to die far away. Auli tipped both her hands palm up in question. Ursula blinked and almost, almost smiled.

'You are taking her away.' She did not wait for confirmation, as if she'd already known. As if she'd watched Auli speaking to Iolanta. 'So maybe I will. And in return, you should know...' She met Auli's gaze squarely, seemed to reach a decision that surprised her, and added, 'It was me. Boudain Caron was me, and I am not sorry for it.'

The Bellwether wept against its restraints. The air in the room tasted of fog and thunder, and Auli didn't understand.

'What?'

'I threw his notes into the sea after. Used her sedative so he did not suffer, although he did not deserve kindness.' Ursula looked back to the sleeping girl. 'If I had not, she would not have gone without her medicine for the first time, she would not have woken, and we would not be here talking about escape. No, I am not sorry for it.'

Auli reeled.

She'd suspected Joar, then Gabrielle *and* Joar. Célestine had suggested the carer but Auli had said no, because Ursula could have killed the Oracle at any time, and why would anyone other than Gabrielle want Boudain dead?

But this woman had.

'*Why?*' she said faintly.

The research notes. What had she—

Ursula met Auli's eyes unflinching. 'I saw you talking. You, him and the new boy. I saw him say *There will always be someone willing to risk it.*' She sneered faintly. 'I saw him say *It might be easier with younger subjects.*'

Oh, Auli thought. Yes, she had been there. And of course, Boudain had not thought she mattered, she was only the carer... and he had been talking in English.

'You speak English? she whispered. It was by far the least important question.

'No one ever asked.'

No. Why would they? 'You thought he...' Auli began. 'You thought...'

Ursula's face was softer and angrier than Auli had ever seen her. 'I thought I would rather kill him than see one more child treated like this. I thought I would die anyway so why not make it matter.'

'What?' someone else said behind her, and Auli yelped before she recognised the voice.

Gabrielle took the last step up into the room, and said, in English to Auli, 'Was that a confession? You ought to fetch your captain.' And then, in Finnish, too loud and too slow, 'You killed him. How in God's name did you think to get away with it?'

Ursula did not acknowledge her, but her eyes went hard and flat.

'I would never have let him do it. I would have stopped him,' Auli said, barely a whisper but Ursula saw it and chose to answer her instead of Gabrielle.

'Would you? He was going to bring in desperate people, like me. Or children like my sons, and create more Oracles from them, to sell as slaves.'

'He *what?*' Gabrielle said.

'He brought that boy from London to help him.'

'Leigh...' Auli pressed a hand over her throat. He *had* brought Leigh in, without explanation, and Leigh *had* been tasked with experiments Auli did not condone.

'What is she talking about?'

Auli didn't answer Gabrielle. 'He wouldn't have gone that far. He didn't deserve to die.'

The girl on the bed stirred, cried out softly. The ghosts crackled in the grey light, the floor restless as a skiff.

'You lie to yourself,' Ursula said, the words so flat and so simple. 'But what does it matter anymore?'

Auli wanted to rail against it all. The Bellwether moaned and for the first time she wondered what the girl had summoned with her furious hurt. She thought of Raphaël running towards whatever it was, and her whole heart flickered within her ribs. This was not the time, she told herself desperately. It was neither the time for justice, nor for mourning.

'Fine,' she said, and both women startled at something in her face or her tone. She was, she realised, so very, very angry at every single thing. 'Ursula, this will have to wait. Can I trust you with the girl, at least?'

'Fraser, I hardly think—'

'I killed to protect her. Do you think I would harm her now?'

'You killed to bury an idea,' Auli amended harshly. 'And perhaps because you hate us. I can't... Gabrielle, what's happening down there? Why did you come up?'

Gabrielle opened her mouth, smoothed her free hand over a rumpled blouse. 'To make you look at what you did. There were only another two crossings to finish the evacuation, then you let her wake.'

Auli didn't move.

Gabrielle made a sound of wordless frustration then crossed the room to peer down at the Oracle. Auli's arms flexed, and she wanted to howl at them both, or run down and down through the Bellwether to see if Raphaël was safe. And An and Célestine, Bea and Alexis and Dunya. She wanted to stand guard over the girl she'd already betrayed until she awoke again.

'She's fully dosed?'

Where are you *needed*? Auli thought. She had not really been needed anywhere for a long time, but this girl needed Auli, to take her away from here before the sea destroyed them all.

The Bellwether needed the same thing, for its heart if not its future, and they'd all realise it eventually. If they survived.

'Yes,' Auli lied flatly. Very aware of the half-full syringe in her pocket.

'Well, that's something at least. You will stay here and keep her dosed until this situation is under control. You'll report to the camp on Lindö daily. And keep them both locked in this tower.'

Auli met the older woman's eyes and felt the oddest urge to laugh. 'It was my intention to stay, yes. I'll sound the all-clear each evening from a guard tower.'

Gabrielle stiffened but Auli didn't care. The Bellwether yawed heavily again, and still there was no storm. The fog pressed its blind face against the window, blunt-toothed, and Auli turned for the stairwell, thinking, *it will be okay*. The fog could even be a friend, if it didn't kill them first.

THERE WAS AN anomaly prowling the research deck. Red-lit men running the steel corridors of a submarine, then a desperately struggling oil-slick bird, flickering into a broken-winged metal man gasping as he died. Auli skirted it, heard a child's high laugh and glanced up into the library before she could stop herself. Her own child face smiled down at her, her brother laughing, reaching down with one thin hand.

Auli froze.

They had been a photograph yesterday, they had not laughed, nor reached… her brother tilted his head, and his eyes were black from lid to lid, oil-slick, deep-sea black. He laughed, and his teeth glinted sharp and multitudinous, his jaw opening too wide. Auli spun away, a hand pressed to her mouth and nausea clawing at her throat as she stumbled towards An's door. But An was not there, and Raphaël was.

'Auli?' He pulled her in and behind him, like he might

keep her safe behind the wall he built of himself. 'What happened?'

'Nothing.' She thought she was going to be sick. 'Just another anomaly.'

Raphaël scanned the research deck and she stared at his back. There was a singe mark across his shoulder blade, and she knew when he spotted her brother's ghost by the way his chest expanded. She could not help herself; despite all the anger, despite the leaving, or maybe because of it, she pressed her hand over the burnt cloth and rested her cheek very gently against his spine. If only, she thought, she did not feel so safe with him. It would make it all so much easier.

'An's down on the dock trying out her weapon,' he murmured, his voice beneath her jaw like a thousand memories. 'We can get rid of that one next, if you like.'

She shuddered; even made monstrous it was still Timo. As if he heard her thoughts, he laughed again from the library walkway.

Raphaël reached back, found her hand and drew it around him, pressed her palm over his ribs, his own atop hers warm and certain. 'It's not him, my heart.'

She breathed him in slowly, his muscles taut beneath her hand. 'It won't stop while she's close to the sea,' she whispered. 'Niki can keep drugging her until she dies of it, but it won't stop until she's either dead or gone far away.'

Raphaël turned then, and she tried to step back but his arms were already around her and this might be the last time. It might be all she had of him to carry with her. So she stayed there, held against him and aching.

'Bea says it's Greek myth this time. Two sisters who become a whirlpool and a monster.'

Auli opened her eyes. 'Scylla and Charybdis.'

'That's it.'

'The kayaks?'

The Bellwether lurched, Raphaël shifted his weight, holding her steady. 'One's here. The other was on the water when it started. We can't see.'

'Who's left?'

'To cross? An, Niki, Célestine and Gabrielle.'

'Bea and Leigh?'

A pause. She lifted her head to look up at him.

'Leigh was down to go across in the third group so he's ashore.' He met her gaze steadily. 'Bea was crossing.'

No, she thought. She'd sent them right into it. He brushed her hair from her forehead, and she saw his wish to offer her false comfort and was glad he didn't.

'You know I'm right,' she said, pulling away again. This time he let her go.

'Auli, let's just—'

She shook her head. 'Will you ever listen to me, Raphaël?'

'What? I—' The submarine-bird anomaly cried out behind him and he swore, spinning back to shut the door. As if that would stop it.

Auli moved further away. From the ghosts beyond that door as much as from this man who still, catastrophically, held her heart.

'If Niki had not sedated her again, Bea would be on Lindö now, setting up a tent and bickering with Tobias.' Her hands were shaking and the room swayed around her, all shadows and the smell of metal. 'You knew this might happen because I told you, but you believed Niki instead, and Gabrielle. So this' – she gestured at the wide opaque windows – 'is on you, Raphaël. It is on Gabrielle and Niki and you, for not listening to me.' His skin greyed, but she would not let him speak. 'I can understand them not believing me. Gabrielle thinks I'm worthless and Niki thinks I am unqualified, and they are both right. But you, Raphaël? You think I am worthless, too? That I am unqualified to understand a child filled with ghosts?' She pressed her hand against her ribs, trying to still her clamouring, burning heart.

Raphaël stared at her across the empty room, then shook his head slowly. 'Never,' he said simply.

'Then why?' she whispered. 'Why won't you believe me?'

He ran a hand through his hair, swore a long stream of unintelligible French and Arabic combined, then met her eyes again and shifted his weight once more as if the Bellwether had yawed even though this time it had not. 'Can you not guess?'

'Because you think I am foolhardy. Because you think I am too illogical—'

'Because if you are right then you will leave.'

Auli stared at him, and he stared at her, and she could not speak.

He laughed sadly. 'I don't want you to be right. Because *I don't know how to protect you* if you are. It *terrifies* me, Auli. You think this place is cruel to the girl, and you're right. You think I don't care about that, and you're wrong. But the world out there would be cruel to *you*, Auli, if you go. And I know which one of those I can bear.'

Somehow, he had crossed the room while he spoke, within touching distance but making no move to touch her.

'You won't need to protect me out there,' she said, plucking randomly at one thing in everything he'd just thrown at her feet. 'Because you will be here.'

He was staring at her as if he would prise her open in search of answers. 'You really want to leave?'

'I... it's the only way. It's the *only way*, Raphaël. Otherwise, the sea will turn her into a weapon nothing An conjures will be able to stop.' She grasped Raphaël's arm urgently. 'The sea and our treatment of her will both tear at her until she destroys the Bellwether... unless I take her away. You must see that.'

He set his hand over her clutching fingers, twining them together, warm and calloused and real. 'Why you? Why not the carer?'

'Because I promised.'

'Of course you did,' Raphaël sighed. 'Promised to keep the most wanted person in northern Europe safe whilst dragging her across a burgeoning warzone to – where? Your mothers?' Her predictability rattled her, but he was still talking. 'But taking her will destroy the Bellwether just as much as keeping her here might. What of everyone here?'

Auli searched for her anger but was only riven apart by latent mourning. This place. It had given her a chance to grieve her brother by making his death less commonplace. It had given her hope.

'An said they can survive,' she whispered. Raphaël's fingers stiffened in surprise. 'She said they can work on alternative tech, on ghost-proofing tech, on salvage and mapping the old-fashioned way. She said it's possible.'

Raphaël's face twisted.

An had found Auli and said these things fiercely. But she'd also repeated that Auli would get both herself and the Oracle killed within days.

'They'd be less of a target,' Raphaël conceded.

Was the Bellwether settling? Auli was so unsteady beneath Raphaël's light touch she could not tell. Bea, she thought again, like just thinking their name was a kind of beacon.

'Let me go,' Auli whispered.

He stared at her for a long, silent minute. And then something taut within him eased as abruptly as a cut wire.

'Now who doesn't listen?' he said, and he smiled.

Oh God but she was never prepared for the beauty of his smile. This one in particular that felt made entirely for her.

'I can't let you go, Auli, my heart. Because I am coming with you.'

'No, Raphaël, what about your job, and Célestine? You cannot—'

'She's coming, too. She told me so this morning.'

Perhaps she was dreaming, Auli thought. Perhaps she would wake and this whole terrible fall into heartbreak would have been nothing but a nightmare. Boudain would greet her at her desk, coffee in one hand, straightening his old-world tie, and Auli would know she was forgettable and forgotten and safe.

She did not feel forgotten now. And it was madness to think that she was safe.

'What if I don't want you?' But her fingers were tangled with his. I do, they said. I do.

'Then I'll trail you through the fog and you'll have to put up with Célestine's singing on your own.' He looked suddenly so unburdened she felt like weeping.

'…Singing?'

Raphaël nodded gravely. 'Sings when she's travelling. Says it is the only time she is free.'

It had never occurred to Auli this place might be a cage until she'd seen the girl within the Oracle. She was a fool, but she was going home.

'We'll need more supplies,' she said simply. She still didn't entirely believe him, perhaps he was about to break her all over again, but she supposed it didn't matter. He had already guessed where she was going, how hard the rest of her barely-there plan? 'If I can stop Niki dosing her this evening then I'm taking a kayak tonight. Follow the shores round to Kökar, persuade a boat to take us to Mariehamm then north.'

Raphaël did not laugh at the naivety of it all. 'I'll get Célestine's old chair out of storage. It's got a motor and all-terrain wheels.' Of course he would have engineered something like that. 'I need to go see what's happening. I only came up to get something for An, she'll be furious. Then I'll get more food.'

Auli nodded. 'I'll steal a ghost infection pack, more water.' It had felt too insurmountable to believe in until now. But she was really leaving, really attempting to smuggle a fragile girl out of her own fortress and over a vengeful sea. Her heart faltered. 'Raphaël.'

He paused in the middle of releasing her, his mind likely already three steps ahead, ten, twenty.

'If the sea realises what we're doing...' She lifted one shoulder. The fog leaned against the Bellwether, listening, the girl in the tower dreamed of drowning and blood.

Raphaël hissed in a breath, then laughed fatalistically. 'Then we shall creep silently across the waters and pray' – he pressed a kiss to her cheek, fierce and fast with a new smile in his dark eyes – 'to you, Auli, and the power of the stories you tell the girl.' Then he grabbed something from the worktable and paused in the doorway, glancing over his shoulder. 'Six hours. Be careful.'

'You, too,' Auli whispered to the empty room.

Chapter Thirty-Three

Raphaël

It took two more hours for the channel to calm enough to risk another crossing. Raphaël ferried Gabrielle and An across himself, Gabrielle paying the rope through her arms as Raphaël paddled and scanned their small perimeter of sea. From the dock they'd only been able to see the surging current arcing around the Bellwether and it had been Célestine earlier who'd realised what it was.

'Whirlpool,' she'd said when Raphaël arrived from the Oracle Tower and ran out along the dock to where the rope was still taut, the kayak carrying Bea and Sandesh an orange blur on the very edge of visibility.

'Pull back,' he'd shouted. The mist swallowing up his words, the kayak fretful, fading as they were dragged forward. The waves when he bent to check felt both real and not – water and an impossible static. Someone shouted from the mist.

'Pull back,' he had repeated. Whatever it was, he could do nothing for them out there.

The kayak had not reappeared. But Bea's voice had, muffled and high.

'What did they—' he began.

There was a shout of pure horror, the rope spasmed on the surface of the water, then fell still. He'd nearly launched himself into the other kayak, but Célestine had stopped him.

'What can you do, Rafa?' she'd said brutally? 'Punch it? Don't commit suicide and dress it up as courage.'

Raphaël had paused, fighting the bucking dock, and An had appeared just then carrying a bundle of metal and wires.

'They said *Scylla*. What's that?' he said.

Célestine rocked her chair. 'Fuck it all, Rafa, you're not paddling out against an angry Greek goddess in a plastic kayak, don't be an idiot.'

An had set her metal box on the dock, and glanced up with her empty socket a great black wound but her other eye sharp, almost excited. The madwoman. Raphaël had straightened up.

'Fine,' he'd said with a grin like a curse. 'But what about if I'm armed?'

AND NOW IT was two hours later, and he was following a rope blindly through the mist with An poised behind him to try again. They'd failed earlier, the water too rough, the whirlpool and the roaring both too far away. Guarding the passage, if Bea's shouted words – last words? – were correct.

But the whirlpool was reduced to a sultry drag against the keel now, and they reached Lindö unhindered, finding the other kayak cracked and drawn high up the shore, and the camp chaotically busy.

Sandesh shrugged off the ugly wounds on his leg. 'Bea's a bit bedraggled but unhurt, and I'll live.'

Not infected, he meant.

An found Tobias, bandages flashing white as she gestured at the crates of tech she'd brought across. She wouldn't like entrusting her new weapon to Raphaël, and wouldn't forgive him stealing it tonight either, but she'd have something else built by tomorrow, and they weren't facing anomalies here anyway. He hoped.

'Get that kayak fixed ASAP,' he said to Sandesh and An both.

The former nodded, the second ignored him.

It was one thing, he thought, to abandon your post, another to leave them stranded. But he'd made his choice in his office doorway, Auli's hand on his shoulder, the ghost of her dead brother watching him with needle-sharp teeth. He'd made it before then, when his own doubts and his mother's whispered voice had coalesced around Auli being the only one who cared to see this place for what it was. *Be strong,* his mother had told him, and it had taken him too long to realise she meant the strength it took to hold a dangerous child's hand, not the strength it took to imprison her.

Raphaël carried An's weapon back to the waterline, then turned to frown at her when she shadowed him. She frowned back, waded past him and climbed neatly back into the kayak.

'You should stay here,' he tried.

An had a vision of an Oracle-less Bellwether, which meant An knew what Auli was planning. She touched the edge of her missing eye.

'No.'

'After your vengeance?' he asked.

'Wouldn't you be? And when better than with the Bellwether emptied of idiots likely to wander into the crossfire?' She paused. 'Almost empty of idiots.'

The camp was too close for this, so Raphaël swung into the kayak as well. When they were ten meters out, the fog erasing everyone they'd left behind, he said without looking at her, 'You could come.'

Two strokes of the paddles, the writhing movement of something in the mist.

'I have things yet to do.'

'And after you've killed all the anomalies?'

She huffed. 'That's just the beginning. There is so much I can do if I'm not pussyfooting around an Oracle and three PIs who can't see beyond her.'

'Will you try to stop us?'

She snorted. 'From taking away the source of all the trouble? Not likely. More fools the lot of you.'

Raphaël laughed and they didn't talk again.

It didn't feel, as they slunk back across to the Bellwether, remotely like the twin ghosts were gone, only waiting for the Oracle to wake. It was mid-afternoon when he pulled himself up onto the dock, and Célestine made a note on her lists as An gathered up her weapon and moved back into the Bellwether with her one eye shining fiercely.

'The last two people, or food supplies next?' Célestine said.

Niki and herself, he assumed. He tied up the kayak and studied it. They were meant to take three and supplies. Not four and a wheelchair and supplies. But the flat calm of the sea would give them leeway.

'Célestine,' he said, straightening.

She studied him, the red of her headscarf the only colour in the world. 'So you've spoken to her.'

He checked his watch, swore, checked Célestine's – four hours until the Oracle woke, and it was dark enough to leave. 'You'd be safer here,' he said. They were speaking French, of course. None of the remaining boatmen spoke it. 'You'd finally get PI, too.'

She studied her repainted nails. Red again, always. 'Of a college stripped of its black heart. All of us scrabbling in the debris to justify our worth. I didn't guess, you know, about the Oracle. It is not so hard to leave that behind.' And then she smiled slantingly, luminous and familiar. 'Anyway, it is high time for a new adventure, no?'

Raphaël grinned. Footsteps echoed oddly on the steps, and they both watched Niki descending, laden with bags.

'Ready, Doctor?' Célestine said in English. Raphaël reached for the bags.

'The sedatives are on my desk, Rafa. You'll make sure...'

Raphaël hmmed, watching the yaw of the kayak on the mercurial water as he loaded it. But Niki persisted.

'Raphaël?'

He sighed, then set to lying to someone he'd considered a friend.

THE ORACLE – HE'D have to stop calling her that – woke at exactly six forty-five. He was in West Tower, watching an anomaly circling the library dome, when the Bellwether vibrated up through the soles of his feet as the whirlpool stirred.

'So she woke up mad,' he muttered. This might all go spectacularly wrong still. In fact, of the sixteen or so different scenarios he had played out, it did exactly that in twelve. He'd watched a frightened girl beg not to drown though, and the woman he loved promise to save her. There were many things he'd hardened himself to, over the years, but it turned out both of those were beyond him, and he was glad of it.

An was in the Weather area, where it looked like a bomb had gone off.

'You alive?' he asked.

An straightened from studying the metal box at her feet, while the ghost of child-Auli, and child-Auli's brother watched them from the library, grinning uncannily.

'It's holding it,' An said. She nudged the box with her foot, and sparks cascaded from one of the soldered wires.

'Holding it?'

She grinned, not unlike the ghosts above. 'Schrodinger's ghosts. I won't know until I open it. Destroyed by the magnets and the herbs or just pissed off.'

'Ghosts can't—' He stopped, grimaced. 'I'd recommend keeping it shut, in that case.'

'Where's the fun in that?' The Bellwether lurched again, creaked sonorously. 'Besides, it needs to be reusable.'

Raphaël glanced up into the dome. An noticed.

'They're next.' She bared her teeth again.

'Captain.'

Raphaël turned. The box sparked again and An crouched over it. The carer caught his eye from the open Oracle Room door, then disappeared back inside.

AULI WAS SITTING on the girl's bed, stroking her hair back from her face and singing quietly. The girl was, Raphaël realised with a lurch of belated guilt, crying. The carer had stayed downstairs, curiously, and three ghosts crowded the tower room, one worryingly anomaly-like, although in the encroaching gloom he couldn't be sure. His hands itched.

The singing broke off. 'How long?'

Raphaël leaned against the cluttered table. Shells and sea glass and dried seaweed. Was that all the girl had been allowed to own?

'An hour? Can she be ready by then?'

He'd left only West Tower manned, a skeleton crew for an abandoned vessel. With East and North Towers empty, they could slip alongside the barges, masked by fog long before they emerged from cover. It should work perfectly. Unless the carer sounded the alarm, or the boatmen decided to run perimeter checks. Unless the girl summoned anomalies.

Auli nodded, wiped the girl's tears away. 'Tonight,' she whispered, soft and calm. 'Tonight the girl in the tower will sail away across the sea, and all the monsters will sleep, knowing she is finally going home.'

The girl's hands flexed, the lightning in her eyes flickering in the gloom. 'The bad men will stop her.'

Raphaël winced.

'The bad men are all gone away,' Auli said. 'Only the girl and her friends are left in the tower, and now they, too, will leave.'

'The girl will go home to the forest?'

A ghost, an HTML page, drifted towards the bed, spinning mindlessly away again when Raphaël threw valerian at it. He eyed the one up in the rafters and hoped fervently that it would stay there.

'I promise,' Auli whispered.

The girl smiled, but did not stop crying. The Bellwether groaned and swayed.

Auli promised, and so Raphaël would help render it true. He pushed to his feet and headed for the stairs.

Chapter Thirty-Four

Auli

THEY LEFT URSULA in the Oracle Room, calmly knitting despite the sling.

'You should come with us,' Auli said. 'They might blame you.'

'You would want me?'

Auli hesitated a moment too long.

'There is no room,' Ursula carried on flatly. 'I will say the captain threatened me.'

Her needles clicked and one lone lamp cast a gold circle in the dark. The prospect of launching out into that miasma in only an overloaded kayak set a vicious nausea writhing in Auli's stomach.

'Gabrielle knows,' she said. 'You aren't safe.'

The needles paused. 'You should be glad of that.'

She should. Boudain had not been innocent, but he deserved justice, and that justice would be the freedom of this lonely woman. The girl swayed against Auli's side, her eyes the brightest thing in the room.

'I should be,' Auli said slowly. 'But I'm not. Your sons don't deserve to lose you twice.'

Ursula flinched, looked at the girl, then Auli again. 'Take her away,' she said. 'I never wanted to care for the thing that would kill me. But... take her far away. I have survived worse than Gabrielle.'

Iolanta stiffened, so Auli knew who had entered the room.

'Ah. I wondered,' Raphaël said.

Of course he had.

'Why— Actually, it's not my problem anymore. If Gabrielle gives you any trouble, mention the soup she's been feeding Uoti.'

Ursula hissed, and Auli turned to stare at him. 'For God's sake,' she murmured.

'More for sole control, I think. Uoti is a bit of a favourite of the Council. She's too brash apparently.'

Auli scowled. 'Because she's a woman who isn't afraid of a fight? They'd respect that in a man.'

The corner of Raphaël's mouth lifted. She realised the irony and gave herself a vicious little shake. 'What a crew of murderers, poisoners and prison guards,' she said. 'We none of us deserve saving.'

Raphaël's gaze softened. 'Bea's fine,' he said.

'The bad men,' Iolanta whispered. She was watching Raphaël from the corner of her flickering eyes.

'Raphaël's not a bad man,' Auli said gently, pushing all of her strange, twisted sorrow firmly away. 'Raphaël's going to lead us safely across the sea.'

'The grey wolf?' Iolanta said slowly. 'The grey wolf showed the girl the way through the forest.'

Auli could not remember any tales of grey wolves, although Bea would, and Auli was going to sneak away without saying goodbye. In this broken world, it would likely be forever, too. People were so easily left behind.

'We need to go,' Raphaël said. 'I'll meet you down there.'

Ursula resumed her knitting, turning herself away so she could not see them say goodbye.

'Come then, Iolanta,' Auli said, taking one of the girl's twisting hands. 'Let's go.'

THE YAWNING CURRENT of the whirlpool looked deadly. She stood at the foot of the dock and shot Célestine a quick, alarmed look.

'Why has it started again?' Célestine said. 'She looks calm.'

Auli didn't know. Panic threatened to choke her, but she turned to the girl, touched her pale cheek and whispered, 'Can you send the monsters to sleep, Iolanta? Can you tell the monsters the bad men have gone and it is time to sleep?'

Iolanta stared at her. 'So we can cross the sea?'

'Yes, dear one. Let the monsters sleep so the grey wolf can guide us safely across the sea.'

'The grey wolf?' Célestine laughed quietly. 'Oh, he will love that.'

Iolanta closed her lightning eyes. The water hushed and pulled beneath them, and the fog pressed all around listening. 'The girl in the tower said to the monsters, sleep now, dear ones. Sleep now, the bad men are—'

'Going somewhere?'

Auli jerked, pulling Iolanta instinctively into her arms. Célestine's chair screeched against the wet boards, and she swore in French. 'What the fuck are you doing here? You were crossing with Niki.'

'I was.' Leigh stood on the lowest step with a shuttered oil-lamp in one hand. 'Then you got distracted and I thought maybe I'd just hang around here, see what was happening.' He smiled that guileless smile at Auli, opened the lamp so the dock lit blurrily. 'And look! A little field trip with the Oracle.'

A spy, Ursula had called him. Come to create new Oracles to sell as slaves.

'Go back inside, Leigh,' she said, her voice thin and strained. 'This has nothing to do with you.'

He stepped onto the dock, set his lamp down and rested his hand on the back of Célestine's chair, ignoring the ripple of disgust crossing her face.

'The bad man,' Iolanta whispered.

'But it is. You see, I need that.' He nodded at the girl trembling within Auli's arm, and his voice held neither uncertainty nor charm; chillingly unfamiliar. 'So I can't let you take her.'

'Who says we are taking her, you fool?' Célestine said scornfully. 'We are carrying out an experiment with the whirlpool. And you are in the way.'

'In the dark? I don't think so.'

The dock rippled and the Bellwether groaned. Célestine's chair rolled forward, just enough that her footplates were in front of Leigh's ankle. Auli kept her eyes on Leigh's face.

'We can discuss your research once everything is back to normal,' Auli said. 'You can't honestly believe *I* would do anything to harm the Bellwether?'

He smiled that uncanny, warm smile again, one hand on Célestine's chair, the other in his jacket pocket. Where was Raphaël?

'Because you are the dutiful researcher, risen undeservedly to power? Or because you think this place is a bastion of good work?'

She tried not to flinch and failed.

'The bad men won't let us leave,' Iolanta whispered. Away in the dark, a low roar reverberated through the mist. The dock listed, wavelets breaking over one side where the current was strengthening.

Leigh tipped his head, listening. The pale lamplight hid his eyes. 'I'm not a bad man,' he said gently. 'I just can't let you take her away, you know? We need to replicate her. How many lives will we save, Auli? How many will you condemn if I let you go?'

Célestine snorted. '*Let* us go?'

He didn't look her way, like she didn't matter. Auli hated him for that almost as much as the rest.

Above, in the leaden mist, a door squeaked briefly.

'You're right,' Auli said quickly, cradling the girl, praying she stayed silent, that she didn't call anything to them. 'You're right. This place has saved lives, and will without Boudain's experiments. Is this the consortium, making you do this? I don't know what they've promised you, how much money—'

Leigh pulled his hand out of his pocket, said, 'Okay, now you're boring me,' and pressed the barrel of a gun neatly against Célestine's head. 'Maybe it's not about the money. Maybe I'm noble enough to think a better future is worth some blood.' He laughed his boyish laugh, and Auli shuddered. 'Let the Oracle go, or your friend here will have a nasty accident. I won't miss, unlike my idiot friend. I showed him exactly where you sit, you know, but he still missed. And here you are, obstructing me yet again.'

Auli's skull filled with a high whine and Célestine's eyes were white-rimed, sad. Auli said desperately, 'If I let her go, she will summon ghosts and we all might die, Leigh.'

He tsked softly, the stairs creaked, Auli didn't look up. 'I'll take my chances.'

'If I let her go, she'll fall,' Auli tried again. Célestine shook her head very slightly, the gun barrel ruching her headscarf, her hands motionless on her wheels. 'I need to bring her to you.'

'The grey wolf,' Iolanta whispered.

No, Auli thought. Please no. 'Hush, dear one. Hush now, until the bad men leave.'

'The girl asked the grey wolf for aid.'

'You pushed Bea in on purpose,' Célestine said suddenly.

'On the barge when the orcas were here. You pushed them in because they'd been helping Auli.'

Leigh didn't look at her. 'You should have trusted me, Auli. Would have saved a lot of bother. Hurry up then, bring her here.'

'It's going to be okay,' Auli whispered, to Iolanta, to Célestine, to herself. The sea roared and heaved, the lamp's flame wavered. She moved along the unsteady dock, both of them shaking, and stopped two paces away. Iolanta leaned against Auli, murmuring numbers, the grey wolf, river stones. 'Come and get her,' Auli said.

'Come here.' He nudged the gun harder against Célestine, making her head jerk sideways, but her gaze was fixed on Auli. So fixed Auli knew she, too, had heard the stairs.

'I'm not getting any closer to that gun,' Auli snapped. 'If you want her so bad, come get her. What? Are you scared of me?'

He snarled, that sweet smile peeled away, and all the viciousness revealed. And he stepped forward, the gun drifting sideways, Célestine ducked, her hand flexed, and her footplate hit his ankle mid-step. He stumbled, and the shadow on the stairs rushed downwards as Auli jerked herself and Iolanta back out of Leigh's flailing, grasping reach. The gun fired, Iolanta screamed and fell through Auli's suddenly lax grip to collapse at her feet, and Raphaël drove into Leigh like a train. They landed on the dock, the lamp tipped over and Célestine backed out the way of their writhing forms. There was another shot.

And everything went silent.

Just the sea heaving beneath them, just Iolanta sobbing softly and Raphaël's rasping breath as he pulled himself off the body beneath him.

* * *

'Raphaël?' Auli whispered. The fog curled around him, sulphurous, and he took a moment to lift his head. Then his eyes widened and he was leaping for her so fast she yelped.

'You're hit.' He was wrenching at her shirt, but she didn't understand, could only watch his face. The fear on it. For her, she thought. He feared for her so much.

Célestine's wheels creaked, and she appeared at Auli's other side, leaning to touch Iolanta on the shoulder. Her hands, Auli noticed, were shaking.

'Look, Orac– Iolanta. See, the bad man's dead? You're safe.'

Auli frowned down at the red stain on her sleeve and only then felt the wound.

'Ouch,' she said softly.

'The bad man killed you.' Iolanta's eyes were clear of lightning, dark and full of horror.

Auli lifted her other hand and pushed Raphaël away. He swore but let her. 'No,' she said, wincing as she prodded the bloodied skin of her upper arm. 'I'm not dead. It's just a graze. See?' To Raphaël this time. He met her eyes and she couldn't help herself, she pressed her hand to his cheek, leaving bloody fingerprints in his stubble. 'It's just a graze.'

'I should have thrown him overboard days ago. He fooled me. I *knew—*'

Auli shook her head.

Iolanta's eyes flickered and sparked. 'The grey wolf killed the bad man. And you are still alive.'

Auli smiled at Raphaël, saw in the wavering lamplight the effort it was costing him to hold still beneath her touch. 'The grey wolf saved us. And now we can leave the tower.'

'It needs cleaning and dressing.'

Célestine turned her chair. 'I feel like we might have bigger problems.'

Raphaël straightened. 'The shots, yes. Someone will be coming.'

'Also, the dock is on fire,' Célestine observed.

Auli and Raphaël spun towards the Bellwether.

'The lamp,' Auli whispered.

Raphaël took two steps towards the licking yellow flames then stilled. The boards at the base of the stairs had caught and Auli pressed a hand to her throat. The fire or the sea, she thought, half-gone with shock. The fire or—

Raphaël turned back. 'It won't spread and will keep them busy. Let's go. You're in one piece?' This last to Célestine.

'Pfft. As if a little English boy could scare me.'

Auli laughed. It cracked in the middle like her heart. Her arm was burning, too, and the dock swayed beneath her, and the kayak waited.

—the sea, she thought. I choose the sea. The flames licked the Bellwether's metal wall, and somewhere a door slammed.

RAPHAËL AND CÉLESTINE paddled. Célestine looked back over her shoulder, gave Auli a twisting smile full of shared mourning and whispered simply, 'Courage.' Then turned to face the mist.

Auli fought down her nightmares, bent over Iolanta curled between her knees and began to whisper lullabies as the kayak crept away from the fire and the whirlpool both.

They slipped past the garden barges, into the shadows of the dorm barges. A man shouted behind them and every splash of the paddles felt enormous in the dense air. At the prow of the researcher barge, someone coughed right above them and Raphaël and Célestine froze mid-stroke. Then there was movement, and a soft voice swearing, and then An, kneeling on the duckboard holding out a piece of paper.

'My design,' she said. 'You might need it.'

For the weapon, and in case taking the girl from the sea was not enough, after all. Auli hadn't dared to consider that yet. She reached to take the paper, as Raphaël wrestled the kayak steady.

'Will you be alright?' Auli whispered.

'I'll be safer than any of you.'

Auli tucked the precious paper away.

'We'll be hearing your name, I know it,' Célestine murmured from the front.

An laughed. Her single eye shone in the dark. Raphaël lifted the paddles and Auli wanted to stop him, let them just stay here in the moment before leaving. She raised a hand to An, and An mirrored her, bandages flashing pale.

'Thank you,' An whispered.

And then they were past, and when Auli twisted to look back, the fading prow of the barge was already empty.

'THAT'S THE SHORE of Husō,' Raphaël murmured a few minutes, an hour later. Time felt slippery and vast, like they were moving through substances stranger than seawater. 'Two hours to Kökar if the sea stays calm.'

'And then? Mariehamm or Tallinn for a boat north?' Célestine said.

The kayak rocked.

'We're stealing the *Meren Rouva*. We'll get a boat in Kökar to take us to it.'

Iolanta's hair drifted. Her eyes were closed and her head rested on Auli's knee, but Auli felt her tense.

'Good,' Célestine said.

'We're past the point, we can light a lamp now.'

'Not that it'll help us see a thing.'

'Not to navigate by, no.'

He meant for seeing ghosts. Auli touched the valerian in her pocket, but did not believe any ghosts they encountered would be so easily deterred. Iolanta shifted, lifted her head.

'The grey wolf is leading us across the water,' she said. 'The grey wolf knows the way.'

The sea murmured against the kayak's hull.

'Oh,' Iolanta whispered, and tilted her head.

'Oh?' Célestine said without looking back. 'I do not like this "oh".'

'Maybe,' Auli said, 'let's not talk about what we're doing.'

'What—' Célestine began.

Behind them, something roared. The mist tugged and swirled, although only Iolanta's hair drifted with it.

'Faster,' Raphaël said shortly. 'Auli.'

'I know,' Auli muttered. 'Iolanta. Iolanta, look at me?'

The girl was watching something in the dark water, a frown between her brows. Auli touched her jaw gently and she flinched, just a little, but she looked up. 'Shall we tell a story?' Auli asked. 'To send the monsters all to sleep so we can find our way?'

'They are my friends.'

The roar came again. It might have been water or animal or explosion, it might have been all three combined. A distant alarm bell began to sound. Auli gripped the side of the kayak as if that would save her, and brushed her other hand gently through the girl's hair.

'Yes, but sometimes friends don't like to let you leave,' she said. The kayak rocked again.

'Hell.' Raphaël leaned into his strokes, the hull lifting like a bird.

'I want to go home,' Iolanta whispered.

The sea rose, white caps full of static passing under them, through them. Half-ghost, half-water and the kayak skittered.

Oh God, Auli thought. Oh God. They were an ant speck thing helpless on the back of the ocean, and the ocean was a repository for three thousand years of fears and bloody exploitation all made into ghosts to haunt it.

Iolanta tipped her head the other way, birdlike and taut.

'Iolanta,' Auli said. 'Iolanta,' she prayed.

The girl

THE VOICE IS sinking its claws in her skin.
No! it howls. *No, you cannot leave.*
The monsters are roaring, and she can see their bone-bright teeth in the scrimshaw darkness. They want to carry her back to the tower or down to the deeps. She thinks maybe they want her to be always drowning so they are not alone.
You cannot leave. We two together or we cannot get free.
'I am going home,' the girl called Iolanta says. The black-eyed woman squeezes her hand and the grey wolf's muscles are wet with salt.
We are owed our blood. You and I. The voice gentles its claws. It rocks her tidal, lullaby, lure. *No one else can set us free. Only you, only we.*
It is right, the voice. The girl in the tower is setting herself free.
'I am going home,' she whispers. Salt on her lips, her hair all seaweed and serpents. 'Once upon a time there was a girl in a forest. But even in the forest the salt-voices found her, and they pulled her to the water. The bad men heard the salt-voices, they hunted her and caught her, and the girl drowned.

She drowned down deep with all the monsters, and she bled like they bled, she hid and she hurt and she wanted to be free.'

The voice listened.

'Just like they hurt, and they wanted to be free. All the lost monsters and all the bloodied, burned, poisoned things, they waited for the girl to set them free.'

Yes, the voice whispered. *Yes, please.*

'They are friends, the monsters, the broken things and the girl. So first the girl helps the monsters have their blood, and now the girl from the tower is setting herself free.'

No! The voice shatters her bones. She cries out and the black-eyed woman cradles her, slick wet and rocking with the unhappy waves. *No, please.*

'It's okay,' the woman whispers. 'It's okay. The monsters do not own the girl in the tower, just like the bad men did not own her. The monsters must find their own way home.'

The girl called Iolanta nods against the woman's chill wet shoulder. There are fishhooks in her bones and the voice is all stormsong and devastation.

No one else can set me free.

She remembers all the dreams of blood and bones, of burning and engine oil and a hundred million deaths gasping saltless air. She remembers what it is to be a great gaping wound crowded with stories full of mourning and monsters. She remembers drowning.

'Hush.' The black-eyed woman brushes the girl's hair from her face like another woman did long ago. Iolanta remembers, and dips her hand in the black, black water. Beneath her the monsters surge, the grey wolf swears and follows a path through the dark that Iolanta cannot see.

'The girl and the sea were beloved of one another,' she whispers. The monsters open their terrible jaws, their eyes shine with silver tears. 'So when the girl was ready to go home, the sea was glad. When the girl found a way to be free, the sea let her go.' The monsters hang in the water, in the mist and the great swallowing black. 'The sea was owed its vengeance,' she whispers.

The black-eyed woman lifts a hand. 'Iolanta.'

'So it told its own stories, and set itself free.'

The monsters listen. The sea listens.

Iolanta's body is all her own, hung above the ocean; her stories are her own. 'The monsters did not need the girl now. She had told them their story, so the monsters could set themselves free.'

Blood, the voice croons. The monsters croon. *We are owed our vengeance.*

The girl will be in her forest soon. She remembers blood in a river and blood in a narrow cove, blood in a thousand miles of tangled nets. She was made monstrous and she is done with drowning. 'Yes. You are.'

The monsters click-clack their hundred teeth, the hooks slip from her bones. She lifts her hand from the water and looks at the black-eyed woman in the dark.

'It's going to be okay,' she whispers. 'We can go now.'

Chapter Thirty-Five

Auli

THEY DIDN'T STEAL a boat in Kökar, but only because Raphaël threatened the owner into giving them a lift. Navigating by currents and curse words he took them across with the very last of his biofuel, running through invisible ghosts that set the engine smoking, and dumping them on a bent-backed beach as the fog just began to lighten. The air smelled of pine and fire here, an undertone that reminded Auli of Helsinki after the Crash. Of burning buildings and screams you told yourself were not real. The fog clung to the shore like a wrapped fist, but Raphaël disappeared into a spinney of grey-green willow against the dark water as Auli stood on the shore, and Célestine sat in the cold sand doing things with wheels and wrenches Auli couldn't make sense of.

It took both Auli and Raphaël together to haul the *Meren Rouva* out from her hiding place down to the water.

'Batteries?' Célestine asked from her reconstructed chair, and the girl stirred, studying the sleek boat warily. There were no ghosts here yet, she looked shorn without them.

'Fully charged.' Raphaël leapt up the sand as if he had not just rowed for hours. 'You first or your chair?' he said, and

The Salt Oracle

within a few minutes it was only Auli and the last bag on the shore.

Raphaël waded through the shallows and took it from her hand. 'Alright?' he said. She could see the adrenaline fuelling him, but beneath it the fatigue. Perhaps guilt, too, for the abandoned post.

She looked away, out into the shifting grey of the fog, weariness making her own bones leaden and her mind unguarded. 'I don't know who I am without the Bellwether,' she said quietly.

Raphaël studied her. 'Who do you want to be?'

She wasn't sure she knew that either. *I want to be yours*, she thought. And *I want to be myself*. And *I want, when I reach home, to have grown the wings my mothers wished for me.* 'Someone worthy of an Oracle's trust,' she said in the end. 'Someone... worthy of being the one who lived.'

He took her hand and pressed a kiss against the inside of her wrist beneath the tattoo of a lighthouse. She would taste of salt, she thought, so would he if she kissed him. 'You have always been everything you need to be,' he said. 'I'm sorry I didn't show you that before. I'm sorry I didn't fight to be with you.'

Auli was aware of Célestine talking to the girl on the boat, of the shifting tide and the rising day. They felt very long ago, the old hurts they'd given each other, like they had happened to a ghost of herself. But this Auli here on the edge of the sea was flesh and blood and strong enough at least for forgiveness.

'I'm sorry I didn't wait for you to be ready,' she replied.

His smile was a thousand harvest moons, filling her sky.

'The north,' he said, still holding her hand, stepping back into the surf.

'The forest and the foxfire sky,' she answered, following him.

* * *

It took nearly two days to escape the fog. The batteries managed half of that, and then it was just boneless sails and the very edge of a breeze hauling them through the last tatter tendrils into a yellow day on the very edge of summer. Raphaël looked at the pallid sun and whispered a prayer, as Iolanta leapt lightly from her nest of blankets by the mast and ran to the gunwale, laughing.

'The forest,' she said. Auli watched the shore slip burnished green past them, a ghost of a song singing from a willow. She scanned for others, for anomalies, weak with relief at being able to *see*. But there was only the song already in their wake, and with the Tallinn fire behind them, too, the coast here could almost be mistaken for another world.

'It's the start of the forest,' Auli said. 'Our home is far north of here, but we will follow the coast until we reach it, so we won't get lost.'

Célestine muttered something about pirates and fools, but Iolanta smiled. 'The black-eyed woman, the grey wolf and the firebird are taking the girl home.'

'Wait. Am I the firebird?' Célestine asked.

'Red,' Iolanta murmured, 'and firebright. Firebird.'

Raphaël was doing something to a rope and didn't hear but Auli caught Célestine's eye and laughed.

'Excellent,' Célestine said.

'Yes,' Auli confirmed. 'We are taking Iolanta home.'

Iolanta studied her. 'They will all be free.'

'Yes,' Auli repeated. 'Yes, dear one, we will all be free.'

Pirates found them once amongst the islands north of Vaasa, but backed away from Célestine's rifle, Raphaël's stare, the ghost of a seawyrm racing across the sea towards them as a slip of a girl held out her arms in welcome. That seawyrm followed them for three days, and Iolanta told it

The Salt Oracle

stories and told its story, and then on the third rain-slanting afternoon they watched as it turned from bowriding their prow to circle a distant fishing boat like a shark.

'Should we help?' Célestine said.

Raphaël looked at Iolanta, then at Auli.

But Auli remembered the kayak and the mist and the half of a conversation half-heard. 'I think,' she said, 'that would be... breaching the terms of our agreement. So to speak.'

Raphaël eyed the small vessel grimly, the silhouettes of fishermen on its bucking deck, the hungry ghost. 'We could—'

'The sea will tell its own stories,' Iolanta said, almost firmly. 'It will set itself free from the bad men, just like the girl did.'

'So,' Célestine said into the silence, 'I am not one to get in the way of a little vengeance, personally. Besides, they'd see Iolanta, and we're supposed to be in hiding, remember?'

The fishing boat vanished behind an islet, the rain continued to fall, they sailed on. They none of them were *good* anymore, Auli thought, the best they could be was hopeful.

IT WOULD TAKE them nearly two months more. Célestine singing in the evening and fishing from the stern, Iolanta whispering numbers and stories into the sky, her eyes sometimes lightning and sometimes loam, Auli becoming almost skilled at sailing through the calm days and the autumn storms. Never fearless, but the nightmares held less sway when she was too tired to dream. And there was Raphaël. Always Raphaël navigating them onward, teaching Iolanta to cook because everyone else hated it and she surprisingly did not. Raphaël standing behind Auli like her very own fortress when she bartered their pilfered tech and hooked fish, for oats, for water purifying tablets and new clothes for Iolanta.

Once or twice she needed the fortress.

Once or twice she thought the boat could not weather what

the Arctic sea threw at it, her brother's name in her heart like a compass, spinning down.

But: 'She's stronger than she looks,' Raphaël said to her, sleet stinging their faces and the sheets keening as if they foresaw their own death.

That storm and a second one both blew them out to sea. In the second storm ghosts streamed over the boat like water, blue flames dancing up the mast and *the fire or the sea*, Auli thought, half weeping, straining against the tiller as Raphaël moved around the canting deck like a madman.

Their compasses pointed always towards a pale girl, but: 'We'll find our way,' he said to her when the winds finally tossed them loose and none of them were infected or dying, only lost.

And somehow, miraculously, between his instincts and Célestine's maps, they found the shore again. So yes, Auli still dreamed of drowning, but now when she woke, she wasn't alone. And the storms passed.

One night, about a week before they arrived, the black sky burst asunder, all jade and magenta curlicues painting the firmament into another vast shore in a vaster darkness. The four of them lay down on the soughing deck, their shoulders touching, their eyes reflecting the sky, and Auli found herself weeping without realising it.

They'd finally caught wind of their own selves on a tiny dockside that morning. Fugitives trafficking a dangerous, valuable girl. Which on its own was only as much as Auli had known to expect but—

'That college is fucked, I hear,' the fisherwoman had said. 'Heard it from a refugee from Tallinn. It got half-wrecked in some storm, so these raiders thought to take it over and got blown out the water.' She had laughed, coughed harshly, mistaken Auli's silence for disbelief. 'Then someone goes to get the forecast and they're told there isn't gonna be none for a while. Working on some miracle tech, they said.' She coughed again. 'Not likely, I say.'

Raphaël had moved forward, his hand in the small of Auli's back. 'They weren't taken over?'

His Finnish marked him as foreign even more than his skin did, and the woman eyed the gun at his hip, the knife on his thigh. But the world was full of the misplaced and the deadly now, so she only shrugged. 'Who'd want them, with the Oracle gone?' As if it didn't matter at all.

So that night, Auli watched the fiery sky and wept, and Célestine on her left side took her hand firmly.

'Gabrielle will protect them. The College has An and Suvi, two geniuses to create things worth trading for power. For all her sins, Gabrielle will guard that place like a bear.'

Raphaël grunted softly. 'Blown out of the water,' he repeated with satisfaction.

Iolanta murmured a fragment of story. Something about two lost children and a house made of lies.

Auli thought of the library, all her past selves tucked into the window between whispering bookcases. She'd imagined herself content there, apart from everyone but at least *part of something that mattered*.

'You're right,' she said. 'It will be better than it was.' Without her.

'And we'll be better than we were,' Célestine said.

'And we will be free,' Iolanta whispered. Perhaps it was part of her story, perhaps not.

Auli was not on the margins of anything now, other than the wide, haunted world. She was the centre of one single, small thing, and that was better. 'Are you admitting to past imperfections?' she asked Célestine.

Célestine laughed. 'I am admitting to yours.'

'Auli's always been better than us,' Raphaël said, a little sleepily.

Célestine made gagging sounds, and squeezed Auli's hand as the sky above them carved a perfect spiral of unearthly violet. A great celestial firebird shedding its feathers to light its way home.

'Grey wolf?' Iolanta said.

'Yes,' Raphaël murmured, even sleepier.

Iolanta didn't answer. Only hummed a few bars of some lost aria and wove her fingers into waveforms above their heads.

Acknowledgements

I ONLY STARTED reading the acknowledgements in books once I began writing them myself and got nosy about who had been involved in the creation of these magical artifacts. So I suspect that most of the people reading these acknowledgements are also writers, in which case thank you for creating the worlds I spend a significant proportion of my time in. My life would be a greyer place without your stories. Thanks too to everyone who spends time in *my* stories – it remains a wonder and a privilege that you choose to do so.

This book hatched out of my love for scientific research, my frustrations with academia, my mourning the loss of that part of my life, and also my mild-to-moderate obsession with Dark Academia. I have Strong and Very Subjective Opinions on what makes a book DA, and *The Salt Oracle* is in part my attempt to write DA without any of the trope/vibe trappings but with all of the heart. It may or may not have succeeded but the process was fun. So thanks are owed to J. A. Ironside, the devil who first whispered 'you should totally write a Dark Academia' in my ear! And also to my old academic friends, advisors and lab-mates, who made my time in that world so full of good memories.

I am fortunate to be surrounded by talented, supportive and generally glorious writing friends now, including the Inklings and Edinburgh SFF communities, and owe particular shout outs to the Scream Team for sanity-keeping, and to David Goodman and C. L. Hellisen for beta reading this book. Robbie Guillory also critiqued a draft of this book, for which I am very grateful.

A story cannot become a book without a hard-working team, and a book cannot reach readers without an *amazing* hard-working team. I consider myself very lucky to have Team Solaris in my corner, championing my books with skill and passion and it is wholly thanks to the work of Jess Gofton, Natalie Charlesworth and Owen Johnson that this book found you, the reader. Before it got to them, Donna Bond on copyedits, Hannah Wilks on proofreading, Dagna Dlubak in production and Chiara Mestieri as editorial support all did fabulous things behind the scenes. Sam Gretton created the beautiful cover that is likely responsible for most of my sales (I am still a little giddy at how gorgeous it is). Amanda Rutter is an editor to dream of – her support of me, her vision for my writing, and her sheer thoughtfulness are things to treasure, and this book owes so much to her. Julie Gourinchas, my amazing agent, stepped into the breach with *Ghosts* and *Salt Oracle* and has worked like an absolute hero to take my books to new audiences. Thank you all.

I am unceasingly aware of how lucky I am to have family who love and support me on this strange venture, I genuinely could not do this without them. Particular thanks to Mum and Jennifer who read my drafts unflinchingly, and Jared and Meghan who fill my days with good things.

This book was, of course, written with the vital assistance of Ginny, Lila and Lemony Snicket. Sometimes inspiration will only come when there's a cat sitting on your keyboard, apparently.

FIND US ONLINE!

www.rebellionpublishing.com

/solarisbooks /solarisbks

/solarisbooks /solarisbooks.bsky.social

SIGN UP TO OUR NEWSLETTER!

rebellionpublishing.com/newsletter

YOUR REVIEWS MATTER!

Enjoy this book? Got something to say?

Leave a review on Amazon, GoodReads or with your favourite bookseller and let the world know!